YOSHE KALB

I.J.
SINGER

YOSHE KALB

**TRANSLATED FROM THE YIDDISH
BY MAURICE SAMUEL**

**WITH AN INTRODUCTION
BY IRVING HOWE**

SCHOCKEN BOOKS NEW YORK

Introduction Copyright © 1988 by Schocken Books Inc.
Copyright 1933 by Liveright, Inc.
Copyright renewed 1961 by Maurice Samuel,
assigned to Joseph Singer
All rights reserved under International and Pan-American Copyright
Conventions. Published in the United States by Schocken Books Inc., New
York. Distributed by Pantheon Books, a division of Random House, Inc.,
New York. Originally published in English translation under the title
The Sinner by Liveright, Inc., in 1933.

Library of Congress Cataloging-in-Publication Data
Singer, Israel Joshua, 1893–1944.
Yoshe Kalb.
Translation of: Yoshe Kalb.
I. Samuel, Maurice, 1895–1972.
II. Title.
PJ5129.S5Y613   1988   839'.0933   87-32408
ISBN 0-8052-0860-7

Manufactured in the United States of America
First Schocken Paperback Edition, 1988

Display Typography by Jessica Shatan

INTRODUCTION

BY IRVING HOWE

*Yoshe Kalb** was first published in 1932, at a time when Israel Joshua Singer was still living in Warsaw. The following year he moved to America and shortly thereafter his book was adapted for the stage by the Yiddish Art Theatre of New York. It proved to be an enormous popular success. I still remember a boyhood visit to the Second Avenue theatre where the dramatized version of *Yoshe Kalb* seemed very strange and exotic—something quite different from the soft-tinted nostalgia through which Yiddish writing usually expressed feelings about the old country.

In the late Maurice Samuel's translation, the novel itself carries a strong narrative thrust: it moves, it pulses, it hurries toward climax. The exotic strain is certainly there, but subdued, I think, to a harsh realism, for Singer was one of those Yiddish writers who meant his readers, both in Europe and America, to face up to some unpleasant truths about Jewish life. For the present-day reader, however, all that is necessary by way of background is a bit of historical knowledge (which this introduction hopes to provide). Upon a first reading, *Yoshe Kalb* may seem alien in its setting, but its passions ought to be familiar enough. We know what is happening page by page, but we are never quite certain what it signifies, and Singer is too austere an artist to supply easy tips. Finally *Yoshe*

---

*Yoshe Kalb means, literally, Yoshe the Calf, or idiomatically, Yoshe the Loon.

Kalb strikes me as an enigmatic fiction, but the enigmas are our own.

In his own day, I. J. Singer* won considerable fame both in Europe and America. He was one of the first Yiddish writers to abandon the familial coziness and drowsy rhythms of *shtetl* fiction, which had served so well the founding fathers of Yiddish literature, Mendele Mokher Sforim and Sholom Aleichem. In the early years of this century, the next, or second, generation of modern Yiddish writers, among whom Singer figured prominently, chose instead to follow the lead of those European novelists who were turning out lengthy and thickly populated social or family novels—novels usually weaving together several plot lines, building upon spacious architectural principles, and focusing upon a single, often ideologically rent family.

Perhaps better than any of his Yiddish contemporaries, I. J. Singer mastered the problems of construction peculiar to the large social or family novel: how to keep a multitude of characters more or less connected within a complex narrative, how to sustain a long-breathed and impersonal prose style, and how to make persuasive a vision of society that endows it with a destiny, perhaps even a "will," overwhelming the lives of its individual members. Singer also absorbed—whether through direct influence or "from the air"—the dictum of Turgenev and Flaubert that the novelist should keep himself (his voice, his opinions) out of his narrative, severely apart from the figures and events he portrays.

This narrative detachment was, in the case of Singer, more than a mere strategy of composition. It reflected the growing secularization of the Yiddish-speaking intelligentsia and the resulting critical stance this intelligentsia took toward the Eastern European Jewish milieu. It reflected, as well, the bent of Singer's own temperament, a somewhat unusual one in Yiddish culture. At a moment when many writers were yielding themselves to social movements and

---

*There are two Singers in Yiddish literature, brothers of talent, though of very different kinds. I. J. Singer (1893–1944) is the subject of this introduction; his younger brother, Isaac Bashevis Singer (b. 1902) is a recipient of the Nobel Prize.

national enthusiasms, Singer remained aloof, a writer of deep skepticism not only about his own immediate Jewish milieu, but, you might say, about the entire human enterprise—he wasn't exactly enchanted with mankind. He might remain closely engaged with the customs and mores of his own Eastern European Jewish culture, but he kept a certain critical distance from its norms. Even when evoking scenes of enthusiasm and piety in *Yoshe Kalb*, the "inner voice" of his narrative seems reserved, cool, apart.

In retrospect I think it fair to say that the large-scale social or family novel, though admired by an earlier generation of Yiddish readers for its "universality," was never quite congenial to Yiddish culture. The world the Yiddish writers had available for fictional representation was not spacious or internally diverse enough, nor were its inhabitants free enough, to supply the grounding for the sort of social or family novel written in Europe during the early years of this century. On the other hand, the Eastern European Jewish experience was still coherent enough—or at least the memory of its coherence was still sufficiently fresh—so that Yiddish prose writers could excel in the short novel and the short story, forms that enable that compression of the cultural signals and references which can flourish in such a society. Things don't have to be explained, a phrase can encompass a whole arc of experience, readers and writers make out each others' meanings at a glance.

As against the received opinion of Yiddish readers, I think that I. J. Singer's most enduring work is not his "big" fiction, good as *The Brothers Ashkenazi* and *The Family Carnovsky* are, but the work he did in shorter forms, such as *Yoshe Kalb* and the stories "Repentance" and "Sand" (both to be found in *A Treasury of Yiddish Stories*, ed. Howe and Greenberg). Here, in tensed narratives, Singer was able to bring together his authoritative grasp of old-world Jewish life in its late-nineteenth-century phase of disintegration and his own distinctive sensibility, that chilly skepticism which is his literary signature. In *Yoshe Kalb* he employs an intimately known subject, but more as a literary occasion than out of any direct emotional or intellectual engagement. By upbringing and experience Singer remains a part of Eastern European Jewish culture, but—so it seems to me, at least—in some unspoken yet crucial way he has distanced himself from it. But before saying anything more about the book itself, let me offer a few bits of information about its setting.

One of the most remarkable and, in some ways, creative phenomena of modern Jewish life has been the movement of religious enthusiasm called Hasidism, arising in Eastern Europe during the late eighteenth and early nineteenth centuries. For a people long disciplined, perhaps overdisciplined, by rabbinic orthodoxy, Hasidism satisfied needs for emotional release: song, dance, joy. Hasidism sought wisdom through flights of rapture and as the fruit of intuition, rather than in theology or legalism. Organized internally on hierarchical principles through the unquestioned dominance of *tsadikim* (holy masters taken to be intermediaries between the divine and the mundane), Hasidism preached a kind of romanticist ethic—a communal romanticism, not individual. "Every Jew," said its founder, the Baal Shem Tov, "is an organ of the *shekhine*, or divine presence."

But as it became an established institution in the *shtetl*, there soon appeared another, and far less attractive, side of Hasidism, one that later generations of Jews, slipping into the comforts of nostalgia, have tended to sentimentalize or ignore. *Yoshe Kalb* offers a picture of corruption in the late-nineteenth-century milieu of Eastern European Jewry, with Hasidism declining from spontaneous affirmation into a squalid turmoil of cliques, each with its petty court and despotic, though also sometimes charismatic *tsadik*. In this phase of Hasidism, as the authoritative Jewish historian Simon Dubnow has written: "The profitable vocation of *tsadik* was made hereditary. There was a multiplication of *tsadik* dynasties contending for supremacy. The 'cult of the righteous,' as defined by the Baal Shem Tov, degenerated into a system of exploitation of the credulous."

This milieu is taken entirely for granted by Singer. He feels no need to explain anything about it; he treats it as a cultural "given" likely to be familiar to his readers, quite in the way F. Scott

Fitzgerald could assume his readers were familiar with "the Jazz Age." The personal disorder which comprises the foreground action of *Yoshe Kalb* acquires meaning through its inseparability from the portrayed disorder of the Jewish community. Things are breaking up.

One sign of this is the rivalry, indeed the hatred, between the rationalistic and cultivated rabbinic family of Nahum, the fearful boy who is the protagonist of the novel, and the coarse but vigorous Rabbi Melech of Nyesheve, a character embodying Hasidism in its decline. Singer evokes this rabbi's petty court—its gabbing clients, its sensual undercurrents, its filial intrigues, its commercial nastiness—with a fine command of detail. And that command, in turn, speaks for the writer's awareness of where he stands, both close and far, in relation to his culture.

Yoshe Kalb offers little in the way of full or dynamic characterization, the kind we have been trained to expect in traditional fiction. Here, in a world of rigid prescriptions and possibilities, the characters appear as fixed, largely unchanging, sharply defined entities. Seldom granted any complicating nuance, they serve mostly as functions of a stringent drama or, if you prefer, as agents of fatality. In this setting the familiar distinction between self and role hardly counts. People are grooved into their destinies; those who would break loose suffer violently. If all this serves to limit our interest in the characters' inner lives—strictly speaking, they hardly have any, nor in this mode of fiction do they need any—it also enables I. J. Singer to achieve a notable energy of narrative.

In thinking about *Yoshe Kalb* purely as a literary composition, what strikes one most of all is Singer's mastery in the art of pacing. This is an art that seems to me largely intuitive: an ability to place the telling detail at just the right point while readily omitting dozens of others, the writer's self-assurance that enables him to hold some things back—a clue, an insight, a twist of action. Watch, when you read *Yoshe Kalb*, how cannily Singer negotiates his transitions from one site of action to another, how his story leaps ahead, past mere substantiation, to light upon essential moments (for example, from Book I to Book II). Now, criticism can point to instances of this art of pacing, but as to what it constitutes, what it actually *is*—well, so far as I know, criticism has rather little to contribute. Perhaps it's just as well: let the deepest craft of the writer evade the categories of the critic; not everything can or needs to be explained.

There is, however, another aspect of Singer's craft about which criticism can perhaps be helpful. As he drives his narrative forward, Singer allows, even entices, his readers—especially those with traditional orthodoxy or those looking back sentimentally upon a lost orthodoxy—to perceive *Yoshe Kalb* in terms of sin and its expiation, that is, as an enactment of an austere moral system drawing upon faith. But at the same time, Singer as narrator—we are not here concerned with Singer the actual person—gives little if any indication in the text of acquiescing in such a moral system. (Nor, to be honest, any sign of denying it.) The story thus opens itself up in a somewhat tricky way: it can be read on the level of traditional morality as a parable about the wages of sin, or it can be read as an instance of inexplicable fatality, as an utterly severe depiction of how costly a deviation from an accepted order can be. As I see it, Singer shrewdly allows us to fluctuate between these two modes of perception, never quite at ease with either of them.

The reality of sin is not questioned by the characters, but in Singer's depiction of that reality, what registers most strongly is less an impulse to moral judgment than a hastening sequence of disorder. The norm of sinfulness may be buried somewhere in the life of the community, but it is the rhythm of deviation and punishment which energizes Singer's treatment of the characters. What matters most is the grip of event upon event.

Sin once committed, Nahum sets out as an exile, wandering dumbly, now Yoshe the Loon, through a maze of Jewish villages. In the second half of the novel he reenacts a tragic parody of his original violation. Like a Dantean figure shuffling through the wastes of purgatory, he is a dead soul without words or will, locked forever in his deed. The novel ends with a struggle between religious sects, disputing for possession of this dead soul. A sainted rabbi comes closest to a final statement: "You know not what you do," he says to Yoshe Kalb, "there is no taste in your life or your

deeds, because you are nothing yourself, because—hear me!—
you are a dead wanderer in the chaos of the world."

The vividness of this book seems to me beyond dispute, but its
meaning beyond certainty. One may marvel at the parabola of
Yoshe Kalb's fate, but what thematic significance to assign to
it . . . I would surmise that the power of this novel derives from a
relationship on I. J. Singer's part to the religious culture of Eastern
European Judaism that is somewhat similar to the relationship
the Hawthorne of *The Scarlet Letter* has to the religious culture
of New England Puritanism—though Singer's skepticism is less
clever, more emotionally ominous than Hawthorne's.

Mulling over this fine work of fiction, I have been struck by how
tightly locked within the premises of his culture the work of almost
any novelist must be. In *Yoshe Kalb* every act carries social and
moral weight; no one in the audience to which the book was first
addressed could possibly have doubted what that weight must be.
Some decades later we must grope and approximate, fearful that
the more ingenious our readings, the more likely we are smuggling
in preconceptions. But perhaps I. J. Singer was in advance of, or
apart from, his culture, and *Yoshe Kalb* reveals itself best to those
who approach it from a distance of time and place. At least, one
would like to think so.

YOSHE
KALB

BOOK ONE

1

The great rabbinic court of Nyesheve hummed with the preparations for the marriage of Serele, the Rabbi's daughter.

The famous Rabbi, leader of thousands of Jews of the Chassidic sect throughout Galicia and Russia, was in a hurry. He was, indeed, always in a hurry, for, in spite of his sixty-odd years and his bulging stomach, on which the ritual fringes lay arched like an apron on the stomach of a pregnant woman, in spite of his age and his bulk, Rabbi Melech was exceedingly temperamental. His bulbous, beer-colored eyes seemed always ready to jump from their sockets with eagerness and curiosity. A furious health radiated from his body; it broke through the thick tangle of his beard and ear-locks, and through the hairy heaviness of his fat nape. A noisy, excitable man, with a pair of full, sensuous lips, which always sucked a thick cigar—sometimes lit, sometimes out— Rabbi Melech was widely known for his resoluteness and insistence. Once he had got something into his head, he contrived, shouted, bullied, cajoled and rushed around until he achieved his aim. And he had got it into his head to marry off his youngest daughter in a hurry. Even the calendar was no obstacle to him. He would not wait until after Pentecost; halfway through the interval between Passover and Pentecost, on the Festival of the Thirty-third Day, the wedding would take place.

The father of the bridegroom, the illustrious Rabbi of Rachmanivke, in Russia, was opposed to this unseemly haste; and not the Rabbi alone, but his wife, his household, his court and his followers.

During the year of the betrothal of Serele, daughter of Rabbi Melech, to Nahum, son of the Rabbi of Rachmanivke, registered letters flew almost daily between the two towns. Invariably the letters of the Rabbi of Rachmanivke—letters written in flawlessly grammatical Hebrew, every phrase, every word, every quotation classically exact—pleaded for delay. Rachmanivke wanted the betrothal to last a few years longer.

"The noble and learned Rabbi (long may he live!)," so ran one letter, "will admit that the bridegroom and bride (long may she live!) are little more than children. They are barely fourteen years of age. And it is a custom with us—a custom dating from the time of our grandfather (his memory be a blessing unto us!)—not to hasten in such matters. Moreover, the bridegroom has just begun a special course of studies under his teacher Rabbi Pesachiah of Zavil, and it would be most unseemly to interrupt it."

When the letters arrived in Nyesheve, Rabbi Melech's great-grandchildren would sometimes tear off the Russian stamps, with the Russian Emperor's head on them, before the Rabbi himself had touched the letters.

"Grandfather," they asked him once, "who is nicer, our Emperor or the Russian Emperor?"

"Our Emperor, of course!" the Rabbi answered angrily, for Rabbi Melech was by way of being an Austrian patriot. And then, with a swish of the hat which he wore on top of his skull-cap, he would send his great-grandchildren scattering. "Don't pester me now. Let me read the letter."

He could not stand these letters of the bridegroom's father; he could not stand the meticulous, graceful orthography, which reminded him of the meticulous and graceful writer. Often there were words—most of them taken from the Bible—which he did not know. And therefore he often skipped as he read, not without resentment at this new-fangled and dangerous preference for the Bible over the Talmud. But he could not stand the letters chiefly because they always pleaded for delay. His fat lips would tighten on his moist cigar, and in a spasm of rage he would look round for his *gabbai*—his visier—Israel Avigdor.

"Srelvigdor!" he yelled. "I'll throttle the life out of you. Don't you see my cigar is out?"

No, Rabbi Melech could not stand these letters, with their monotonous refrain. The constant delays were intolerable. More than twelve months had passed since his third wife, the mother of Serele, had left him a widower. She had been thirty-one years old at the time of her death, and she was buried with the little one she was suckling, for together they succumbed to scarlet fever. The death of his wife had been a great blow to Rabbi Melech; but the little one had been of less importance, for his first two wives had brought him a great many children, mostly daughters.

The yards swarmed with his children, grandchildren and great-grandchildren. The entire clan lived together in the massive, ramshackle house of the patriarch. With its bare walls and high windows, with the revolving ventilators on the roof, the house had looked, years ago, like a barrack. But as the clan expanded, the house expanded too. New wings were added, new walls, new attics, a patchwork without style or taste, till the structure became fantastic, till, with its new accretions huddling against the original building on one side, and the synagogue on the other, it made one think of a blind beggar wrapped in a multitude of rags. In this swarming house there was a constant flutter of festivities, major and minor; somebody was always being born or circumcised or betrothed or married or sent to *cheder* or being confirmed or being called up to the reading of the Law for the first time—celebrations of one kind or another almost daily. There were such swarms of children about the place that Rabbi Melech, whose mind was not particularly lively, often drove them out of his presence without knowing whether they were his own children, the children of his children, or the children of his grandchildren. The confusion in the Rabbi's mind was the cause of much resentment and heartache.

The death of his youngest child had therefore been no great loss. Not so the death of his wife. He had loved her more than his first two wives. And he remembered, too, an odd remark she had made to him one night, when he had returned from a ritual bath.

"If you didn't have such a big beard," she said, "you'd be quite young."

A very odd remark for a woman to make!

In fact, it was not what might be called a decently modest remark. Neither of the first two wives would have made it; they had been too frightened—too frightened and respectful. In fact, they had hardly ever spoken to him. But the odd remark had flooded him with happiness. He had never forgotten it; and at her funeral, while he lamented her loudly, and expatiated to his Chassidic followers on her godliness and chastity and modesty, it sprang suddenly into his mind. Then his lamentations doubled in force, and the tangle of his beard and ear-locks trembled with his emotions. His followers wept with him, as openly as the women. They were sure that after such a calamity he would never marry again.

The Rabbi's sons, too, were of this opinion. "He's not so young any more," they said benevolently, gently, speaking as Rabbis' sons are wont to speak when the father has been occupying the Rabbinic throne too long.

His daughters, great, lumpy women, discussed the matter with their husbands. No, they did not believe that Rabbi Melech would marry again. Being women and unlearned, they knew little about the Law; but they had read, in the little, popular books which are specially prepared for women in the Yiddish vernacular, that a Jewish daughter must not marry a man who has buried three wives, for he is known as a Katlan—a wife-killer.

And their husbands, who were afraid of the addition of new heirs to those already waiting (not impatiently, God forbid!) for the day of their ascension, reassured them: "No, no, it is impossible! What Jewish daughter would be willing to risk her life?"

But Rabbi Melech of Nyesheve had his own way of looking at things, and it differed decidedly from everyone's else. Rabbi Melech had, in fact, made up his mind to marry again; and not a widow, either, but a young virgin whom he had already chosen.

Among the Rabbis and the Rabbinic broods which followed the court of Nyesheve, there was a certain Reb Mecheleh Hinever, the son of a Rabbi, destined originally to a Rabbinic career of his own. This same Reb Mecheleh was, however, a stammerer and a simpleton, and an uncle of his drew away his father's following on his death. Reb Mecheleh was compelled to travel from town to town, from village to village, as a superior sort of beggar, living on the claims of his dead father. From time to time he turned up at Nyesheve.

In the house of Reb Mecheleh, in Przemysl, there lived with his wife a young orphan girl, his niece, likewise of a Rabbinic family, but without the smallest dowry. As often as Reb Mecheleh visited Rabbi Melech of Nyesheve, he gave the latter a prayer-note, asking him for his intercession with Providence on behalf of the orphan girl. "Pray for a decent match for her," he pleaded.

Rabbi Melech did not forget.

He acted, characteristically, as his own matchmaker.

Suddenly, and without warning, he began to shower honors on Reb Mecheleh, whom till that moment he had scarcely deigned to notice. At the banquets, where the followers of the Rabbi scrambled for his attention and for the choicer morsels, Rabbi Mecheleh was singled out for both. Israel Avigdor, the *gabbai*, was bidden to find for Reb Mecheleh a place of honor among the most important guests, and to see to it that he got several helpings of wine. The astounded Reb Mecheleh understood nothing until one day, as he was about to leave Nyesheve, Rabbi Melech sent for him.

The interview took place in the Rabbi's own room. When Reb Mecheleh came in, the Rabbi rose, locked the door and handed the stammerer a cigar, together with an amber mouth-piece.

"Mecheleh, I noticed you using an ordinary, wooden mouth-piece, fit only for a wagoner or a woodchopper, and very unbecoming to the son of a Rabbinic house."

And without further ado, Rabbi Melech came to the point and announced that he would marry the orphan girl himself.

"Mecheleh, I want you to know that I am still in possession of my manhood. Tell the girl that she will rejoice in men children. And she must not be afraid of taking a *Katlan*; it is not the Law, but only a custom, and a very foolish custom, too. I don't believe in it."

His bulging eyes twinkled at the little man opposite. He sucked joyously at his extinguished cigar, then grabbed Mecheleh affectionately by his sparse, scattered beard, and said rapidly, urgently: "You'll be a relative of mine then. Do you understand, a relative of the Rabbi of Nyesheve? I'll have you permanently at my table."

The word "relative" had such a shattering and delirious effect on the poor simpleton that he followed Rabbi Melech about, while the latter, still holding on to his beard, strode up and down the room, beside himself with happiness. And at last, forgetting even to stammer, Reb Mecheleh burst out in one breath: "That's absolutely the right idea."

He was suddenly aware of an access of courage; he wanted to add something, a witty simile, a parable from the Talmud; and he remembered something he used to hear from his father years ago, whenever a sensible idea was suggested—something about a comely dish on a comely platter. But the excitement was too much for him, and he choked on the words. Then Rabbi Melech let go of Reb Mecheleh's beard and took hold of his own.

It did not even enter the mind of Rabbi Melech that the girl ought to be consulted. She was an orphan, was she not, without prospects and without a dowry? She was living in the house of her uncle, who was all but an ordinary beggar. Here she would suddenly become the wife of the great Rabbi of Nyesheve. Had her wildest dreams contained anything as ambitious?

The only obstacle, it seemed to him, was Serele, his youngest daughter. To take to himself a new wife before he had married off his own daughter would have been too much even for Rabbi Melech; he would not have dared to face his outraged sons and daughters and sons-in-law and daughters-in-law. And then there were his followers. . . . Not that they would have said anything. If the Rabbi thought something fit and proper, then clearly it was the fit and proper thing. Still, they would not have been too happy about it. And therefore Rabbi Melech was in a hurry to get his daughter married in order that he might, soon after, lead the orphan girl under the canopy to become his fourth wife.

"A beautiful creature," the stammerer told him. "She c-couldn't be lovelier. That's what the women say."

Although he had never set eyes on the girl, Rabbi Melech almost imagined that he knew what she looked like. He pictured her to himself in the likeness of his dead wife, and his heart yearned toward her.

The negotiations for the marriage of his youngest daughter were carried out in whirlwind fashion.

He himself, Rabbi Melech of Nyesheve, wrote the first letter to the Rabbi of Rachmanivke, proposing the match. The Rabbi of Rachmanivke answered promptly enough, but his answer was neither here nor there. Rabbi Melech did not let the grass grow under his feet. He took the first train to Carlsbad, where the Rachmanivke Rabbi went every summer for his gall-stones, and where he was at that moment. Rabbi Melech explained to his followers that he was not feeling well; he needed the warm baths of the famous *Kurort*. And there in Carlsbad, on the walk to the springs, Rabbi Melech met the Rachmanivke Rabbi, and set himself to the task of beating down all resistance.

He was so urgent, so obstinate, so insistent, so importunate, in brief, so insufferable, that the Rachmanivke Rabbi had no real chance against him. He gave way, reluctantly—and relieved.

Rabbi Melech even sacrificed his dignity. He was older than the Rachmanivke Rabbi; he had, moreover, a much larger following; and yet he pleaded almost like an inferior, and pledged a much more substantial dowry than he had given with any other of his daughters.

"No matter," he said, sighing heavily. "A thousand gulden more—let it go. You've got the young man—you're the boss."

The Rachmanivke Rabbi did not like the expression.

"The boss!" he muttered to himself and pulled a face. "The boss!" But he said nothing aloud.

He was the exact opposite of the Nyesheve Rabbi.

He was as slender as a willow; his beard was sparse, in color black, touched with gray; it was almost lustrous with neatness. His eyes were deep, dark and mystical, and his face had a sickly, transparent delicacy, reminiscent of the shimmer of olive trees. His fingers, long and thin, played wearily but nervously with his small golden snuffbox, or with the snow-white carefully ironed rabbinic collar which overlay his well-tailored *capote*. The contrast with the Rabbi of Nyesheve was extraordinary. The latter, hirsute, gross, lumbering, could not pass through the streets without awakening the derision of small Christian boys, who shouted after him: "Hey, nanny goat! Meh-eh-eh!" The Rachmanivke Rabbi, passing through the streets of Carlsbad, awakened the admiration and interest of blonde young ladies, who turned round shamelessly to get a longer view of him. "Oh! Look at that perfectly gorgeous wonder-Rabbi! Just like Jesus!" they whispered to one another. "Those black eyes! What a lover he would make!"

The Rabbi of Rachmanivke found his prospective relative insufferable. He was ashamed of him, ashamed of his wild voice and his wilder gestures, ashamed of the noisy way he sucked his cigar and spat on the floor, ashamed of his shapeless, unbuttoned satin *capote*, his unkempt beard and ear-locks, his indelicate language, and his whole vast body, covered with hair and reeking of sweat, cigar smoke, leather, food and drink.

The furious gestures of Rabbi Melech were positively dangerous. He would step close to the Rachmanivke Rabbi, sometimes treading on his feet, sometimes forcing him against a tree, as if to prevent his escape, and sometimes grabbing a button or a lapel. He would repeat the same idea, in identical words, a dozen times; his speech was thick, hasty and only half intelligible; a thin spray burst from his lips. To top it all, he would sometimes take hold of the other man's neatly combed beard, in a special attempt at intimacy.

It dawned on the Rachmanivke Rabbi that he would never get rid of this monstrosity except by yielding. And he yielded. He could no longer carry on the conversation. He was wearied of the constant bargaining over dowry and wedding presents, weary of the man's enthusiasms, and weariest of all of his smell. Throughout the length of the negotiations the Rachmanivke Rabbi kept his snuff box close to his thin nose.

And this was how the marriage was agreed to.

One half-victory the Rachmanivke Rabbi carried away in defeat; he had refused to fix a date for the wedding. Hence the ceaseless flow of letters between Nyesheve and Rachmanivke. The Rachmanivke Rabbi was thoroughly informed of the reasons for this haste. His *gabbai*, Mottye Godul, a Jew with a sharp-beaked nose, like that of a vulture, a tongue that delighted in scandal, and a heart filled with hatred and contempt for the Chassidim of Galicia, never failed, as often as a letter arrived, to poke fun at the father of his Rabbi's prospective daughter-in-law.

"Another letter, Rabbi! Your relative-to-be is in haste about the marriage! His own marriage, I mean. That young virgin keeps his mind off the study of our sacred books. I'm not surprised, either; he's buried three already...."

"Mottye! Your tongue is too long! It will drag you down into Gehenna."

But Mottye knew that the Rabbi was not displeased by such talk. In fact, the Rabbi seldom read the letters of Rabbi Melech himself. He would have them read to him. And the truth was that the Rachmanivke Rabbi begrudged his colleague of Nyesheve his happy prospects. Such a young girl!

"God forgive me," he said to his wife, a pale, nervous woman, on whose parchment-like face was written the sickly heritage of generations of aristocratic inbreeding. "Such impatience is unseemly! The man is on fire! I could understand it in a young widower—but at his age..." And he sighed several times, faintly, hurriedly.

The Rabbi's wife was not a foolish woman; with that fine, delicate vanity which is not uncommon among sickly women, she understood the envy which ate at her husband's heart; and the thought of it was like a touch of ice-cold steel on an exposed nerve. She bit her pale lips, and said softly:

"Let that man do what he likes. I am not going to send my darling Nahum to Galicia. A child—why should we hurry?"

And so the Rachmanivke Rabbi sent back his cautious, carefully phrased, classical letters. He tried to hide his loathing under mountains of praise, of grandiose titles, of Biblical and Talmudic verses cleverly interwoven; and always he was evasive. In all these graceful phrases there was no answer.

The father and mother both knew—though they did not admit it openly—that their beloved Nahum was literally and physically too young to marry. He was frail and slender, like his father, or rather, like a young girl; he was nervous and sensitive, like his mother, having inherited through her the long-enfeebled aristo-cratic constitution. He was, moreover, sunk in mystic specula-tions, in dreams of the Kabbala. His father pleaded with him that at his age—was he not over thirteen, and therefore a man in the eyes of the Law?—he should be sharpening his mind on the keen problems of the Talmud. Nahum listened, but did not yield. He hid himself away, locked himself in rooms, and returned to his secret mystical studies. In general there was something queer about little Nahum. He was silent and uncommunicative. He kept his eyes wide open, staring at everything about him and seeing nothing. But in secret he was preparing for a great apotheosis. He had read about that great Kabbalist, the Ari, who had brought doves into being with his magic formulae, and he was preparing to imitate him. Very frequently Nahum would purify himself in the ritual bath, the *mikveh;* he would learn by heart and repeat the fantastic names of angels; and he would often deprive himself of meals.

His father tried to change the course of his mind. The Rabbi of Rachmanivke was very much of this world; he enjoyed things of the flesh, as well as things of the spirit. He had taste, too, and wanted to be surrounded by grace and charm. He could not un-derstand the boy's secretiveness, his willful self-isolation and obstinacy.

"Nahum, my son," he said, gently, "your grandfather, of blessed memory, used to say that even in heaven they don't like a fool."

He did not relish consigning his son to the noisy fanatics of Nyesheve. He was afraid that in such surroundings the boy would lose his wits completely.

The mother disliked the match not less than her husband. More than once, when her son refused to eat, or wandered about the house like a lost soul, she wept quietly into her silken kerchief. Besides, she had already had an opportunity of seeing the bride, Serele, when the two families met in Carlsbad. The girl seemed to resemble her father; at thirteen she was a big, fleshy creature, with solid legs, a shock of red hair, strong teeth and the fully developed breasts of a mature woman. She had scrutinized this girl-bride with the close, grudging scrutiny of snobbish, upper-class women who do not forgive plain women their plain womanliness. Delicately she made the gesture of spitting out against the evil eye.

She compared her own boy, her delicate, frail Nahum with this hoyden, and her heart ached.

"If God wills it so, it may be for the best," she murmured piously. "My poor son."

She would have liked to speak openly, frankly with her husband. But in this super-aristocratic, super-intellectual house, things were not called by their plain names. People were supposed to understand one another by hints. Once she even dared to write a few words to Rabbi Melech about her devotion to her child, about their closeness to each other. She wrote an excellent Hebrew, quite like a man, and she closed the letter perfectly with a verse from the Bible, the words of Judah to Joseph, when the latter detained Benjamin in Egypt. "My soul is bound unto the soul of the child."

Rabbi Melech replied to the letters of the Rachmanivke Rabbi; the letter of his wife he ignored.

"The illustrious Rabbi knows," he wrote—the letters were clumsily formed, they were thick, ungainly, like himself; the words were misspelt, distorted—"the illustrious Rabbi knows that among our grandfathers it was the custom never to delay a marriage for more than a year after the betrothal. As to the studies of the bridegroom (long may he live!), these are no obstacle, for, God be thanked, we are not short of scholars in Nyesheve; and if it please the young man better, he may bring his tutor with him here to Nyesheve, and keep him as long as he likes, at the expense of our house."

This letter was accompanied by a gift for the bridegroom, a great heavy watch of gold, together with a thick double chain, also of gold; watches like these adorned the great stomachs of the parvenu householders of Nyesheve.

And so the two sides in this match kept up the game with each other; they despised each other, spoke contemptuously of each other and sent each other exaggeratedly courteous letters. Nor did they fool themselves. But there could be only one outcome. Rabbi

Melech was nothing less than a monomaniac. It was impossible to withstand him. Besides his letters, there were telegrams, and personal embassies. And the match having once been made public, a retraction was out of the question. There was the world to think of. And so the Rachmanivke Rabbi, having given way once, gave way a second time. He consented to an early wedding.

"If you must tear something," he said subtly to his wife, "let it be parchment rather than paper."

His wife understood him; the Rabbi considered a divorce preferable to a broken betrothal. She tried vainly to obtain one further concession: that the wedding might be delayed until the end of the summer, so that she might make one more visit to Carlsbad in the company of her son. She wanted to prepare him for his great, coming trial, and she thought, at the same time, of consulting some professor in Vienna about his condition. But Rabbi Melech was obdurate.

"The illustrious Rabbi knows," he wrote, "that among us it has been a custom handed down by our grandfathers to celebrate weddings on the Festival of the Thirty-third Day."

And for that day the wedding was fixed.

2

THE TUMULT OF PREPARATIONS BEGAN IN THE COURT OF THE Nyesheve Rabbi soon after Passover, several weeks before the wedding day.

The young students who sat all day long in the synagogue, absorbed presumably in the Talmud, were caught up in the restless expectant spirit. Routine was forgotten. They unbent from their folios and talked of profane and even blasphemous things. Only when the Rabbi was expected, at prayer-time, they flung themselves upon the tattered pages, and the chant of their audible studies suddenly filled the synagogue.

The hangers-on of the Rabbinic court, the beggars and camp-followers, freshened up. Occasions like these were rare. They clustered round the village Jews who came to consult the Rabbi, and to ask his intercession with Providence, and demanded double and treble the usual gifts. They beleaguered the front door of the Rabbi's house, and when a woman stepped out, they burst into such loud blessings, and were so insistently benevolent, that there was no escape. And the women were compelled to thrust their hands down and haul their purses out from their bosoms, or even to dig into their stockings for a few coins, in order to be able to pass.

But the kreutzer—the smallest currency—which it was customary to give these beggars had become too cheap.

"What's this?" they yelled. "Kreutzer when the Rabbi's daughter is going to be married? Pfui! We won't take them."

Begging, threatening, bargaining, they often forced visitors to part with their last coins, leaving them without return fare. A general license of misbehavior descended on the court. Beggars stole the phylacteries and prayer-shawls of the poorer or more niggardly members of the household, and pawned them for drink. They hung around the kitchen, snatching up whatever they could lay their hands on.

Even older and graver householders of Nyesheve yielded to the spirit of festivity. They wore their satin Sabbath mantles throughout the week, or even their Sabbath skull-caps, with their thirteen dangling tassels. Some of them went so far as to give their skull-caps a rakish tilt.

The daily morning, afternoon and evening prayers were gabbled hastily, and long patches were omitted, as on the Day of the Rejoicing of the Law. Never again would the Rabbi of Nyesheve marry off his youngest daughter! Minor festivities, like preludes, sprang up here and there. From surrounding villages and hamlets beggars and drones streamed in. Men left their wives and families and settled for weeks around the Rabbinic court.

"*Mazel-tov!* Good luck!" The words were heard everywhere, as often as a glass of whiskey or of mead was swallowed. It was everybody's wedding. "*Mazel-tov!* God be good to all of us!"

In the kitchens of the Rabbinic court there was a ceaseless boiling, frying and sizzling. In the confusion of those weeks, the Rabbi's sons usurped their father's privileges; each one set up a little court of his own, gave banquets, distributed morsels to favorites, propounded the Law and drank wine. There was bitter rivalry between the minor courts, each one fighting for the largest number of followers. While such banquets were in progress, guards were set about the rooms, to give warning lest the Rabbi himself approach and see with his own eyes how his sons were fighting, during his lifetime, for his Rabbinic empire. The servants worked as they had never worked before. But as they could not keep pace with the mounting celebrations, Israel Avigdor impressed into service a horde of beggars and hangers-on, thin, half-starved Jews in rags, who spent their days loitering about the synagogues, singing Psalms.

"Into the kitchen with you!" he shouted, grabbing them by their *capotes.* "The Lord has had enough of your Psalms. Into the kitchen with you! Potatoes have to be peeled! Onions! Cabbages!"

And the beggars peeled potatoes and onions and cabbages; they dragged up logs from the outhouses, brought water from the wells, scrubbed the hair off calves' feet, washed the raw meat of newly slaughtered animals, rubbed sharp horseradish on the graters. The tears ran out of their red eyes onto their sunken cheeks. The servant girls, vast, shapeless creatures on stumpy legs, perspired from over-work and over-feeding. Their hands were dipped into great, greasy pots, or were lost in masses of yellow dough; they blew up the fires, shifted the pots and pans, burned themselves and vented their rage on the beggars and on the dogs and pigs which had wandered into the yard, drawn by the smell of cooking and by the bones and offal constantly being thrown out.

"Hey, you beggars, drive away the dogs and the pigs," the girls yelled at their helpers. But the beggars were afraid of the dogs, and the sight of pigs filled them with loathing. They only stood at

a distance and yelled "Out of here! Pfui!" till the servant girls
came with pails of water, sometimes hot, sometimes cold, and sent
a shower over the animals. It was no use. They only shook themselves, and stood waiting patiently.

And Israel Avigdor, the *gabbai*, the Rabbi's right-hand man,
was in his seventh heaven.

He was a stocky, sturdy man, with a red beard, and a face—
wherever it was visible—covered with freckles. He wore silk and
satin; but in every movement and word and gesture he betrayed
the vulgar ignoramus, the one-time errand-boy, who, by cunning
and flattery, had risen to power, and had become the chief *gabbai*
of the Rabbinic court. His big nostrils were always stained with
snuff, and his red-haired hands were everywhere. Now he grabbed
a youngster by the ear and nearly twisted it off, now he pulled
some beggar's hat down over his eyes, now he quarreled with the
synagogue boy, and crawled onto the table with his muddy boots
—right among the books and papers—to take down a lamp
chimney and show that it was dirty.

"Idiot!" he growled. "Is this the way to clean a lamp? Come
here, I'll show you how it ought to be cleaned."

And seizing the skirt of the boy's *capote*, he wiped the smoked
lamp glass with it.

Israel Avigdor was invariably provoked by youngsters who
were not seated at the table studying the sacred books; but he had
no knowledge of his own, and his quotations of texts were gro-
tesquely and coarsely wrong. From the synagogue he would hasten
into a kitchen, look into the big pots, pinch one of the servant girls
and shout instructions. And always he was faithful to the interests
of his Rabbi's court.

"More water in that bean soup," he ordered. "You don't have
to give such thick soup to the beggars. They're not used to it;
they'll break their teeth on it."

He always steered clear of the Rabbi; that is, except when some
follower of the court sought admittance with a petition for intercession. And then Israel Avigdor was always on hand to get his
little rake-off. As often as the Rabbi yelled for him to come and re-
light his extinguished cigar, Israel Avigdor was somewhere else.

The Rabbi threatened that he would drive him out of the court; but Israel Avigdor paid little attention. For he knew that the Rabbi needed him more than he needed the Rabbi.

No one knew the workings of that court as well as Israel Avigdor. No one knew the faces at table as well as he. He knew exactly how many bottles of wine had to be put down to each visitor, whether he wanted it or not. He knew all the rules of precedence, knew exactly where to seat people—and particularly the rich Jews—in such wise as to offend no one. He knew what morsels went to whom, who was supposed to receive a generous portion, and who could be fobbed off with a half-empty plate. He had the knack of holding back a mob at the Rabbi's door, while admitting the important personages. But, above all, Israel Avigdor was irreplaceable when he accompanied the Rabbi on money-gathering journeys. He could throw the fear of God into the Chassidim, and demand unheard-of sums which they dared not refuse.

He was excellent even outside the Jewish field. He never failed to get a private car when the Rabbi of Nyesheve traveled by train. He persuaded country magnates to place their carriages at the disposal of the great Rabbi. When he accompanied his chief to some local celebration of Chassidim, he managed to arrive with such pomp, and made so much noise, that at once the local Rabbis shrank into the background, and seemed to become the guests, rather than the hosts, of the Rabbi of Nyesheve. He had a lordly way of commanding the local *gabbais*; they obeyed him like errand-boys.

But the most important thing about Israel Avigdor was his knowledge of the inner machinery of the Rabbinic court. In fact, he knew a little too much. He knew the quarrels, the secrets, the kitchen intrigues, the family feuds and pretenses. He saw, heard, felt, smelt everything. No room and no incident was private to him. It was told that one Saturday, after the festival meal, he even burst in on the Rabbi himself during a moment of connubial intimacy with his third wife.

It was no sin he had stumbled upon, God forbid! But from that moment on he looked the Rabbi straight in the eyes, with a leering, knowing look; from that moment on, too, he became deafer than ever to the Rabbi's yell of "Srelvigdor! I'll throttle the life out of you."

Now, with the approaching wedding of Serele, Israel Avigdor unfolded his wings and soared. He was never to be seen near the Rabbi; when called he sent someone of the lower hierarchy of servants. He was either drinking mead with the Chassidim or flitting through the kitchens, slyly, observantly; and wherever he went, the smell of his snuff went with him.

On the Festival of the Thirty-third Day, that is, the day of the wedding, thousands of Chassidim, followers of the Rabbinic dynasty of Nyesheve, gathered in that town. Rich Chassidim came from Krakow in special cars; they said their prayers jubilantly and in chorus at the railway station; they danced, sang and told each other stories and legends of the wonder-working Rabbis of the Chassidim. To these special cars neither non-Jews nor Jews who had no beards were admitted. The conductors drank joyously with the Chassidim and wished them the best of luck; so infectious was the mood that even the most German or Polish or Ruthenian conductors, as they changed relays, began to speak Yiddish with the gelatinous Galician pronunciation. Poor Chassidim came, not by train, but on foot, sometimes begging or stealing a lift from wagoners, and being whipped off the cart as often as not. The inns of Nyesheve were jammed; private houses, stables, barns, garrets were filled. And on top of the flood of Chassidim came the flood of beggars.

It was forbidden to bathe in the river until after Pentecost; but the young Talmud students were too impatient. Right in the midst of the Seven Week period between Passover and Pentecost, they went down to the river in a body, stripped and plunged in. They swam, dived, shouted at the top of their voices, just as they did in the steam-rooms of the ritual baths, when the heat drove them up the highest steps and their bodies tingled and sang. "Oh, good, good!" they shouted.

From the river they went to the big barn in the Rabbinic courtyard. There they put on Cossack uniforms. According to an immemorial custom in Nyesheve, young men would dress themselves, before a Rabbinic wedding, in Cossack uniforms, and thus ride out to encounter the bridegroom.

These uniforms lay in bundles under heaps of hay and straw in the barn. From wedding to wedding they lay there, decaying and rusting. The boys drew on the long, tight trousers, closed at the bottom with cross-laces, the Hussar coats, also laced across, and the high boots. Cossack uniforms they were called. Actually they were a mixture of styles: Hungarian cavalry, operetta hussars and old Polish infantry of the time of Jan Sobieski. The most fantastic part of the uniform was the head-gear, a towering hat of fur crowned with a stiffened horse-tail. In this weird rig-out the lean and hungry Talmud students, with their sunken faces, their dangling ear-locks and their slouching bodies resembled no known military on this earth—unless it was the "Turkish Soldiers" which children in Jewish villages used to cut out of paper and show in a magic lantern which consisted of a paper box, a candle and a hole.

In keeping with the custom, the wagoners and the well-to-do Jews placed their nags at the disposal of the Talmud students. The nags were even remoter than their riders from the Cossack spirit and appearance; but they seemed to resent the travesty. Starved and bony and spiritless as they were, they put up a resistance, bucked and refused to go forward. The riders hung to the manes, yelled, dug their spurs into the horses—without success.

Meanwhile a number of Chassidim had carried into the barn a huge barrel which was generally used for the preparation of red beet soup for Passover. Others brought pails of hot water from the kitchen. Richer and more privileged Jews stood over the barrel and squeezed lemons into it, the juice running over their fingers, and emptied bags of sugar into it. They were preparing the famous Nyesheve punch for a Rabbinic wedding. A wild babel of voices went up; Jews quarreled, pushed one another, gave instructions, everyone being of the opinion that he alone was the true inheritor of the traditional recipe for Nyesheve punch.

"Idiot! That's all wrong! Let me show you!" No one took offense; no one paid any attention. And when the brew was finished, everyone tasted, smacked his lips and cried ecstatically: "Marvelous!"

A magnificent coach, drawn by four glistening white horses, drew into the yard. Whenever a Rabbinic wedding took place in Nyesheve, Count Olcha sent his private coach to be used by the bridegroom as he came from the railroad station to the town, a distance of a few kilometers. In exchange, the Rabbi of Nyesheve ordered all his followers to vote for the Count when he stood for election to the Austrian Parliament. The Count's coachman, a gigantic peasant with a pair of drooping blond mustachios which lost themselves in his sideburns, swallowed great portions of cake and brandy brought out specially for him. When his spirits had reached the right pitch, he picked up his whip and cracked it so loudly above the heads of the old horses that they started forward in terror, forgetting their years and their resentment.

"Yow!" he howled. "Forward, Sheenies!"

The cavalcade streamed out of the yard, the students clinging to the manes of the horses; the Count's coach lumbered after them down the road, and the procession was swallowed up in sunlight and dust. Everything vanished: the frightened students yelling their death-bed confession, the clattering hoofs, the coachman standing up and cracking his whip.

At the station the Cossacks crawled off their mounts and waited. When the train drew in they made a rush for the bridegroom's car, singing in chorus:

"Welcome, bridegroom! Welcome, *mazel-tov*, good luck to you!"

Pale, tired, astounded, Nahum stared at the throng of masqueraders, the like of which he had never seen in Rachmanivke. His eyes opened wider than usual, till they looked unearthly. He was both terrified and ashamed; the public reception was too much for him, and he shrank from the milling crowd and from the hands thrust in his direction. They were hot, sweaty hands; he touched them with his thin, boyish fingers and shrank away from them.

"Easy there!" cried Mottye Godul, the *gabbai* of Rachmanivke, glaring at the crowd.

He hated these Austrian Chassidim and their Chassidism. The nostrils of his beaked nose quivered, like that of a hawk scenting prey. But no one paid any attention to him. The crowd closed in tighter on the bridegroom. Mottye Godul lost all his self-control.

"Lunatics!" he yelled. "Keep back! Heathens!"

Israel Avigdor was not the man to let this pass. No Russian Jew was going to talk to *his* Chassidim in this tone of voice.

"Heathen yourself!" he yelled back. "Heathens come from Rachmanivke! In Nyesheve we have only decent, God-fearing Jews!"

The two *gabbais* stood up to each other with flaming faces. Mottye's nose had gone as red as Israel's beard. They resembled two cocks working themselves up for a battle.

"Gangway for the bridegroom," Mottye Godul ordered.

The bridegroom stumbled forward. He had lost himself completely. In his short silken *capote*, neatly tailored, his little, lustrous boots, his snow-white, ironed collar spreading over the *capote*, and his half-orthodox, half-German head-gear, he looked even younger than his years.

His mother, the wife of the Rabbi of Rachmanivke, was very modishly dressed. Her hat, with its high feathers, was copied from the fashion plates of the Gentile aristocracy. She went up to her son and, taking out a little kerchief, wiped away the sweat from his face, as tenderly as if he had been not a bridegroom on the day of his wedding, but a little child still in the cradle.

"Nahum, darling," she said, "don't be afraid! I'll look after you! Let whatever happens be on my head."

The Chassidim heard—and were offended. They were offended before they heard her speak; her dress was too Gentile. No ordinary Jewess of Nyesheve—let alone a Jewess of the Rabbinic court—would ever have dared to attire herself thus. But they were doubly offended by her words, and by her attitude toward her son.

"*Litvaks!*" they thought, contemptuously. "*Litvaks!* Snobbish, infidel Lithuanian Jews." Whoever came across the border into Galicia was in their eyes a Lithuanian.

And for a moment they were even aware of a vague distrust for the whole wedding. Why should Nyesheve import a bridegroom out of Lithuania? But they said nothing. If the Rabbi had arranged it, it had probably been ordained on high.

Only the Count's coachman spoke out. He looked with an expert's eye on the bridegroom, pulled his mustachios, and said vigorously to the conductors and porters: "*To dopiero narzeczony* —some bridegroom. He'll need his mother around to button him up."

A burst of laughter came from the Gentiles, but their voices were drowned out by the chorus of the Cossacks:

> *Ein k'elohenu*
> There is no one like our God,
> There is no one like our King.

3

ALL THAT LONG SUMMER DAY THE BRIDEGROOM TOOK NOT A MORSEL of food.

Serele fasted too, according to the Law, but she bore it well. She was hungry, but quiet and self-possessed; no shadow of distress crossed her face.

She had been quiet and self-possessed throughout all the period of the betrothal, obeying the laws, doing what she was told, less like a young girl than a grown woman. She had received the news of her betrothal calmly from her father, and had asked no questions. Calmly she received all the wedding presents in their satin-padded boxes.

Her one remark was: "Isn't that beautiful!"

And just as calmly she listened to her older sisters—blowsy women whose mothers were not her mother—when, a few days before the wedding, they taught her the first duties of a bride.

They approached the subject mysteriously, indirectly and allusively, so as not to shock the fourteen-year-old girl.

"Serele," they said, "you know that we women do not need to learn and study in the sacred books, like the men. But the Lord has given us our own commandments, and to obey them is just as important as the study of the Law."

And they quoted instances from the Bible, alluded to the matriarchs, to Sarah, Rebecca, Rachel and Leah. They looked for the most delicate words, in order that the child bride might not be shocked. They might just as well have spared themselves the trouble.

This big, overgrown girl heard everything, did everything, in simple, straightforward fashion. Not a suspicion of a blush passed over her cheeks, not a single shy smile disturbed the even luster of her cold eyes.

It was thus that she went, the night before the wedding, to the women's ritual bath in the Rabbinic court. She was accompanied by her sisters, by the wives of *gabbais*, by beggar-women, by a motley crowd. The town orchestra went along, adding to the din. Her sisters looked with envy at the young firm body, at the full hips and bosom, and, to drive away evil spirits, they spat out and repeated: "Pfui! May no evil eye harm her!"

They brought her oranges, to strengthen her; most brides need to be strengthened after the ritual bathing, and after all the other ceremonies.

"Eat, bride," they coaxed her. "You must be feeling weak."

But she needed nothing. She felt perfectly well, perfectly healthy.

With the same calmness she greeted the old woman who came to shave her head.

In Nyesheve it was the custom to cut off the bride's hair, not on the morning of the wedding, but the day before. The sisters of Serele began to prepare her for the ordeal; they remembered their own terror. And they were very tender with her. They caressed her, passed their fingers through her thick locks and expressed their admiration.

"Such a forest, such a thick forest," they said to one another, softly, mysteriously. And as they unbraided and rebraided her locks, they remembered their own first blossoming and the quick withering that followed. "May this be a sacrifice, Serele, like the first fruits which the Jews used to bring up to Jerusalem in the time of the Temple."

Serele was not conscious of any sacrifice. This was the law, and she obeyed it as she obeyed all the other laws. The old woman who cut her hair was filled with astonishment at the precocious piety of the bride.

"Such a pure soul," she sighed, dipping a piece of cake into brandy. "May the sun shine on her life, dear God in heaven, as her young cheeks shine now."

With her big scissors she began to cut criss-cross; then she passed the razor over the skull, making it look like the hide of a new-shorn lamb.

"Mazel-tov, mazel-tov, good luck and happiness," her sisters cried, and they covered the suddenly diminutive head with a satin kerchief.

"Mazel-tov," Serele answered, and tied the ends of the kerchief in a knot under her chin, with the deftness of an elderly woman.

The old woman went from one relative to another, to collect "shaving money." Then, coming to the bride, she said: "You ought to give me a kreutzer for every hair. Please God, may we soon see the birthday of your first son."

"And may you soon see the same among your daughters," Serele answered tranquilly in the usual formula.

With the same tranquillity she sat later in the bridal room, among her sisters, and read aloud in the book of woman's duties, a great book with ivory covers and a gold clasp. She read out the archaic sentences evenly:

"And she shall be willing in the time of their union—" Serele's voice took on the traditional chant of feminine prayer—"and she shall not, God forbid, be a cause of pain or suffering to him; but she shall show him comfort and love, and she shall be willing in the good and pious deed, as the commandment and custom thereof is; so that thus may be born of her men children...."

No such peacefulness reigned in the soul of Nahum, the bride-groom.

The long day of the wedding, as well as the brief night which preceded it, had been a time of intense suffering for him. He had spent the preceding twenty-four hours in the train. And he needed rest. But rest was the last thing they thought of giving him. There were, first of all, thousands of people who felt entitled to greet him and pay him their respects in person. Many of them had come hundreds of miles in order to be present at the marriage of the Rabbi's daughter. Nahum had to receive them, return their handshakes, reply to their words of greeting. Very soon his hand began to ache, and his throat became dry.

And when he was through with the public reception, his father-in-law took him into a private room for a long heart-to-heart talk. Rabbi Melech had observed the laws of hospitality, and had eaten cake and drunk brandy with each newly arriving group. He was not drunk; he was merely in a condition of misty exhilaration. He wanted to talk—to talk much—without interruption. And so he talked rapidly, swallowing half his words; and he chanted most of the sentences after the fashion of a Rabbinic sermon and in the Galician dialect, so that poor Nahum of far-away Rachmanivke understood one word in five. The Rabbi, uncertain of himself, was trying to show off his erudition; and he remembered some parable which he had invented for his own wedding sermon, fifty years back; and he repeated it for the benefit of Nahum. He repeated it more than once, and with every repetition his delight at his own ingenuity became more enthusiastic. It reached a point where he grabbed Nahum affectionately by the chin—for lack of a beard—let go of it, clapped his hands together, thrust the boy against the wall, and kept on saying:

"That was clever, that was. But you've got to get the point; it was like this. . . ."

When Rabbi Melech talked he sprayed; and thick cigar smoke brought the tears to Nahum's eyes. It crept, too, into his dry and empty stomach and made him sick. He was choking. He coughed several times, but his father-in-law did not hear; he seldom did hear anyone else.

"You've got to get the point," he said, enthusiastically.

When at last Rabbi Melech released him, he fell into the hands of the Rabbi's sons. They led him from apartment to apartment, from room to room. In every room there was a crowd of wedding guests; everyone ate and drank—no one thought of the boy's fast.

"*Mazel-tov! L'chaim!* Long life!" they shouted, lifting up their glasses, draining them, and then shaking the boy's hand vigorously.

Almost worse than these revelers was the queer creature who was introduced to him, in one of the rooms, as the "genius" of Nyesheve. Every Jewish town of note had its genius, its brilliant youngster destined to greatness in the Law. The genius of Nyesheve was a young man who carried his head on one side and made complicated gestures to help out arguments; uncouth, uncivilized, he fastened onto Nahum, determined to give him a dazzling display of learning. But he scarcely enunciated a sentence without catching himself up and saying: "Of course you can always take the opposite point of view, can't you?" Nahum listened, and the perspiration dripped down his cheeks.

The ritual bath which they prepared for Nahum was heated, although the day was warm and summery. The closeness in the baths was stifling; Nahum nearly fainted.

Several times, on the morning of the wedding, his father tried to persuade him to break his fast.

"Rabbinic children," he said, "don't need to fast on their wedding day."

But Nahum would not yield. His frightened mother wanted to invoke authority. "My child," she said, "I want you to eat! The commandment concerning obedience to parents is of more weight than the commandment concerning the bridegroom's fast. And I shall command you to eat."

"Mother," he begged, "don't make me unhappy. I won't eat."

All day he carried around with him a volume of the Kabbala, and on the rare occasions when the pressure on him was released, he dipped into it. Also his teacher, the Rabbi Pesachiah of Zavil, a tremendously learned Jew and tremendously pious, would take him away for a few minutes and make him repeat his wedding sermon.

"Bridegroom!" he said. "Be a credit to your father, bless him!
Let not shame come on your parents and your town. There will be
learned men at the wedding dinner!"

The great synagogue, where the tables were laid, was filled to
overflowing with guests and visitors eager to catch a glimpse of the
bridegroom. The Chassidim blocked windows and doors; younger
people had crawled under the tables. If they could not see the
bridegroom, they would at least be privileged to hear his wedding
sermon. The air was thick, almost palpable. The candles in the
small candlesticks and in the elaborate candelabras added to the
heat, and melted and bent over as they burned. The guests perspired and stuck to each other clammily. And the waves of heat
beat strongest toward the upper part of the synagogue, where
Nahum, the bridegroom, was seated, surrounded by the nearest
relatives and the guests of honor.

His head swam. He wore, in addition to the skull-cap, a great
fur hat, which pressed on his temples. The sweat ran down his ear-
locks and stained his white collar.

In the women's rooms, where the bride was being prepared for
the ceremony, the atmosphere was different. Here it was cool and
spacious. Girls danced together, lifting up the ends of their bal-
looning skirts; or else they stopped, and talked affectedly with
the musicians, trying to make their Yiddish sound like German.

Waiters in short coats flitted from room to room, distributing
cold drinks. They wore Jewish skull-caps on their heads, but they
tried to sound non-Jewish and elegant, and also mutilated their
Yiddish in the hope that it would sound like German. "*Wollen Sie
etwos geniessen?*" they asked. Little girls in new dresses and huge
bow-knots were made to curtsey to the grown-ups, and went from
person to person flirting their fans. More than anyone else the
relatives of the bride and bridegroom were showing off their elegance and their culture. Gold and silver and jewelry and silk and
brocade flashed and glowed in the rooms. The only man in the
women's rooms was the *badchan* or jester, a high functionary of
all Jewish weddings. This Jew had put on the clothes of a non-
Jew; he had combed his beard in the manner of a high Austrian
official; and now he strutted about reciting bits of German, into
which he wove Hebrew quotations and Yiddish expressions; now

and then he burst into improvisation. He shouted, gesticulated and winked at the girls; all in all he thought he was giving an excellent imitation of a comedian he had once seen in a city cabaret.

> O, *hören Sie mal aus, hochgeschäzte Braut und ihre liebe*
>   *Mädchen,*
> *Sarah, Rivka, Rachel und auch Rosa und Grätchen;*
> *Das Sterben,* chalilah, *und die Heirat kann niemand meiden,*
> *Dann die liebe ist doch fur die junge Leute ein* wahres
>   gan-eden.
> *Die Rösen duften wenn sie frisch sind, sagt der grosse*
>   *Dichter,*
> *Darum freuet euch und liebkost euch, ihre schöne Gesichter.*
> *Und wie die liebe Sonne, Kalah, soll dein lichtig* mazal
>   *scheinen,*
> *Und beim* Rebono shel Olom *ein glückliches Schicksal*
>   *ausweinen.*

But in the great synagogue there was neither air nor gayety. Every now and again one of the Chassidim would faint; he was dragged out of the room and taken to the well in the courtyard, and left there. Little boys, hopeless of getting into the banquet hall, amused themselves here by pumping water over him till he came to.

Then the grand moment came. The teacher leaned over to Nahum, saying: "Now, bridegroom; a congregation of Jews is waiting to hear your word."

When, at the end of his sermon, which lasted over an hour, Nahum had to go to the bride, to cover her with a veil, he could not walk without assistance. He was so weak that, before he threw the white silk kerchief over the bride's face, he dropped it on the floor.

"Oh!" A shudder passed through the women. It was an evil omen.

Then followed the banquet. The bowl of golden soup—symbol of golden years—came first, and Nahum could take nothing. The bride ate with relish. She would have liked to tell him to eat too; it was good for him. But she could not talk. At this point her self-possession failed her, and she was shy in the presence of this strange boy whom she now saw for the first time and who was her husband. She therefore ate in silence. At last Nahum took one spoonful of soup from the common dish which, as is the custom, was placed before bride and bridegroom at the wedding dinner. He was so exhausted and frightened that he did not even think of taking a look at his wife.

The rest of the dinner he ignored. Long after it was over, late in the night, two toothless old Jews, honored householders of Nyesheve, led him aside, and conducting him toward the bridal chamber, talked a great deal and mysteriously about the first duty and commandments of a husband. They thrust him into the room and slammed the door behind him. And Nahum was lost, helpless, like a child abandoned by its mother in a strange place.

Out of the sea of soft white cushions and covers, a pair of open eyes stared at him. He took one sharp frightened glance at them, at a pair of flaming cheeks, at the strange feminine head bound in a white kerchief with red ribbons. He was dazed. Cold sweat broke out over his body.

In an agony of fear and shame, he whispered, soundlessly: "Mama."

The next morning his father-in-law called him into his room and bade him take a seat. Rabbi Melech sat down opposite him, and pulled the chair closer and closer. He thrust his face into Nahum's, and all his hairy covering of beard and ear-locks trembled with anger.

"It's a bad business!" he said, grimly. "Very bad! Disgusting! We don't understand that sort of thing in Nyesheve. It's no way to behave! Disgusting!"

Nahum shrank inward, became smaller than himself. His tongue was paralyzed. He was conscious only of a nameless fear. He was afraid of his father-in-law, with his terrible beard; he was afraid of the hordes of men who surrounded him; he was afraid, even, of that face in the sea of white cushions and covers, and of the open eyes and crimson cheeks, the memory of which still dazzled him.

His lips formed the single word "Mama!" but no sound came out of them.

4

THE SEVEN DAYS OF THE SEVEN BENEDICTIONS—THE FESTIVITIES
which follow a marriage—were for Nahum like the Seven Days of
Mourning which follow the death of a near one.

Night after night there were these banquets of the Seven Benedictions, uninterrupted eating and drinking and rejoicing and talking. Night after night his father-in-law bade him get up and utter
words of learning and wisdom for the assembled Jews. Night after
night the same two toothless old Jews took him aside and babbled
things into his ears which made his olive-pale face flare up with
shame; night after night they led him to the bridal chamber and
slammed the door behind him.

And every morning, immediately following the first prayers,
Rabbi Melech sent his eldest daughter to talk things over with the
bride. The daughter returned with the same report. A contemptuous shrug of the shoulders and the word: "Nothing."

In his anger, Rabbi Melech drew for several minutes at his
cigar, without noticing that it was out.

"God in heaven!" he shrieked at last.

On the last of the Seven Days of the Seven Benedictions the
Rabbi sent for Serele herself.

She came to him in a long dress of yellow silk. On her shaven
head she wore a velvet bonnet on which nodded a garden of
cherries, leaves and flowers. Her father bade her sit down in the
big chair which was always reserved for the most important visitors and sat down opposite in his own armchair. He fixed his
eyes on her so ferociously that she felt a stab of cold pass through
her bosom, and she covered it with one hand. The look on her
father's face reminded her of the terrible ceremonies which took

place when some village girl was brought to him to have a demon exorcised.

"Well?" he asked at last, in a chanting voice.

Serele was silent.

"What's going to be the upshot of this?" he asked; and his chant changed from the Talmudic to the mercantile, as if he was trying to make the best of a bad bargain.

Serele stared back at him dumbly.

"Was he with you?"

"N-n-no!" Serele burst into tears; she wept not only with her eyes, but with her mouth and nose and body.

"Idiot!" the Rabbi said. "Get out of here." He motioned her to get up and pushed her to the door. "Get out of here, you idiot," he repeated.

Rabbi Melech then sent a servant for several volumes of the big Lemberg edition of the *Shulchan Aruch*, the code of Jewish laws. They were brought to him, old books in linen bindings, with dirty, wrinkled pages. And Rabbi Melech sat down alone to find, in that ocean of tiny text, the laws relating to husband and wife.

He had made up his mind to write a letter to the bridegroom's father, the Rabbi of Rachmanivke, who had returned home with his wife the very morning after the wedding, without waiting to take part in the Seven Benedictions. He was going to tell him of the shocking outcome of the match, and to take first steps toward a divorce. But he wanted to be sure of the law; he wanted to know how much he could claim in the way of damages for the shame and humiliation inflicted on the bride; also how much he was entitled to in the way of expenses, and how he was to set about the recovery of presents and dowry.

A day and most of the night Rabbi Melech thumbed the old pages. He had never been much of a scholar. Ever since assuming the rôle of Rabbi of Nyesheve, he had given up his studies. Only at odd intervals would he pick up the *Zohar*, the book of the Kabbala, and look for something easy to quote at a banquet. Besides being the Chassidic Rabbi of Nyesheve, he was also the Rabbi at large; he was therefore bound to answer all ritualistic questions and settle disputes according to Jewish law. But he had never done this himself. He kept a learned assistant for the purpose.

He might have asked his assistant to ferret out the law. But he was unwilling to expose himself to the ridicule of the court. And so he wandered blindly and painfully through obscure texts, losing his way in the commentators, perspiring over the difficult and obscure words which they threw in profusely. And at last he found what he wanted. He was ready to write his letter.

In the morning, after prayers, he sat down again, prepared to teach that learned snob of Rachmanivke a lesson, and to arrange that his helpless son be shipped back to him with nothing more than the clothes he had on. He rolled back his sleeves and began. He had already got as far as the high-sounding introduction, which he tried to make all the more magniloquent, so as to be able to follow with an effective insult, when the door burst open, and his oldest daughter rushed in, leading Serele by the hand.

"Father! *Mazel-tov!* Good luck!"

Rabbi Melech's eyes opened wide; they bulged until they seemed ready to jump out.

"What?" he cried. "Do you mean that . . . ?"

"He was with her last night," said the oldest daughter, triumphantly. "Unexpectedly. Serele, tell Father. You don't have to be ashamed."

Serele, the strong colors fixed on her cold face, told everything simply.

"Well, well. God be thanked," the Rabbi said, and smiled with all the bushiness of his hairy face. "It must have been a touch of the evil eye. I should have thought of that, and done something. God be thanked!"

He paused a moment, then, in his usual fashion, began to thrust the women out of the room, but this time more indulgently.

"Go, go, you little silly," he said to Serele. "Go, and be a good, dutiful Jewish wife. It's all right now. . . ."

The letter to Rachmanivke was never finished. Instead, the Rabbi sat down at once and wrote a letter to the stammerer, the uncle of the orphan girl. He bade him, on receipt of the letter, come to Nyesheve without delay, in order to arrange the marriage between the Rabbi and the orphan girl Malkah. And to save time, he wrote, they would dispense with the two ceremonies of writing out the betrothal, and then waiting for the marriage. Marriage and betrothal would take place together. In the meantime, a verbal understanding would suffice. In the letter Rabbi Melech enclosed a twenty-gulden note. When it was ready to be sealed, he stood holding it in his hand. Perhaps he had made a mistake. Fifteen would have been enough for that pauper. But the words of the man came back to his ears:

"A beauty! A beautiful creature! That's what all the women say."

Instead of taking out the twenty-gulden note, he added another five-gulden note, and sighed a mingled sigh of resentment and satisfaction.

"A son of the Rabbinate, after all," he said to himself. "A few extra gulden won't do him any harm."

He was about to seal the letter when he remembered something else. He added that, with regard to the usual presents for the bride, the girl need have no fear. He, the Rabbi of Nyesheve, would provide everything; he would adorn her in a manner becoming to the loveliest bride. Her clothes would be in keeping with her descent—she was the granddaughter of great Rabbis, and her honor would be guarded accordingly. At the bottom of the letter the Rabbi added something more, in all but illegibly jammed-in lines: She was not to be afraid of the intrigues and quarrels of the Rabbinic court. He, the Rabbi, would spread his wings over her, and she would be sheltered under the mantle of his greatness. Furthermore, he wrote, though he himself would have been content with a quiet, private wedding, he knew that, according to the law, she, being a virgin, was entitled to a joyous public wedding; and therefore he, at his own expense, would arrange for a wedding with many guests, with music and with much feasting; and that wedding should take place, according to the custom, in the home town of the bride.

He added his name at the bottom, likewise his father's name, his grandfather's and his great-grandfather's, to four generations. He licked the envelope thoroughly, and closed it. Then he sent for one of his grandsons and bade him write the address. He himself, the Rabbi of Nyesheve, could not write the language of the Gentiles. He watched the boy writing, admired his talent, and gave him a gulden.

The letter gone, he sat down contentedly in his armchair, cut himself a fresh cigar, and shouted:

"Srelvigdor! Srelvigdor!"

This time Israel Avigdor was on hand. He was being called, as he knew, not merely to light the Rabbi's cigar. He was to introduce into the room the rich Jew of Kiev, Reb Paltiel Hurwitz, who had come all the way from Russia to the wedding of the Rabbi's daughter, and who now begged a private audience.

Reb Paltiel Hurwitz was a great timber merchant; huge stretches of forest were his monopoly; he was the owner of a sugar factory; he was a familiar of the Russian Gubernator of Kiev, and himself spoke Russian—it was said—magnificently. On top of all this he was an ardent follower of the Rabbi of Nyesheve. Several times a year he gathered up his sons and his grandsons, had passports prepared for them and made a pilgrimage to the Rabbi.

To the wedding of the Rabbi's daughter Reb Paltiel Hurwitz brought not less than one thousand rubles, besides separate gifts to the bridegroom, to wit, a costly skull-cap and an enormous silver candelabrum. His children, and even his grandchildren, also brought presents. But Rabbi Melech was not satisfied. He was after something else. Paltiel Hurwitz had told him that he stood a good chance of buying up, from a Russian general, a great stretch of forest which would yield him a fortune. But there was a hitch; the purchase had to be made indirectly, for if the government found out that the purchaser was a Jew, there would be trouble; prison, very likely. And somebody would be sure to find out and betray him. And therefore he had come to the Rabbi for advice.

No sooner had Rabbi Melech heard the story than the idea flashed through his mind that Reb Paltiel Hurwitz could not do better than take him, Rabbi Melech, in as partner. At this particular time, what with his daughter's marriage and his own, he needed money. A partnership would be a godsend. Reb Paltiel Hurwitz would not dream of asking his Rabbi to invest something.

That was never done. Followers of the Rabbi had often made him partner in some transaction. This time, of course, the transaction was of such dimensions, that the giving away of a partnership looked, at first, out of the question. And Rabbi Melech was afraid to broach the subject. This important merchant might take offense, and might transfer his allegiance to another Rabbi. That would be a blow to prestige and income. And yet—Rabbi Melech reflected—this business was a dangerous one, was it not? The shadow of the prison, of Siberia, lay over it. How much securer Reb Paltiel Hurwitz would feel if he had, as partner, the Rabbi, who would give him a definite promise that God would be on his side, and everything would pass off well.

And so Rabbi Melech had refused to let him depart. The manner of it was simple: he would not admit Reb Paltiel to private audience for leave-taking and parting benediction. Rabbi Melech knew that this kind of treatment always confused a follower, a Chassid; and it worked best with followers of importance, business men harried by big affairs. In the case of Reb Paltiel it would work best of all; for Reb Paltiel was worried and distraught, he was afraid of treachery, and the cruel delay weakened his will and made him more amenable to the Rabbi's will.

As often as Reb Paltiel sent Israel Avigdor in to the Rabbi, the Rabbi answered: "No, no; Paltiel mustn't hurry away so soon."

And Paltiel Hurwitz was becoming frantic. Appointments, transactions, persons waited for him in Kiev. Telegrams came in sheaves daily. Paltiel Hurwitz thrust a fistful of uncounted notes into Israel Avigdor's hand, and said:

"Israel Avigdor, go to the Rabbi again. Tell him I must leave. Russian generals are waiting for me—don't forget—Russian generals."

But the Rabbi would not be moved.

Paltiel Hurwitz was beginning to lose patience. His loyalty was being stretched too far.

With all his adoration of Rabbis, Paltiel Hurwitz was a man of affairs, not unacquainted with high society. He had even drunk wine with nobility and officers; he had eaten with them once or twice, and that like a Gentile, without a hat on his head. Nor

would the food have borne Rabbinic scrutiny as to whether it was
kosher. Yes, on his visits to St. Petersburg, Paltiel Hurwitz's piety
was not above reproach. And sometimes it happened that during
his travels in the forests a young peasant woman would wait on
him, the wife of some keeper; she would smile up at him as she
drew the long boots off his feet before he went to bed; she would
beg him to raise her husband's pay. Then he did not say no; nor
did he refuse to let her kiss his hand out of gratitude when he had
put out the light . . .

These sins of his haunted Reb Paltiel Hurwitz; but they also
brought a touch of bewilderment into his faith—and at one time
even a touch of doubt. In any case, his impatience with Rabbi
Melech was yielding to resentment. The Rabbi is the Rabbi, he
thought; true enough; but business is business. Rebellion was
awakening in the heart of Paltiel Hurwitz.

And on one occasion, when Israel Avigdor brought him the
usual refusal, he burst out: "All right! If he won't, he won't. I'll go
away without his benediction."

But within a few minutes he had changed his mind. He remembered that his complicated business affairs were not always above
suspicion. He was surrounded by enemies, by envious Jews, who
might some day betray him to the authorities. Such things had
been done before. And behind the shadow of prison there loomed
the red shadow of something worse—the fires of hell. He was a
sinner. He had never done any pious reading in the holy books; he
had been remiss in his prayers, often gabbling only half of them.
Yes, he had even gone so far as to neglect putting on his phylacteries of a morning. And there were other sins—great God!—
hideous sins. And God remembers everything. He is a God of
vengeance, even visiting the sins of the fathers on the children.
Who can escape Him, without intercession? And who is fitter to
intercede than His Rabbis, His beloved ones? When they plead for
mercy, God inclines a gracious ear. Those that believe in His
Rabbis win forgiveness from God. True enough, these beloved
Rabbis of His were, it seemed sometimes, a trifle exorbitant. They
lived on the fat of the land, dressed themselves and their wives
and children and grandchildren in silk and satin, went every year

(they and their wives and the rest) to the warm spring baths. And their children were never few. There were births, weddings, confirmations without number. And always they wanted presents. But, when all was said and done, they were worth it. They were a refuge and a comfort in times of sickness, or when treachery threatened. Something to rely on, to look to. It was good to have a buttress, even if you were rich and powerful. For what, reflected Reb Paltiel Hurwitz, is man, and what is his strength?

He regretted his evil thoughts and his sharp words. Who could tell what was in the Rabbi's mind? Perhaps this delay had some hidden significance. Perhaps the Rabbi foresaw or forefelt danger, disaster, treachery, murder, God save us! The world was filled with robbers, betrayers, envious souls.

So when, at the end of a week of torment, Israel Avigdor came to Paltiel Hurwitz and announced joyously: "Reb Paltiel, the Rabbi sends for you!" Paltiel approached the presence humbly, timidly, filled with faith and ready to do whatever the Rabbi commanded.

The Rabbi received Paltiel with a countenance that beamed as if with good news.

"Sit down, Paltiel!"

And when Paltiel Hurwitz was sitting, the Rabbi himself went to the dresser, brought forth cake and wine and filled a silver beaker.

"Rabbi!" exclaimed Paltiel Hurwitz, startled. "The Rabbi himself deigns to serve?"

The Rabbi did not answer. He continued to pour until the wine overflowed, and stained the table-cloth. Paltiel Hurwitz saw in this a good omen, a cup running over, bringing good luck, much money.

Then, before giving him the wine, the Rabbi took his hand, and said quickly:

"Well, Paltiel, I see you are frightened. And in order to remove all fear from your heart I, the Rabbi, will go in with you as partner in this forest affair. For I see that such is the will of heaven."

Paltiel had not a word to say to the contrary.

"May heaven send us success!" he answered, pressing the soft Rabbinic hand in his own. Then he drank the bad wine which Israel Avigdor brewed and then sold to the Rabbinic court as genuine Hungarian.

When he had blessed Paltiel, and had sent him away, the Rabbi sat down, and drew heavily and with relish at the thick Havana cigar which the merchant had given him. The smoke curled about his beard and head, and he rubbed his hands several times, murmuring:

"Blessed be the dear name of God!"

His morning's work was not through yet. He poured himself out a beakerful of wine, drank it down and ate a good-sized piece of cake. He was in excellent mood. His mind was filled with thoughts of festivities, of marriages, of his bride, the young orphan. He brought his brows together in an effort of imagination. What would she look like, this girl he had never seen? There came up before him the misty image of his third wife, the last one, the best beloved.

He sat down quickly at the table. He had just sent off a letter to the girl's uncle; but he immediately wrote another. He reiterated in this letter that he wanted no delay. Speed! And even if the uncle was preparing, as he received the letter, to set out on one of his money-raising expeditions, he was to give it up at once. He, Rabbi Melech, would make good the damage; he would reimburse him double, four times—any number of times.

I can afford it now, he thought. That forest affair is not going to fail. My faith is in God, and He will not let it fail. No Jews will betray Paltiel Hurwitz this time, for Jews are, after all—God be thanked for it!—Jews.

5

In the turbulent rabbinic court of Nyesheve Nahum moved about, a lonely, abandoned soul.

He no longer heard complaints and reproaches. After the first few days of childish terror he had suddenly shown himself a man.

Those seven days had been a nightmare to him; the daily festivities, the benedictions, the two toothless graybeards who had taken him aside and had muttered secrets into his ears, the meaningful sighs and glances of the sisters of the bride, the angry muttering of his father-in-law, the impatience and expectation that filled the air—all this had lain like an incubus on the soul of the fourteen-year-old bridegroom. And at night, when they thrust him into the bridal room, and slammed the door behind him, he did not see Serele, his young wife, lying in the sea of shimmering white bedclothes; he saw only a kerchief with crimson ribbons, a pair of eyes, a pair of flaming cheeks. He was conscious then only of terror and shame and helplessness. These were the only emotions that filled his sleepless nights.

Serele waited and waited for him, and longed. But in her longing there was no element of fear and mystery and timidity, that mingling of emotions which is best fitted to awaken in young boys a responsive longing. It was the dumb waiting of brute femininity, the heavy, patient expectancy of primal instincts.

She was healthy and precociously ripe, like most Jewish girls, ready, at fourteen, to bring forth children. She had been prepared for her rôle by the lessons of her sisters, and by the ritual which is prescribed for women. She waited, in a massive kind of desire, for her predestined husband to approach her; but in her waiting there

40

was no coquetry or playfulness. She was devoid of art; she had no tender word, no gesture even, with which to attract him, no unspoken promise of caresses and happiness. She only waited, silent, submissive and heavy, under the weight of the bedclothes, until she fell asleep; and in her sleep she uttered thick half words, unintelligible and unconnected, which reminded him of her father. And this only served to drive him further from her.

Only later, when in the court of Rabbi Melech all hope was abandoned that he would prove himself a man, when the pressure had been relaxed, when they no longer tormented him with instructions and expectations, and when they no longer conducted him to the bridal chamber and slammed the door behind him, only then did something awaken. Suddenly power and ripeness flooded his body. A sweet, irresistible strength expanded his heart, and ran through his nerves and muscles. The flood flowed faster and hotter.

Then a change came into his eyes, too. They became crystal clear. Instead of the white kerchief and the crimson ribbons surrounded by mist, he saw a woman; not the vague fantasy of the Talmudic pages, not the diaphanous visions of the Kabbala, but a woman of flesh and blood and body, clear cut against the whiteness of the bed.

The sudden awakening of desire to possess and to master was so strong that he approached her the first time with the certainty and strength of a full-grown man. And Serele conceived a great love for him, loving him both as a man and as a child. She was suddenly bound to him with the deep affection of a strong woman, who seeks in a gentle, frail husband not so much the man as the child which she can fondle and serve and sacrifice herself for.

On the morning when she told her sisters the good news, their thick eyes lit up with joy. They had actually become afraid of this strange young Nahum. They did not trust his Jewishness; and they did not trust him with their sister. They had, in fact, made up their minds to take their sister away from him, and to sleep with her, in turn, during those nights when the law forbade him to approach her.

"Remember, Serele," they warned her. "Be a good Jewish

woman. For three sins a young wife is taken early from this world
in childbirth: for the sin of not pinching off the piece of dough
from the Sabbath bread and throwing it into the fire; for the sin of
not lighting the candles on the eve of the Sabbath; and for the sin
of impurity. A wife should love her husband, but she must love
the Torah even more. In the time of your impurity, remember, you
must keep away from him; you must not let him touch you."

Serele nodded obediently, though she knew in her heart that she
would never be able to oppose her Nahum in the slightest wish.
Already her attitude toward him was one of utter adoration and
submission; to her, simple, earthy, the frail dark-eyed boy-
husband was something set on high. Though she was in her impurity, when it was a deadly sin to let a husband touch you, she
could not have denied him if he had stretched out a hand to her.

But all these warnings and precautions were superfluous.
Nahum did not even try to come near her when they were left
alone in their apartment. He was silent even during meal-times.
And when she put a second portion of chicken on his plate, he
pushed it back silently, without looking at her.

From the first moment that he saw her, Nahum knew that he
did not like her. She repelled him with her charmless heaviness,
her thick peasant-woman speech, her panting breath, her dull
piety; she would often sit over a simple book of devotion, printed
in the vernacular, and she would read the contents aloud, with a
queer chant, such as might be heard on the lips of some devout
elderly Jewess. And he was repelled by her expressionless red
face, which was made all the grosser by the bonnet on her shorn
head, with its little forest of cherries and blossoms.

He was alone and abandoned in Nyesheve, and his mind turned
back with longing to Rachmanivke.

His childhood home rose constantly before his eyes. He saw the
big yard of the Rabbinic court, with its whitewashed walls, with its
pump in the center; he saw the green well, with the carved lion's
head; the jaws of the lion yawned; and out of them cold, clear
water streamed joyously, and fell on the clear white stones, which
were rubbed smooth and clean by the ceaseless flow. In his home
the rooms were big, broad and well lit. The windows were always

clean; over them hung snow-white little curtains. These summer
days the windows would be open and the curtains would be fluttering in the wind. After the Feast of Tabernacles, Naphthali, the
yard servant, would pour sand between the double windows, and
Mariashka, the servant girl, would cut high cones out of red
paper and stick them in the sand; and she would throw into the
sand fluffs of cotton wool looking like flakes of snow.

In his father's room the walls were covered with gilded paper and
tapestries. It was filled with the warm, friendly odor of tea, which
his father drank from a red-painted glass. His father smoked thin,
sweet-smelling cigarettes, which sent up, into the still air, long,
bluish columns of smoke, forming into vague clouds. In the mahogany case, with its glass windows, stood many spice-containers,
and the smell of the spices seeped through the door and windows
of the case.

And at moments he saw his father, sitting over a book, chanting
softly to himself. And he saw his father look up, as he himself,
Nahum, came in. And his father smiled, not like a father, but like
a young comrade. "Well, Nahum," he asked, "how are your studies?"

His mother's apartment was on the second floor. The rooms
were large, but somber; the windows were covered with heavy
curtains and plush portières. A big, round-bellied samovar always
stood on the table, and always hummed. On the doors of the
clothes closets were carved lion's heads; they held big rings in
their closed jaws; they had fierce manes hanging down to their
shoulders; but the lions themselves were not fierce; they were
friendly, gentle house-lions. On every side there was the subdued
glimmer of silver candle-sticks, candelabra, cups, beakers, trays,
vases, colored glass, crystal.

He saw his mother, with the brown kerchief on her head, drawn
down to the eyes. Often she was not well; she had a headache. But
it seemed to him now that this headache, too, was a friendly,
gentle house-headache. His mother sat always on the ottoman, her
feet hidden under the silk dress. Only the tips of the little black
satin shoes peeped out. Most of the time she was reading.

Somewhere in the house there was a distant aunt of his, a

haughty magnificent person; a Rabbi's daughter or granddaughter;
a divorcee who had not been able to get on with some very snobbish Rabbinic husband precisely because of her magnificence and
haughtiness. And so she had come to the Rachmanivke court,
where there was room and tolerance and people minded their own
business.

The Rabbinic court was closed off from the Jewish town, almost after the fashion of a regular Gentile castle. The second
story, which contained the apartments of the Rabbi's wife, had
nothing to do with the ground floor, which belonged to the Rabbi
and to his chief followers. Even Mottye Godul, the *gabbai,* never
showed himself upstairs. On rare occasions some very important
visitor, a Chassid of Moscow or St. Petersburg, in the heathen
dress of the big cities, would be invited to the apartment of the
Rabbi's wife, and would be received by her and by the distant
relative. They sat at table, and drank wine and ate cakes genteelly;
and the ladies would listen eagerly to news from the big outside
world.

Nahum was no longer a child. He studied, under Reb Pesachiah, the famous scholar, the most difficult folios of the Talmud,
the laws of marriage and divorce. Matches were already being
proposed to his parents. He was even turning toward the Kabbala.
But his mother would not understand all this; she would still draw
him on to her lap, stroke his head, and sing an old cradle song, a
foolish song, which he still remembered clearly:

> A day and a night the phoenix flew,
> The palace windows were all pulled to.
> "Princess, awaken, the message I bring
> Comes to your heart from the lips of a King."

He would tear himself away from his mother's lap. But his
mother held him tighter.

"Nahum, my child," she said, tenderly. "You mustn't make
your mother sad. Stay here, and let me sing to you."

He was ashamed; but it was warm and snug in his mother's lap.

His relative, the distant aunt, also tried to treat him like a child.
She would catch him to her, and kiss his eyes; and the more he

tore himself from her, the more eagerly she held him, kissing him
and crying: "You stupid little boy! You lovely prince! You have
wonderful eyes!"

He fought these memories down. He turned to his books, and
tried to forget himself in texts and mysteries. But the yard, the
house, the rooms, the faces came up through the pages. Here, in
Nyesheve, there was no beauty and no intimacy; everything was
strange, repellent, even disgusting.

There was something loathsome about the buildings, ugly and
formless and tattered, clustering round the courtyard. The well
was dilapidated, the chain rusty, the windlass creaked whenever it
was used. Heaps of filth lay in front of the synagogue, the rendezvous of cats, dogs, pigs and crows. From the ritual baths always
came the revolting odor of steam and stale water; it filled the yard
and penetrated into the rooms. He could not stand the mobs that
filled the Rabbinic court of Nyesheve: filthy hangers-on, beggars,
followers, retainers, in rags, unkempt, unmannerly; their like was
unknown in Rachmanivke.

He could not stand the big barrel which stood in the middle of
the yard. It was supposed to contain clean water, so that Jews
could dip their hands, according to the law, before they entered
the synagogue to pray. It never contained clean water. At the
bottom stagnated a greasy liquid. The Chassidim bent over,
moistened their fingers, thrust them into their pockets to dry them
—and they had fulfilled the law! He could not stand the great
synagogue, naked, without ornaments. It contained long, bleak
benches, and dirty bookshelves. On the shelves lay, in utter disorder, old tattered volumes, the pages and the sackcloth covers
falling to pieces. He could not stand the tremendous, clumsy
oven, behind which all sorts of filth had accumulated: rags, leav-
ings of meals, discarded bundles. The place stank with the sweat of
the beggars and wanderers who made this their temporary home,
who slept here, smoked, ate, quarreled and counted their takings.
He could not stand the way the Jews of Nyesheve prayed, wildly,
incoherently, flinging themselves about. Their words were unintelligible to him, their melodies outlandish. He could not stand the
Rabbinic banquets in the synagogue, with the eager, gabbling

crowds, with the thick food, with Israel Avigdor, who would take
morsels of meat in his filthy, snuff-stained hands, and carry them
to the most important guests at table. Often the great Rabbi himself condescended to take a piece of fish in his own hands and
transfer it to Nahum's plate, but Nahum could not eat it. It stuck
in his throat. He could not stand the taste of the "genuine Hungarian wine" which Israel Avigdor brewed. He was terrified by the
family hordes, by the children and grandchildren and great-grandchildren, by the bulky men and women, with their hard, unfriendly
eyes.

He could not stand the apartment to which he had been assigned; the rooms were filled with massive wardrobes, hard leather
chairs and gigantic beds heaped to an extraordinary height with
bedclothes. Feathers were always flying about the rooms. He
could not stand the ill-cooked food, the over-soaked meat, the
mutilated chicken wings, the badly scraped calves' feet, the wrinkled sweetbreads, sticky, thick, tasteless. He could not drink the
tea, which was served in thick glasses and which reminded him of
the stale water in the ritual baths. The smell of that water was
everywhere.

And he could not stand his wife, his Serele, with her kerchief
and bonnet, with her brutish body, with the shapeless clothes that
hung upon it, with her noisy, clumsy footsteps.

Her face lit up a dull red whenever he came in; she was always
busy with something—busy and submissive. But she never had a
word to say. She had only one way of expressing her tenderness;
when they sat at table she would take a piece of chicken with her
fingers out of her own plate, and put it into his.

And he would thrust the gift from himself.

At such moments a keen longing seized him; it was almost
physical, like a steel cord drawn tight round his heart. He wanted
his mother, his father, even that distant aunt of his; he wanted the
sunlit rooms, the well-head with its lion, the flashing silver in
the rooms, the blue smoke ascending from his father's cigarettes,
the intoxicating odors of the spices seeping through the doors and
windows of the mahogany cases.

The thought of them made his delicate nostrils quiver.

6

THE MARRIAGE OF RABBI MELECH OF NYESHEVE AND THE ORPHAN girl Malkah was celebrated with great pomp soon after the Sabbath of Consolation.

When the Ninth Day of Ab—the day of mourning for the destruction of the Temple—had passed, thousands of Chassidim set forth for the village of Kiteve, in the Carpathian mountains, where the marriage was to take place. The young bride did not want her bridegroom to come to her in her home town of Przemysl. Her uncle had tried to impress her with the extraordinary honor that was being conferred on her, when the Rabbi of Nyesheve, with thousands of his followers, came all that distance for her sake. But she would not hear of it. She was ashamed to have all the town, and all her friends, see with their own eyes the graybeard husband she was going to take; and she threatened to run away on the day of the marriage if the ceremony was not arranged in some distant village.

Her uncle, the stammerer, heard her and trembled. He was afraid of the anger of the Rabbi of Nyesheve; but he was still more afraid of the bride. He knew his niece only too well, and he knew that she had earned honorably her nickname—Spitfire. She could be as good as her word. Nor would it be the first time that she had run away from home. And therefore the uncle would rather try to make his peace with her than with the Rabbi. He tried to explain to the latter. In carefully chosen words, with hints and remote suggestions, he conveyed the situation, softening the impression. His embarrassment made him stammer more than usual, and as he talked the sweat ran down his face. But to his astonishment the Rabbi of Nyesheve showed no anger.

"Well, well," he said, "she's only a child. We mustn't be hard on her."

He had picked out for the wedding the remote and obscure village of Kiteve, far up among the mountains. The Jews of Kiteve were plain folk, of simple faith. Kiteve was a sacred place. Among these mountains the Baal Shem, Master of the Name, founder of Chassidism, had dug lime; and along these roads he had driven his wagon to market. In the little river which ran through Kiteve the Baal Shem had bathed; the river was narrow and shallow and level, and it ran swiftly and noisily down its stony bed between rocky banks. Only in one place it was deep enough to reach a man's chin; and in this place the Baal Shem used to wash the crusted lime off his body. Sick women and barren wives came to bathe here, in order that the Baal Shem might help them. Rabbi Melech, too, intended to dip himself here. Not that, God forbid, he did not feel himself in full possession of his manly powers; but it would certainly do him no harm to steep his body in these holy waters—the more so as he was looking forward to the begetting of men children.

The wedding was celebrated in grand style. Apart from the thousands of Chassidim and local Jews who attended, the Gentile mountain folk, shepherds and peasants, turned out by the hundred. They came in hay carts, yokels in feathered hats, rosy peasant girls in balloon blouses, with heavy folds of beads on their bosoms. They danced in the Jewish inns, and shot off their guns to the health of the young couple. The peasants brought their flocks with them; lean, long-mustachioed peasants took their horses from the plowing, carpeted their clumsy wagons with straw, and transported Chassidim to the wedding. Such an opportunity came once in a lifetime; they earned such large sums that in the night they held celebrations of their own, lighting big bonfires of dried branches. Several Jewish orchestras, and a number of wedding-jesters, had come to town; there was even a non-Jewish orchestra, consisting of fiddles, shepherd flutes and a *kozba*—a sort of bagpipe made of goatskin, played by an old, barefoot peasant in sheepskin.

The morning after the wedding a long caravan set out from

Kiteve and descended the winding roads and paths toward Nyesheve. Several peasant carts had to be hired for the wedding presents. These headed the procession; immediately behind came the Rabbi and his intimates, in a superb coach. After him, in less pretentious coaches, came the wealthier Chassidim; after them, in peasant carts padded with straw, the plain folk; after them, on foot, in rags, with bundles, the beggars and hangers-on. At the end of the caravan came the young bride, surrounded by women and servants. The dust went up, the sun shone, the Chassidim sang without pause.

But neither the magnificence nor the jollity could rejoice the heart of the sexagenarian bridegroom, Rabbi Melech.

He was an unhappy man. He was returning from Kiteve to Nyesheve not as if he had just celebrated his own wedding, but as if he had just buried a near and dear relative. The singing of his Chassidim and the ministrations of his attendants made him feel bitter.

Melech, the great Rabbi of Nyesheve, had reason to be sad.

On the very day of the wedding, his young bride, Malkah, had given him a hint of what he might expect.

In the Rabbinic court of Nyesheve it was the custom to shave the bride's head not on the very morning of the wedding—as is done everywhere among pious Jews—but on the day before. No one in Nyesheve had ever dreamed of challenging the custom. Accordingly, on the day before the ceremony, three old women came to Malkah, and one of them carried the fatal shears and the flashing razor. But as soon as Malkah saw them, she uttered a shriek, fastened her hands in her thick black hair and flew into a corner.

The Atropos of the party, the official bride-shearer, a hard-faced, scrawny old woman, with a pointed chin and a single tooth in her hideous mouth, grinned at the bride. "That's all right," she mumbled. "They all fight. They all fight but it does them no good."

She flashed her scissors. "God in heaven! If I only had as many gulden as the heads I've shaved. Come, bride, come, darling."

Malkah cowered in her corner like an animal at bay.

Women were sent for, and they pleaded with Malkah, soothed her, promised her all sorts of presents—a hundred gulden if she would only submit quietly. But Malkah gripped her hair convulsively and shrieked: "I won't let you. You'll have to cut my hands off first!"

"But child, what's the difference?" they urged. "You know you'll have to give in before you go under the canopy. Why make all this fuss for the sake of one day?"

"I'll let you do it tomorrow," she said, between her teeth. "Not today. And if you try to come near me, I'll scratch your eyes out, I'll bite!"

And she showed her long white teeth in a snarl of rage, so that the women shrank away from her.

The Rabbi himself came to plead with her.

"Bride!" he said with dignity. "You are about to become the wife of the Rabbi of Nyesheve! You must conform to the customs of Nyesheve. It is my will that your head be shaved today."

"It is my will that my head shall not be shaved today," she snapped back, and glared at him unafraid.

A sudden chill contracted the Rabbi's heart. It was the first time in his life that anyone had dared to oppose him, or had even dared to talk back.

Malkah's uncle, the stammerer, almost fainted. Something terrible was going to happen! He was certain that the Rabbi would fly out in a towering rage and give immediate orders to pack up everything for an immediate return to Nyesheve. But nothing happened. Rabbi Melech only smiled softly and said:

"An obstinate child, the true daughter of a scholar. Well, it isn't a *law* that her head should be shaved the day before the wedding. It's only a custom, nothing more. Let be. Tomorrow will do."

But this little prelude was as nothing to what took place later. All day long Rabbi Melech prepared himself for the bridal night. Marriage was no new experience to him; three times he had stood beside a "destined one" under the canopy; every time the destined one had been a virgin. But never before had he felt so uneasy, so excited and confused. Hours at a stretch he pored over the laws of a bride and bridegroom on the night of the wedding, for all the

world like a young and unripe boy. He repeated prayers; not
ordinary ones, such as are to be found in the usual prayer-books,
but obscure ones, printed only in special volumes, and that only in
old editions. He began suddenly to comb his thick beard and ear-
locks with his stubby fingers; he had not used a comb for years.
He did not fast through the whole day, as is the law; he excused
himself on grounds of weakness, and took some cake and some
brandy. He had an old Jew come in to exorcise from him the evil
eye. The old Jew washed his hands and intoned:

"*Sholosh noshim* —three women stood on a cliff. One of them
said, 'Sick!' The other said, 'There will be neither sickness nor
weakness.' If any man has done thee evil, may the hair fall out of
his head and his beard. If any woman has done thee evil, may her
teeth and her breasts drop out. As the water has no path and the
fish and the mosquito have no kidneys, so may neither sickness
nor weakness nor pain nor harm nor evil eye come unto Melech,
the son of Devorah Blumeh, for he is sprung from Joseph the Just,
against whom the evil eye could not prevail. I therefore abjure all
eyes: evil eye, dark eye, bright eye, green eye, narrow eye, deep
eye, bulging eye, eye of a man, of a woman, of a graybeard, of a
girl that has not yet known a man; I abjure you that you may find
no approach to Melech, the son of Devorah Blumeh, neither when
he is awake, nor when he sleeps, nor in any one of his two hundred and forty-eight parts, nor in any one of his three hundred and
sixty-five veins . . ."

While the Rabbi prepared himself, the women prepared
Malkah, the bride. For the hundredth time they explained to her
the incredible, the unexpected good fortune which had befallen
her; thousands of women would have given years of their lives to
change places with her who was about to become the wife of the
great and powerful Rabbi of Nyesheve.

"The angels in heaven," they said, "must have wrought this
wonder for you. You should be dancing with joy."

Over and over again—until she was sick of it—they explained
to her what was due to her husband, the illustrious Rabbi.

Then they caressed her head, and spat out piously against the evil
eye. At night they were very tender to her. They dressed her in a
long white gown which reached from her toes to her throat, so that

no part of her was visible. Malkah did not oppose them; passively
she let the women do whatever they wanted. And for that reason
the women forgave her for whatever she had done before, and said
only sweet things to her. They combed her coal-black hair with
their fingers, and covered her head with a blue kerchief tied with
satin ribbons. They tucked in every separate strand of hair, saying:

"Hide it away, bride. At least let not your shame be seen."

Then they kissed her head and stole out backwards from the
room, murmuring: "Good luck! Good luck! In nine months may
we celebrate the birth of your first son!"

And when the Rabbi came into her room, she still said no word.
She only watched his every motion with alert and curious eyes.
She saw him throw off his velvet *capote*, and draw his ritual
fringes over his head with trembling fingers. She saw his lips in
motion; he was muttering prayers to himself. She heard his heavy
sighing, and behind him she also saw the grotesque, mocking
shadows on the wall. But when he put out the light, and began to
rub his skull-cap back and forth on his head, she leaped out of bed
with the swift motion of a young goat, and poised herself right in
the middle of the room, her black eyes fixed on him with a phosphorescent gleam.

For a little while the Rabbi stood there paralyzed. Something, a
confusion of ideas, passed through his old, weary mind.

"Spirits! Evil spirits! They always come to poison Jewish festivities!"

He shook from head to foot. His helpless hands looked for the
protective ritual fringes. But soon he came to himself, and his eyes
opened so wide that the eyeballs might have fallen out.

"God save us!" he muttered. He was lost! He had not the
slightest idea of what to do now. He was prepared for everything
but this.

In his long career as husband, which stretched back half a
century to his thirteenth year, he had met all sorts of situations.
His wives had not all been alike. Now, in his aged mind, a variety
of thoughts, memories, experiences, all kinds of nights, all kinds
of situations, recurred. There had been nights of great joy and

nights of weeping, nights of tormenting inadequacy, and nights of womanly abandonment, lightheadedness. But *this!* Such—such— mockery! Such contempt! And directed against him, against the Rabbi of Nyesheve!

If only her uncle had been here, her uncle, the stammerer! Rabbi Melech would have turned on him and rent him limb from limb. The pauper! The beggar! Did he know how lucky he was to have the Rabbi of Nyesheve as his relative by marriage? Had he ever explained to this penniless orphan girl how lucky *she* was? Had he ever made her understand what was due to her husband, the Rabbi of Nyesheve? But the uncle, the stammerer, was not here! It was with her, the orphan niece, that he would have to talk now, this ungrateful, disrespectful, penniless bride of his, who did not know what honor had been bestowed on her. And Rabbi Melech did not know how to argue with a female. He had never done anything but command. He had never carried on a conversation with any one of his wives; and the only other women he had ever talked to all were the mothers who came to him for his intercession with the powers above, weeping women who trembled in his presence. What was there to *say* to a woman?

He did not want to argue with her. How can you argue with a woman? And such a young, brainless one, too. But—but he could say something about her health, could he not?

"You can't stand in the middle of the room," he growled. "You'll catch cold, God forbid."

She did not answer. She only glared at him with her phosphorescent eyes.

This subject being exhausted, Rabbi Melech bethought himself of Jewish piety.

"Come, come! A Jewish daughter! A Jewish wife! A family of Rabbis. No, no! It is a great sin to torment a bridegroom."

But this did not help either. And finding nothing else, Rabbi Melech passed into a towering rage. His beard and ear-locks danced in the darkness.

"Impudent!" he yelled. "Ignorant, impudent creature! Have you no respect, no reverence?"

In his fury he forgot who he was and where he was. He began

to crawl out of bed to catch her, to teach her, with his own hands, the insolent woman, how the Rabbi of Nyesheve ought to be treated. For the world was not yet coming to an end. . . .The world . . . But at this point his strength deserted him. His arms and his legs shook as in a fever. He suddenly felt all his age, and he began to groan and whimper. He was old, broken, not like a bridegroom on the bridal night, but like a grandfather who needed rest and peace.

And as he lay there, almost sobbing, his bride approached him, and began to stroke his skull-cap quietly. But he was too weak, too broken, to stretch out his hand to her. She tucked him in carefully under the thick, heavy cover, placed a big cushion over his feet, and watched him fall asleep.

Now, sitting in the midst of his worshipful followers, in the magnificent, upholstered coach which was taking him back to Nyesheve, Rabbi Melech kept thinking of what had happened the night before, and his head was as heavy as a lump of lead.

"Fooled!" This word recurred to him again and again. "Fooled!"

The singing of his Chassidim galled him; their voices seemed to be filled with mockery. Several times he wanted to make a gesture for silence, but he restrained himself. Why betray himself? No one must know that he was suffering.

As he sat there in the lumbering coach, he realized that a divorce was out of the question for him. In the first place, it would be too much for the Chassidim, his followers. They had been not a little astonished by his fourth marriage. But they had said nothing. It was the will of the Rabbi, and therefore the will of God. And they turned out for the wedding in full force, and brought gifts. What would it look like if he divorced his bride? Would not their astonishment change to something else? And then the other Rabbinic courts, the Chassidic groups throughout the length and breadth of Jewry! What laughter would there be! What a byword and a mockery the Chassidim of Nyesheve would become among those that hated and envied him. No, no, he would not tell.

Besides, there was his own family. Sons and daughters and sons-in-law and daughters-in-law—they had all been against the marriage. They would all laugh at him. There would be no respect for

him in the very court of Nyesheve. No, it must not come to such a
pass.

But the last, the most important consideration was Malkah herself, the young bride in the other coach, with her women attendants all about her. What a pity to lose her! True, she had tormented him, she had hurt him, she had conducted herself in a
manner unbecoming a true daughter of Israel. Perhaps she had
even—God forbid!—made a sick man of him. He was old! He
could not stand suffering! He needed gentleness, consideration,
softness! If they were cruel to him he would break down, as he had
broken down in the night. Who could tell if that torture had
not—God forbid!—taken away the last bit of his manhood? He
did not feel the same man as before the wedding. That morning
hundreds, thousands of Chassidim had wished him a son of his
old age. Surely the benediction of thousands of Jews was not without meaning or power! And yet he was weak and old. And *she*
was to blame! God in heaven! Had such a thing ever been heard
of before? Perhaps among the heathens, the non-Jews, or among
the lowest orders of the Jews, the laborers. . . . Ah! Rabbis and
Rabbinic courts had fallen on evil days, if such things could take
place in their midst!

He felt hatred toward the virgin bride in the other coach. And
yet he did not want to drive her away. For what did he have left in
the world besides his—his wife? His children were enemies to
him. They were waiting for the day of his death in order that
they might divide the heritage of his Rabbinic empire among
themselves. Israel Avigdor hated and despised him. There was not
one person to warm up to. And she—she was so young, a beautiful creature, the women said.

And therefore Rabbi Melech did not prevent his Chassidim
from singing their joyful songs. He fought the sickness in his heart
and tried to appear joyful too. Nothing was going to be changed.
No one was going to know—except, perhaps, the uncle. For here
he was undecided at first. He thought of telling the uncle, the
stammerer. What a relief it would be to grab this idiot by the
throat, to pour out all his rage and bitterness and outrage on this
submissive, helpless, crawling thing! And then perhaps the uncle,

in the agony of his terror, might move Malkah herself to better behavior. On second reflection Rabbi Melech saw the hopelessness of it. He himself would have to bring her round, with his own strength of will. The main thing was to recover his confidence and power. He might go to Vienna and consult a professor. But no one had to know about all this; he must not humiliate himself.

And so Rabbi Melech, in the jolting coach, argued with himself and, frowning, summoned back his self-confidence. He tried to forget his weakness and his humiliation. He began to smoke one cigar after another.

"Srelvigdor!" he commanded every few minutes. "Fire!"

Israel Avigdor struck one match after another, and as he carried the flame toward the Rabbi, he looked into the Rabbi's eyes mockingly, impudently.

Something had reached his ears—what would not reach the ears of Israel Avigdor?—through the talk of servants. *They* had heard something from the women who had gone early that morning—after the Rabbi had departed for prayers—to wish the bride good morning. There had been talk, hints, quarrels. There had been much examination of the bedclothes; there had been—so it was rumored—reproaches against the bride. So it seemed to Israel Avigdor that the pool of the Baal Shem, in the river that ran through Kiteve, had not done his master much good. And he looked straight into the Rabbi's eyes, mockingly, impudently.

Bridegroom! Take heart! he thought, and took a great pinch of snuff.

A little later the Rabbi shoved his hat vigorously to one side, as he always did when he had taken an important decision.

"Srelvigdor!" he said firmly. "Listen to me! I want these Seven Days of the Seven Benedictions to be celebrated as no such days have ever been celebrated before in Nyesheve! I want the tables set every day in the synagogue. Do you hear me, Srelvigdor?"

7

DURING ALL THE FESTIVE SEVEN DAYS OF THE SEVEN BENEDICTIONS,
the aunt and uncle of Malkah lived in an agony of fear. Malkah
was gunpowder! Malkah could explode at any moment! Malkah
could get up in the middle of everything, leave Nyesheve and
disappear without a trace.

From the day on which the stammering uncle came back from
Nyesheve and announced that the great Rabbi wanted Malkah to
be his bride, he and his wife had not known peace. Side by side
with the incredible joy of the event—they, the obscure, the fallen,
the penniless house of a long-dead Rabbi, were about to be lifted
into an alliance with the world-famous head of the dynasty of
Nyesheve!—together with that joy, almost intolerable in itself,
there was the unremitting fear of their niece, Malkah Spitfire.
Their lives were in her reckless hands. One characteristic gesture
of hers, and they would be back in the dust from which the Rabbi
of Nyesheve had raised them. And there was not one moment in
which their happiness was not overshadowed by distrust and anxiety.

When the stammering uncle came home and imparted the news
to his wife, she looked at him pityingly, contemptuously, and
answered in one word:

"Idiot!"

Aunt Aidele wore the trousers in that house. She considered
herself the brains of the family. The proposal made by the Rabbi
of Nyesheve, and brought home enthusiastically by her husband,
was ridiculous.

"*The* match for our Malkah Spitfire," she said, mockingly.
"And if you want to have your beard torn out by the roots, just tell
her about it, that's all."

57

But in the first momentum of his joy, the stammerer rushed straightway to Malkah. Without preparation, and only fearing that his wife would interrupt and silence him, he broke the news.

"M-m-*mazel-tov*, good luck! Congratulations!" he babbled at his niece. "You're g-going to be the wife of the Rabb-bi of Nyesheve!"

Aunt Aidele rushed after him in time to hear these words, and she became quite white with fear. But Malkah Spitfire only laughed. She laughed naturally at first, as at a good joke, but gradually her laughter worked itself up into an uncontrollable spasm. She could not stop. And when the laughter exhausted itself for a moment, she did not ask what kind of man this famous Rabbi of Nyesheve was, what he looked like, how old he was; she only panted until the fit of laughter returned and doubled her up.

"Oh, Mama!" she cried, and continued to laugh.

They stared at her.

"Are you mad?" her uncle stammered. "Don't you want the Rabbi of Nyesheve?"

Malkah mastered herself for a moment. "Of course I want him! Only you've forgotten the cake and brandy to celebrate with . . ."

The stammerer looked at his wife. This was the first victory he had ever scored over her, probably the first he had ever scored over anyone. In his exultation he forgot his fear. He became aware suddenly of qualities of manliness. He approached his wife, tucked his thumb between two bent fingers, and thrust it derisively under her nose.

"Well!" he crowed. "Aristotle! Who's the wise one now?"

Taken aback, Aunt Aidele turned up her eyes to heaven and murmured: "God grant it!" Then she turned them back on her husband and said, warningly: "But be sure to get your bear before you skin him!"

And so the match was arranged.

When the news became public, every relative of Malkah, close and distant, took on a new dignity. But everywhere, mingled with that dignity, was uncertainty. They could only explain Malkah's acquiescence to the fantastic match with the aged Rabbi as one of

her characteristic, mad tricks. Malkah was capable of anything—
just like her mother. By the time she was sixteen years old Malkah
had run away three times; and three times she had been brought
back, and the matter had been hushed up.

"Wicked blood!" they said of her in the family. "She has it
from her mother. She took it in with her mother's milk."

Malkah's mother, a daughter of a Rabbinic house, and daughter-
in-law of a Rabbi, had also run away—but successfully. She had
been, in all, fifteen years older than her daughter. They had married her off at the age of fourteen, and within a year she had given
birth to Malkah. Eleven years after the mother's marriage, when
Malkah was already ten years old, and marriage proposals were
already coming in, the great tragedy took place. The twenty-five-
year-old wife of the Rabbi of Przemysl left her husband and her
daughter to run away to Budapest with a cavalry officer of the
local garrison.

The family cursed her and wiped her name from their records.
Her husband, a sickly scion of a Rabbinic house, died of loneliness and humiliation. But no one outside the family knew the
truth. It was given out that the Rabbi's wife was a very sick
woman, and that she was living abroad in a sanitarium under the
constant care of doctors.

Malkah the orphan was taken over by her aunt Aidele. Aunt
Aidele had had no children by her husband, the stammerer; and
as she was widely known for her irreproachable religious life, the
family decided that she should have the upbringing and education
of the orphan. Malkah was to be made, by her aunt and uncle,
into an example of Jewishness and God-fearing piety.

The stammerer set to work at once. The ten-year-old girl received, every day, long instructions in the duties of a daughter of
Israel. For hours at a stretch her uncle explained the laws to her,
and read her fearsome passages from morality books, in particular
the descriptions of hell and its fires. The stammerer was a scholar
and an authority on the infernal regions; he knew all the paths,
fiery rivers and lakes, all the instruments of torture, the grids, the
blazing pitch and sulphur baths, the white-hot prongs of the devils,
and all the beds with their upright spikes. His wife, not as learned

as he, had her own way of instilling reverence and dutifulness into
the little girl. Lazy by temperament, too poor to have the many
servants she would have liked to have, she taught the girl obedience by making her fetch and carry, by turning her into a mixture
of scullery maid and personal attendant.

But the little girl already had a character of her own. She stood
up against her aunt and uncle, and gave as good as she got. She
would listen once to any story her uncle told her about hell and its
compartments. The second time she rebelled.

"I've heard that!" she said sharply, and turned her back on
him.

After the first instant of submission, she ignored her aunt's
orders. She had to be called a dozen times before she answered.
And when her aunt, emulating her husband, began to recount
stories of the saintly lives of Rabbis and their chaste spouses,
Malkah exploded.

"I don't want to hear that! I want to hear about my mother in
Budapest!" she cried, right in the middle of a tale about the Master of the Name and his battles with a spirit from the nether
regions.

Aunt Aidele tightened her lips and answered frigidly: "Don't
ever dare to mention her name. You have no mother. I am your
mother."

"No, you're not!" Malkah shouted, stamping her foot. "My
mother is my mother. You're only my aunt!"

The family began to be afraid of the little spitfire.

"Her mother!" they murmured, horrified. "The dead image of
her mother, may her name be blotted out!"

Like her mother, Malkah grew swiftly into a tall, slender
woman. She had blazing, dark eyes, but with all their darkness
they were not Jewish. They had the wildness of the gypsies in
them. Her hair was thick and black, with a blackness that glim-
mered blue. It lay on her head straight and smooth, without a
suggestion of a curl. Equally black and thick and smooth were her
eyebrows, which met above her thin, straight nose. Only toward
the tip her nose broadened slightly, curving into the wide, sensitive
nostrils.

As her aunt combed the little girl's hair, and braided it, she sighed.

"Nothing Jewish about *you*; the same smooth black hair, the same straight Gentile shoulders as—*she* had."

"*She*" was the mother, who was never mentioned by name. *She* had had a sharp tongue, and had spared no one; Malkah was the same. Malkah was wild and obstinate and rebellious. There were times—days at a stretch—when Malkah behaved like some young untamed animal. She laughed at the top of her voice, without rhyme or reason, ran from room to room, shouted, leaped on and off chairs. And there were times when, equally without rhyme or reason, she sat silent, obdurate and motionless.

"There's something evil in that child," the aunt said frequently to her husband. "A devil, a spirit out of hell!"

That something evil showed itself whether Malkah was in high spirits or in low. Her playfulness was not like the playfulness of other children. It was furious, ungovernable. She would fill the house with children, upset the leather chairs, shove the furniture around, pull the drawers out of the desks and scatter her uncle's papers on the floor. Her favorite games were to build a train, seat the children on it, and set out on a journey to Budapest, to her mother, or to make marriages.

Next to this she liked most to play at marriage. She would pull out her aunt's dresses and furs and crinolines and hats, and deck herself out as a bride. She would unearth her aunt's jewelry— brooches, chains, necklaces, stickpins—and cover herself with them from head to foot.

Her aunt, coming in, would scream: "Malkah! You'll ruin me! Malkah! Am I not poor enough already?"

Malkah was unmoved. As soon as her aunt left the house, she was at it again. She infected the other children with her own spirit. She yelled, danced about the room, sang, turned the house into a bedlam. "Shout!" she commanded. "You're on the train! We're getting near Budapest!"

The "marriages" were as noisy as the "train-rides." On one occasion a neighbor came to Aunt Aidele, confused and horrified. Malkah had made herself a bride, and had chosen an eight-year-old boy to be her bridegroom. After having gone through a mock ceremony, Malkah had commanded two of the little girls to conduct bride and bridegroom to their bed! The children, going home, told their mothers, and the "bridegroom's" mother came in, weeping.

"I can't understand that," she complained. "Where does that child get it from?"

For a long time Aunt Aidele tortured Malkah to find out who had told her about bride and bridegroom going to bed. But Malkah set her teeth and did not answer. In the night Aunt Aidele, unable to sleep, woke her husband.

"Listen, you," she said, tugging at his skull-cap. "That little demon will bring shame on us, as her mother did."

Malkah developed an intemperate love of little children, a love so wild that children ran away from her, and mothers were frightened. Whenever she could lay her hands on some tot, she would press it so fiercely to her bosom, kiss it so rapturously, that the little one began to scream.

"The demon!" mothers exclaimed, when they saw her in the distance. And they pulled their children into the house. Under their breath they muttered: "Salt in your eyes! Pepper in your nose!"

It came to such a pitch that whenever a child fell sick in the village, the mother would come to Aunt Aidele, and beg her for a thread from one of Malkah's shawls. A thread from the shawl of a possessed woman was a specific against the evil eye. Aunt Aidele wept with the shame of it.

At the age of thirteen Malkah ran away for the first time.

With nothing but the clothes she had on, without a coin in her purse, she boarded the train for Budapest, where she knew her mother lived. What her mother was doing there, she did not know; nor did she have an address. She only knew that she was going to find her mother. She was stopped by the train police and turned back home. Aunt Aidele thought that, on being brought back, the child would weep, would be frightened and ask to be forgiven. But Malkah was hard as stone. She stared at her aunt out of eyes which already showed the first hunger of adolescence and said:

"Wait! I'm going to do it again! I'm going to find my mother!"

Then Aunt Aidele and her husband explained things to Malkah. Day after day they spoke against her mother, explained what an evil woman she was, how she had brought shame and humiliation on the family and how, because of her, Malkah's father had died before his time. That woman, they said, had a forehead of brass and a heart of stone. She had cared nothing for her husband, nothing for her child.

Malkah was unmoved. "I'm going to my mother," she repeated.

"If you go to your mother, they'll make you eat swine."

"I'm going to my mother."

"You'll have to live with non-Jews."

"I'm going to my mother."

"They'll make you wear a cross."

"I'm going to my mother."

Malkah was as good as her word. She ran away twice. But she did not find her mother. The woman had disappeared, had been swallowed up, and Malkah had to return to her aunt and uncle. And after her last attempt something came over the girl. Her silences became more obstinate. She no longer played with other children. She sat at the window by the hour, staring at the garrison officers as they passed down the street, staring mutely at them as they approached and as they receded into the distance.

It was at such a moment that her uncle burst in on her with the great news from Nyesheve. No wonder he and his wife were beside themselves with joy, for, apart from the good luck which it meant for them in the way of prestige—and something more substantial than prestige—it also meant that they would be relieved of their impossible niece. What hope had she? Poor, friendless, eccentric, evil-tempered, she might well stay on with them until her hair turned gray or until (God forbid!) she stooped to marry some laborer.

They could hardly believe it.

"If it was only over! If I only could see her standing under the canopy!" her aunt repeated. And she prayed to all her ancestry, to the Rabbis and pious wives in paradise, to stand by and see the match through.

They stood by, and Aunt Aidele saw her niece standing under the canopy side by side with her bridegroom, the Rabbi of Nyesheve. She went along to Nyesheve herself, and took part in the Seven Benedictions. And she was still incredulous. *Something* was going to happen. Malkah *always* had something in reserve.

"I don't understand it," she said nervously to her husband. "It's too good to be true. My heart tells me something is going to happen."

But nothing happened. During the months that passed between the announcement and her marriage, Malkah asked no questions about her bridegroom. She danced with joy over every present he sent her. He sent her a great many—diamond rings, earrings, brooches, bracelets and even diadems set with precious stones. All of these had been worn by one or another of the three wives he had buried. As each one of these had died, her respective daughters had claimed their mother's jewelry. But the Rabbi had accumulated a three-fold store, and even when the third wife died he still refused to divide the heritages. He locked the jewels away in the big iron safe which stood in his room, and he never let the key pass out of his possession. He was in no hurry. He had calculations of his own. Now he sent the jewelry piecemeal to Malkah, and Malkah danced with joy. She covered herself with precious stones from head to foot, and tried to see herself all at once in the single half-size mirror which stood in her aunt's room. She strutted from one end of the room to the other, and made great gestures, such as she imagined proper to a princess or a countess. Besides the jewels, the bridegroom sent large sums of money for her trousseau. At first he tried sending her some of the costly clothes which had been worn by his three wives, priceless satins, silks and furs. But Malkah would not have them. It took a long time to make Rabbi Melech understand that clothes may be made of the finest materials, and may be as good as new, but if they are no longer in the fashion, they cannot be worn.

"So?" he said in astonishment to the stammerer, who repeated from memory, phrase by phrase, what his wife had told him to say. "Not in the fashion? There's no understanding these strange creatures."

He therefore sent money, and plenty of it. All day long Malkah
flitted from one shop to another, buying silk, velvet, satin, wool
and linen. She brought the brightest and most striking colors,
materials as stormy as her own moods. She bought at first glance,
luxuriously, in fantastic quantities. And she refused to let her aunt
bargain.

"Lunatic!" her aunt exploded. "What do you need all that stuff
for? You're throwing money out."

"I want it!" was the sharp answer.

The tailors brought their sewing-machines into the house to
make up her wedding clotl_es. The older men sat with crossed legs,
crooning melodies, the younger men sang snatches of German
songs that had been carried by devious routes into the village, and
made eyes at the bride. The whirring of the machines, the singing,
the constant dressing and undressing, the measuring and remeasur-
ing, filled Malkah with happiness. She even caught her aunt
around the waist and kissed her furiously on both cheeks.

"Lunatic!" her aunt panted. "Let go of me! You're leaving red
marks on me."

The idea of the wedding, too, filled her with ecstasy. She did not
think of her husband to be. She knew he was old; and therefore
she demanded that the wedding be held in another town. Then she
forgot Rabbi Melech completely. When the wedding came, she
liked it. She had always liked the game, and here she was, playing
it on a grand scale, with real clothes, real ceremonies, real banquets and wine and musicians. Even the preliminary clashes with
her husband did not upset her. The first time, when he asked her
to let them shave her head, he had given way easily. The second
time—in the dark room there—he had been terribly angry, an
angry, scolding old man. It did not matter. She was even pleased
by the spectacle; she had almost laughed aloud.

She did not look into the future. The excitement of the moment,
the crowds of Chassidim, the flattery, the noise, the good wishes,
the importance bestowed on her—everything was good while it
lasted.

She liked, too, the long ride from Kiteve to Nyesheve. It was
jolly. The Jews of the villages on either side of the road came out

to see the Rabbi of Nyesheve and his bride pass by in state. They asked for his blessing and they brought presents. They brought their children to be blessed, and they paid for it with bottles of wine and jars of honey. The wives of the village Jews begged to be allowed to kiss Malkah's hand.

"Like a queen!" they exclaimed. "The Spirit rests on her face."

Wherever the procession stopped for the evening, there was a public festival; lanterns were hung up; there was dancing, drinking and singing. Malkah was in a continuous fever of excitement. She jumped up and down, and clapped her hands. Her attendants, the pompous womenfolk of the Rabbinic court of Nyesheve, blushed for her.

Her reception in Nyesheve was all love on the surface, all hatred underneath. Daughters, daughters-in-law, grandsons— all sorts of relatives of the Rabbi who had not come to the wedding—met her with smiles and compliments which did not conceal their envy and hatred. One after another the daughters of former wives of the Rabbi approached her, looked at her ornaments and sighed:

"Oh, that was mother's, blessed be her memory. May you wear it many, many years."

Malkah was not at all displeased. She felt the envy and liked it. She realized at once that this place was filled with hatreds and intrigues and gossip, that the court was divided into hostile cliques which watched each other venomously. She had not been there one day before attempts were made, by flattery, by ill-natured reports concerning the attitude toward her, to win her into some of the cliques. She liked it all. Malkah Spitfire felt at home in this atmosphere; it appealed to her love of mischief and her hunger for domination. She was happy, and Aunt Aidele—if she had but known it—had as yet no grounds for anxiety. These, in fact, came into existence only when, satisfied and reassured, she returned with her husband, the stammerer, to Przemysl.

After the seven days of tumult and excitement, came days of quiet and boredom. The visiting Chassidim scattered to their homes, the orchestras were silenced, and Malkah was left to her own devices in the big Rabbinic court, in the huge bleak rooms

with their naked walls and their old-fashioned wardrobes filled
with the moldering dresses of her three predecessors who had
lived and died there. The big unwashed windows stared out upon
the yard—a prospect of cracked plaster and mud. Malkah pulled
aside the curtains and glued her eyes to the pane. She saw the
crooked walls, the shapeless attics, the patched roofs and the rusty
well which creaked from morning till night. She saw mangy cats
and dogs, and Chassidim in filthy rags loitering at the doors. She
felt the burden of all the years to come; for ever and for ever she
would have to look out on this scene. And suddenly she was aware
of an acute longing for Przemysl, for the windows of her aunt's
room through which she had watched the garrison officers approaching and receding. She longed for distant things, the hooting
of the trains, the swinging lanterns of the conductors in the night;
she longed for Budapest and for her half-forgotten, far-off mother.

In all her apartment there was not one mirror; such vanities
were forbidden the wife of the Rabbi of Nyesheve. When she put
on her jewelry she could admire herself only in the silver trays and
boxes on the tables, and the little hand-mirror she had stolen from
her aunt before leaving. She looked at herself and bit her lips
when her eyes rested on her own head, shaven and diminished.

She thrust her tongue out at herself.

"Monkey!" she said spitefully into the mirror.

She drew the black silk kerchief down till it touched her heavy
eyebrows and pulled faces at herself. Then she wearied of the
game and sat down to think.

What was she going to do with herself in this place? She remembered that she had jewelry—lots of it. And dresses. She took
out the jewels, weighed them in her hand, let them run through
her fingers. "With these," she thought, "I could travel a long way.
Some night, when I can't stand it any more, when I'll be dreaming
about Budapest . . ."

The thought of the horror which would descend on the place
when they found the nest empty, the thought of the white faces
and the gabbling, and the thought of her aunt and uncle in hysterics when the news reached Przemysl, made her shout suddenly
with laughter. The bare walls redoubled the strange sound, and

Malkah's servant, a stumpy, gray-haired elderly maid, came running in.

"I got such a fright," she panted, one red, scratched hand under the left breast.

"Fright?" Malkah asked. "Why?"

"The others—the ones before"—the maid stammered—"they never used to laugh."

The maid's half-incoherent words lay like stones on Malkah's spirit. A chill settled on her, and the laughter died on her lips. The room became intolerably close; she heard the far-off voices again.

And then, one day, something happened—something astounding and unexpected and impossible—something that changed the whole Rabbinic court for Malkah, and made it the one place where, she felt, she could spend the rest of her days. Her longing for distant places died; it was as if it had never been. Here, in the ugly court, among the bleak, peeling walls, was her happiness and destiny. She had seen a face.

When the Seven Days of the Seven Benedictions were over, there were dull, little minor affairs: visits from one apartment to another. Every branch of the family—every daughter and daughter-in-law of the Rabbi—invited Malkah, the new "head of the household" in turn, and entertained her with cakes, jams, jellies, flattery and two-edged, poisonous remarks. The last of the invitations came, naturally, from Serele, the youngest daughter of the Rabbi.

Serele was perhaps the only one in the family who looked forward with genuine hope to the coming of the new wife of the Rabbi. She had neither the sharpness nor the malevolence of her sisters. She was young, simple and utterly absorbed in her Nahum; court politics did not penetrate to her. Heavy, slow, good-natured, she had no room in her make-up for hatred or envy or calculated flattery. She wanted a friend, a young married woman of her own age; like every newly married young woman who is in love with her husband and has no masculine companionship, she needed a friend of her own sex to whom to pour out her heart.

Serele made great preparations for the visit of Malkah. She

heaped up cakes, cookies, candies, jams, wine, fruit-juices and almonds. She had no other way of expressing her anxiety to please. And she had no notions of conversation. Malkah was something strange, too: half sister, half mother; sister in age, mother by position. She did not know whether to talk to Malkah in the familiar second person singular or in the more formal second person plural. She therefore avoided the use of any pronoun, and this embarrassed her so dreadfully that she had to cling to one sentence:

"Oh, dear, Malkah doesn't like my cakes and my wine." And while she said this she played with her stepmother's necklace.

Malkah was bored both by the food and by the clumsy affection of Serele. They were alike—heavy, sweet, cloying. She made the visit brief and rose to go. Just as she reached the door, and stretched out her hand, it was opened from the other side, and she stood face to face with Nahum. They started, and made an attempt to ignore each other.

It was Saturday night. Candles burned on the table, filling the room with a dim light. Nahum wore a flowery silk dressing-gown, which made his body look more slender than it was. The white Rachmanivke collar lay on his shoulders, setting off the brown of his throat. He stood there hesitant, graceful, steeped in the mystery of the Sabbath half-light. Opposite him stood Malkah, with her black silk kerchief drawn over her brown face to her eyebrows, a slender figure to match his. For an instant they looked at each other, a wild, unconscious joy lighting their faces. Then, catching themselves up, they looked away, and remained standing, paralyzed.

Perhaps if Serele had been able, even then, to intervene, and say something natural to break the tension and the astonishment, the incident might have passed off. But she too stood wordless, looking at both of them, understanding nothing. Her hands hung down; she stared like some servant girl who has dropped a vase and does not know what to say. Nahum was the first to come to himself. With a sudden gesture, partly of shyness, partly the result of long training, he covered his eyes in order not to look at a woman, stepped aside, and murmured: "Good evening."

The words woke Malkah out of her trance. A red flood rose from her throat to her eyebrows, and a cry escaped her lips. "Mama!" Then she slipped past Nahum and ran for her apartment as if she were being pursued. In her room she tore her dress off, and liberated herself from the tight lacing and whalebone which choked her. Love and pity and happiness had filled her suddenly. The boyish figure in the flowery silk dressing-gown had brought back to her the impulse which, in earlier years, had made her snatch up little children and kiss them frantically. He was a man and yet a little boy. She was confused; she wanted him, and she wanted a child too, at the same time; a child she could pick up, press to her breast, suffer for; a child that looked like him, dark, gentle and tender. All the furious impulses of her nature, without discipline and without compromise, rose up in her. She bared her firm, shuddering breast, and cupped both hands under it, so that she felt as if she were suckling a baby.

Nahum lay on his bed, restless with fever. He heard the voices of the Chassidim in the courtyard singing the closing song of the Sabbath night—"Farewell to the Queen!" Someone was drawing water from the well. And nothing was real but the figure standing in the doorway, slender, black, the kerchief drawn down to the glowing eyes. In the darkness Nahum stretched out his arms to Serele; he began to caress her, at first shyly, hesitantly; and then, forgetting himself, more boldly and fiercely.

It was the first time that Serele had known such an outburst of passion on his side. In her bewildered gratitude she did not hear him whisper once or twice a name that was not hers.

8

Nahum steeped himself in Kabbala. He read:

"*Sod ha-zivug tolui bashlemus*—the secret of the union lies in its completeness. Let the strength of the man and the strength of the woman really unite, become one body. And the man, the predestined one of this woman, waits with fainting eyes and with great longing for the time of the coming of the beautiful and desired one; and he runs to her and embraces her and gives her happiness; and after he has kissed her and thereby united their spirits, meaning the inward union, there follows the outward union—hand to hand, mouth to mouth, eye to eye. And the kiss of two is made into one breath. And she, the beautiful maiden, the lovely virgin without eyes, she who makes all others look dim and without beauty, she whom all the loves of all men and all women imitate, and in whom they are all united, she . . ."

He could not study Talmud any more. His teacher, Reb Pesachiah of Zavil, who had been imported especially for him into the court of Nyesheve, was anxious to have his pupil shine in the Law; and he had prepared for him a difficult program. But Nahum stared at the pages and saw no letters. He only saw a face. He saw it everywhere: on the carved cover of the sacred Ark which held the Scrolls of the Law, on the velvet mantles which covered the Scrolls, in the red evening sky toward which his glances wandered, and even in the dread letters of the Ineffable Name of God, above the Ark. Only when he looked into the pages of the Kabbala could he read, for these words spoke to him of her.

Reb Pesachiah was startled and puzzled by the sudden change in his pupil. With the utmost difficulty he managed to get the young man's attention upon some subtle interpretation of the

71

Law, and just when he thought that Nahum had absorbed everything, he was aware of a blank. Nahum was not paying attention.
He was staring at a fly, at a sunbeam crawling over the wall, at a
bird which had touched the window with the tip of a wing.

"Nahum!" said Reb Pesachiah softly. "What are you looking
at?"

"Nothing!" Nahum answered, as if awakened from sleep. "I
forgot myself."

Often, like some inattentive child taking his first lessons,
Nahum lost the text and could not find it. Reb Pesachiah suffered
greatly. Ascetic and moralist that he was, his thoughts were full of
the world to come, and of the torments of the damned in hell. He
knew that it was a deadly sin for a man to interrupt his studies of
the sacred Law with vain and trivial thoughts, to exchange the
words which are eternal for some fleeting worldly reflection which
was without worth. More than once he had told Nahum about Elijah of Vilna, that mighty man of learning, who had been wont to
keep his feet in cold water while he studied, in order that his mind
might remain alert. And there had been pious men, scholars, who
had stabbed themselves in the eyes, blinded themselves, in order
that they might never again be tempted by the follies of the world
to divert their attention from the pursuit of God's word.

Reb Pesachiah never spoke angrily. He had ordered his life
according to the teaching of the moralists, and he had conquered
all his evil inclinations. He knew that anger was evil; to yield to
rage was equivalent to bending the knee before an idol. He knew
too what the sages had said: An angry man cannot be a teacher. In
all the years of his labor as a teacher he had never, even under the
extremest provocation, spoken a sharp word to one of his pupils.
He only taught them the sayings of the moralists. He had never as
much as looked sternly at Nahum, in the old days, in Rachmanivke; how much less liable was he to do it now, when Nahum was
the son-in-law of the Rabbi of Nyesheve! All that he permitted
himself with Nahum was a moral sermon, a page or two from one
of the good books of the saintly sages.

These warning words penetrated Nahum as if they had been
steel foils. The voice of Reb Pesachiah was low, calm and deadly.

It issued from between his thin, pallid lips, which were visible under the colorless hair which covered them, as from a grave. When, on Saturday afternoons, Reb Pesachiah chanted one of the chapters from the Ethics of the Fathers, it sounded like a dirge over the vanity and futility of the life of a man.

In the same voice he intoned, for Nahum's benefit, passages from the morality books. Whenever he caught Nahum dreaming over the Talmud, he began to murmur:

"Rabbi Chanina, the son of Rabbi Chachinai, says: If a man wakes up in the middle of the night, or if a man goes alone on a road, and permits his heart to dwell on vanities, he has forfeited his life. Rabbi Jacob says: If a man walks on a road, and interrupts his own meditations on sacred law, in order to say: How beautiful is that tree! or, How beautiful is that field! such a man, it is written, has forfeited his life."

Nahum trembled. He made another effort to collect his distracted mind and to concentrate it on his studies. He put his hand over his eyes, to keep out the world. But before he knew it he was again looking at some foolish thing, and the law was far from his mind.

There were no trees in the courtyard. But beyond the gates of the yard stretched the level, plowed fields; and somewhere on them could always be seen the figure of a peasant bending over the soil, or following his horse. Sometimes a stork came down, and, poising itself on one thin red leg, stood there for hours, stood there as if it had been hired to keep watch. So emptily, so motionlessly, Nahum could sit at the window hour by hour, looking at the flat fields or at the fluffs of cloud which drifted under the hot sun.

Toward the other side of the house the meadows lay on a rising slope. They were always green and moist; they were always filled with sounds of life: the humming of insects, the shrilling of crickets, the crying of birds, the quacking of geese, the croaking of frogs. Most he suffered from the deep humming of the insects, which was a never-ceasing accompaniment to the other sounds. It crept into his flesh, and drew him away from his books. And when he looked into the meadows, he was drawn, too, by the mottled cow, with its head tied to its foreleg; by the big-horned goats, chained to logs of wood; by the tethered horses swishing their tails; by the herds of white sheep and by the flocks of geese swimming peacefully on the river.

A hundred times Nahum determined fiercely not to look on these things. What was there to look at? The same thing, over and over again. But his eyes wandered to the window, and remained there. They could not get enough of the green of the fields, the white of the geese, the yellow of the buttercups. And in spite of his torments, Nahum felt unutterable joy streaming out of these things. It was a joy without meaning; it rose from a sunbeam breaking through leaves, and throwing a spot of gold on a horse's head; from the white ruffling of the water; from the patchwork on the back of a cow. And utterance came out of the thousand sights; something secret and significant, bound up in some way with her who sat at that moment in some other room. He heard her name in the piping of the shepherds' flutes and in the crack of the wagoners' whips.

There were moments when the peaceful creatures on the meadows were seized by a fit of restlessness. This happened mostly after a heavy rain, when the sun burst out between thick clouds, and a great arc of color rose from the dark horizon to the zenith. Then tethered mares began to neigh wildly and longingly, the raucous sound filling the damp, steaming air; and some stallion, held close for his breeding value, would crash through the door of his stall, and make with such fury for one of the mares that the shepherds could not beat him off with whips or staves.

Young goats, which till then had amused themselves by running from one hedge to another, their little tails stiff in the air, became fierce with new-born desires; they attacked the mothers which, only a few months before, had suckled them. Even old, heavy rams, uncouth, unshorn, began to chase frightened sheep, bleating after them with unsatisfied longing.

Nahum knew that he was defiling himself by looking on these things; he knew that for such sins he should have fasted for days at a stretch. He reminded himself that he was no longer a child, but a man, a married man. He struggled with himself, but the manifold joy of the field was stronger than he. The hand which he placed over his eyes, the thin weak hand of a helpless boy, was pulled away by an overmastering force. And he looked again.

He saw the same restlessness manifest itself in the shepherds. They paid no attention to their flocks and herds, letting them wander at will into closed-off fields, while they themselves ran after the shepherd girls. He saw the girls shamelessly throw off their upper clothes and plunge into the river, the men after them. And one older girl, whom he had seen often at a distance, a dull creature fit for nothing better than watching geese, uncovered herself completely as far as the waist, and showed her naked body to the surrounding world.

Then Nahum's thoughts focused themselves definitely on Malkah. His body became rigid as he imagined himself kissing her, holding her body to his. He lifted his hands blindly, and only when his convulsive fingers closed on emptiness did he come to himself.

Sin! Deadly, mortal, unforgivable sin! He was crumbling to pieces, here in the Rabbinic court of Nyesheve. He knew from the books that the sin of desire was the same as the sin of possession. There was no flame in hell hot enough for him who had even lusted after the wife of another. And he lusted not after a stranger, but after the wife of his Rabbi, of his father-in-law, the stepmother of his wife!

In his anguish he turned to the books of the moralists.

"And there are demons," he read aloud, chanting the text and swaying back and forth, "there are demons which have a thousand eyes, and they torture the sinner only by looking at him. And there are fires which are named Death and Darkness and Curse and Abyss, and many others. And the smallest of these fires is sixty times hotter than the hottest fire on earth. And the screaming of the sinners is a greater torture even than the fire. And still greater is the torture of their shame, inasmuch as they must pay, for one minute of foolish pleasure, with so much agony. And the demons standing around mock the screaming of the sinners."

Nahum leaped from his chair and stood trembling. He looked at his hands; they were thin and frail; they could not bear pain; a little scratch on that transparent skin made him wince. He saw these thin hands of his clawing the white hot coals; he felt the white hot prongs piercing the sensitive flesh under his nails.

Sweating from head to foot, he sat down again, and forced himself to go on with the text. Hoarsely he chanted:

"And there was a goldsmith, an artisan, who had much to do with women, for he made ornaments for them. And being neglectful of his soul, this man touched the hands of the women, and he touched their naked throats when he placed necklaces on them. So the women desired him, because he was good to look upon. And therefore the demon Lilith fixed her heart upon him, and she came to him whenever he thought of her; she came to him naked and full of desire, and laid herself on a golden bed and called him to her and he sinned with her. And after his death—God help us!—millions of demons ran after him and called him father, and his shame was a greater torment to him than the fires of hell, which are sixty times fiercer than the fiercest fires on earth. . . ."

He closed his eyes and saw the sinful goldsmith running down blazing alleys of hell, pursued by millions of demons. And then the figure of the goldsmith yielded to the figure of Lilith, and she was slender and dressed in black, and a black silk kerchief came down as far as her eyebrows. Then she too changed; beautiful and lustful, she called to him; she lay naked on a golden bed, calling him with wanton words to her wanton body. And it seemed to him that he was sinning with her, and crying "Malkah! Malkah!"

But his nights were filled even more terribly than his days with the stranger whom the Rabbi of Nyesheve had brought into his court.

In his dreams he would see her not as the wife of the Rabbi, but as his daughter. He was being married to her. At the wedding feast he rose to his feet, and propounded a subtle parable for the assembled scholars. Then he covered her face with a silken kerchief, and the kerchief fell from his hands, and the women moaned in terror. Then he sat alone with her in a room, and they tasted the golden soup out of one dish. Then the two old men came, and led him toward the bridal chamber, and slammed the door behind him. This was Malkah, the daughter of the Rabbi. But Serele was, in turn, the daughter of the stammerer. She was sick, and she died. Then the Rabbi of Nyesheve turned into a sexton, and with a big spade dug the grave for Serele. Nahum wept for her, but Malkah, his wife, wiped the tears from his eyes, just as his mother used to do, and told him that it was forbidden for a bridegroom to weep.

These dreams became intolerable. In long prayers he invoked angels to keep guard over him and to drive away evil dreams. It was no use. The dreams returned, and their theme was always the same. In the morning he was haunted by a sense of guilt toward Serele, and was ashamed to look at her, as if she knew of his visions in the night.

He took to fasting, and to subduing his flesh.

Serele suffered too. She prepared the tastiest dishes for him; she baked cakes with onion parings, and scattered poppy and caraway seeds on them. She knew he loved these things. But he did not eat.

"I've had evil dreams," he said. "I want to fast."

He became lean. His eyes seemed to grow bigger, and circles of brown and blue formed around them. Serele began to be afraid of her husband. She watched him dumbly, not knowing what to ask. And then, in despair, she took a daring step. She wrote to her mother-in-law in Rachmanivke about Nahum's fasting, and Nahum's mother sent him a long letter in Hebrew, in which she implored him to give up his ascetic habits, and above all things to take care of his health. He must not dare to fast, she wrote. She even proposed that he come home for a long visit though he had been married only a few months.

She closed the letter in homely Yiddish, as she always did when she wanted to pour out her heart. "Darling child, your mother is waiting for you. She will make you happy and whole again."

Nahum did indeed give up fasting, for he found that a long fast, instead of subduing, only provoked to more fantastic activity the evil thoughts for which he was doing penance. But he did not go home to his mother. Over him, too, a change had come in relation to the Rabbinic court of Nyesheve. He too discovered that the dirty windows and the creaking pump and the peeling walls were near and dear things. Everything was part of her. He sat by the hour at the window of his own little study in the attic, looking down into the yard, waiting till she should pass. He had always avoided his father-in-law; now it became a habit with him to make visits, the pretext being a book, a question of ritual, a point of law, or—nothing at all. She was there, in the room adjoining. He felt her presence through the wall, and shivered.

But before long it became a habit with her to come into the room when Nahum was there. A sudden and alien fit of thoughtfulness toward her husband would come over her; without being asked, she would bring her husband a glass of milk, or his medicine.

The Rabbi was astounded, and, scarcely aware of what he was doing, actually spoke to her with tenderness in the presence of another. "My dear! With your own hands?"

Nahum did not dare to lift up his eyes to her. His heart seemed to have stopped beating. She, however, did look at him, and he felt it. She even passed so near him that a fold of her skirt brushed his knee, and a quick little wind passed over his burning face. For days the touch of her skirt and the cool breath of her passing were with him.

Once she was able to seize his hand, and to hold it tight for several seconds. This happened right in the Rabbi's room, and in his presence. Rabbi Melech was surprised and gratified by the change that had come over his son-in-law. Instead of evading him, the young man now came frequently, and of his own accord, to discuss legal questions and to indulge in plain, human conversation. He therefore commanded Malkah to receive her son-in-law with some special attentions; to bring in cakes and wine and fruit for the visitor. On one occasion she herself served Nahum, and in her agitation she caught her foot in the train of her dress. She stumbled, and Nahum leaped to his feet. Instead of catching at the arm of the chair, which was nearer to her, Malkah snatched at

Nahum's hand. He stood petrified, unable to help her, letting her lean a moment against him, till she had righted herself.

The bottle of wine she was carrying had crashed to the floor. Rabbi Melech got up anxiously, and took Malkah by the hand.

"The wine!" she cried, dismayed.

"Never mind the wine," he answered. "As long as you didn't hurt yourself."

She fled from the room.

For some time after this incident Nahum again avoided the apartment of Rabbi Melech. It seemed to him that his hand would betray him. He washed it and rubbed it, to cleanse it of all traces of her touch. But it could not be cleansed. Often, while he sat over the Talmud, or over a book of moral sayings, his hands would be under the table, and one hand would caress the other meditatively. Once, when no one was with him, he bent down and left a shy, frightened kiss on the hand she had held.

And all this time fear grew in the heart of Serele. She was afraid for him, as well as of him. She thought that perhaps he ought to see a doctor, but did not dare to suggest it. In the nights her husband avoided her. She knew from the books which dealt with the duties of a wife what was due her. On nights when she had been to the ritual baths, she said many prayers, imploring grace, in order that her husband might find her desirable. She tried to give him hints, when the days of her impurity were over, that he might approach her. But it seemed that his eyes and ears and heart were locked; she could not reach him.

And once, all of a sudden, he drew her to him, and began to kiss her and fondle her frantically. This frightened her more than ever; she became rigid, and did not know what to say or do. In the little books of feminine duties, written in Yiddish, there were a great many commands concerning the way of a wife with her husband. But there were no commands regarding such wild behavior as Nahum now indulged in. Serele needed some one to confide in. Her mother was dead; her sisters were much older than she—and they were not really her sisters. She had no one but Malkah to turn to, and because Malkah was her only hope, she clung to her with dumb, heavy affection, told her everything, down to the slightest details of Nahum's strange treatment of her.

Malkah listened hungrily. She, the stranger in the Rabbinic house, hated by all others as an interloper, was nearer than anyone else to her daughter-in-law.

"Serele," she whispered, kissing her, "tell me more—tell me everything, as if you were my sister."

9

MALKAH NOW BEGAN TO LIVE IN SERELE'S APARTMENT MORE THAN in her own. She took her meals in her own apartment, and slept there. The rest of the day she was usually with her step-daughter.

She brought a tempestuous spirit into the dull, repulsive rooms, and turned everything upside down, much as she had done in the house of her aunt in Przemysl. She changed the position of the furniture, hung new curtains at the windows, adorned the walls with colored cloths, and even re-arranged the dresses in the wardrobe. She did everything with such fury that Serele stared helplessly.

"Wait, Serele, you'll see. I'm going to get pictures for the walls. I'll make it beautiful in here. I'm going to get you a big mirror."

Serele stared with fear.

"Malkah, darling! You can't do that. No one dares to have a mirror, here in Nyesheve. If my father gets to know . . ."

"Let him know!" Malkah answered, unabashed. "I want your rooms to be pretty!"

When she was done with the rooms, she turned her attention to Serele herself. Her ideas of dress and deportment were taken from one or two old fashion journals she had seen, and from the few story-books that had fallen into her hands. She made Serele change her dress several times; she told her how to hold and flirt

a fan, and how to walk with the train of her dress hanging over
one arm. Then she seized Serele round her clumsy waist and tried
to make her dance a quadrille. Serele lumbered after her helplessly
—the only dance she knew was called, among Jews, "the dance of
piety," in which the partners are separated by the length of a
handkerchief. Malkah whirled her round and round wildly, until
Serele became dizzy and fell. Then Malkah's shrill laughter rang
out so loudly that it was heard in every corner of the court.

"Malkah, darling. You mustn't laugh like that. Nahum will hear
you."

"That won't do him any harm," and she laughed louder.

Serele was disturbed by Malkah's wildness. Such things were
not done in the Rabbinic court of Nyesheve. Not that she dared
say a word to her young step-mother. Even when Malkah tore the
clumsy bonnet, with its nodding cherries, off her head, and pinned
on a silk kerchief, she did not protest. But while Malkah was
making the change, Serele covered her head with both hands.

"But why are you holding your head?" Malkah asked.

Serele answered in the chanting voice of one who reads from
a book of religious commandments: "A daughter of Israel may
not show her naked head even to the four walls of a room."

Malkah let her remain bareheaded for several minutes, and
laughed at her. "You look like a little lamb that's just been
shorn," she said, mockingly. "Ba-a-a! Ba-a-a!"

She wanted to make this great lumbering creature angry, to
force her into a quarrel. But Serele, not knowing how to talk, did
not know how to quarrel. She could only weep, the big tears
rolling down her stupid face. And then Malkah would change
suddenly; she would become gentle and contrite; she would em-
brace her daughter-in-law, comfort and kiss her. And when Serele's tears were dried. Malkah was off again; she tried a new
combination of ribbons on Serele's forehead; she made her take
out her wedding clothes and try them on.

"Serele! I'll make you look like a princess! Nahum won't recognize you."

"Nahum never looks at me," Serele said, dully. "He's always
with his books."

"*I'll* make him look at you," Malkah answered, swiftly. "*I'll* make him pay attention. Only do what I tell you."

She began to teach Serele new habits. She told her to stop taking glasses of tea up to Nahum's attic study; if Nahum wanted tea, he could come down to the apartment for it. But Serele was afraid.

"You're a little fool," Malkah explained. "Don't you know he's from Rachmanivke, and in Rachmanivke they aren't as provincial and as stupid as in Nyesheve? In Rachmanivke men *talk* with their wives. And if you want Nahum to love you, you've got to act with him as if it was Rachmanivke. Do what I tell you!"

It worked. Nahum did not complain when tea was not brought to him. He came down, said "Good day" briefly, and sat down at table. Malkah sat down next to Serele, and taking Serele's kerchief, stretched it to cover her own head too.

"Won't you have some poppy-seed cakes?" she asked Nahum, as if she were the hostess; and she pushed the tray closer to him.

Nahum was silent. In Nyesheve it was not the custom to converse with strange women, or to eat with them at the same table. But Malkah was not easily beaten. Brought up as she had been in the atmosphere of the Rabbinic dynasties, she knew the standing, the history and the relationship of all the Galician and Russian courts; and she insisted on finding out how—apart from his present marriage—Nahum was related to her. In that complicated inbreeding of the Rabbinic courts, it was unlikely that she could not find some bond.

"If the Rabbinate of Rishineh," she said, like some crone showing off her knowledge of family precedence, "if the Rabbinate of Rishineh is allied by marriage to the Rabbinate of Karlin, then Nahum and I must be related on my mother's side. . . ."

Serele sat on the edge of her chair, and stared at Malkah as if she were a freak. Even wives must not speak to their husbands before they are spoken to; and here was a stranger in the house addressing Nahum as if it were the most commonplace thing in the world; there was no sign of shyness on her face or in her voice. She even spoke his name out boldly. Serele, married to him for several months, had never yet dared address him by his own

name; it was immodest. But the greatest wonder of all was that
her husband answered! True, he answered without looking at the
strange woman, keeping his eyes fixed on the table or the floor; he
answered in a low, almost inaudible voice, and his sentences were
curt. But he answered!

It became a custom for Nahum to come down for tea at a fixed
hour, and to find Malkah with Serele. Malkah always played the
hostess. She made Serele fetch and carry; she sent her on errands,
as if she were a servant girl.

There was hardly an afternoon when she did not manage to be
alone with Nahum in the room for a few minutes. She knew quite
well—this she had learned at home, and she would soon have
learned it in Nyesheve—that a man was not permitted to remain
alone in a room with a strange woman, especially if that woman
were married. But the prohibition gave a sharper edge to her joy;
and something rebellious and delicious stirred in her as she
watched Nahum wriggling with embarrassment and shame.

Something was always missing at table: raspberry juice, or
cakes that were locked in a cupboard in another room. Or else
Malkah was suddenly cold, and snuggling close to Serele she
would say, with all the sweetness at her command, "Serele, darling, do find me a shawl."

Serele, too, knew that it was sinful for a man to remain alone
with a woman; the little books had taught her this much. She knew
that her husband could censure her severely for having left him
with Malkah. But she did not know how to refuse Malkah's re-
quests; it was not in her nature to oppose anyone's wish—least of
all Malkah's; Malkah was so much cleverer, knew so much more
of the world. Heavy-footed, she left the room, walking sometimes
through the entire house before she found what she was sent
for.

The moment Serele was gone, Malkah found some reason to
move round to the other side of the table—to offer cake, or to put
sugar into the tea, or to move the trays and plates. She always
managed to brush his face or his body with a sleeve or a fold of
her dress; sometimes she dared to touch his knee with hers, or,
with almost obvious deliberateness, pass her hand across his.

"Nahum," she said softly, "your tea's getting cold." All the love and warmth that flooded her then spilled over into his name; and he became so helpless that things dropped out of his hands.

Once, when Serele was gone from the room, Malkah, wilder than usual, lingered round Nahum, whispering his name while she pretended to be occupied with the plates. His agitation and distress and fear provoked her to tease him the more; still whispering his name, she lingered close to him when the heavy, dragging footsteps of the returning Serele were already audible. Only at the last moment, when it seemed that the hand was on the door, did Malkah make a leap back to her own side of the table, a soft, cat-like leap, so smooth that it left no trace of motion on her face or body. At the same instant, Nahum, in an agony of helplessness, dropped his glass.

She found a special joy in this dangerous, provocative game, in which the elements were the sensitiveness and terror of Nahum, her own daring, and Serele's thick-witted good nature. She developed a subtle technique, a mode of invisible communication, which kept up a tense relationship between herself and Nahum in the presence of Serele. She conveyed in hints, looks, gestures, intonations, allusions—in a thousand ways perceptible to him and her—all the shades of her emotion. There was a constant stream of communication between them, strong and unmistakable; only Serele was not aware of it.

Then this game, too, began to lose its flavor. She wanted something more—greater risks, closer intimacy. She tried to meet him outside Serele's apartment, alone. If she had only dared, she would have stolen up to his study in the attic. But this was too much even for her. She satisfied herself with passing under his window and looking up. Seldom did the little curtains fail to divide hurriedly; seldom did the black, eager eyes fail to respond.

She knew the exact hours of his coming and going. She knew on what days he went out to walk in the fields, along the paths which led by the river and through the woods, and among the hills on the other side of the woods. She began to haunt him on his walks, setting out in another direction, circling round quickly and meeting him face to face. When they encountered each other, she did not try to stop him; she only whispered his name as she passed.

Nahum would then redouble his footsteps, turn down a bypath and run rather than walk home. He made up his mind not to go walking again; or, if he did go, he would take Reb Pesachiah along, so that they might talk of sacred things while they walked. But he went again, alone. He went along the same paths, knowing that she would come to meet him, waiting to hear the whisper of his name.

On a hot day, later in the summer, he stole out of the courtyard and took a new path out of the village. The dust rose from the dry roads in faint puffs and spirals; storks flew from roof to roof in the village. Behind the hedges of the orchards ripe pears and apples nestled in the heavy green foliage. The feeling of the end of the summer was in the air. In the open fields the peasants were mowing and stacking the hay, and slow, warm waves of odor were carried to Nahum's nostrils. Nahum walked on dreamily till he came to the woods. Beyond these woods, far away, lay the mountains. He walked and looked at the ant hills under the trees; he heard the sound of the woodpeckers, and tried to catch glimpses of them; he saw the black and red squirrels leaping, with a rustling sound, from branch to branch, from tree to tree. Suddenly a wind began to agitate the needles of the pine trees; the sky became black, and a furious rain came down, almost without warning; the lightning played across the sky, and after every flash the thunder cracked and rolled through the woods.

Nahum saw in front of him a huge and ancient tree, one side of which had been hollowed out by age and by storms. He shrank into the hollow, and, stretching out his hands to the rain that dripped from the overhang, washed them in order that he might utter the benediction for thunder. Before the words had crossed his lips he started back; Malkah was at his side, her clothes soaked through, her eyes staring with fright. She nestled into the hollow of the tree, so that her body touched his. Her hand was on her heart.

"Nahum! I'm frightened! I got caught in the storm. I'm so frightened."

He did not ask her where she came from, and how she came to

be here. He only felt the tingle of his blood from the roots of his scalp to the soles of his feet.

They stood silent, staring at the fine spears of rain slanting down from the black sky, at the threads pouring from the leaves and branches, at the rivulets making an involved tracery on the ground. The thunder began again, and with every burst Malkah snatched at Nahum's hand.

"I'm frightened!" she gasped.

Nahum forced himself to say something. "You should not be afraid. You should wash your hands and say the benediction for thunder."

She tried to obey. She stretched out her hands and washed them; then she tried to remember the words of the benediction for thunder. But in that instant a furious line of whiteness split the entire sky, and for an instant the woods were steeped in terrific light; almost simultaneously the thunder broke overhead, beginning with a deafening crack, and continuing in a deep, tremendous roll of sound, dying, then beginning again louder and more terrifying, accompanied always by innumerable echoes in the wood. Malkah uttered a scream, "Mama!" and throwing her arms round Nahum, clung to him like a terrified child.

He tore her arms from round his neck. A second flash, as bright as the first, seemed to spring out from every corner of the sky, a whip of fire with a thousand lashes, the fire of God for the punishment of sinners. He uttered a cry and dashed out into the rain.

He heard her voice, dying: "Nahum! Nahum! I'm frightened!"

He came into the courtyard soaked to the skin, and beside himself with fear. The men were already assembled in the synagogue for afternoon prayers.

He lay in bed several days with fever. When he recovered, a change had come over him.

He had become more silent than before. He never left the little study in the attic, and Malkah haunted the apartment in vain. Every day she went out into the fields and woods, along the paths he had always frequented, but she never found him. Her favorite waiting place was the withered old tree where she had seen him last; she spent hours there, though she knew that he would not come again.

But while he avoided Malkah, he was more tender and more intimate with Serele than he had ever been before. He did not converse with her, but he had become a dutiful husband again, and behaved toward her as the little books told her he ought to behave. Flushing with happiness, she told Malkah:

"He's not the same, since that sickness."

Malkah did not give up. She continued to visit Serele, just as she continued to walk through the yard, looking up at the curtains which never divided for her now. She was waiting. The dread month of Elul, the month of the High Holidays, the Days of Awe, had set in. She thought that when this time of prayer and penitence was over, he would be the same toward her. He would have to be! In the night she thought of new devices to draw him closer to her when the penitential month was over; she could think of nothing else, of no one but this boy who alone made her life in Nyesheve tolerable.

But when the month was closing a special messenger came from Rachmanivke to bring Nahum home to his parents for a visit.

His mother's patience had come to an end. To all her letters imploring him to return to her for a while he had given evasive answers; and one day she called in Mottye Godul, the *gabbai* of the Rabbi of Rachmanivke, gave him money for a passport and expenses, and told him not to dare to return without her son.

Mottye Godul undertook the high commission with malicious joy. He hated the Chassidim of Galicia; but he hated those of Nyesheve with a special, separate loathing. He had been opposed to the match from the beginning; and his opposition had taken on a sharper edge when it was too late, when, at the wedding, he had made his first contact with the uncivilized court of Nyesheve, and with Israel Avigdor, the *gabbai* of Rabbi Melech. It would be a pleasure to snatch Nahum out of their hands, if only for a respite, a pleasure all the greater because there had been no mention at all of Serele, his wife.

Mottye Godul, armed with his mandate, descended grimly on
Nyesheve. He sought out Nahum at once, and, scarcely waiting to
exchange greetings, began to scold him. "Is this the way," he
asked, "to treat your parents? Don't you know that your mother,
God bless her, is sickening for the sight of you? And have you
forgotten everyone in Rachmanivke?"

He would have picked Nahum up at once, carried him off like a
prisoner, without a chance to change his clothes or to say good-by
to anyone. The Chassidim of Nyesheve tried to placate Mottye
Godul; they begged him to stay a while with them. He would not
listen.

"I'm in a hurry!" he said, coldly. "The wife of the Rabbi of
Rachmanivke is waiting for her son."

He avoided the Chassidim of Nyesheve. The only man he con-
versed with freely was Reb Pesachiah, Nahum's teacher. As to the
others, he had only one word: "Get Nahum ready! I have no time
to lose."

The preparations which were made for that journey would have
sufficed for an expedition. The women began to cook and bake
and pack; they prepared cakes, biscuits, cold chicken, fruit-juice
—provisions enough for a small army. Serele was torn between
two emotions: a wretchedness that nearly paralyzed her and a
desire to show her mother-in-law in Rachmanivke how well she
looked after her son. But Mottye Godul kept shouting:

"You don't need all this, I tell you. Do you think I've come
from Rachmanivke without provisions of our own?"

But as against this, he demanded that all of Nahum's clothes,
including his furs, be packed at once. "You'll need them all,
Nahum," he said, significantly. "Your mother won't let you go
back in a hurry to Nyesheve. There's plenty of time for *that*."

Reb Pesachiah, the teacher, was also coming along.

Serele attended to her duties half blinded by tears. Her sisters,
who usually kept away from her, had suddenly become very atten-
tive; they were hurt—for her sake, of course—because her mother-
in-law had not invited her to Rachmanivke; they wanted to
console her, and their consolation took the form of bitter and
contemptuous remarks about the snobs of Rachmanivke, who

thought themselves too good for the simple Jews and Jewesses of Nyesheve.

"My lady of Rachmanivke! She wouldn't soil herself by touching her Nyesheve daughter-in-law," they said, imitating the haughty grimaces of Nahum's mother.

And to Nahum she could say nothing, neither ask him when he thought he would return, nor tell him how she would long for him, nor even implore him to write often. Things like these are not said by the wives of the Nyesheve court to their husbands! They are presumptuous and immodest. And if she had been able to overcome her fear, she would have lacked the words; the very tradition of such language was not in her life. When Nahum had taken farewell of his father-in-law and his brothers-in-law, he came to take farewell of her. He did not put out his hand to her; he did not utter a single loving or regretful word. He only said: "Keep well!" Even her name did not cross his lips.

"God be with you," she answered. Then, forcing herself to add something, she could think of nothing better than: "Keep yourself well wrapped. You mustn't catch cold." The effort sent the blood into her cheeks.

He took his farewell of Malkah as briefly and coldly, his hands at his sides, his voice low, his eyes fixed on the ground.

Serele stood petrified, not knowing whether she even dared ask to accompany her husband as far as the railroad station. It was Malkah who shook her out of her trance, saying angrily:

"You can at least walk part of the way with the coach. Come!"

They walked behind the coach, and Serele kept her eyes fixed on the frail, shaking figure of her husband. He did not turn round. When the coach curved off the muddy lane on to the hard, broad road, the coachman whipped up the horses, and the coach disappeared in a cloud of dust. Then Malkah, who had been holding Serele's hand in a fierce grip, sat down on a stone by the roadside and burst into hysterical sobbing.

Serele stared at her in wordless amazement. What was this? An idea asserted itself in the confusion of her mind, and bending over Malkah, she asked, anxiously:

"Malkah! Are you—did—are you going to have a baby? Don't

be ashamed, Malkah! And don't cry! Father will be very happy."

Malkah stopped crying. She lifted up her eyes to Serele, and began to laugh wildly.

"Mama!" she screamed, and her laughter became more and more hysterical.

10

DAYS FILLED WITH RESTLESSNESS AND DESPAIR, WITH SENSELESS pain and rebellion, ensued for Malkah.

Her one place of refuge was Serele's apartment; over and over again she listened to her dull, thick speech, over and over again pushed aside the sticky cakes and jams prepared to tempt her appetite. She came to Serele not because she wanted to, not because it had a meaning, but because she did not know what to do with herself. Only once a week a letter came from Nahum. Serele let Malkah read it. It was brief, cold, confined to news of health and regards. But Malkah read the few words over and over again.

The answering of these letters gave Malkah something to do. Serele wanted, for her own and for her husband's sake, to make an impression on her mother-in-law. She knew that she passed for a fool, but she would prove that they were mistaken. She knew, too, that she could not write a passable letter. Apart from the fact that her script resembled her father's, being ugly and clumsy, she had no idea how to begin or to end a sentence. As a child she had been taught—like her sisters—the elements of letter writing by an illiterate schoolmaster, considered good enough for women. He had shown her how to produce a form letter in affected, Germanized Yiddish, ending always with the Hebrew phrase:

"From me, Sarah Serele, daughter of the holy Rabbi of Nye-sheve." Even most of this she had forgotten. She begged Malkah to write out the letter for her, and she would copy it word for word.

Those letters became Malkah's preoccupation day and night. It was quite clear to her that Nahum would not be fooled; and therefore she turned every word and phrase over in her mind, till she felt it conveyed the right degree and shade of tenderness and longing and devotion. She wrote that she was waiting for him; that life had no meaning for her apart from this waiting. She described the dullness of the days and the loneliness of the nights; she gave rein to her passions and fantasies, keeping always within the limits of the fiction that it was Serele who wrote—a patient, loving Jewish wife, pious and submissive. And she knew that Nahum in Rachmanivke would read, in every line of clumsy, blotty script, *her* words, and know them to be hers.

As long as the autumn remained dry, Malkah frequented the fields and woods where, in the summer, she had so often encountered Nahum. But as the autumn advanced the skies hung lower and darker, rains fell continuously, the roads and fields became soggy, so that even women had to put on boots. The woods were chilly and misty; an unceasing dew dripped from the branches. She had to remain at home, watching pigs wander into the yard, scraping their ugly hides against the walls, grunting with a disgusting sound. The days became shorter—a brief interval between twilight and twilight, and the lamps were again lit, throwing more shadow than light around themselves.

She paced the house then like a caged animal, feeling herself going insane.

She found her husband—who of late had become more affectionate than ever—loathsome, repulsive, unbearable even in thought. When the Great Holidays had passed—the New Year and the Day of Atonement—the visiting Chassidim left Nyesheve. Then Rabbi Melech found less to do than ever. He went to bed early. Moreover, the rains and mists got into his old bones, and he needed to be in bed, near this fourth wife of his. After all, he had paid so much for her! More than for all the other three combined.

"Well," he would yawn, when he had finished saying the night prayer, "it's time to go to bed. It's no good to stay up late winter nights."

She would not answer. She would go into her own room, and sit down quietly; and she would listen with a mixture of rage and satisfaction as he pottered about the room and as he undressed, groaning with the pain in his joints.

She had an active hatred of him. Just as Nahum, desiring Malkah, had not hated Serele but had been drawn toward her, because, like every man who loves another's wife, he felt guilty and compassionate toward his own, so Malkah, like every woman who loves another's husband, felt hatred toward her own.

Often she lay down to sleep in another room. And sometimes, if she had gone to bed with him, she would get up in the middle of the night, put some things on the floor, and go to sleep there, with the heavy quilt drawn over her head.

Rabbi Melech would feel his heart slowing up.

"Malkah, Malkah!" he would cry to her, in a stifled voice. "You mustn't do that. It's not right. You may catch cold. . . ."

She did not answer.

Sometimes her hatred was not content with passive contempt. She wanted to hurt him actively, tease him, insult him, until, tormented into an outburst of rage, he was on the point of collapse. And then she would stand over him mockingly, as he lay shivering and moaning in his bed, and make fun of his age. He looked so ridiculous, so helpless, this old man whom thousands exalted as the great saint, whom tens of thousands sought out that he might intercede with Providence in their behalf. Where was his power now? Why did he not intercede with Providence in his own behalf? He looked so comical with his bushy, disordered beard, with his panting, shapeless belly; he reminded her of the hideous stone figures which stood in the town garden of Przemysl. And the recollection sent her into fits of laughter—Rabbi Melech standing up in the middle of the town garden of Przemysl!

With an old man's longing, and more than an old man's vanity, Rabbi Melech could not understand why Malkah treated him so.

Something—some specific thing—was wrong. All that he had done for her! From poverty and obscurity and probable spinsterhood he had lifted her, with one gesture, to wealth and prominence. She had not a stitch of clothing on her which he had not paid for. She had not a copper coin which he had not given her. What was it then? What demon was in her? Something—something definite—there was a solution. . . . Over and over again he rehearsed in his mind the benefits he had conferred on her, and found nothing, nothing at all, lacking. And then, suddenly, he did find it! Fool that he was! Of course! *That* was the key to her dissatisfaction!

The stupid young woman did not feel herself secure! Of course he was no longer a young man; true, he had many years ahead of him, but in her eyes he probably looked older than he really was. And she was afraid. If he—God forbid—were to die before his time, what would happen to her? And perhaps, from her point of view, she was not wholly wrong. Those sons and daughters of his were not a dutiful lot. They were waiting only too eagerly for the day (let them wait another hundred and twenty years!) when they might divide among themselves the great Rabbinate of Nyesheve. The moment he was gone, she would be driven out—back to Przemysl, or anywhere at all; it was none of their business.

A great light had burst upon Rabbi Melech. *That* was it. And the stupid creature, being young, had not dared to suggest the truth to him. And Rabbi Melech chuckled. There was an answer to everything. Within a few hours of the revelation he sent Israel Avigdor for the notary of Nyesheve; and in due legal form he transferred to his wife, there and then, part of the great house, most of the jewelry and a considerable sum of money. Then, sending the notary away, he rubbed his hands, took a glassful of brandy, treated Israel Avigdor to the same, and growled: "Thank God! *That's* settled!" His heart was full of joy and certainty.

He kept the secret to himself all day, but went to bed earlier than usual. He intoned the regulation night prayer, and added a few others for good measure. And when he crawled into bed, he grinned happily at Malkah, so that a kind of joy suffused the thick and tangled growth on his cheeks, his lips, his chin and his throat.

"Malkah!" he said suddenly. "Good luck! You became a rich woman in your own right today."

She stared at him.

"You've become a rich woman!" he said again, laughing. And he explained exactly what he had done.

To his horror she did not respond with one word of gratitude; not the slightest sign of satisfaction showed in her face or eyes. Rabbi Melech felt the world tumbling about his ears.

His sufferings were all the sharper because there was not a soul he could confide in or seek advice from. He who was the universal counselor, the fount of wisdom for thousands of others, was quite alone in his difficulty. Children, relatives, followers, worshipers, numberless dependents surrounded him; but he was alone in the shame which this orphan whom he had raised from the dust had brought upon him.

"An evil spirit!" he muttered. "A demon sitting in her heart!"

His health began to fail him. He could not eat or sleep. Even cigars gave him no pleasure; they all tasted bitter. He consulted doctors, took cold baths, swallowed medicines, hoping to forget the torment. And all this failing, he began to absent himself from Nyesheve. He undertook long journeys; he made the rounds of his Rabbinic territories, finding excuses for new levies on his followers. His rapacity had grown to inordinate dimensions; he was ruthless as well as insatiable; and in the collection of funds he found a partial anodyne.

Malkah began to miss even the hateful pleasure of tormenting her repulsive old husband. Except for the letters to and from Nahum there was nothing at all. She had no interests and no occupation. Through the interminable nights she listened to the cracking of the ice on the walls, to the creaking of the frozen windows. She lay awake, begging hopelessly for sleep. Then, in moments of hysteria, she sobbed, tore the cushions with her teeth, and cried out the name of the boy who was separated from her by the Austro-Russian frontier and hundreds of miles.

She thought of him alternately with unbearable longing and with hatred. What right had he to go away like this, leaving her in this ugly wilderness, without friends, without hope? She clenched her fists, and felt that if she could strike him, scratch him for his cruelty, she would feel better. This passing, she felt desire for him awakening like a sweet poison in all the veins and nerves of her body. She heightened her torment by reading exciting love tales which she obtained by stealth. Unlike Nahum she could not sometimes transform her love into pure, lofty thought, confusing his image with the spiritual imagery of the Kabbala. The provocative books made her think of him as a man, flesh and blood and arms and lips, to be taken and possessed. The savagery of her desire drove her mind into hallucinations. She knew he was far away; but an accidental noise, a footstep in the distance, made her leap convulsively with the thought: "He is coming! It is Nahum!" Yes, she *knew* he would not come, but her blood and body took no account of what she knew. They had their own perceptions, born of animal hunger.

When this passed, and when her rage against him was exhausted, her fury turned toward the horrible court of Nyesheve, toward her scheming aunt and uncle who had sold her, toward her indifferent mother living gayly in Budapest with her Gentile officer. It spread like a poisonous flood, this hatred, covering all the world, all the men and women she had ever known. It rose so high that even Nahum was engulfed in it, and the world was transformed into a black deluge of hatred. One night she sprang out of her bed and smashed the grandfather clock to the floor; she could not bear the sound of its ticking, and the booming of the hours, separated from each other by an eternity. And in another impulse she pulled out her German romances, with their Gothic letters, their woodcuts of chivalrous gentlemen in frock coats and ladies in lace shawls, and ripped them all to pieces.

Other nights, filled with pity toward herself, she rose, lit the lamp, ransacked the wardrobe, and put on her most gorgeous clothes and ornaments. Alone, she walked up and down the room, posed, and made gallant gestures to the emptiness; and tiring of this, she began to waltz, to turn swiftly until she became dizzy and fell down on the bed.

One night she went in her chemise to the window, opened it

wide, and sat with chattering teeth, looking out at the wastes of snow and at the pale shadows of the buildings in the moonlight. She would have liked to catch cold and die. But nothing happened to her.

She began to think of the three women who had lived here before her, and had died in this room. Perhaps they too had spent hours as mad with loneliness as hers. She thought of herself dead, carried in the coffin to the cemetery, with a long procession following, Nahum among thousands of others. She thought of the clothes she was wearing hanging unvisited and untouched among the clothes of the other three, hanging till the moths ate holes in them and the mildew wore away what was left.

She would not have that! She would not mingle with them! She ran one night to the wardrobe, pulled out the old-fashioned dresses which her predecessors had worn, ripped them, cut them to pieces. Then she stripped herself naked and examined her own young body, sobbing for its neglected beauty, caressing her own shoulders and breasts and thighs.

Some nights she slept with Serele, snuggling close to her and caressing her.

She talked interminably, not always knowing what she was saying. Then moments came when her caresses became tempestuous, and she hugged Serele as she had once used to hug little children, saying, in a stifled voice: "Serele! I could eat you up!"

Sometimes she compelled the maid to sleep with her—or at least to spend the night with her, for she did not let her sleep a wink. She had curious, unpredictable impulses. She would insist on presenting one of her best dresses to the astonished elderly woman, demanding at the same time—this was in the middle of the night—that she get up and put it on. Then she would begin to question her: Why had she not married? Had she never had any offers? Had she never been engaged? Then, springing up, she would grab the clumsy creature round the waist and swing her round the room in a crazy waltz.

The maid would never have dared to approach her mistress so close, or to touch her. She shrank from the contact. She began to be afraid.

One night Malkah took out some of the Rabbi's clothes from the wardrobe, dressed herself solemnly in his dressing-gown and hat, and told the maid that she was about to receive the potent benediction from the great Rabbi of Nyesheve.

The maid broke into a frightened, neighing laughter: "My God! If somebody were to see us!"

The idiotic laughter of the woman infected Malkah; she doubled up and screamed until the tears ran down her cheeks and her sides ached.

Toward the end of the winter she invited Aunt Aidele to visit her, and Aunt Aidele came. But from the first hour of her visit she lectured Malkah on the duties and commandments of a pious wife in Israel, and wanted to know how soon her niece was going to become pregnant. Malkah sent her aunt home, making her many presents of clothes to expedite the departure.

At last she could no longer bear the house. Unseen, she stole away again into the covered fields and naked woods, and wandered alone through the half-darkness. Sitting on a stump or leaning against the iron bark of a tree, she listened to the disconsolate calling of the crows gathering on the boughs and scattering as senselessly as they had come together. Wrapped in black, wandering among the ghostlike trunks, she looked like some gigantic crow. At moments she began to hop about, like one of them, and to flap her arms as if they were wings. An occasional peasant, seeing her at a distance, crossed himself.

She began to think again of distant places, of trains, of the lanterns of conductors and of her mother. And she made up her mind that when spring returned she would run away from Nyesheve.

But a few days before Passover a telegram came from Rachmanivke with the news that Nahum had left for Nyesheve. When Malkah realized what this meant, she threw her arms around Serele, and kissed her with such fury that Serele broke loose and thrust her away.

"You silly, you; you nearly choked me."

11

Spring descended on Nyesheve from the surrounding hills, drenching it in freshness and restlessness. The hard snow crumbled and melted in the fields, the icicles dripped from trees and eaves, and the tinkle of tiny rivulets in the streets and yards filled the village. New estuaries carried into the river the fragments of rotted branches, the unearthed bones of birds that had died in the frosts and had been half eaten by ravenous beasts, and millions of pine needles that had lain on the ground since the autumn. The country was being washed as it awakened from sleep.

Spring came down from the hills and the skies; but it also seemed to ascend in spirit from cracks in the earth and from hillocks of garbage. The sunlight, lying on these, and on the tattered roof of the Rabbinic court, and on the iron crosses of the Catholic church, startled them, as if against their will, into renewed life.

In the warmth of midday the black fields sent up a mist. The first blossoms of grass, impudent little blades, pushed their way through the heavy loam. The winter corn started out, so fresh, so radiant in its greenness, that the peasants blessed it, put up scarecrows, and threw sods of earth to frighten away the robber-birds. The snowdrops laid a new shimmer of white on the uncovering fields. The storks came back from the south, flapped their wings over the houses they had nested in and looked for new lodgings. During the nights the frogs again took up their forgotten chorus. The warm rains washed the roofs and ran down in threads, tinkling into the pails placed there by unmarried girls, who knew that soft spring rain was best for thick hair.

All that fullness and motion, the flowing and awakening and drenching freshness, echoed from Malkah's heart.

Nahum came back from Rachmanivke clear-skinned, clear-eyed, developed almost into a man. His mother had kept watch over him. By loving deceptions, by persuasion and by command, she had broken through his ascetic habits. She insisted that he eat in the mornings before the long first prayers. "It is permissible for a Rabbi's son," she said, speciously. And when he objected and argued, she changed her ground to the old, familiar warning: "I want it! And a mother's commands are more important than prayers. Honor thy father and thy mother; those were among the first words spoken by God to His people. But fasting before morning prayers is not a command, it is only a custom."

Nahum yielded more to her insistence than her logic. She went further; on the minor fasts of Esther and of the Tenth Day of Tebeth she made him eat.

"It is permissible for a Rabbi's son," she said again. "Your father will absolve you."

His body became fuller. A faint down, such as might still have belonged properly to a dark-skinned young girl, showed itself on his upper lip, the first sign of approaching manhood. His eyes had become deeper; there was a new warmth in them that sent a shiver through Malkah the first time she met him in Serele's apartment. Her hand went up with a sharp gesture to her breast, as if this were the focus of her sudden nervous reaction.

Neither then nor afterwards could she get a word out of him. He no longer went walking in the fields, and she haunted the old places in vain. But instinct told her that he had not forgotten, and desire in him was as strong as when he had fled from her through the storm. When she caught a glimpse of him at a distance, she read, in the disciplined expression of his face and in the movements of his body, all her own passions subdued only by his unsleeping will.

After the spring came hot days, in which burning suns alternated with fierce showers and short thunderstorms; the air was charged with lightning. Spring military maneuvers began near Nyesheve. Several regiments of infantry and cavalry came down, and the fields round Nyesheve were dotted with encampments. These were, apparently, important maneuvers, for the highest commanders came from Budapest and Vienna, accompanied by members of the Imperial household. During the days the booming of artillery filled the air; at night the sky was brilliant with rockets. The streets of Nyesheve became bright with the uniforms of Hussars; young Hungarians, with all the elegance of the metropolis in their carriage, with the deliberate insolence of rank in their eyes and in the curl of their black mustaches, walked in twos and threes, their scabbards swinging at their sides, their spurs ringing at their heels.

They were always in high spirits, these young officers, who wore monocles and whose chests were covered with medals. They were much amused by the queer Jews, who wore ear-locks and had ribbons (how could the officers know that these were the sacred ritual fringes?) hanging from under their waists down to the boots. The Jewish stores were always filled with buyers; the officers bought everything: candies, cigarettes, curios; and they never chaffered; sometimes they even shoved the change back. But they also reached out to chuck the Jewish girls under the chin or to pinch their cheeks:

"*Hübsch, Schwarzkopf, sehr hübsch!*"

The mothers said nothing while the officers were there; they only smiled submissively. But as soon as the officers were gone, they turned on their daughters and sent them home. "May they drop dead before they put a finger on you again!" and they spat in horror.

They were everywhere, the soldiers and officers, and wherever they went they brought with them tumult, gayety and singing. Malkah could not have avoided them if she had wanted to. On the streets they looked at her coolly, appraisingly and addressed her:

"*Warum so einsam, schönes Fräulein?*"

As soon as the maneuvers began, a carrousel immigrated into Nyesheve; and the blare of its organ mingled all day long with the sound of guns and the shouting of the crowds. Soldiers, holding hefty peasant girls round the waist, careered round and round on the wooden boars and horses and griffins. Soon after, another amusement turned up in Nyesheve—a field cabaret for officers. Its owners were a dark-faced couple who looked like gypsies, but were obviously not. They set up their big tent on an open place, adorned it with streamers and Chinese lanterns of all colors, set up a bar and put their one musician and their many dancing girls to work.

It was soon known in the village that the dark-faced couple who looked like gypsies, but spoke German, Hungarian, Polish, Czech, Roumanian, Serbian and even Turkish and Romany talk, were Jews from the Bukowina. Rabbi Melech at once smelt sin in his village. Unsavory stories were told about the doings behind the flapping walls of the pavilion, and Rabbi Melech sent his *gabbai* Israel Avigdor to bid the sinful couple appear before him. But the gypsy-faced Jew was not perturbed in the slightest. He refused to come. He told Israel Avigdor that inasmuch as he, the cabaret owner, was not interfering in the business of the Rabbi, it would be fitting for the Rabbi not to interfere in his business.

After this visit the music in the cabaret became even louder; it was heard in every corner of the village; it echoed in the Rabbinic court. It interfered with the Rabbi's sleep, and in the night he turned on his bed and groaned: "A sinful generation! Seed of evil!"

Malkah, too, was kept awake, but not with resentment. The excitement in the village was slowly waking her blood into a frenzy. She had never felt as rebellious as now. Strange faces and strange manners transformed Nyesheve into a pandemonium. She heard, under all the shouting and singing, the voices which had haunted her childhood, the sound of distant trains, the hooting of engines; she saw in her dreams, more clearly than ever, the swinging lanterns of railroad men walking along the track. Her mother haunted her, her distant mother living with a Gentile in the tumultuous capital of Hungary.

The lunacy that gripped Nyesheve became more pronounced from day to day. A stream of peddlers, beggars and mountebanks was drawn toward the encampment. Among soldiers and officers it became a fashion to visit the strange wonder-Rabbi of Nyesheve, and uniforms were as numerous in the Rabbinic court as the rags of the Chassidim.

There was no rest for Malkah. At night she threw off her bedclothes and lay panting with fever. As long as she could bear it she stared up at the ceiling, listening to the tumult in the streets of the village. Then she sprang out of bed and ran up and down the room, wringing her hands, crying in a voice that was almost audible outside: "Nahum, Nahum! Come to me!"

Very late in the first night of Pentecost she sprang from her bed, feeling that the walls of the room were closing in on her, to crush her to death. She could not breathe. In the darkness she fumbled for her clothes, drew on a dress and stole out into the darkness.

There was no light in heaven, either of moon or stars. The noises in the village had died, and the night breathed heavily, as if in drunken sleep. The wind of its breath was laden with lilac and acacia blossom, and with the darker odor of the brooding meadows.

The preceding day had been the wildest since the coming of the soldiery. Count Olcha had arranged a hunting party for the officers, followed by a ball in the castle. During the day hundreds of peasants and Jews had driven the game, making a big circle round the woods and closing in toward a clearing. Armed with staves, accompanied by excited dogs, they had beaten the woods all morning; and all afternoon the crack of the guns resounded through Nyesheve, mingled with the pealing of trumpets and the harsher cry of the shepherds' horns. Now the village slept, exhausted, torpid.

In all Nyesheve there was only one wakeful spot—the synagogue. There the Rabbi and his followers were saying the night prayers that ushered in Pentecost. A faint light came from the dusty windows. Malkah neither listened to the voices of the worshipers, nor saw the light of their candles. She saw only the darkness of the night, and listened only to the dumb voices that came to her from the woods. There was a faint whispering out there, a conspiracy of suggestive secrets and odors. As she drew away from the court, and came nearer to the woods, she began to distinguish the separate odors of trees. Her nostrils were quivering like those of a hunting animal. Her eyes were wide open, following eagerly the faint paths, and focusing on the sudden, thin trails of glowworms. She began to distinguish the phosphorescent glimmer of decaying wood. The black night was alive for her.

She hurried, as if something or someone were waiting for her. She hurried through fields and thickets and clearings. Her footsteps disturbed watchdogs, which bayed at her, wakening the horses in the stables. Frightened, she changed her course, bruised herself against hedges, and almost lost her way.

At last, exhausted in body, but more restless than ever in mind, she turned back to the court.

When she entered she saw the lantern hanging on the wall of the big barn. Without knowing why, Malkah reached up and took the guttering candle out of the lamp. The door of the barn stood open and, holding the candle, she crossed the threshold, and stopped abruptly, her throat muscles contracted by the foulness of the air. In this barn lay the Cossack uniforms which rotted from wedding to wedding; they lay in heaps, together with other rags, under a covering of straw. Filthy, decaying barrels and mildewed matting—the nightclothes of beggars when the court was crowded —were scattered about.

In that pestilential uncleanness Malkah recognized, through her tense confusion, the whole horror of the Rabbinic court of Nyesheve. The barn, the yard and the village revolved about her. The candle in her fingers guttered and dropped thick white lumps of fat, which burned her. With a gesture of loathing which shot through all her body, she flung the candle into a heap of straw in front of her. She stood breathless, expectant, not knowing what was happening. When the first little tongue of flame crept out, she started away, and with cat-like footsteps ran across the yard and up into her own room. She pulled a chair quickly to the window, and stared down into the yard.

When the Jews in the synagogue first saw, through the dirty windows, the flames in the barn, the fire had already spread to the walls. And the first cry was not for water, but: "Jews! Save the scrolls of the Law!"

But when these had been carried out of the synagogue, no one seemed to know what should be done next. These Jews were helpless. They were not accustomed to action of any kind; Chassidim, Rabbis, students, beggars—they ran about, yelling, weeping, watching the flames mount. It was only when the despised wagoners and workers arrived from outside the court that water was brought. But by then one half of the synagogue was wrapped in flames.

The village was now wide awake. The church bells were ringing furiously, and crowds of women and children, huddled together like frightened sheep, watched from a distance, whimpering.

Malkah ran about wordless, panting, drunk. She was looking for Nahum. She was hardly conscious of the fire; she only knew that the night was illumined, and she could look for him whom the night had always hidden till now. Like an animal in rut, she ran from group to group, her eyes wide open, her mind frantic with one idea. Now! In this confusion! In this mad night!

She found him standing alone at a distance from the crowd. He was clasping a torn book to his breast and staring in front of him.

She approached him swiftly and took one of his hands. In a tone of sure command, such as a mother might use to an obedient child, she said, "Come!"

He followed her!

Quietly, unseen, they hastened across the fields toward the woods, to the spot where they had stood together in the storm. They had no word to say to each other. One impulse moved them both.

Their footsteps were firm and certain, and they found their way without hesitation in the darkness which enveloped them. A light wind played about them. They heard the crunch of dried pine-needles and the crackle of fallen twigs under their feet. They reached the gnarled tree which she had so often visited in the days of absence, and, still wordless, they sat down close to each other. Then, with a soft moan, they turned, and clasped each other and became one.

She cried aloud in the first happiness of her life; she cried into the spring night, drenched in the odor of lilac and acacia. In the distance the sky took on a fiercer tinge from the blazing synagogue of Nyesheve.

12

THE COURT OF THE RABBI OF NYESHEVE WAS DESOLATE.

The pride of the court, the great synagogue, was in ruins. Blackened walls and cracked chimneys stood gaunt under the blue skies of the late spring. The heat of the fire had barely died down when a host of ravens came to make their nests in the ruins, and their incessant croaking was like an augury of greater evil to come. Besides the synagogue, two wings of the court had been destroyed by the flames. The outer walls had tumbled, and the insides of the apartments, blackened with smoke, stared dismally at the world. The remaining apartments had been saved from the flames, but smoke and dirt had penetrated into every corner of them, and whatever had not been carried out by the wagoners and workers, had been made unfit for use.

The Rabbi, together with most of his children and grandchildren, had left Nyesheve for the warm springs. It was his custom to go abroad at this time every year; but the catastrophe had made his visit to the baths and clinics more necessary than ever. He felt himself a broken man. His joints had gone stiff, and the horrible experience of the great fire had affected his heart. The doctors whom he called told him that, in addition to the usual warm baths, he needed mud baths for his joints; but inasmuch as the mud baths would be a strain on his heart, he would have to take additional potions of the medicinal waters to counteract the effect of the mud baths.

But a third reason drove the Rabbi of Nyesheve to the springs: he needed money—more money than he had ever needed before.

The warm springs were, at this time of the year, the rendezvous of thousands of rich Jews. Among them were pious followers of the Rabbinic dynasty of Nyesheve. They would have to rebuild the synagogue and house for him; they would have to replace the clothes, ornaments, furs, linen, furniture and vessels which the fire had destroyed. And above all they would have to reimburse him—without knowing about it—for the most awful loss of all: the bank-notes which, in the tumult, had been stolen out of one of the volumes of his private Talmud.

No one besides himself (and possibly one other—God's curse on him!) knew about that loss. In the heavy Tractate *Chulin*, one of the tomes of the big Talmud which the Rabbi kept locked in its case, he had laid away, in notes, thousands of gulden. This was his secret treasury, hidden from the eyes of the envious. And this he had lost. The fire, it is true, had not reached as far as the Rabbi's apartment; but Israel Avigdor had been tremendously active in rescuing the Rabbi's things from possible damage. His greatest concern was for the sacred books; and he considered more sacred than the others the books which stood in the locked case. Israel Avigdor had shown himself a hero in this rescue work. He had not snatched things at random; he had endangered his life by waiting long enough to force open the lock of the case, and he had carried the Talmud, for safe-keeping, to his own house, at some distance from the court. It was the first thing that the Rabbi missed, and the first thing he began to yell for when the panic subsided and he became coherent. Very proudly Israel Avigdor told him that the precious Talmud was safe. He would bring it at once from his house. And he did bring it. But when the Rabbi, with trembling hands, opened the pages of the Tractate *Chulin*, there was not a single note among them. Everything else was there: hairs from his beard, hidden away piously, an old fringe that had fallen from his ritual body cover, and smudges of snuff. But no bank-notes; not one.

Rabbi Melech lifted up his blood-shot eyes to Israel Avigdor.

"Srelvigdor," he croaked. "The money!"

Israel Avigdor knew nothing about any money.

"Srelvigdor!" the Rabbi yelled, and murder was in his eyes.

Israel Avigdor looked back coolly, haughtily.

"If the Rabbi suspects me of anything," he said, "I am ready, after thirty years of devoted service, to go out alone into the world. I am ready to swear, on the Holy Scrolls . . ."

The Rabbi bit the stump of the cigar which he held in his mouth, and supported himself on the table. He looked from Israel Avigdor to the open, empty tome, and back again. He remembered that without Israel Avigdor he was helpless.

"Who wants you to swear?" he asked bitterly. "Why don't you light my cigar for me?"

With unusual devotion Israel Avigdor struck a match, held it to the Rabbi's lips, and let the Rabbi puff the smoke into his face.

"Rabbi," he said, affectionately, "I think we ought to put up a temporary wooden tabernacle in the courtyard, and by the summer after next we ought to have a new, permanent synagogue, a bigger one than before, one that will hold several thousand worshipers."

The secret hatred of Rabbi Melech for Israel Avigdor was impotent. The latter remained the greatest influence in the Rabbinic court. At this moment his energy and loud-mouthed persistence were needed more than ever. He alone could prepare a journey in proper style; and he alone could be counted on to put the right degree of pressure on recalcitrant Jews for contributions to the new court and synagogue. The preparations for this journey—since the Rabbi's absence from Nyesheve would be longer than any previous absence—were of the most elaborate kind. In the private railway car which Israel Avigdor obtained from the government, the Rabbi carried all his portable possessions, from laundry to silver. In the Rabbinic suite were a special ritual slaughterer, a special cook and a servant. The Rabbi of Nyesheve did not rely, for kosher food, on strangers; least of all on impious German Jews who did not even wear beards, but shaved every day after the fashion of Gentiles.

The sons and sons-in-law of Rabbi Melech did not accompany him to the watering place; each of them had a resort of his own. They set up their own little Rabbinic courts, preached the Law, dispensed favors and gathered funds. The most reliable source of income was from barren wives, who supplemented the treatments in the baths with special prayers which they bought at high prices from the holy visiting Rabbis.

Serele did not stay behind in Nyesheve. She accompanied one of her brothers to a *Kurort*. For a year had passed since her marriage, and there was no sign of pregnancy. Her older sisters commiserated with her, clucked their tongues and asked regularly:

"Well, Serele?"

And Serele always had to answer: "Nothing."

"When I was your age," each of them said in turn, "I was already carrying the second one."

Unhappy by reason of her barrenness, and suffering under the compassion of her sisters, Serele made up her mind to visit one of the springs. Her father readily assented to this, the more so as he was worried by the barrenness of his own wife, and it seemed to him that he could the more easily persuade her to accompany him to the springs if Serele had decided to try the same cure. He anticipated a bitter struggle with Malkah; she was likely to oppose his wishes merely because they were his wishes. But to his amazement she said nothing. She would go with him to the springs. Grateful and astonished, Rabbi Melech promised himself that when the season was over, and he had gathered what he could at the springs, he would undertake a new tour, and return to Nyesheve richer than he ever had been; and of his new wealth he would set aside for Malkah a greater portion than before.

The day before the break-up of the Rabbinic court in Nyesheve, a host of Jews gathered from surrounding villages. They came with presents of food and money. They escorted the Rabbinic coach to the station, and they kept their eyes fixed on the private car until it was no longer visible.

And then desolation descended on the court of Nyesheve. Chassidim and hangers-on melted away. A handful of wretched beggars who had not the initiative to move hung about the yard and the kitchens. The servants had nothing to do now except look after themselves, and they either lay in bed or dozed in the sunlight. Malkah's elderly maid, who was supposed to keep her mistress' apartment in order until her return, got wind of a match, gathered up her forces for a last desperate effort, leaving the apartment to decay, to vermin and to rats. She heard that in a village not far from Nyesheve a poor Jew, a potter, had become a widower, and there was a host of little children to be looked after. Malkah's maid saw her chance; she was forty years old, gray-haired and shapeless—but God was good, and miracles had happened before. She spent half her time in the other village, scrubbing the floor, washing the verminous heads of the children, and putting patches in the trousers of the widower.

"A man's a poor body to be left alone," she sighed at him.

In the yard itself the workers were busy making preparations for the rebuilding of the synagogue, slaking lime, digging, hammering. But in the night the place was like a forgotten cemetery, or like a city that had been sacked and abandoned generations since. And on this grisly darkness Nahum stared down from his study in the attic, which the fire had spared.

He had refused to budge from Nyesheve. Serele had implored him dumbly; his father-in-law had stormed at him. His one answer was:

"I must remain here. I can't go away."

For days at a stretch he did not leave his study. He did not even go out to join the quorum of worshipers downstairs. He was never seen in the streets of the village. He returned to the ascetic habits which his mother had made him abandon in Rachmanivke, but with a fervor which he had not shown before. The servants who brought meals up to his room frequently removed them untouched. They saw him either concentrated on a book, or sitting immobile at the window staring down at the ruins of the fire.

"And greatest of all the sins which a mortal can commit," he read to himself, "is the sin of defilement with the wife of another man. For a man who uncovers the shame of his neighbor—so says Holy Script—shall surely die, both the man and the woman who has transgressed; they shall both be destroyed from the midst of the people. Woe to the wicked who sin with the wives of others, for it is as if they have asked for the fires of Gehenna in the world to come; but even there they will not be admitted, for great is their sinfulness. And they shall be tossed from one end of the world to the other, and they will be reborn imprisoned in animals and wild beasts and fowl and creeping things and fish and plants; great shall be their anguish and greater their shame. When the earth will cover them, demons will come in the form of oxen and tread on them; and the Angel of the Great Silence will crack a fiery whip over their graves and cry: Who art thou, sinner, and what is thy name? And the sinners who have defiled the Jewish people, and, above all, those who have brought bastards into the congregation will not be able to remember their names. Then demons will come, like the sands of the sea for number, and they will smite and torture the sinners, and mock them; and the screaming of the sinners will be heard at a distance of four hundred miles. And the sinner will repent, but the demons will answer him in mockery, saying: Now it is too late to repent!"

Night after night he saw the fires of hell, and they were like the fire which had destroyed the court of Nyesheve. In the center of the place where the synagogue had stood gaped the abyss of hell. Angels stood in velvet *capotes* round the walls of hell, saying the night prayers of Pentecost. In their midst stood the Rabbi too. Then suddenly demons came, and began to mock the Rabbi; they grabbed him by his *capote* and they dragged him into a forest, and showed him an old tree, hollowed by decay and storms. And he, Nahum, together with Malkah, was running away, and both of them were naked. A multitude of Jews ran after them, caught them and led them to Jerusalem, where the Temple stood. The Rabbi raised his voice, shouted to the assembled priests, and pointed to Malkah: She has sinned. But Malkah denied it. Then the High Priest rose, an angry-faced Jew with a black beard which came down to his girdle, and he forced Malkah to drink water of bitterness, and he cried in a loud voice: If you have sinned and have defiled yourself, and have practiced falseness upon your husband, let the water cause your belly to swell, and let your thighs burst open, and you shall become a curse in the midst of your people. And Malkah screamed: Nahum! Nahum, darling. He tried to shield her with his body, but all the Jews picked up stones, and threw them at him, shouting: Let the man be utterly destroyed who has uncovered the shame of another man's wife; let him and his blood be utterly destroyed!

He would wake up in the night and find himself wailing with fear; his body was doubled up.

In waking moments too he saw visions. They came mostly out of the twilight, when he sat at the window watching the onset of evening above the cracked chimneys which stared into his room. An echo of many voices came from the corners of the sky and from the corners of his room. Forms entered, not through the door, and spoke to him in the half-darkness.

"And he is blind," said one form, "who thinks that if one has stumbled and fallen there is no more hope; for God is merciful, and he has given man the power to repair his own evil. And though your sins be as red as a scarlet thread, they can through repentance become white as snow. And the sinner must torment his body and fast and put ashes on his head; and he must repent with a full heart, for as fire cleanses the iron of rust so does suffering cleanse the sinful body of contamination. And it is better to torment the body in *this* world, while there is yet time, than to suffer a thousandfold in the *next* world. . . ."

Another form laughed scornfully: "The fool thinks that with fasting and self-torment he can approach the great unity. Fools! They do not know that the thought of man is a thousand times stronger than sin itself; and meditation on a sin which is not committed is more evil than the committing of the sin; for the sin itself is but fleeting while the thought is eternal. For when the man has yielded to the evil inclination, and has sated himself, then the sin is no longer in him, for he has liberated himself from it. Then the brain is cleansed and the mind is clear and it can understand the higher things. But when the man fasts and thinks of nothing but food, and when the man separates himself from women and the lust of women, and thinks of nothing but uncleanness, then his brain is befouled and his mind is dark and he cannot serve God. He is steeped in horror and in evil thoughts, which are like defilement. And there have been many saints who have sought through sin to hasten the coming of the Messiah—inasmuch as the Messiah will come when all are saints or all are sinners. Moreover, sin too is of God, and the Evil One no less; and the powers of darkness are part of the Godhead; and God is present in all sin, for God is in everything. For it is written: I will rest with you in your uncleanness. . . . And as the black cannot be made white, so that which has been defiled cannot be made pure. Therefore it is best to cleanse oneself by surfeit of sin, till it is vomited and spit forth out of overfullness; like the glutton who eats and eats until he spews out food and desires it no more. And thus one reaches the Godhead."

And Nahum listened to this voice and to that, and his confusion was increased, and he did not know what to do with himself.

On some days he afflicted his flesh, refused food, slept on the bare floor, would not change his linen even if it was the Sabbath; and if the day was cool he would plunge into the cold ritual bath, and feel the death-chill trapping his blood.

On other days he would not utter a single prayer; he would not don his phylacteries, because he did not want to defile them through contact with his unclean hand and brow. He would not let one sacred word pass his lips, lest it be made filthy by the passage. And voices said to him: Go, fool! Defile yourself! For you will never attain to purity again. Therefore lie and whore and sin, for it is written that I will rest with you in the midst of your uncleanness.

The two forces in him maintained constant war, with alternating success and failure. Sometimes they were evenly balanced, sanctity and defilement, good and evil; and in such moments he did not remember who he was. In the midst of the most passionate prayer, he would suddenly snatch the phylacteries from his head and hasten from the room. He would walk with hasty steps toward the fields and woods. Walking, he would talk continuously to himself. He would stop on the bank of the river where peasant women, half naked, squatted over their wash; and he would fix his eyes on their uncovered red legs. He would stare long at the crosses on the spire of the village church, and evil thoughts would rise in him.

Sometimes it seemed to him that he was not Nahum at all, but another, a reincarnation which was taking on again its previous form. Just as often he was sure that he was not one person but two; and then he became terrified, and cried out loudly to himself:

"Who are you? Tell me!"

When the Rabbi and his retinue returned from the springs for the High Holidays, they scarcely recognized Nahum.

Life began with fresh zest in the court of Nyesheve. Rabbi Melech had had an immensely successful season. The catastrophe had softened the hearts and loosened the purse strings of his followers, and he returned to Nyesheve with large sums of money. His sons too, in their various courts, had reaped rich harvests. Chassidim, followers, guests, hangers-on filled the barn, the new wooden synagogue and the outhouses. It was known, moreover, that the Rabbi's fourth wife was pregnant, and it was going to be a son; the Rabbi himself had hinted as much, and he surely knew.

Nahum alone absented himself from the numerous festivities. He spoke with no one, refused even to attend the official banquets over which Rabbi Melech presided. And in the court they began to speak of him with awe.

"He has his own ways," they said to each other, quietly. "He is not easily to be understood."

The High Holidays came and went; months passed; and Serele suffered. Her husband never came near her. When she gathered up all her courage and tried to say something, he turned silently away. Till at last, in despair, she burst in on her father.

"Father! What shall I do? He has separated himself wholly from me."

Her father thought a moment, then, as was his habit with women, drove her from the room.

"Go, you little fool," he growled at her. "I'll speak to him myself. He shan't bring these tricks to Nyesheve—Nyesheve will not put up with them. Wait!"

And he did intend to speak sharply to his son-in-law. But he put it off from day to day. He had much to do that fall and winter. Nyesheve was crowded with his followers; there was money to be gathered. And those followers who had not come to the court had to be visited in their home towns. The Rabbi was frequently absent on his tax-collecting expeditions; and when he was at home his mind was taken up with other matters than his daughter's complaints. So he put off speaking to Nahum. Finally he set a date; he would speak to him, publicly, at the Feast of Purim. He thought to himself: There will be a big banquet. Everyone will drink, everyone will be merry, and then, in the midst of it all, I'll get up and make fun of him. I'll say: "I married much later than you, young man! But I got there first, you Rachmanivke skeptic!"

But before the festival of Purim came round, a second calamity befell the Rabbinic court of Nyesheve.

On the coldest night of that year, which fell, strangely, just when spring was due, Malkah, the wife of Rabbi Melech, was taken with violent labor pains, and could not bring forth her child. A sleigh with three fast horses was sent to the nearest town, to bring the old doctor who had always attended the wives of the Rabbi. But though he came in all haste, he arrived too late.

Malkah died, together with her unborn child.

Rabbi Melech sat alone in a closed room and wailed loudly. None of his children would approach him.

"She should not have married a *Katlan*—a wife-killer!" the women folk muttered.

A day and a night woman worked over the dead body of the Rabbi's wife in order to bring out the child that it might be buried separately, according to custom. But Malkah would not give up the child. They said Psalms over the dead woman, immersed her body in the ritual bath, and begged her to be merciful—all to no effect.

A Tribunal of three Rabbis was summoned, to lay its command on the dead woman.

"Malkah, daughter of Shifrah," the Tribunal said, "we lay upon you the command that you give forth your child from your womb, according to the Law."

The dead woman held to her child. Open-eyed, she glared back at the Tribunal, her upper teeth fastened on her lower lip.

The village of Nyesheve was filled with fear. This dreadful thing was an omen of things more dreadful to come.

In the night, when the Tribunal and a host of witnesses were gathered round the corpse, lighting candles and saying prayers, Nahum opened the door of his study room in the attic, descended quietly, unseen and unheard, and disappeared.

They found the next morning everything that belonged to him except the clothes he had on and his phylacteries and prayer-shawl.

Messengers were sent out along all the roads leading from Nyesheve. Proclamations were made in the synagogues of all the surrounding towns and villages. The police was pressed into service, and notices were even published in the Gentile newspapers. The Rabbinic court of Rachmanivke was appraised by special messenger of the disappearance of Nahum, but they were as helpless as the court of Nyesheve. He was gone, as if a wind had lifted him out of the world.

Serele took a brick and placed it on the kitchen fire till it became red hot; then she muttered over it:

"Stone, stone, as you glow with the heat of the fire, so let the heart of my husband glow with desire for me. Come, come, come!"

Nahum did not come.

When several weeks of fruitless search on the part of both courts had yielded no result, Rabbi Melech sent for his daughter. He did not ask her to sit down; he did not even look straight at her.

"Know," he said, "that you are an *agunah*, an abandoned wife. Are you pregnant?"

Serele burst into tears, but her father made no effort to comfort her.

"Go," he said.

She went to her apartment. She took the satin cover off her head, and wrapped herself in a plain, gray woolen shawl, such as the poorest women wear. She put on an old black dress, and placed a pair of loose, worn slippers on her feet.

She looked now like an ordinary woman of the village whose workingman husband had gone away to America, and had never been heard from again.

BOOK TWO

13

THE MUDDY ROADS WHICH LEAD TO BIALOGURA IN RUSSIAN POLAND, hard by the Galician frontier, were alive with travelers.

It was the time of the great annual fair which every year, shortly before Christmas, brought together the peasants of hundreds of surrounding villages. Rich landowners, in red furs, came in wagons, accompanied by their families; behind the wagon always followed an ox, tied to the rear axle by the horns. Poor farmers came on foot, leading a pig at the end of a rope. Beggars swarmed on the roads; with their huge white beards and flowing robes they looked like the gingerbread figures of St. Nicholas which are made for children. At every cross-road ikon, at every painted image, dilapidated and unrecognizable, they kneeled in the snow, crossed themselves and muttered prayers. Jewish peddlers and shopkeepers, caterers, tailors, hatmakers, cobblers, furriers came in light carts with their families. Young apprentices, full of high spirits, steered the carts among the pedestrians and the heavy wagons of the rich landowners. As they rolled by the wattled hedges of farms and villages, they waved to the peasant girls and shouted in Yiddish:

"Hey, calf's foot, did you ever taste a piece of *kosher?*"

The older people turn on them angrily: "Blackguards! Keep your mouths shut! Are you looking for trouble?"

The apprentices pay no attention.

They pass a stupid-faced peasant boy carrying to market a score of eggs in a red kerchief. "Hey *huptchy-kuptchy!*" they yell.

"Want to buy? Want to sell? What have you got?"

The boy stops, shoves his ear forward with his free hand and listens to the strange language.

"What?" he shouts back, in Polish.

The apprentices go into fits of laughter and pinch the girls sitting by them in the carts.

Jewish junk-dealers and rag merchants, with clipped beards and faces bronzed by suns and storms into a gypsy color, drive their carts, on which are laden their canvas booths, boxes of wares, dishes, pots and pans, flutes, glass beads, wire thimbles, necklaces, brooches, all sorts of bargains, some to be sold, some to be exchanged for rags and bones. They stop in every village, ring their bells, blow through gilded earthenware, figures of cocks and hens, and chant to a synagogue melody a rhyming gibberish in Polish, Yiddish and Russian:

> Peasant girls, mistresses, maidens and witches,
> Beads for old blouses and bracelets for breeches;
> Brooches of silver and genuine stones,
> For rags from the attics and buckets of bones.
> Bring out the bundles of ruins and wrecks,
> Scramble, old mares (and break your necks!);
> Bring out your pennies, I'm here again,
> And ready for business, Amen! Amen!

Czech jugglers with monkeys on their shoulders, gypsies with copper kettles and pans, hungry Ruthenians, mountaineers of the Carpathians, wire twisters who wander thousands of miles each year from village to village and farm to farm, mending broken pottery—all plod along silently, sullenly.

Sometimes they lift up their hands to passing carts carrying Galician Jews in Rabbinic hats and long dirty *capotes*, Jews, flitting across the frontier with woolens and silks, lift up their hands and beg: "Brother! Something to eat! A dried crust! Anything! My guts are falling out! God'll pay you."

Jewish horse-dealers stream toward Bialogura from the Russian interior, gigantic Jews in high boots, with heavy sheepskin coats and sheepskin hats. They quarrel violently with their competitors, horse-dealers of Galicia, Jews with long ear-locks and clerical cloaks, who sell and buy horses for the Austrian cavalry.

The long caravans of horses—young, fiery horses neighing for the warm stalls and the mares from which they have been driven —throw the road into a turmoil. At the head of one caravan rides a Galician Jew, his red face bursting with health. He rides bareback, his legs dangling, his long cloak almost brushing the mud; his beard and ear-locks are lifted by the wind, the ends of his ritual fringes fly behind him, his greasy Rabbinic hat teeters on one side of his head; but he cannot be thrown even by the fieriest mare.

"Hep! Hep!" he yells, driving the caravan along the muddy roads. "Faster, you dogs' bodies!"

Russian competitors, catching up with him, or passing, let out long yells of laughter at the antics of the horse-dealer in Rabbinic garb.

"Hey! Galician goat!" they shout, and turning in their saddles they take cuts at the flanks of his horse, to unseat him. "Galician goat! Red-head Rabbi! Bean-soup and onions!"

"Russian swine!" the "Rabbi" answers, in full gallop. "I spit on your father's carcass!"

The Great Synagogue of Bialogura, with tremendous walls and semi-circular barred windows, which made it look like a fortress of the time of Jan Sobieski, was jammed. Visiting Jews, peddlers, wagoners, hucksters, dealers at the fair, begged local Jews for a loan of prayer-shawl and phylacteries.

"It won't take long," they promised hoarsely. "One-two-three, and I'm through before you can spit twice. I haven't the time for long prayers."

The city Jews did not feel like lending their sacred vestments to the visitors.

"Next time," they said, "don't forget, that's all. You didn't forget to take your whiskey along, did you? But you did forget prayer-shawl and phylacteries. Heathens!"

"That's enough now!" one wagoner pleaded, rolling back half a dozen successive sleeves of coats and sweaters and shirts from his left arm, baring it for the phylactery strap. "Come on now. All I want to do is throw the harness on and off, kiss the fringes, spit out once—and hep! I'm through. I've left the horses outside and not a soul to watch them."

While, in one corner, some stood at prayers, in other corners Jews ate and drank, drove bargains, argued and bought hot, peppered peas from an old woman who kept a supply under a mass of rags.

"Good health! God's blessing on this fair! Good business for all of us!"

The regular frequenters of the synagogue, youngsters of Bialogura, or imported newly married boys who lived with their in-laws and pursued their studies, sat at heavy tables, over their tattered folios of the Talmud. They made much noise, but they studied little. The license of the fair was in their bones. They envied those of their comrades who had been taken away by a father-in-law from studies, to serve in a shop or to boss the hired peasant girls. They could not sit still with the noise and the new faces around them. Now and again a couple of them made an effort to resume the chanting study:

"Now let us take the following case: *shor shenogach es haporoh*, an ox having gored a cow . . ."

Like all synagogues, this one was provided with a gigantic stove, built like an oven with shelves above to accommodate travelers, beggers and poor students. Behind the stove in the Bialogura synagogue was a huge pile of wood; and round the woodpile hordes of beggars, for whom the fair was the most important incident of the year, were encamped. Strictly, it was not the fair-period itself which was *their* harvest time. During the days, the Jews are absorbed in the business of the fair—little use then making the rounds; in the evenings Jews are busy making up accounts and preparing for the next day—no use knocking at doors then, either. Only a few went out during the fair. The days *after* the fair were the beggars' days. And therefore, during the fair proper, the beggars were assembled, most of the time, round the woodpile at the back of the stove. Separated from the rest of the synagogue, warm, intimate, the place was their own. They sat all day on heaps of rags, on their own canvas and burlap wallets, or on the floor; they counted their groschens and kopecks, or the lumps of sugar which some niggardly housewives had given them instead of currency.

They wrapped the sugar in separate little bags, weighed it in their hands and estimtaed its worth; sugar could be sold; it was used for making jams and jellies; and the owners of cheap inns bought sugar from beggars to sweeten the tea for their guests.

Some sat on the floor hunting the lice in their beards and clothes; others unwound the rags from their swollen feet, and recounted stories of unfortunate week-ends when, for Sabbath charity, they were taken into the house of a pious Jew intent on the letter but not on the spirit of hospitality to the wanderer. They had some system in their wandering; they divided the country into fifty-two sections, one for each week in the year. And to each section they gave the name of the particular division of the Pentateuch which was read that Sabbath in the synagogue. Thus they avoided visiting the same village twice in one year. But thus it also came about that they knew no names of villages: they knew only the Pentateuchal divisions attached to them.

"My Genesis is a bit of all right," one said, sighing. "Fish and calves' foot jelly and good pudding and stewed carrots and cake and as much whiskey as I want. And lots of beet soup and potatoes. I wouldn't sell that Genesis for three gulden."

"My Leviticus," said another, bitterly, "is lousy. I hope to God it burns up. A piece of fish as big as your finger nail, white bread just enough for the benediction, and after that nothing but black bread."

Toward one side, taking no part in the conversation, sat a young beggar in flimsy, tattered clothes. His face was white and hollow; a thin black beard outlined rather than covered it. He held in his lap an old prayer-book, and chanted, in a continuous monotone, passages from the Psalms.

All day long he had been seated there, indifferent to the commerce around him. At last an attempt was made to draw him into the crowd.

"How much sugar have you got?" said an old beggar, leaning over. "I'm buying sugar."

"I've got no sugar," the young man answered, and went on with his Psalms.

"Have you got any *prutos*?" another asked. "I'll give you a groschen for five."

Prutos were the lowest form of charity, next to bread and sugar. They were paper slips, redeemable on the community chest at a fixed value much below that of the smallest coin in currency.

"I have no *prutos*," said the young man, and continued with his Psalm-reading.

A blind begger felt him with shaking fingers. "Listen," he said. "Let's go partners. You'll show me the way, and whatever we get we'll go fifty-fifty."

"I don't know the roads myself," the young man answered.

"What do you know?" several asked at once.

"Nothing."

"What do you do?"

"I sing Psalms."

"Off his head," one said, briefly.

"No—a faker," said another. "Look at him; he's not a cripple and he's not sick. He's young, too. So he plays the pious, and gets it that way."

One beggar with a red beard and a wooden leg was outraged by this revelation. "What the hell does he want here? He has no right to be a beggar; we're not respectable people here—just low-down, lousy beggars!"

"Hey, Psalm-singer! No room for you here."

The crowd began to laugh.

"Pull down his hat over his eyes," some jeered.

"Open that sack of his. I bet it's full of groschen."

But for some mysterous reason they approached him carefully. The young man did not make even a gesture of resistance. He went on intoning Psalms. A couple of beggars picked up his sack, unbound it and emptied it. They found nothing but the phylactery bag and a stone to give weight to the sack.

"Let him alone," some elderly beggars said. "He's got nothing."

"Let him get out of here," others shouted. "We don't want any saints round here."

"Let him get out," insisted the red-bearded beggar with the wooden leg. "There's no room here—and I want to bring someone in anyway."

Without waiting for the Psalm-sayer to move, he went out and returned in a few moments with a dark young woman. One of her eyes was out; she wore a man's *capote* gathered at the waist with a rope.

"Sheindel," said the one-legged beggar, "there's room for you here. It's warmer than outside. You there, make room for her."

A loud cry of protest went up from the beggars.

"Hey, you can't bring a woman in here! You can't have a woman in the synagogue! Throw her out!"

"It isn't his wife, either," someone howled. "He took her away from her husband, a blind man. I know."

"Send her down to the lodging house. She can't come in here."

The red-bearded beggar thrust out his chest and bellowed:

"Bastards! You're jealous! I'm going to bring her in here, and you can all burst."

He thrust his way forward like a steer. With one hand he held on to the young woman, with the other he cleared a path. Then, in the center of the crowd, he planted his wooden leg against a log, stood like a rock, and glared at the beggars. His eyes fell on the young Psalm-sayer.

"You! Get off there and make room."

The beggars howled: "Don't you do it. We'll call the beadle. Don't you be afraid."

The young beggar said nothing. He picked up his sack, went quietly from his warm place near the fire to a bench near the draughty door, sat down again, and went on intoning Psalms.

"Idiot!" the beggars yelled at him. "Loon!"

The young man paid no attention to them. His eyes were riveted on the prayer-book.

In the evening the respectable Jews of Bialogura assembled in the synagogue for prayers. Then the beggars lined up near the door. During prayers their behavior was exemplary. They followed the text closely, gave the responses eagerly and loudly,

and tried, by their postures, to expose their stock-in-trade of
wounds, diseases and scars. The red-bearded beggar shoved his
wooden leg forward for all to see. He had sent his consort away
before the arrival of the first householders. Seen from the front he
seemed to be a model of piety and misfortune; from the rear,
however, beggars could see him reach out and pinch those who
shoved forward and obstructed the full public view of his wooden
leg. During the prayer of the Eighteen Benedictions, which is
whispered or murmured quietly without interruption from beginning to end, the beggars stood up faithfully, their lips moving in
apparent devotion; but their words were not from the prayer-
book. They were quarreling viciously among themselves, uttering
furious curses and trying to scratch one another without disturbing
their pose.

When prayers were over, each householder picked out one of
the beggars to take home. The wanderer would get a meal and a
bed to sleep in.

The synagogue emptied. The beadle made the rounds, and put
out the lamps. He looked around to make sure he was alone, and
began to put out, likewise, the memorial candles placed that day
in the synagogue by the poor. The memorial candles of the rich he
did not dare to touch; but the widow of a workingman would
make no complaints, and if she did, she could be outfaced. These
candles he gathered up and hid under a bench in a corner. Then he
went to the door, chanting a synagogue melody under his
breath.

At the very door he nearly stumbled over someone. He
stopped, frightened.

"A corpse!" The thought flashed through his mind: "A corpse
whose candle I took away."

But the next instant habit triumphed over instinct: the habit of
a beadle and sexton and grave-digger who had been handling
corpses cold-bloodedly for years. No, this was no corpse; and even
if it were, there was nothing to be afraid of.

He bent down and saw the huddled figure of a young man. He
heard the whisper of a voice, chanting Psalms.

Sternly he asked:

"Who are you?"

"A stranger."

"What do you do?"

"I wander."

"Where were you before, during prayers?"

"Here in the synagogue."

"Why didn't you stand at the door, like the others, and get a householder to take you home for supper and a bed?"

The young man was silent.

"I'm not going to find a householder for you now," the beadle continued, angrily. "What will you do?"

"I'll sit here and sing Psalms."

The beadle looked closely at the stranger. He frowned, and then shrugged his shoulders.

"A loon," he muttered.

He hesitated, and made up his mind to leave the young man where he was; if he hadn't brains enough to get himself food and lodgings like any other beggar, it was none of the beadle's business. But when his hand was on the door, he stopped, and something flashed through his mind. Zivyah! His half-witted daughter, beyond the marriageable age! His only child. He turned back.

"Who are you?" he asked. "What are you? A bachelor? A widower?"

"I am a homeless wanderer," the stranger answered.

"What's your name?"

The stranger thought a moment. "Yoshe," he said.

A curious idea occurred to the beadle. It might be, after all, the hand of God. He told the stranger to get up and follow him.

"Yoshe, Yoshe, you're a loon as sure as there's a God in heaven," he said, stumping down the muddy alley of the synagogue toward the old cemetery. The stranger followed him silently.

They passed the bath house, which loomed, a square of deeper blackness, in the black night. They went past the beggars' lodging house of the community, and reached the stone hedge about the cemetery. From behind the hedge came the rustling of the wind in heavy trees.

"This is the cemetery," the beadle said. "Are you afraid of dead men?"

"I'm afraid of God," the stranger answered.

The beadle said nothing more. There was something queer and unnatural about this silent stranger. They came to a large gate with a little door on one side.

"Bend down!" the beadle said, after the stranger had knocked his head against the gate.

They came first into the smaller room which contained the washing-board and the box for the corpses of children. By the light of a candle they saw a cat, surrounded by kittens.

"*Pshick!*" the beadle shouted, and waved his stick. "Blast your bones, have you nowhere else to sit?"

The cat and kittens fled. The beadle led the stranger into a low room, from the ceiling of which hung a Sabbath candelabrum adorned with paper flowers. On opposite sides of the room stood two beds piled high with cushions and quilts and covered with chintz sheets with gayly colored designs.

As they entered, the beadle called out: "Zivyah! Put something on the table. I've brought a guest. He'll sleep on top of the oven, and you'll give him my old fur to cover himself."

The stranger did not notice the huge woman who turned round from the oven into which she had seemingly pushed the upper half of her body. A shock of matted, straw-colored hair covered her head. Her eyes were green, like those of a cat. She did not answer her father, but snatched a herring from the cupboard and began to chop it to pieces on the table. Her big breasts and fleshy hips swung as she brought the knife down. She seemed unable to touch anything without making it crash. She fixed her green eyes on the stranger and giggled.

"What are you laughing at, Zivyah?" her father asked.

She giggled louder, and chopped more fiercely at the herring. Several hens which had been roosting on the shelf above the oven were startled, woke up with a wild fluttering of wings and began to cluck noisily. A cock strained his body up and crowed. Zivyah lifted up her apron and chased the cock down from the shelf.

"Asha-a-a!" she shouted.

The stranger sat with downcast eyes. He ate little, but did a lot of praying. The girl laid steaming hot potatoes before him. She busied herself near him, approaching him so closely that her big breasts touched him. Her body gave off an animal heat which mingled with the steam of the potatoes. The stranger squirmed in his chair. The girl giggled. After the little he had eaten, the stranger added, to the usual benediction, several extra prayers. These he followed up with a number of prayers before sleep, and then at last crept onto the top of the oven. The girl covered him with an old, tattered fur, giggling all the time; she tickled his sides and feet as she tucked the fur round him, and in the midst of her giggling she kept repeating: "You! You be Zivyah's husband, eh? You be Zivyah's husband."

The small lamp hanging on the wall trembled continuously, so that the blobs of shadow danced.

In the night, when the clock, wheezing through all its machinery, gathered the remnants of its strength and struck twelve times, the stranger awoke and began to intone penitential prayers. A thin, half-choked wailing came from his throat; he sat up and beat his breast unceasingly. Hour after hour his lamentations continued, accompanied by the heavy snoring of a man, the lighter snoring of a woman, the rustling of the trees outside, and the occasional shrilling of a cricket under the oven.

14

THE MORNING AFTER THE FAIR THE BEGGARS TOOK THE TOWN BY storm.

As always, the householders tried to distribute *prutos*, but the beggars would have none of these. The fair had been unusually successful; the beggars knew this, and they would take nothing less than actual coins. They were on strike; they would accept neither *prutos* nor sugar nor corners of loaves. The latter they flung back in a rage.

"Choke yourself on that! Give us money!"

The householders groaned, and dug out groschens. Rich men even gave kopecks.

One begger took all the *prutos* offered him; that was the stranger, the beadle's guest.

In the evening he went to the town *gabbai*, the chief official of the community, to exchange his *prutos* for cash.

The *gabbai*, a short-winded man with a big stomach, asked him: "How many have you got?"

"I didn't count."

"Why did you let them give you nothing but *prutos*?"

"I took whatever they gave me."

The *gabbai* shrugged his shoulders. "A loon, so help me God!" Slowly he counted the filthy paper *prutos* which the stranger handed him; to count them he wet his thumb from time to time, and turned the notes over to examine the Hebrew letters stamped on them: "One *Prutah* of the Holy Congregation of Bialogura." Counting, he sighed every time he put his thumb to his lips.

As he had not counted the *prutos* when he handed them to the *gabbai*, so the beggar did not count the money which he received in exchange. He only picked up the small heap of coins and dropped them into his pocket. Then he turned, kissed the *mezuzah* on the lintel of the door, and went out.

The beadle was waiting for him.

"How much did you make?" he asked, sternly.

"I don't know. It's in my pocket."

"Let me count it."

The stranger took out the coins—three-groschen pieces mostly —and handed them over to the beadle. The latter counted them by the light of his lantern and dropped them into his own pocket. The stranger said nothing. He only drew the rope tighter round his ragged *capote* and turned to go.

"Yoshe! Where are you going?"

"Into the world."

"At night! Aren't you afraid of danger?"

"There is danger everywhere."

"God! Yoshe, what a loon you are!" said the beadle. "Come! We're going to the synagogue."

The stranger followed. In the synagogue the beadle handed him a broom and ordered him to sweep up round the stove. When he had finished, the beadle ordered him to replenish the pile of wood from the yard, and to heat up the stove. Meanwhile he sat and watched, contentedly. Late in the night he took the stranger home with him again, fed him and told him to go to sleep on top of the oven.

The stranger remained in Bialogura as the synagogue servant, the assistant to Reb Kanah the beadle.

He was not really the assistant; he was, as far as work went, the beadle. He worked from early morning till late at night. At dawn he was up to attend to the stove in the synagogue; the wood-pile had to be replenished, the stove made red hot. He brought water from the well, bucket by bucket, to fill the barrels. He swept all the huge synagogue, picked up carefully the leaves of sacred books and carried them into the garret. He cleaned the lamp chimneys for the evening studies and prayers.

If, between tasks, he sat down and took out his prayer-book, the voice of Reb Kanah the beadle was heard all the way across the synagogue. 'Let's have no laziness here. There's work to do; you can read all the Psalms you want on the Sabbath."

Reb Kanah had fallen on easy days. He attended now only to the more honorable and more lucrative services of a beadle; he arranged for the lighting of memorial candles and stole as many of them as he dared; he carried the folded canopy to be erected over a bridal couple at the marriage ceremony; he went among the crowd at funerals and rattled the charity-box, crying: "Charity saves from death." But, as to getting up in the early morning, and making the rounds of the Jewish houses to call the householders to prayer, this he left to Yoshe.

Yoshe went from door to door after he had prepared the synagogue. He tapped on the shutters with his wooden hammer and called out weakly: "Jews, rise! It is time to serve God."

Not knowing which were the Jewish and which the non-Jewish houses, Yoshe got into trouble. There were a few Gentiles in the heart of the Jewish quarter. From these, until Yoshe learned to avoid them, came curses—and once a bucket of ice-cold water. Yoshe shook himself, and went on from shutter to shutter.

If someone had died the day before, Reb Kanah the beadle said to him: "Yoshe! Tomorrow morning you've one call less to make. There's a dead man in town."

On Fridays Reb Kanah sent Yoshe through the town to knock at the doors with his hammer and remind the housewives it was time to light the Sabbath candles. In fact, Reb Kanah took things so easy that he even abandoned to Yoshe the task of beating the drum in the market-place on the days when the great stove in the public baths was being heated. He hung the drum around Yoshe's neck, showed him how to handle the sticks and sent him out.

"That's a grand old age Reb Kanah is having," Jews said, enviously. "He lives like a king."

If it chanced that, during the day, Yoshe found a free moment, and Reb Kanah was not around to drive him, the Talmud students found things for him to do. They had errands for him: "Yoshe, get me some cigarettes. Hey, loon, a pail of water. Yoshe, a bottle of whiskey—someone's having a memorial anniversary today."

Yoshe went without asking questions.

The most insistent, the most vicious of the students were the sons and prospective sons-in-law of rich Jews, young fellows who carried gold watches and chains. They had no real work to do; they ate well; they sat over their Talmud folios, time hung heavily on their hands and they were restless with unused strength and desires. Those that were engaged were not acquainted with their brides, and therefore could not write to them. But they had to write—and they did write—to their prospective fathers-in-law. These letters were show pieces; it was proper that they should contain a few learned allusions to Talmud and ritual, likewise a point or two of ingenious exegesis. They were invariably written by the teachers, and copied out by the students. As to their brides, the boys had no idea what they looked like, and they let their imaginations play about them. All of them waited with burning impatience for the day and the night of the wedding. In the meantime, they tried to still their desires in the lustier passages of the Talmud, and in the ritual books which dealt with the duties and problems of the woman. The relevant pages of the Talmud were always the dirtiest and greasiest. Often they were in tatters. But it was easy to get sick of this amusement. They gathered in small circles and spoke of forbidden, wanton things. Sometimes they gathered round Yoshe, when the beadle was absent, and teased him.

"Yoshe! Did you ever have a wife? Yoshe! Have you ever obeyed the first commandment toward a woman? Yoshe loon, answer!"

Yoshe did not answer. His lips moved, but he was intoning Psalms. His lips were always moving in this way—he never stopped chanting Psalms, not on his errands, not while he heated the stove and not even while he swept the synagogue. It was only in the night that he said something that was not in the Psalms. At twelve o'clock he awoke without fail, and, if the lamp was not burning, crept down in the darkness to find a little water to pour over his nails. He put on his ragged *capote*, tied the rope round his waist and said the midnight penitential prayers. By heart he repeated, in a wailing voice, passages from the Zohar, the Book of the Kabbala, and from the book of prayers for Divine forgiveness. He beat his breast, and sometimes took a handful of ashes from the stove and poured it on his head.

This, at least, was his practice during the first nights of his life in the home of Reb Kanah the beadle. But before long his nights were tormented by Zivyah, Reb Kanah's half-wit daughter.

She wanted Yoshe; she wanted him in a simple, shameless animal way. She showed it as soon as he entered the house, and when a few days were gone she was not content with tormenting him during the day, but pursued him in the night too. When he came in for his meals she watched him with her green eyes; her broad nostrils opened wide, her lips drew back in a grin, revealing her pointed teeth. She was catlike in her pursuit of him, leaning against him, rubbing herself against him, like a cat which arches its back, raises its tail and rubs itself against a person's leg. He avoided her and repulsed her, but she could not be discouraged. She returned to him, grinning, eager, half-witted. She pushed her body against his and breathed into his face, giggling. He averted his face and, setting his teeth, repeated prayers grimly.

When she came to him in the night for the first time, he started out of his sleep with wild terror at his heart. Something was near him, something that pressed and breathed hotly on him. When he understood what had happened, and the terror, receding, was replaced by loathing, he drew his body away toward the brick wall.

"You!" she said, with an idiotic giggle. "You—my husband—father said, 'Zivyah's husband—' "

She crawled nearer to him, so that he had to put up his hands and elbows to keep her away.

"Go away," he moaned. "I'll wake your father. Go."

She paid no attention to his threat. Her hands fumbled over his body. He tried to push her away, but she was stronger.

"You, Yoshe loon," she whispered, and began to kiss him wildly, putting her lips to every part of him that she could reach.

He began to cry out: "Reb Kanah! Reb Kanah!"

But Reb Kanah could not be wakened. He was fast asleep under two heavy covers, one his own, one that of his dead wife. His snoring was louder than Yoshe's cry, an angry snoring, as if he were quarreling with someone in his sleep.

With a last convulsive effort, Yoshe tore himself free from the embraces of the girl, slipped down from the oven and crawled into a corner. Zivyah gave up. He heard her shuffling heavily across the floor and heard her throw herself into her bed. Again Yoshe began to repeat his prayers, but again the girl interrupted him. Now she did not seek him, but, lying on her bed, she wailed from between clenched teeth, wailed like a wounded animal. The sound of it froze his blood—the dumb call of an abandoned beast. She stopped, and he began again to pray. But after a short silence she lifted her voice again, more desperate than before.

And now her wailing, instead of freezing his blood, sent a wave

of heat through it. He had fled from contact with her body, but the
sound of her agony drew him toward her. He wanted to go to her,
put his hands on her head, comfort her in the darkness. The
thought of it made him shudder, and he shook his head in violent
negation. He pinched himself furiously, bared his flesh and tore it,
to drive away his evil thoughts. But in the midst of his self-
torment he realized that the pain was pleasurable; it was sweet; it
tasted like the blood which he had once sucked from his own
finger when he had cut it.

So he sat in the corner, trembling, until the wailing stopped. He
crept back to the oven and drew Reb Kanah's tattered fur coat
over his head. Sleep did not come to him; his blood was awake.
He forced himself to keep his eyes closed; but the heavier the
pressure of his lids, the more vivid the visions he saw: women of
all kinds, naked, insolent bodies, arms stretched out to him, lips
that called him. The Evil One stood at his head, in the likeness of
the town doctor—a thin man with a little pointed beard and with a
cane in his hand. The doctor grinned.

"Idiot!" he said. "You drive away from your side a girl, a
virgin, an orphan, so that you may sin in thought with filthy
demons and whores of dreams. . . ."

He slipped down again from the oven, dressed himself hurriedly
and found his way to the door. He would run away in the night,
run anywhere, so that he might never look on this house again. In
the darkness he felt for his wallet, and for the phylactery bag. But
at the door something held him, a force that was not himself, a
force stronger than his will. His legs were heavier than lead; he
could not lift them or push them forward.

For, before he had even opened the door, a homesickness, a
longing, came over him for this home, for the dark warmness of
its nights, for the shrilling of the cricket under the oven, and for
the sound of the woman sunk in heavy sleep. Something poured
through his limbs, filling them with sweet desire for sleep; sweet
desire and faintness overwhelmed his thoughts, and made him
forget himself. If she had come to him then, he would not have
had the strength to repulse her.

Clothed as he was, in *capote* and boots, he crawled onto his bed again. He began once more to chant Psalms, but his voice shook, and tears ran down his face into his open mouth.

"God," he begged, "why hast Thou forsaken me? I call to Thee in the day and Thou answerest me not; I cry in the night, and Thou art silent."

15

THE ROADS AROUND THE CEMETERY OF BIALOGURA WERE FILLED with terror in the night.

Wagoners passing that way long after sundown, with their loads of salt or kerosene, could hear, above the creaking of their own wheels and the steady klop-klop of their horses' hoofs, a whispering, a fluttering, a sliding through grass, between trees. Peddlers— Jews who wandered from village to village, sometimes selling, sometimes gathering pigs' bristles and rabbit-skins—reported that, in the nights, they had seen lights wink and dance in the cemetery.

The community of Bialogura took fright. Jews took to examining their ritual fringes minutely; perhaps something was wrong with the twisting, the number of threads, the spacing, or another of the rigid prescriptions. Wives did not dare to leave the house after sunset unless they wore a pinafore. Men and women were reluctant to pass the cemetery even in the day; they ran till the stone wall was out of sight, and then panted with exhaustion and relief. At night none of the inhabitants of Bialogura could be tempted to go that way. It came to such a pass that even the hardy wagoners, who were not afraid to drive alone from sunset to sunrise through the thickest depths of Count Zamoiski's forests, which were filled with wolves and robbers, would not pass the cemetery at night except in groups. Even thus, they went lumbering past at top speed, cracking their whips to drive away their fear,

herself hastily, covered her head with a tattered shawl, and vanished into the cemetery. She made her way by the glimmering stones, under overhanging boughs, to the place where she saw the cigarette tips of the smugglers flitting through the darkness. There she remained for many hours.

They did not drive her off, as Yoshe the loon had done. They gave her roast chicken and roast duck, and let her drink Austrian cognac from their bottles. They even gave her presents, silk kerchiefs and colored ribbons. And in exchange she went with them under the cover of the four-pillared dome which covered the grave of the sainted grandfather of Reb Boruch'l. On the stony floor of the mausoleum bundles of wool made a bed.

In the darkness she giggled idiotically, not seeing the face of the man who was with her: "You—Zivyah's husband—my bridegroom—father said—"

Yoshe, lying on the oven, awake, tormented, heard every sound in the cemetery. His flesh burned, and he tore it with his nails to drive out evil thoughts. Hour after hour he repeated by heart long passages from the Zohar, the Book of the Kabbala.

16

AT THE END OF THAT WINTER, SOON AFTER THE FESTIVAL OF Purim, a deadly pestilence broke out among the children of Bialogura.

It began in the poorest outskirts of the town—the sandy section adjoining the barracks and stables of the Don Cossacks. Village peddlers, military tailors, wagoners, cobblers, lime-carriers—plain, ignorant folk—lived there; and in this section was likewise a brothel for the use of the soldiers.

On Shushan Purim—the day which follows Purim proper, and which is given over, even more than Purim, to feasting and rejoicing—the child of a certain widow, who made a living by peddling sunflower seeds among the soldiers, became violently sick; without warning it fell and began to gasp for breath.

The widow removed a stocking from her foot, filled it with hot salt, and wrapped it round the child's neck. This brought no relief, and the child continued to choke. Terrified, the woman ran through the town to the house of Samson, the healer and musician. She rushed in, wringing her hands, and began to scream:

"Reb Samson, quick! My child! Help me! I'm a widow! My child!"

Reb Samson the healer very slowly drew on his eight-cornered hat with the velvet button, passed his hand through his short, wiry beard, picked up his box of leeches and followed the widow reluctantly.

He was angry. "Shushan Purim!" he said bitterly. "She couldn't pick out another day. All the way through the sands at the other end of the town!"

"Reb Samson, you good angel," the widow panted. "I wouldn't go to Yeretzki, the doctor. I wouldn't. He isn't fit to clean your shoes. You've got more in your little finger than he's got in all his stupid head. . . ."

Reb Samson liked to hear that. He loathed his enemy and rival, the trained and official doctor, Yeretzki, who in turn despised the half-trained, half-educated, semi-official healer.

"All right, all right," he answered. "I'll save the child." And he quickened his pace.

He did not save the child. He had scarcely taken it into his arms when it gave up the struggle for breath, opened wide its glazed eyes and died.

Reb Samson stared at the dead child. "I see," he muttered under his breath, and returned home with his box of leeches. The thought that *this* was beginning in town, and that it would probably reach its height during the Passover, consoled him for his useless trip through the sands. In her horror and despair, the widow had not paid him the gulden to which he was entitled.

The next morning the widow ran to the Burial Brotherhood, to have the child taken away. But the members of the Burial Brotherhood were still drunk after their feast of Shushan Purim. They had been drinking most of the night, making the rounds of the town, breaking into houses with the license of Purim, snatching dainties from tables and stealing wine from cellars. They would not listen to her now. To her cries the *gabbai* of the brotherhood answered joyously: "A happy Purim to you! Cursed be Zeresh!" He was too drunk to know what he was saying.

From the house of the *gabbai* of the Burial Brotherhood, the widow ran to the head of the community. He too refused to listen.

"What is this?" he answered angrily. "On a day like this! All the way through the sands!"

The widow returned to her hovel. She went to a dark corner where her old wedding dress still hung under a sheet. She took down the sheet, cut it and sewed grave-clothes for the child. She emptied the basket in which she carried her sunflower seeds and laid in it the wrapped-up corpse of the child. Wailing, she carried it to the cemetery, and gave Reb Kanah a gulden to do what was proper. And coming out of the cemetery she dropped the black shawl from her head and lifted her two bony arms over the town and cursed it.

"Sodom!" she screamed. "You shall not escape! You shall feel my pain and my despair, and pay for the shame of the widow and the orphan."

From the huts and hovels on the sands the pestilence spread toward the town. It attacked first the narrow streets of the workers. Then it passed to the marketplace, round which were clustered the houses of the merchants and the rich. Bialogura no longer slept; the nights were as loud as the days with the wailing of women.

"Jews! Have mercy! Save my loved one!"

During the first days of the pestilence the Jews depended on the doctors. From the poorest lanes and alleys a stream of women in tatters poured toward the door of Samson the healer. He could not attend to all of them. Day and night they beat on his door with their fists.

"Murderer! Open!"

The middle class went to the Polish doctor, Yeretzki, an eccentric, bad-tempered man. He hated Jews. He shouted at his Jewish patients as if they were inflicting an injury on him; he had even been known to strike them.

"*Pupik* show!" he said sharply, in mock Yiddish. "Moishe! Let me see, *oi veh!*"

"Prince!" the Jews begged him, their heads uncovered. "First comes God and then you, Professor."

The rich Jews went to the Cossack doctor, Shalupin-Shalapnikoff, a general, with a beard down to his waist. He was always good-humored, even in the presence of the last agonies of a patient.

"*Nitchevo*, darling, *nitchevo!*" he always said consolingly, in a deep voice.

The doctors worked, examined, diagnosed, prescribed and washed their hands industriously in hot water. It was of no avail.

The pestilence grew from day to day.

From the doctors the Jews turned desperately to Reb Boruch'l, whom they called the women's Rabbi.

They kept him busy through the nights, writing amulets, some of the usual kind, some with special power against a visitation of general evil. They also asked for dried herbs, which, ground and tied in little bundles, had powers of their own. Reb Boruch'l had, in addition, certain rare and valuable specifics against disease and death; pieces of amber on which the long dead Maggid of Kozhenitz, of blessed memory, had said prayers; fragments of black sugar which had touched the lips of the saintly Grandfather of Shpoleh, strings of wolves' teeth, black devil-fingers, girdles of remnant strips, blessed oil from the Holy City of Safad in the Holy Land. The four deaf and dumb daughters of Reb Boruch'l worked with him, packing herbs, pouring oil, cutting parchment and sewing girdles.

Women thrust their way at all hours into the synagogue, tore open the doors of the Ark of the Scrolls and cried aloud to the Word of God. Their faces covered with their shawls, they approached the men and wept:

"Jews, pray for Leah, the daughter of Hannah Dvorah; Jews, say Psalms for Simchah Meir, son of Feine Hodel. . . ."

The Jews chanted Psalms; they changed the names of their children; or to sons' names they added *Chaim*, which means Life, so that they might live long, or *Zeide*, which means Grandfather, or *Alter*, which means old. They changed girls' names, or added to them *Chayah*, *Alte* and *Bobbe*. Some even added the three names at once; so that if, in heaven, a decree had gone out against them in one name, they might be saved by the second, and if against the second, they might still be saved by the third. Mothers who had lost all their sons but one before the pestilence now dressed the last one, the remaining *kadish*—remembrancer after death—in white linen robes. In the street, the children of the poor ran after the white-robed only sons of rich mothers, threw stones at them and yelled:

"Mama's darlings! Angels of Death!"

But the mothers insisted on the white robes and the white hats, saying: "If you are destined to put on the white clothes, put them on while you live, so that you may not, God forbid, have to wear them of a truth."

The beggars of Bialogura came into their own. No more crusts and pieces of sugar, no more *prutos*, but whole groschens, and sometimes two- and three-groschen pieces. Yes, even ten-groschen pieces were handed out by the rich. In the night, Reb Kanah the beadle would go into the synagogue, and with a bent wire extract coins from the filled boxes of the Palestinian charities. He no longer bothered gathering up candles. It was small game now; besides, he had stacked a whole corner with them.

"When things start," he said, sagely, "they go by themselves."

And the pestilence grew from day to day.

The women turned their attention to the cemetery.

When a child died, the women shouted into the Ark of the Scrolls, begging the dead child to intercede.

"Run," they shouted, "to the Holy Mothers, Sarah, Rebecca, Rachel and Leah. Tell them it is enough."

Candles were lit at the graves of the saintly dead, and prayer-notes were written and deposited there. Tables were carried into the cemetery; men sat there with pen and ink, and took eighteen groschen for writing out a note—eighteen because the letters of the word *chai*—which means Life—stood, in Hebrew, for eighteen. Mothers came by the score, and the scribes worked fast.

"The child's name and the mother's name," the scribes said, hurriedly. "And eighteen groschen. Quick! Others are waiting."

Women who were barren took lengths of linen, measured off with them the circumference of the cemetery, and gave them away to the charities for the trousseaux of poor brides. Other women twisted wicks for candles, and with these, too, drew a line round the cemetery. By all these means they hoped to draw an impassable cordon round the Eternal House of the Dead, so that it might receive no more of the living. But nothing availed.

The pestilence grew from day to day.

Reb Meir'l, the Rabbi of the city, called the householders of Bialogura to a meeting.

"There is sin in the city!" he cried. "Jews, repent! Perhaps God will be merciful to us. For the sins of one man, all the little ones of a city may perish."

The Jews of Bialogura trembled. They began to look for sins, each man watching his neighbor. Women stood guard round the house of Samson the healer and musician, to make sure that on the Sabbath evenings, at practice, the musicians did not touch the servant girls. It was rumored in the city that dances had taken place in the house of Samson the healer. The owner of the brothel on the sands was sent for, and the Rabbi commanded him to drive away the one Jewish girl whom he kept among the Gentile girls. The owner, a Jew with a Russian blouse hanging down over his wide trousers—he was half Russified, having served many years in the garrison in Podolia—began to argue.

"Rabbi," he pleaded, "I've got to have one Jewish girl. The swine have to have one. . . ."

The Rabbi was obstinate, and the owner appealed to the laws of justice and charity. "Rabbi," he said, "where shall the girl go? She is an orphan, poor thing, without a friend in the world."

The Rabbi flew into a rage. He swore to the owner of the brothel that after his death no son of his would be permitted to recite *Kadish* for him in the synagogues of Bialogura. The Jewish abomination had to be driven from the city. The owner of the brothel was terrified by the threat and drove the woman out.

A committee of wealthy Jews called in the chief attendant of the ritual baths, to ask him the names of the women who were remiss in their visits. Husbands were bidden to keep close watch on their wives, to see that their heads were properly covered and that no lock of hair stray out from under the cover and be seen over the ear or at the back of the neck. Fathers instructed their daughters sternly not to uncover their necks and not to go out with bare arms.

Likewise the Rabbi of the city had a great proclamation published; its style and content were like those of proclamations hundreds of years old. Students of the Talmud were ordered to copy out the proclamation in the finest script, and copies were posted on all the walls, from the yard of the synagogue to the hedge of the beggars' lodging house.

"With the help of the Supreme, Blessed be His Name! It hath been reported to us that sinfulness hath broken out in Israel. It hath been told to us (God defend us!) that sundry wives of this Congregation do still keep their own hair under their perukes, which is after the manner of the heathen. Likewise they do not cover their hair on their brows and near their ears, and this is a great sin and a great shamefulness which, it is known unto all, should not be in Israel. Moreover, wives who give suck unto their children are heedless of passers-by, and they uncover at their doors their breasts, which may be seen by men and by young men, and this may be likened unto shamefulness. Moreover, young girls are likewise heedless, in that they gad about with uncovered necks; neither do they wear sleeves on their arms. They also sing aloud, which is sin, for the voice of a woman and of a young woman singing is shameful, and no benediction may be made in its hearing. It hath further been reported unto us that young girls do comb their hair on the Sabbath, which is as if they lit a fire on the Sabbath. Wherefore, because of all this sinfulness, the punishment of Heaven hath been visited upon our little ones, which have not sinned in any manner whatsoever, and have fallen because of the anger wherewith Heaven is angered. Now let Death be destroyed forever, Amen! We therefore call out in the gates of Israel: let the shamefulness be removed from our midst. Let the women bethink themselves, and the young women also. Let all beds be separated, one from another, by a distance of one ell, and let the wives shave their heads. Those wives that are poor, and cannot pay for the shaving, them, with the help of God, the congregation shall cause to be shaved; and they may go every day to the woman who shaves women, at the ritual baths, and they shall be given the counter of the Congregation, that they may be shaved; also they shall be permitted to bathe themselves in the ritual bath of the women, which is of this Congregation, and they shall not pay therefor. Let deliverance come upon Israel, and let the Supreme say unto the Evil One: It is enough! And let Death vanish. These are the words of those who are broken, and who write with trembling hands and a broken spirit. Take away the shame that is in your midst."

Here followed the signatures of Reb Meir'l the Rabbi and of Reb Boruch'l, the second Rabbi, whom they called the women's Rabbi; and both were entered with the full titles of their humility.

"The young and small Meir Judah, the son of the great Rabbi and mighty spirit Reb Samuel Zev, of blessed memory, the Rabbi of the Holy Congregation.

"The small and utterly unworthy Boruch, the son of the divine angel, the fiery column, Reb Nisan of Torbin, and the grandson of the martyrs, Preacher in the Holy Congregation."

A fever of piety set in among the Jews of Bialogura. The women did as they were bid, and pulled down the ends of their wigs over their ears; they covered their faces with their shawls, and exposed to the world only the tip of the nose and their eyes. Young men who had just married did not permit themselves to be gay with their young wives. The fright having spread to the school children, even they were caught up in the wave of piety, and said all their daily prayers without omissions or curtailment. Workers no longer sang questionable songs at their work, and servant girls going to the river for water no longer stopped to flirt with the wagoners. But it availed nothing.

The pestilence grew from day to day.

Reb Meir'l the Rabbi, and Reb Boruch'l the preacher, whom they called the women's Rabbi, again called together the Jews of Bialogura, but this time in the synagogue, and they laid the curse of full excommunication upon him who had sinned and had not confessed. Having said midnight penitential prayers in the middle of the week, Reb Kanah the beadle lit the great candles, as if this were the eve of the dread Day of Atonement. Yoshe the loon brought into the synagogue the washing-board of the dead, from the cemetery, and stood it up in a corner. The chief men of the synagogue took the Scrolls of the Law from the Ark. Kanah the beadle struck three times with his hammer on the pulpit, and the Rabbi read out in a grave voice from a parchment which lay before him:

"With the knowledge of the Congregation, and with the sanction of the Tribunal thereof, we call upon those that have sinned —whether they be men or women, whether they be young men or virgins, whether they be dwellers here or sojourners—to confess their sins before the Congregation, for a great calamity has fallen upon our city, and our little ones die like flies. And it were incumbent upon us to do that which was done in the days when we dwelt in our own land, to wit, to go forth before the gate of the city and to say: Our hands have not shed this blood. For the sinner in our midst may be likened to one who has risen in a field and slain a man. The blood of the little ones cries out against us. But before the Holy Temple was built, the Tribunal was likened unto a Holy Temple; and therefore we, acting as the Tribunal, may proceed with full rigor. And therefore we stand at the gates, and we cry: Cursed be they who hide their sins, whether they be men or women, or young men or virgins, or dwellers here or sojourners, and may their names be blotted out, and may evil grip their loins, and may their memories be a mockery and a shame in Israel. And if it be a man may his hands lose their cunning and may his legs fail him, and may his loins wither, and may he beget no more. And if it be a woman let her presence be wiped out, and let her children perish, and may they be forever a byword in Israel, Amen."

"Amen!" the men and women answered, weeping.

"Sound the *shofar!*" the Rabbi called out.

The *gabbai* lifted the ram's horn to his lips and blew three blasts.

A deadly silence descended on the whole synagogue. Not a breath was heard. Only a bird, which had entered the synagogue through a broken window-pane, fluttered wildly round the carved lion on the Ark of the Scrolls. The worshipers waited in tense silence.

And suddenly Reb Moses, the scribe, rose from his place, ran up to the pulpit and cried out loudly:

"Jews! I confess!"

A shudder passed through the congregation.

"Jews!" Reb Moses cried, and his eyes burned. "I am full of sin, I am covered with corruption from head to foot."

And running down the steps, he flung himself at the foot of the pulpit and begged hoarsely:

"Jews, tread on me, spit on me, bring shame upon me!"

But no one stirred from his place. Only the Rabbi, and the preacher, whom they called the women's Rabbi, ran up to Reb Moses, and lifted him to his feet, and pleaded with him:

"Reb Moses, let your virtues intercede for us in heaven. Pray for us!"

Women, hidden in the gallery of the synagogue, wailed: "Holy man, save our children."

Neither did the curse of the full excommunication avail. Kanah the beadle was still busy all day long rattling the charity-box at the funerals of children, and saying hoarsely: "Charity saves from death."

The pestilence grew from day to day.

Abish the butcher took it upon himself to find the sinner in the congregation. He was a huge man, the head of the butchers' synagogue in Bialogura. On the Sabbath afternoon which followed the excommunication, he addressed his fellow butchers in the synagogue:

"Excommunications! *Shofars!* Hens cackling! That's no way to make a sinner confess. Butchers! We'll take the job on ourselves. Let's look through the town, and by God, when we find the sinner, we'll tear him limb from limb and turn him into mince-meat, as I'm a Jew. . . ."

Abish himself was most on the alert. He watched the women who came to his butcher shop; he listened to gossip, he lingered at doors. And on the fifth day of his search he found it.

He found it accidentally.

At the end of a long row of women who had come to lay in meat for the Sabbath, was Zivyah, the daughter of Reb Kanah the beadle. Her father was doing well, and Zivyah bought heavily.

The other women being gone, Abish the butcher could not keep his hands off Zivyah—as off any other woman who was alone with him in the shop. He had sworn so often to himself to behave, to be decent and pious, especially in these bitter times. But as soon as he came into the butcher shop he was lost. He could not prevent his hands—they seemed to move by themselves—from creeping toward a woman's leg or breast, to take a little pinch of flesh, to snatch a caress. His wife Beileh Dobbeh, a lazy, slatternly woman, no longer watched or cared. She might even be dozing in a corner of the shop when she heard the voice of some women raised in shrill anger:

"Abish'l! If your hands could only be paralyzed!"

His hands went, of themselves, to Zivyah; they pinched and patted—but Zivyah did not scream or twist away from him. She only giggled:

"He, he, he, Abish'l butcher!"

And suddenly the trained hand of Abish felt something, and stopped dead; and at the same instant a thought clove through his brain, like an ax cleaving open the head of an ox. Abish the butcher saw light.

He flew to his wife Beileh Dobbeh, who was dozing in a corner, bent over her, shook her violently and panted: "Beileh Dobbeh! Beileh Dobbeh! I've found it! I've got it! Take a look there at Kanah's precious daughter—look!"

He closed one eye and winked the other at the girl's figure.

"You don't know what you're talking about!" his wife answered, angrily. "You're crazy."

"Crazy?" Abish roared. "I'll show you if I'm crazy."

He strode over to Zivyah and, suddenly placing both hands on her stomach, squeezed.

"Mama!" the girl screamed, and Abish spat out in his wife's direction so violently that he almost hit her.

"The bastard's already kicking in there," he shouted. "Come here, Beileh Dobbeh! Come here, and see who's crazy. Feel!"

But without waiting, he ran to the door and bellowed into the street.

"Women! This way! I've found something for you!"

The wives of the butchers came running. Zivyah tried to escape, but a dozen hands held her firm. She tore the wigs from their heads, she bit and screamed, but she could not tear herself free. They lifted her, laid her down on the butcher's block and felt her.

"The fifth month!" one woman screamed. "God in heaven! May it run out of her stomach."

Another woman, who had lost a child in the pestilence but eight days before, and was out now for the first time after the seven days of confined mourning, leaped at Zivyah, thrust her hands into her hair, and howled: "This for my little Chaskel, ten feet underground, because of you, beast!" And she tore at Zivyah's hair.

With one despairing effort Zivyah lifted herself from the block, dashed to the door and, still screaming, fled down the street in the direction of the cemetery and her home. But Abish the butcher was after her. He seized her again and roared to the crowd:

"Take her to the Rabbi's house! Take her—but don't bring her there dead!"

Four butchers lifted her up, each one throwing a hand or leg over his shoulder, as if she were a slaughtered animal. Screaming and struggling, she was carried in procession toward the house of Reb Meir'l, the Rabbi. Women and children, hearing the wild yelling in the street, came running out and joined; they left the soup to boil over, the meat to burn, and they ran along with the rest. Workers joined them, carrying scissors and hammers, cobblers with a boot drawn over one arm, men without coats, their ritual fringes flapping in the wind. Water-carriers even forgot to put down their shoulder-pieces and pails, but ran with their burdens. In front ran Abish the butcher, like a marshal.

"We've caught her," he roared to every side. "Zivyah, Reb Kanah's daughter. We're taking her to the Rabbi."

There were some men who laughed, but the women, with hatred in their blazing faces, shook their fists toward the struggling, panting girl, and screamed:

"Stone her, the whore! For the sake of our little ones, stone her!"

17

REB MEIR'L, THE RABBI OF BIALOGURA, SAT IN HIS BIG, HARD judgment chair, an old volume open before him; though the day was warm, he was wrapped in his red velvet fleece-lined dressing-gown; his long pipe was in his mouth, and from time to time he sighed.

"Lord of the Worlds," he murmured. "How long? If we need not the Deliverer now, when shall we need Him?"

The soul of Reb Meir'l was in torment. Besides the torment of the pestilence, and the weeping of the women who broke in upon him daily to beg him to pray for their children, he had many difficult and painful problems. There was, for instance, this new and terrible decree, issued by the Emperor himself, forbidding Jews to wear ear-locks, girdles and skull-caps unless they were Rabbis and teachers. The police had never taken such pleasure in enforcement of the law. The rich Jews could, as always, manage to buy themselves out. But the poor ones were helpless. The Chief of Police of Bialogura had issued the strictest instructions to his force, and it was dangerous for a Jew with ear-locks, beard and girdle to leave the house. He was not sure of sleeping in his home that night. Nor did he escape the great shame, for the policeman did not wait for trial; he whipped out his sword and removed the ear-locks on the spot; frequently a handful of beard and several pieces of skin went with the ear-locks; then he appropriated the girdle and skull-cap as material evidence, and marched the Jew off to the prison. If the Jew had three rubles for the fine, he was released; otherwise he served three days.

A number of Jews thought of the same device simultaneously: on leaving the house they tied a kerchief round their faces, as if they were suffering from toothache. The policemen would have let this pass, but the Chief of Police, astonished by the supplementary epidemic of toothache, caught on almost at once, and ordered his men to remove all kerchiefs from male faces.

"*Shacher macher!* Swindlers!" the policemen snorted, and laughed. "*Peisinke davoi*—let's have those ear-locks!"

And early one morning, in fact before he had yet said his prayers, Reb Meir'l was called before the Chief of Police, and listened to stern and angry language.

On the preceding day Reb Moses the scribe had been grabbed in the street by a policeman, and had lost an ear-lock. It happened in this wise: Reb Moses had reached the Ineffable Name of God in the Scroll of the Law which he was writing; therefore, rising from his table, he had gone to the ritual baths to purify himself before he put pen to parchment. On the way back from the baths he ran rather than walked, hoping to preserve all his purity, and not to encounter on the way an uncircumcised unbeliever, or even a Jew without learning. Such was his haste that he had not even dried himself properly after the immersion. He ran with eyes which were wide open but saw nothing around him; and in this way he ran plump into the policeman's arms.

"B-r-r-r! Whoa, there, daddy!" the policeman growled, and shoved his rounded chest up against the astounded little Jew. "*Peseleh, garteleh*, little sheeny, *oi veh. . . .*"

Reb Moses the scribe started away in horror. He put up both hands and covered his ear-locks; and when the policeman drew his sword and threatened to cut his hands, Reb Moses did not flinch; better lose a hand than an ear-lock. The policeman lugged Reb Moses to the jail, and with the help of other policemen bound the

Jew's hands behind his back; then he removed the right ear-lock down to the skin and threw Reb Moses into a cell occupied by several drunkards.

The Jews of Bialogura were in a turmoil. A deputation went at once to the Chief of Police, and pleaded:

"Prince! Let him out! He is a holy man, a Rabbi, a scribe."

The Chief of Police sent for Reb Meir'l, the Rabbi, and questioned him sternly.

"Who is the Rabbi in this town?" he shouted. "You, or this other one?"

Reb Meir'l did not understand a single word, and therefore could not answer. He could only shiver with fear. The Chief of Police sent for the State Rabbi, the Russified Rabbinic official whom the government recognized as the representative of the Jews. The State Rabbi interpreted.

"Tell him," begged Reb Meir'l, "explain to him, that I am the Rav, the teacher, the interpreter of the law; but Reb Moses is a scribe, a saintly man, and that is greater than a Rav."

The State Rabbi explained in excellent Russian; but the distinction was too much for the Chief of Police.

"*Shacher macher!* Jewish swindlers!" he shouted. "Don't I know your sheeny tricks?"

But Reb Moses could not be abandoned. A committee of Jews made the rounds of Jewish houses, and gathered in a red kerchief enough coins to exchange for a gold piece. Reb Samson the healer was entrusted with the task of slipping the coin to the Chief of Police, which he did with great skill while pretending to grab the official's hand in supplication. Reb Moses was released; but Reb Meir'l was still shaken by the incident.

"Woe!" he sighed at his table. "Such a saintly man! And such unclean hands have dared to touch him!"

And as if the decree against ear-locks, girdles and skull-caps were not enough, there were now reports that the government was contemplating compulsory Gentile education for all Jewish children; Jewish boys would be dragged away from the *cheder* and from the study of the Sacred Law to learn Russian and atheism. The State Rabbi himself had read about it in the Russian newspaper. The Emperor himself was about to issue the new decree.

Reb Meir'l knew, of course, that the Jews would not take such a blow lying down. He knew that many saintly men, rich Jews, Rabbis and others would be moving heaven and earth against the approaching evil. It was further rumored, in fact, that great sums of money were being gathered—hundreds of thousands of rubles —to purchase relief. The money would be taken to St. Petersburg and handed to the Minister himself, the right-hand man of the Emperor. Jews, moreover, were fasting and praying. This was not the first time that decrees of compulsory apostasy—and was Gentile education less than that?—had been contemplated against Jews. There had been the effort to force German upon the Jews. And there had been the effort to turn the Jews into land workers, peasants, scattered among Gentile villages, where the Word of God would never reach them, and they would become like the ignorant peasants around them. Oh, there had been many evil decrees. And Jews had always fasted and prayed and gathered money; and God had been merciful and helped them. Jews had remained Jews.

But, on the other hand, Reb Meir'l reflected bitterly, it was said that Jews, wicked Jews, were actually responsible for decrees of this kind. There were Jews (God help us!) who actually begged the great Gentiles in St. Petersburg to open such schools for Jewish children. Jews had actually persuaded the great Gentiles to admit Jewish young men into the army, where they ate food which was not *kosher*, and worked on the Sabbath. And these same Jews (was it credible?) had started the movement against ear-locks, girdles and skull-caps. They wanted, like the Sadducees of old (blast their name!) to apostatize the Jewish people. Yes, there was double exile for the Jewish people; it was surrounded by the hostile nations from without, and betrayed by Jews from within.

"It is the day of the Messiah!" the thought flashed through Reb Meir'l's mind. "Things cannot be worse; and therefore He is due. And there are other signs of His coming."

Just a few days before, Reb Meir'l lighted, in an old book, on a few words which indicated clearly that the Messiah was to appear this very year. He had shown the words to a few intimate friends, scholars like himself, and they agreed with him that nothing could be clearer. More than this, he had found an ancient commentary which declared that when Javan would be at war with Ishmael, the deliverance would come. And now he had heard, during a conversation in the ritual baths, that Russia and Turkey were on the point of war. Russia was of course Javan, and it had always been known that Turkey was descended from Ishmael, the son of Hagar, the handmaid of Sarah.

"It cannot be otherwise," the Rabbi muttered, and his excitement increased.

For an instant an unworthy and un-Jewish doubt flickered up at the back of his mind. For, ever since he had had a mind of his own, Reb Meir'l had been accustomed to find hints, secret indications, dark allusions, to the Redemption which was due there and then. Whenever a war broke out, Reb Meir'l stumbled upon some ancient commentary which, in words that could not be clearer, proved that this was the very last war; at its close the Messiah would appear. And the Messiah had not come! The Jews were still in exile! And a saint like Reb Moses had had an ear-lock cut off!

The doubt flickered up and died down. Reb Meir'l knew that he had sinned; beyond the shadow of a doubt this was the work of the Evil One. A Jew must believe! He must have faith! He must be prepared, every day, every hour, every moment, to hear the trumpet of Deliverance. Why, Reb Meir'l's grandfather had always slept in his clothes (leaving off only his dressing-gown) for fear the trumpet should sound in the night and catch him unawares. And Reb Meir'l remembered clearly how his grandmother used to argue with her husband at least to take off his socks. But her husband had replied: "What? And if the Messiah comes, shall I first go looking for my socks?"

Reb Meir'l, remembering his sainted grandfather, was strengthened in his faith. Bit by bit the wretchedness and brokenness of his spirit were replaced by the certainty of deliverance. He forgot the evil decrees; he forgot the unspeakable Chief of Police, before whom he had stood trembling. He no longer saw the miseries which overwhelmed the faithful and the pious. In his old ears a far-off clarion call sounded, traveling from end to end of the world.

There was no clear picture in Reb Meir'l's mind as to how the

Deliverance would come. He remembered, from many old books, a variety of preliminary portents. Some books said that the Messiah would come in thunder and storm. Three days before, there would be thunder and lightning such as the earth had never seen; a great terror would descend upon all living things; and then a voice would echo from heaven, announcing the glad tidings. But other old books said, on the other hand, that the Messiah would come very quietly, while Jews were still busy buying and selling and chaffering in the market-place. He would come on a white ass, like a poor man, without noise, without storm and without portents. But Reb Meir'l knew one thing: in whatever fashion the Messiah elected to come, His coming would be good for the Jews, and good, above all, for Jews who were pious and learned.

Of course, he thought contemptuously, plain people, ignoramuses, picture it quite simply: roast leviathan to eat, and roast meat of the Great Ox; wine without limit to drink; and the Gentiles of the world to act as servants. And Reb Meir'l smiled at the simplicity of such folk, and at the poverty of their imagination. And perhaps, he thought, God will indeed prepare such low joys for workers, wagoners and other ignoramuses; what other delights would they be fit for? What understanding was theirs? Far different, however, were the delights prepared for the learned. For *them* eating and drinking and comforts were not an end in themselves. Not for this had they so long suffered and labored and been faithful. Their reward was higher and nobler.

He saw it all so clearly: a world illumined with a light which children of this earth cannot imagine; a light which God had hidden away and kept for the end of the world; a series of tables, round which were ranged the saints and the scholars of all ages, each one ranked according to his saintliness and scholarship; the patriarchs, the holy patriarchs, would be seated there too; and Moses and Aaron and all the angels and all the prophets and all the sages and teachers. And He, the Infinite and Almighty, would sit at the very head, and He would chat with the saints, and expound the Law to them.

Great is the Law, Reb Meir'l knew; it is full of secrets. In every word, in every letter, and in every dot, great truths are concealed.

And, as Reb Meir'l knew further, there had been men of sublime learning and sublime clarity, who had expounded many of the secrets of the Law. For thousands of years Jews had studied the Law, and delved into its hidden treasures. How many books had they not written! Shelves and shelves of them, countless shelves. Why, he himself, Reb Meir'l, who was a dolt and an ignoramus compared with those great men, had done his share and written several books, adding his trifle of enlightenment to the infinite task of the Law. And perhaps he would be found worthy, after all, of a place at one of the tables. True, it would be the lowest place at the lowest table; still—he would be there. For the Almighty loves those who are preoccupied with the hidden meanings of the Law. But for all that, Reb Meir'l knew that much, much, remained yet to be made clear in the words of the Law. It was, in fact, as if the task had not even been begun. And how great the rejoicing would be when the Almighty, for whom the Law contained no secrets, would reveal to his saints all the depths and all the glories which had been beyond them!

Joy seized Reb Meir'l, a great joy which warmed all his old bones.

"*Ani maamin!* I believe!" he began to say aloud, fervently. "I believe in the coming of the Messiah! And though He delays, I wait for His coming every day, every hour, every second."

His eyes, turned upward, did not see the low, smoky ceiling; they saw a great illumination. The sound of pealing trumpets grew clearer in his ears. A mighty voice was drawing nearer and nearer. He heard shouting, whistling, crying, a multitude of voices. A chill crept into his heart. Still he waited. The voices drew still nearer, footsteps became clear, many footsteps. And suddenly the door was flung open and a horde of Jews rushed in.

"Rabbi!" loud, joyous voices announced. "Rabbi!"

Reb Meir'l leaped to his feet.

He has come! flashed through his mind. And the thought flashed from his mind through his body, through that frail, tense body which for so many years had suffered in the expectation of the Messiah. He is here!

There was a sudden crash at the door. Four bloody Jews staggered in, and flung to the floor a vast bundle of flesh and rags and hair which wailed in a loud voice.

"Rabbi!" thundered Abish the butcher. "I've found her! Reb Kanah the beadle's daughter, the whore!"

Reb Meir'l stood paralyzed, gripping with both hands the rail of the judgment table.

"Who are you?" he croaked at the butcher.

He did not recognize Abish, who came to him nearly every day with the liver and lungs of some animal, to find out whether they were defiled or not.

18

Zɪᴠʏᴀʜ, ᴛʜᴇ ʙᴇᴀᴅʟᴇ's ᴅᴀᴜɢʜᴛᴇʀ, ʟᴀʏ ᴏɴ ᴛʜᴇ ꜰʟᴏᴏʀ ɪɴ ꜰʀᴏɴᴛ of the judgment table, just as she had been flung there.

"Slut! Get up!" several voices cried. "How dare you lie on the floor in a house of judgment?"

She did not seem to hear; she lay there and howled like an animal.

Abish the butcher approached her with clenched fists. Reb Meir'l stopped him sternly.

"No force!" he said.

Reb Meir'l tried gentleness. Without looking straight at the girl, he addressed her. "You," he said. "Stand up. A human being should not lie on the floor, like an animal."

She did not answer him nor turn toward him.

The Rabbi's wife approached her.

"Maid!" she said. "Have you no shame in you? There are men in the room."

Zivyah did not answer.

The Rabbi's wife whipped off her big apron and covered the half-exposed legs of the girl.

"An idiot!" the Rabbi said pityingly, and looking round at the Jews, who were spitting in disgust and muttering curses, he added: "I will not have it! Jews are forbidden to curse!"

He turned and ordered someone to go for Zivyah's father, and then again began to question the girl.

"Daughter of Kanah," he said, "say whether what is said against you is true—that you have, Heaven defend us, sinned and played the whore."

The girl now lifted her eyes to him, but did not answer.

"You are silent!" the Rabbi went on. "You do not deny. It means, then, that you confess. If you confess, then declare before this Tribunal who the man is with whom you have sinned."

The girl lay silent and immobile.

"Do not be afraid," the Rabbi continued. "You are in my house, which is a house of judgment. No harm can befall you here. Did you sin willfully, out of your own wicked desire, or were you taken by violence, and did some man work evil upon you against your will?"

The girl looked at him out of wide-open eyes.

"For if evil was done unto you against your will, if force was used against you"—the Rabbi's voice dropped into the traditional chant, as if he were teaching a pupil—"if you cried out and no one heard your voice, then you are not guilty, for you have been afflicted against your will. So says the Holy Law. If a man find a woman in the field, and force her to lie with him, thou shalt do nothing to the woman. For as a man rises against his brother and slays him, so is this thing. For he found her in the field, and she cried out and there was none to help her."

The girl now watched with curious, childlike interest, as if some beautiful story were being read to her from a book.

"And even if," the Rabbi chanted, "even if it was not done with violence, but a man persuaded you, and you let yourself be persuaded, then you must declare to the Tribunal the name of the man. For he will then be called before the Tribunal and he will be judged according to the Holy Law. If he be unmarried, he shall be

compelled to marry you so that you shall not—God forbid!
—bring a bastard into the congregation. And if he be a man with
a wife, he shall be compelled to pay damage money to you and to
your father for the evil and the pain he has inflicted upon you, and
he shall be made to do penance for the great sin which he has
committed."

The girl continued to stare, open-eyed. It was the first time that
anyone had addressed such strange, musical words to her. She
liked it.

Reb Meir'l wrinkled his lofty forehead, and continued:

"And even if you were not persuaded with persuasive words,
but—God keep such things from Jewish daughters!—did this
thing of your own will, that is to say, you did desire the evil, then,
even then, you must also speak out the name of the sinner who
sinned with you, whether he be with or without wife, whether he
be an old man or a young man, a dweller in this town or a
stranger. For even then the Tribunal will bring the man here, and
compel him to take you to be his wife, or to recompense you with
money. Only speak out the truth, for you are in the presence of
the Tribunal, which is as if you were in the presence of the Almighty Himself."

She did not answer.

"Perhaps you are ashamed to confess in the presence of many,"
Reb Meir'l continued. "In that case you may go into another
room, or I shall compel these people to leave this room. And only
I and one other Jew will remain, according to the Law, to listen to
you."

Zivyah still lay on the floor, uttering no sound.

The sweat was pouring over Reb Meir'l's face. He took out his
handkerchief and dried himself. He turned now from the Law to
appeal to human emotions.

"You," he said, not knowing how to address her. "Because of
you and of the man with whom you have sinned, the little ones of
this city have been cut down before their time. The Tribunal must
know with whom you have played the whore. For the Tribunal
must purify the Congregation, in order that the anger of Heaven
may be turned from it. The lives of human beings are at stake; do
you not understand?"

Still there was no answer.

"You must not be frightened," the Rabbi pleaded, "if the man with whom you have sinned happens to be rich or powerful or strong and cruel, or if he gave you money for the sin. Because in the presence of the Tribunal the rich and the poor and the weak and the strong are alike; and the man of importance is like the man who flays carcases for a living. Confess your sin, and call out the name of the sinner. And the anger of Heaven shall be turned away from the innocent souls, from the little children, who have not committed any sin whatsoever."

The girl stared at the Rabbi, lifted her pinafore and blew her nose. The crowd lost all patience.

"Slut! Answer! It is the Rabbi who is talking to you!"

Abish the butcher could not contain himself any longer.

"Rabbi!" he begged. "Let me! I'll make her answer! I know how!"

But Reb Meir'l waved him away. Seeing that it was useless to plead, he raised his voice and addressed the girl sternly.

"Do not think," he cried, "that the Congregation will let this thing pass. You will be pursued and punished; you will be hunted like a wild animal. The child which you will bear will be a bastard, and it is written in the Holy Law that a bastard shall not come into the Congregation, and it is forbidden to anyone to marry a bastard. You too will not be taken by any man in marriage. You will be scorned and mocked, and you will bring shame upon your father's house. Your father may be driven from his place as beadle, for the sins of children are visited upon the parents. But if you will confess and you will name him who has sinned with you, we shall compel him to marry you, and the shame will be taken away from you and from the generations which you will bring forth. The Tribunal desires your welfare. Speak!"

Abish the butcher could stand it no longer. Unobserved by the Rabbi he had edged up close to the girl; suddenly he bent down, lifted her violently to her feet, and delivered two terrific slaps, one on each cheek.

"Answer, you whore! It's the Rabbi himself, God bless him, who's speaking to you."

He let go of her and she collapsed again, howling, kicking

furiously and uncovering her legs to the thigh. The room was in a tumult; the Rabbi spoke sternly to Abish the butcher, but his weak voice was lost in the angry, approving shouts of the audience. They liked Abish's methods better than the Rabbi's.

"Kill her!" they yelled. "Tear the skin off her!"

The girl might have been torn to pieces there and then if the door had not been flung open at this instant by Reb Kanah, her father. He came in, his lantern in one hand, his staff in the other, not like a suppliant, but erect, raging. He plunged into the crowd, thrusting men and women aside, till he stood at the center.

"What is this?" he roared. "Have you forgotten where you are? This is the house of the Rabbi, the Tribunal! Out of here, all of you!"

Not his voice or even his fists restored order, but his utterly unexpected insolence. He was not the responsible father of a sinful woman; he was Kanah, the beadle. The sudden silence of bewilderment descended on the packed room.

Kanah bent down and lifted up his daughter. He covered her bloody and tousled head with her shawl and, supporting her, turned toward Reb Meir'l.

"What is it you want of this poor orphan?" he asked, sharply. "Don't you see, all of you, that the poor thing is a cripple, an idiot, a helpless creature. Why don't you send for him, for the loon, the sinner in Israel. He's the man who ruined her."

The Rabbi's brow turned into a wide net of wrinkles.

"What loon?" he asked, startled. "What are you talking about, Kanah?"

"The loon, God blast his name!" the beadle shouted. "Yoshe the loon, my assistant. This is the way he has paid me for my kindness. I took him, when he was a homeless dog, into my house. I gave him food and put a roof over him—and this is his return."

"Yoshe?" The name was murmured in every corner of the room. "Yoshe—the Psalm-sayer? Yoshe the loon?"

The voice of Abish the butcher was suddenly heard. "The loon? Do you call that a loon? He's got too much sense—that's what's the matter with him!"

Reb Meir'l was black and white, like the walls of his own

judgment room which the community had not had whitewashed for many years. Woe unto the Jews of Bialogura! What unspeakable evil Satan had wrought here—and right under the Rav's nose, in his own synagogue! And he, the shepherd of the flock, had been blind. A beadle's daughter! With an assistant beadle! And the place! The cemetery itself, the House of Eternity! Great God! A Congregation so fallen could never be lifted up again!

The Rabbi stood leaning on the hard wooden arms of his chair.

"Kanah! Go at once and bring the assistant beadle to the Tribunal. At once!"

The order was unnecessary. Abish the butcher had already slipped out of the room, and with him half a dozen young butchers. They sped through the streets toward the synagogue, and the voice of Abish was heard, bellowing: "Loon! He's no loon. He's got too much sense, that's what he has, as I'm a born Jew!"

Yoshe the loon sat in the synagogue.

In all that congregation he was the only one who did not know that Zivyah, the daughter of Kanah the beadle, had been caught in sinfulness by Abish the butcher. He had been aware of an unrest; people were excited; they ran; they argued; they cursed; they laughed. But, as was his wont, he approached no one and asked nothing. His life was circumscribed by these things: his labors in the synagogue; the care of torn pages from sacred books, which he picked up carefully and stowed away in the attic; the rounds with the wooden hammer in the early morning; the chanting of Psalms all day long; the return to the cemetery in the evening; the saying of midnight prayers. Nothing else existed for him, and nothing else interested him. He spoke with no one of his own free will, only answering questions that were put to him. And, when he could, he answered with one word: Yes or No.

At this moment then, when the entire city was in a tumult, he sat apart from everyone, in the synagogue. He had filled all the barrels with water, arranged the books, carried away the torn pages; and now he sat near the door, reciting Psalms. The synagogue was deserted, and he was able to pray undisturbed. There were no errands to go, no rowdy Talmud students to pester him.

For the thousandth time he went through the entire book of Psalms, chapter by chapter, uttering every word clearly to himself, and fixing his mind on its meaning. Suddenly he was aware that the door had crashed open violently, and heavy boots were clattering on the wooden floor of the synagogue. Before he could rise to his feet, violent hands were laid on him.

"There he is! Grab him!"

He turned his frightened, astonished eyes from face to face, but he said nothing. He never interrupted a Psalm if he could help it; and just now he thought that this was another of the stupid jokes to which he had grown accustomed. More than once the Talmud students and others had laid hands on him, stretched him face downward on a bench and applied a strap to his rear. But this time Yoshe saw something in the faces, felt something in the hands which was quite out of the ordinary. Nor were these faces at all familiar to him; these men were not frequenters of his synagogue.

He made dumb noises, indicating that they must not force him to speak in the middle of his prayer. He lifted his arms toward them, but one hefty young fellow seized them, threw a belt about them and tied them fast. Yoshe became genuinely afraid.

"*Mafsik,*" he shouted in Hebrew, warning them against interrupting him.

The only answer was a burst of abuse and laughter.

"Stop playing the loon!" Abish shouted, furiously.

And another added: "Poor little saint; he just doesn't dare to speak in the middle of a prayer. You didn't wait with Zivyah till you finished your prayers, did you?"

The words were incomprehensible to him, and he could not imagine why they were addressed to him. One thing he did understand: that some terrible danger was hanging over him. There was too much hatred in the faces and voices of these strangers. He suddenly forgot his prayer and began to scream: "Help!"

As the word escaped his mouth Abish the butcher gave him a fearful blow in the face, so that on the instant the blood burst from his nose and lips and ran over the little black curls of his beard. He lost consciousness. This was the kind of blow with

which Abish the butcher used to quiet the more obstreperous
animals which were being led to slaughter.

"Pick him up! In fours!" Abish ordered.

They threw him on their shoulders as they had thrown Zivyah
on their shoulders, and in exactly the same way they carried him
through the street. He looked, in fact, like a slaughtered animal.
His hat had slipped from his head, which hung down sideways,
dripping blood.

"We've got him," Abish proclaimed through the streets. "And
he's not a loon either—got too much sense. We're taking him to
the Rabbi; let him play the loon there."

Crowds followed them, as they had followed Zivyah. Women
spat, and little boys threw stones.

"Stone him! Sinner in Israel! Murderer of innocent children."

Behind the procession ran a poor little Talmud student in a pair
of big charity boots, carrying Yoshe's blood-stained and muddy
hat.

19

FOR HOURS ON END THE JEWISH TRIBUNAL OF BIALOGURA QUES-
tioned Yoshe the loon and could get no straight answer from
him.

The Tribunal consisted of three judges. At the head sat the
Rabbi himself; on his right was Reb Shachnah, an assistant Rabbi,
a choleric man with a chronic catarrh who never stopped blowing
his nose into a huge red handkerchief. On the left of the Rabbi sat
Reb Tevel Borer, a timber merchant who was enough of a scholar
to be able to answer all questions of ritual, but who generally
refused to act in the capacity of Rabbi. On two long benches were

ranged the rich and influential householders of the community. Along the walls and round the oven were clustered the workers and poor people. The doors and windows were jammed with women, children and beggars.

The Rabbi began, as always, very gently.

When Yoshe was brought into the room, covered with blood, the Rabbi became pale.

"Shame!" he cried. "Blood! That is no way for Jews to behave! Shame on you!"

He came down from his bench, took Yoshe by the sleeve and led him into an ante-room where a barrel of water stood. He took up the copper dipper, and himself served Yoshe, helping him to wash.

"Woe is me!" he moaned, turning his head to one side. The sight and smell of human blood made him feel faint.

He helped Yoshe to wipe himself, led him back into the judgment room and even bade him sit down. Yoshe remained standing.

"Yoshe," he said, "a sin has been uncovered in the Congregation. The daughter of Kanah the beadle has played the whore, and she is pregnant with a bastard. Her father, Reb Kanah, says before this Tribunal that you are the guilty one; you, he says, persuaded her to it, and you sinned with her. I therefore ask you, is what he says true?"

Yoshe did not answer.

"Yoshe," said Reb Meir'l. "You stand before the Tribunal. You must answer when you are asked. I ask you: are the words of Reb Kanah true, or are you innocent of that sin?"

"I do not know," said Yoshe.

"What does that mean, you do not know?" Reb Meir'l asked, astounded. "You *must* know what the truth is."

"I do not know the truth," Yoshe answered, in a low voice.

Reb Meir'l thrust his hat back on his head.

"Yoshe," he said, "Reb Kanah accuses you of a mortal sin and crime. If you are innocent, you must show it, and keep your name clean. If you will remain silent, you will do yourself wrong. The Holy Law says that silence is equivalent to confession. Do you know that?"

"Yes."

"If that is so, what have you to say to the words of Reb Kanah?"

"Nothing."

Reb Meir'l the Rabbi felt himself growing hot. He knew Yoshe only vaguely and from a distance. He had noticed him in the synagogue, serving, or sitting at the door, reciting Psalms. Now he looked at him very closely, and the longer he looked the more uncomfortable he felt. There was something queer, something disturbing, about this town loon. Rabbi Meir'l was even slightly frightened by the man and his answers.

"Who are you?" he asked Yoshe, suddenly.

"I do not know."

There was laughter in the room. Reb Meir'l felt himself growing hotter.

"I do not understand this," he said, and became silent.

Reb Tevel the timber-merchant, the third member of the Tribunal, made the next attempt. He approached the matter coldly, factually, like a merchant. First he banged the desk, and exclaimed: "Order here!" and then turned toward Yoshe.

"Yoshe, tell the Tribunal where you come from."

"I come from the world."

"And why did you come to our city?"

"I do not know."

"What do you want here in our midst?"

"Nothing."

"Who are you? Are you an orphan, or have you parents? Are you single or are you a widower? Are you divorced, or have you left a wife somewhere?"

"I am a stone," Yoshe answered.

The laughter was louder this time. Reb Tevel did not even rebuke the audience.

"A loon," he said, audibly. "Impossible to talk with him."

Reb Shachnah, the assistant Rabbi, blew his nose violently, angrily, and turned furiously to the task.

"Yoshe, can you deny, in the presence of the Tribunal, that you have slept nights in the house of Reb Kanah?"

"No," Yoshe answered, in a low voice.

Reb Shachnah's nose became redder with satisfaction; he was getting the Tribunal somewhere at last.

"Yoshe," he said, "you are not a scholar. But you are able to read, and therefore you know that a Jew may not remain alone with a woman, not even if she is a virgin."

"Yes."

"Then, if you know, why did you remain alone with her? Why did you not avoid it?"

"I don't know."

"If that is the case, Reb Kanah the beadle may properly suspect you of this sin."

"Yes."

Reb Shachnah grabbed himself by the beard with both hands.

"You admit then Zivyah is pregnant by you?"

"No."

"But you have admitted, have you not, that one may properly suspect you."

"Yes."

"But if you yourself say that you may properly be suspected, we are justified in interpreting this to mean you confess."

"I do not know."

Reb Shachnah flew into such a rage that he nearly pulled his nose off with his red handkerchief.

"Sinner!" he yelled. "Answer plainly!"

He rose in his place and thrust his two arms out of their wide sleeves. It looked as if he was going to run over to Yoshe and assault him. But Reb Meir'l caught him by the arm, and said:

"No anger, God forbid."

Reb Shachnah mastered himself, sat down again and began on a new tack.

"Yoshe," he said, trying to keep his voice calm, "how old are you?"

"I don't know."

"You mean you don't remember. All right. But you are certainly not a child. You are a grown man. Why have you no wife?"

"I do not know."

"Is it because you are not—God save us—all a man; because you are crippled?"

"No."

"You are then, a normal man, with normal instincts and normal appetites?"

"Yes."

"Why have you not taken a wife to yourself, as all Jews do? Why did you not ask this congregation to find some poor orphan for you?"

"I don't know."

"What then—are you stronger than the evil impulse?"

"No."

"You confess, then, that Zivyah is pregnant by you?"

"No."

Reb Shachnah grabbed himself again by the beard.

"Sinner!" he yelled. "Heathen! Insolent!"

Reb Meir'l tried to stop him, but Reb Shachnah did not lower his voice.

"Yoshe," he went on yelling, "the Tribunal knows that Kanah's daughter has had nothing to do with other men. Confess your sin, or you will rue it."

Yoshe remained silent.

Reb Shachnah leaned over and shook a warning finger.

"Yoshe! If you will confess, the Tribunal will exonerate you; and you will be married to the daughter of Reb Kanah. The Congregation will even gather a little money for you, so that you may take up some business and provide for your wife. If you will confess and do penance, you will be forgiven; and in the fullness of time, after a hundred and twenty years, you may even become the beadle of the synagogue. Or you may become the sexton and grave-digger. But if you will remain obstinate, you will be tied hand and foot in the yard of the synagogue, and in the presence of the entire Congregation you will receive the lash."

Yoshe was silent. Reb Shachnah shook his finger still more violently in Yoshe's face; it was the finger, crowned with a long nail, with which he was wont to test the sharpness of the slaughterer's knives, to see if they met ritualistic requirements.

"Do not imagine," he cried, "that this will be all. When we are done with you we will turn you over to the Gentiles. They will bind you in chains and send you away to Siberia. Such a sinner in

Israel may in all virtue be turned over to the Gentiles."

Yoshe was silent.

Reb Shachnah tried his last threat.

"Yoshe! You will be sent away into the army."

But this too failed to elicit an answer from Yoshe.

Reb Shachnah collapsed in his chair, looked round and said weakly: "He has exhausted me completely. Let me rest a little."

Abish the butcher, standing near the wall, began to stamp furiously. Like a dog straining at the leash, he had been growling in his throat.

"Rabbi!" he burst out. "Let me! If I get him into my hands I'll chop the words out of him."

An approving shout went up from the audience. Men's and women's voices were lifted ferociously.

"Let him! Slaughter the sinner! For the little ones he has murdered."

Again the Rabbi interfered. "Kanah," he said sharply, "bring your daughter before the bench. Perhaps she will say something direct to the accused."

Reb Meir'l had not much faith in his own suggestion, nor had the audience. A murmur went through the room; most of those present had sat through the first cross-examination of Zivyah. "What does he think he'll get out of her now?" they asked each other.

But something unexpected happened now. When Zivyah was brought before the bench, she seemed to be a different woman. Instead of opposing a brutish silence and indifference to all questions, she seemed to be alert to whatever was happening, and at the signal from her father answered without hesitation.

"Come, Zivyah," her father said firmly and quietly. "The Rabbi wishes to speak with you."

Zivyah took hold of her father's sleeve and approached the bench.

"Cover your head," her father said. "You may not stand like that in the presence of a Rabbi."

Zivyah shoved the shawl forward over her head.

"The Rabbi himself is going to question you," her father said.

"You must not be afraid of him—he is a Rabbi, bless him, and he won't do you any harm. You must answer him, do you hear?"

"Yes. Good." She nodded eagerly.

The Rabbi addressed her as if she were a little child. Pointing to Yoshe, he asked:

"Do you know that Jew?"

Zivyah giggled, and nodded again. "I know," she said.

"What is his name?"

"Yoshe the loon," she said, proudly. Her face lit with joy, as if she had forgotten everything that had happened to her before.

"You must not," said the Rabbi patiently, "call a Jew by such names. His name is Yoshe."

"Yes, Yoshe." She giggled once more.

The Rabbi took courage. Turning to his colleagues, he murmured: "She's answering like a human being now." But now came the difficult part of his cross-examination of Zivyah. He could not address her by her name; he had never uttered a woman's name. And the questions he had to put were delicate. He hesitated before speaking.

"Tell the Tribunal," he began, embarrassed, "whether this man, Yoshe, ever remained alone with you."

The girl giggled, louder than before. Her father gave her a stern look. "Don't laugh, Zivyah," he ordered. "The Rabbi is asking you whether Yoshe ever remained alone with you in the same room. He did remain alone with you sometimes in the night, when I used to be called out to see about someone who had died?"

The girl nodded. "Yes! Yes!"

Reb Meir'l uttered the next question with great difficulty.

"Did he ever try to behave indecently toward you?"

The girl did not understand. She stuffed a corner of the shawl into her mouth to prevent herself from giggling aloud. The Rabbi tried again.

"I mean," he asked, "did he behave lightly and frivolously toward you? Did he ever take you by the hand? Did he ever try to persuade you? Did he ever say he would be your husband?"

The girl took the corner of the shawl from her mouth. In the full presence of the Tribunal and the audience, she sidled toward

Yoshe, just as she had been wont to do in her father's room, and touched him with her body and her hands.

"Husband!" She had caught this word. "Yoshe, Zivyah's husband—Yoshe. . . ." She burst into laughter which resembled the neighing of a horse.

A fierce hum rose in the room. "Listen! Did you hear that?"

There was not the slightest doubt in anyone's mind, not even in the mind of Reb Meir'l. He had, indeed, been convinced before, but he was doing his duty in obtaining the last piece of decisive evidence.

He went further.

"Kanah's daughter," he said suddenly, addressing her for the first time, and with the title which was used for respectable and decent women. "Tell the Tribunal if between you and Yoshe occurred that which must occur only between husband and wife."

She did not understand.

Reb Meir'l tried simpler language.

"Did he unite himself with you?"

Still she did not understand.

For a few moments Reb Meir'l rubbed his hat back and forth over his head. He sought a word which would pierce through the thick mind of the girl before him. He became red, and he felt a sudden, uncomfortable heat in all his limbs. And in his embarrassment he returned to the simplest of the words in the Bible.

"Did he lie with you?" he asked.

The girl shoved the corner of the shawl back into her mouth and choked back her wild giggling. Kanah the beadle suddenly struck the bench and in a voice which boded evil thundered, "Zivyah! Answer!"

"Lie with me," she gabbled. "Yoshe—on the oven—up there."

The fierce humming rose again, swelled into a shout. In vain did Reb Meir'l thump the bench with his fists. The voice of Abish rose above the others: "I tell you he's no loon."

Men began to close in from the walls. In an instant Reb Meir'l was at Yoshe's side. "Jews!" he cried. "Go to your homes! The Tribunal, with the help of God, will do whatever must be done, and the Congregation will be informed of it."

It needed the combined efforts of the Tribunal and of Reb Kanah to clear the room. Abish the butcher was the last to be cleared out. He kept begging: "Rabbi, let me stay in a corner! Let me hide behind the oven. You won't even see me."

But no one except the Tribunal remained in that room, not even Kanah, the father of Zivyah. The moment the three judges were alone, Reb Meir'l, with the lightness and energy of a boy, pulled the stepladder over to one of the bookcases, ascended rapidly and brought down several large, dusty, leather-bound volumes. He opened them on the bench, and the three men sat down to discuss the case.

They sat through the night, consulting and arguing.

The case was not an easy one. The guilt of Yoshe was clearly established in the minds of Reb Meir'l and his assistants. But, in the last analysis, there were no witnesses; and the law demanded the evidence of witnesses who had been present during the commission of the crime. On the other hand, the orphan girl had made a clear statement before the Tribunal. Still, there was a good reason for discounting her evidence; she was directly involved in the case. But, again, the girl was a simpleton, and therefore it was to be deduced that she had spoken the truth. If Yoshe had at least denied it! But he had denied nothing. He had answered all questions evasively—half answers, meaningless answers, with no denial in them.

The case would have been infinitely more difficult, however, if the woman had been the wife of some man, or even if it was suspected that somewhere a husband of hers still lived. But they were dealing now with an unmarried girl. True, there could be a doubt as to whether Yoshe himself was married or not. No one really knew who he was and what he was. In the city of Bialogura he was accepted as a bachelor, and there was no reason to think that he was not. Therefore he could be accepted as such. But even if this was not the case, if Yoshe was not a bachelor, it was not an insuperable difficulty. For according to the Holy Law a Jew may have several wives. Monogamy was not a law but a custom, and it dated only from the time of the injunction of the great and saintly Rabbi Gershom. In the Holy Land there were still pious and saintly Jews who had two wives. And the Tribunal had to bear in mind that the destiny of a Jewish girl was involved, a Jewish orphan whom it must, if it only could, rescue from eternal shame.

These points were argued and clarified through the long hours of the night. The final decision, however, was definitely the result of an inspiration. Reb Meir'l suddenly remembered that in a time of visitation such as this, it was recommended that a community commend itself to the mercy of the Almighty by the performance of a specially virtuous act—to wit, the marrying off, in the cemetery, of a poor boy and girl. Indeed, the poorest, the most obscure and most forlorn were chosen—such as, without the intervention of the community, could never have achieved the holy state of wedlock: fools, cripples, God save us, a woman beyond marriageable age, or even a fallen woman, and a man whom no woman would look at. For the sake of such an act of charity and humanity, said Reb Meir'l, the anger of Heaven would be withdrawn. And he recalled the many cases in which pestilences had been arrested in Jewish communities by just this specific.

Yes, the more he talked, the more obvious it became that the hand of Providence had arranged this situation; Heaven had shown them the way out. He closed the heavy books and, a great light shining on his weary face, he said to his assistants:

"I say that this is the only answer. We will marry them off at once, and in the grounds of the House of Eternity. For the sake of this good deed, the anger of Heaven will be stilled."

Reb Shachnah was impressed. He blew his nose and said: "They have lit this fire. They shall extinguish it."

Reb Tevel stretched his aching limbs and smiled briefly.

"A very suitable settlement," he said. "What could be more suitable than an idiot and a loon?"

Greenish light of dawn filtered in through the window and lit their haggard faces. Rabbi Meir'l looked out, frowning. He was wondering whether there was enough light by which to distinguish between a blue thread and a green; if there was, then, according to the law, it was time for the earliest morning prayer. Not that this helped him much, for in the best of lights Reb Meir'l was not quite sure which was green and which was blue.

"What do you think, gentlemen?" he asked his assistants. "Is it time yet for the first prayer?"

In the outer room Yoshe the loon lay sleeping near the barrel. Utterly exhausted, he did not wake up at his usual hour when it was his duty to make the rounds of the community and call Jews to prayer. The first light of morning touched his childlike face with fantastic blue and green colors.

20

IN A SPIRIT OF GREAT FAITH, WITH ENTHUSIASM AND GENEROSITY, the community of Bialogura celebrated, on the cemetery grounds, the marriage of Zivyah, daughter of Kanah the beadle, to Yoshe the loon, assistant beadle in the Great Synagogue.

For no sooner had the Rabbi pronounced from the pulpit, the very morning after the trial, the decision of the Tribunal, and the principal reason for it—to wit, that it was a specific against the pestilence—than all the men and women of Bialogura saw in Zivyah and Yoshe the salvation of the afflicted community. Where the doctors and Reb Boruch'l had failed, these two would succeed; what the prayers, the girdling of the cemetery with linen and candle-wicks had not done, this marriage would do. The market-place, the synagogue, the streets echoed with the praises of Reb Meir'l.

"A saint!" they said. "A saint and a sage. Such an idea could have come to him only from heaven itself."

And the hatred toward the two sinners, the half-wit girl and the simple-minded Yoshe, was converted on the instant into pity, and even affection.

"The poor orphans!" women sighed, and busied themselves with the preparations. They were going to make this wedding in the cemetery a grand and joyous affair, a credit to themselves, an irresistible appeal to heaven. The welfare of Zivyah and Yoshe became a matter of concern to everyone; God forbid that anything happen to them before the marriage. God forbid, above all, that Yoshe the loon take it into his head to run away from Bialogura, disgrace the town again and bring further evil upon it.

His behavior troubled them. Not a trace of joy, or even of relief, was visible on his face. He was as silent as ever. And the Jews of Bialogura tried to draw him out. They treated him with the consideration and respect due to a bridegroom of high social standing. They invited him to their homes for supper. They forbade the students in the synagogue to tease him; and when one student flung the mocking question at him: "Hey, Yoshe! Was it nice on top of the oven?" he was set upon by older Jews, who cried: "Heathen! Leave him in peace! He is a bridegroom!"

To all these overtures Yoshe paid no attention. He would not accept any invitation; he would not be drawn into conversation. Day after day he sat near the door, murmuring Psalms. At night he slept on a bench in the synagogue.

"Yoshe!" they said to him. "You have done penance enough. It is not proper for a bridegroom to be downcast. It is proper for him to rejoice."

But Yoshe would not rejoice. If anything, he became darker, gloomier than before. Pious and godly women brought him hot meals into the synagogue. He would not touch them. He chewed on a piece of hard bread, drank water after it and made long benedictions. He spoke with no one. Only from time to time he would go to the window and stare out at the open fields. The Jews observed him and trembled. They divided the day into watches and stationed responsible men with him. He could not even go into the yard without being accompanied.

"It is dangerous for a bridegroom to be alone," they said soothingly to him.

There was not a woman in Bialogura who was not taking part

in the preparations for the wedding; but busiest of all were the women of well-to-do households and the wives of synagogue officials.

The last batches of linen which were used for the girdling of the cemetery were converted into shirts, cushion covers, bed-sheets and table-cloths for the bride and bridegroom. Groups of women met, to measure, cut and sew. Pious brides went so far as to adorn the collars of Zivyah's night-shirts with attractive patterns in red. And poor women, with elderly, unmarriageable daughters on their hands, murmured enviously: "The luck of that girl!"

Abish the butcher, who had been ready to tear Yoshe limb from limb, was the most active of the men. With a big sack slung over his shoulders, he made the rounds of the houses, gathering gifts for the bridegroom: *capotes*, prayer-shawl and phylacteries, hats, skull-caps, even girdles. And he would take nothing but the best.

"No old things, please," he said. "Nothing torn or patched. It's not decent to offer them to a bridegroom."

The Burial Brotherhood sent out men with baskets among the shops and stalls of the market-place. They gathered flour and eggs, raisins and goose-fat, for the wedding. The women gave generous portions.

"God have mercy on us all," they said, lifting their eyes to heaven. "May this be a redemption from our affliction."

Mothers whose children had died in the pestilence gathered up the little shirts and dresses of their dead, and brought them to the pregnant bride. "You'll be needing them soon," they said. The special virtue of this kind of gift was the protection of the living.

The richest women of the town descended on the Widow Shprintze, the cake-baker, commandeered her oven, and baked the wedding cakes and loaves. They did everything with their own hands; they even brought the water from the river. They could not feel themselves intimately enough associated with the good deed which was being done in Bialogura. They could not make the cakes rich enough, and almost spoiled them with excess of eggs and sugar.

On the day of the wedding, which was a Tuesday—a lucky day—the shops and stalls of Jewish Bialogura were closed. Not a man, woman or child, of whatever age, of whatever social standing, was to be absent from the wedding. The preparations of that morning were proportionately generous—a whole city was to be entertained; and only the city could cope with the preparations. There was such baking and frying and cooking in Bialogura as had never been witnessed before. Abish the butcher collected from his section of the town whole sides of beef and dozens of hens and geese. The fishermen were sent out to the river, with instructions to bring in the greatest haul of their lives. Samson the healer and musician gathered his orchestra and trained them for days in new wedding marches and bridal music. Every *cheder* in Bialogura was closed.

In streets and homes the phrase *mazel-tov*—good luck—was heard on all hands. "Good luck to all of us! Good luck to the Jewish people! Let God's mercy come upon this Congregation, for the sake of this poor couple!"

Ambitious girls, anxious to look their best at the wedding, washed their hair the night before in fresh river-water. Daughters of well-to-do homes lent out their woolen Sabbath clothes to poor seamstresses and servant girls, to enable them to attend; they themselves laid out their finest silks and satins. The mothers of well-to-do homes went, in this riot of piety, to help the poorer girls put on the clothes, and looked at them uneasily as they drew on their unaccustomed finery.

"Girl," they said, "by the grace of this great event let the city of Bialogura be helped; it is proper that you should look your best there."

And at midday the entire community streamed out toward the cemetery.

Chassidic Jews, followers of wonder-working Rabbis, wore satin *capotes* and velvet hats. Working folk came in their Sabbath *capotes* of broadcloth, split behind, and broadcloth caps on their heads. Rich housewives, in silk and satin, took down from the shelves the lace which they had worn at their own weddings. Young wives put on their finest hats, old-fashioned structures of wire and buckram and gauze, on which gay birds were perched with outstretched wings ready for flight. All the brooches, necklaces, diamond pins, earrings and bracelets in all the jewelry boxes of Bialogura were taken to the cemetery that day. Yente, the money-lender, opened her heart that day, and loaned out to needy housewives the jewelry which they had in pawn with her.

Rich girls put on white stockings and patent-leather slippers, and carried little, highly colored umbrellas delicately, as if they were made of glass. Poor girls in borrowed clothes blushed as they met acquaintances, and prayed to God that the clothes they wore might be mistaken for their own. Their hair was twisted up in a stiff, damp coil, with a colored cockade at the tip.

A space round Kanah's house, which adjoined the purification room in which the dead were washed, had been covered with fresh, yellow sand. Chinese lanterns dangled from the branches of the trees—the special work of *cheder* boys. Young girls had adorned Kanah's room with paper flowers; they had converted a plain chair into a throne by covering it with plush; and on this throne sat Zivyah in her new white wedding dress. Her face was washed, her hair combed; she neighed and giggled alternately with the sheer joy of it all.

Samson the healer outdid himself that day. He wore a German topcoat, with ribbons dangling from the sleeves and lapels; he had a four-cornered silken skull-cap on his head; his beard was newly trimmed, and through the cleft of it shone a streak of white chin. He worked, indeed, as if he were ministering to the richest couple in town. He played his flute, directed his orchestra, and broke in with genuine improvisations after the approved fashion of traditional wedding jesters.

> Musicians, the best that is in you
> Serve up on the musical menu!
> Play up your tenderest, fiddle,
> For the daughter of Kanah the beadle!

Women pushed their way through the over-crowded room to greet the bride. "*Mazel-tov*, bride," they said sentimentally, and kissed her. "*Mazel-tov*," gabbled Zivyah right and left.

Richer girls competed for the privilege of calling the dances.

"Reb Samson! A waltz. Ten kopecks for a good waltz."

"Twenty kopecks for a polka-mazurka, Reb Samson!"

They danced stiffly, haughtily, one arm delicately round the partner's waist, one arm in the air, little finger held delicately aloof and aloft. Reb Samson blew into his flute until his face was purple. The louder he blew, the haughtier grew the attitude of the dancers. They looked severely at one another, with pursed lips, a touch-me-not expression on their faces. It was their idea of grand, ball-room behavior.

Unfortunately they could not dissuade Zivyah from joining the dancers.

"Bride, bride," they said to her, gently. "A bride should rest; she is weak."

But Zivyah bellowed to Reb Samson, "More! More! It's good! Zivyah likes it!"

The men sat outside, since the one room was monopolized by the women. Barrels had been placed in rows under the trees, long boards were laid from barrel to barrel, and the improvised table was covered with a cloth. Cakes, fruits, jams, jellies, wines and whiskies were set profusely on the tables.

"*Mazel-tov*, bride and bridegroom! *Mazel-tov*, Yoshe!"

But, as if Zivyah's joy was enough, and more than enough, for both of them, Yoshe sat at the table silent and morose. They could not force a single sentence out of him. His mouth was clamped tight; his eyes looked starkly in front of him. He let them do with him whatever they liked; but he himself was not a participant. He let them take him to the ritual bath; he let them clothe him in new clothes from head to foot; he let them conduct him to the cemetery; still silently, as though mind and body were of two persons, he let them place him at the head of the elaborately set table, in the midst of the most prominent and most important members of the Congregation.

They did their best to bring life into him; they were not only oppressed, but a little frightened by his silence. It was a bad omen. So they leaned over him, jested, clapped their hands and insisted:

"It is the duty of a bridegroom to be merry. Bridegroom, rejoice!"

Samson the healer undertook to perform what the important citizens at the head of the table could not do. He brought the orchestra over right in front of Yoshe; it was a famous fact that the gloomiest soul in Bialogura could not hold out against Samson and his orchestra if he had a mind to make everyone laugh, and Samson was in that humor now. New jests, improvised rhymes and witty epigrams poured from him. He contorted himself, turned his *capote* inside out and made fantastic flourishes with his flute while he kept his lips glued to the mouthpiece. Yoshe was unmoved. Young workers who had taken several glasses of whiskey shoved the tips of their beards forward into their mouths, lifted up the skirts of their *capotes*, and went off into a genuine Russian *kazatzky*. The audience was convulsed with laughter; even Reb Meir'l permitted himself a chuckle. But on Yoshe's pale face there was not a glimmer of amusement or even of interest; it was as stony and as immovable as when he had stood before the Tribunal.

The wedding, though lavish, was shorter than most weddings. The Jews of Bialogura did not want to drag it out beyond evening. They would not remain in the cemetery at night.

Close by the mausoleum of the sainted grandfather of Reb Boruch'l, where on winter nights bundles of wool had made a bed for Zivyah and the smugglers, the bridal canopy was erected. To the tune of a lively march which Samson had picked up from the orchestra of the Cossacks, a long procession of Jews and Jewesses bearing lighted candles conducted the bride and bridegroom to the canopy.

A short, unpleasant incident occurred during the march.

A young woman, the mother of a child who had died in the pestilence, caught sight of the new grave, and dashing out of the line flung herself on the little mound with an hysterical cry.

"Chaim'l, little one! What have I done with you? Where have I left you?"

Other women dropped their candles and began to wail with her.

But the Rabbi himself, Reb Meir'l, sternly interfered.

"Women!" he ordered. "There must be no weeping now! At this wedding there must be only rejoicing!"

Samson gave the signal to his orchestra to redouble its din. The wailing of the women was drowned out by the music.

"Bravo!" men shouted aloud. "Long live bride and bridegroom! Long live Samson and his music!"

Some women picked up a huge wedding loaf, covered with gilding in a gay design of birds and flowers, and holding it aloft in a circle of hands, broke into a dance, shouting:

> Hip! Hop! Bride and Bridegroom!
> Hip! Hop! Bride and Bridegroom!

Men tried to snatch the loaf from their hands; the women thrust the men away and went on dancing.

Little girls made a wheel of their own, spun round, singing shrilly:

> From the attic to the cellar
> Put new things in every room,
> All in honor of the bride,
> All in honor of the groom.

Zivyah could scarcely stand still under the canopy; she wanted to go on dancing. Yoshe stood at her side, rigid, unheeding. He did not even move when they made the bride hold out her finger to him for the ring.

"Bridegroom!" the Rabbi ordered, cheerfully. "Sanctify the bride to you forever!"

He did not move. Two men lifted his hand for him, and somehow the ring was on Zivyah's finger. No one heard him say the words which made Zivyah his wife: "Behold thou art consecrated unto me according to the Law of Moses and of Israel." There was too much shouting and urging. Only Kanah the beadle asserted loudly: "Yes, he said them! I heard him!"

The Rabbi wrinkled his forehead, hesitated and accepted the word of the beadle.

"Be it so," he said at last. "*Mazel-tov!*"

At the table, after the ceremony, Yoshe touched no food. The bowl of golden soup, from which bride and bridegroom must eat together, so that their married life be golden, was placed before them. Zivyah dipped and swallowed noisily, rubbed her hands together and jogged Yoshe with her elbow.

"Yoshe! Good! Soup! Yoshe!"

Nor did he answer the loud toast of *"L'chaim!"*—to life!—which sounded on every side of him. And when the Rabbi himself proffered his hand, he did not seem to see it.

"Well," they said angrily, among themselves, "what can you expect of a loon?"

The wedding broke up and the guests hastened from the place before twilight had fallen. In spite of the merriment and the drinking, they all felt better at a distance from the stone wall of the cemetery. Only when the crowd approached town did some bethink themselves of certain things which had been better left unthought—certain things concerning a bride who was pregnant at the ceremony. Thoughts like these were unfit for the sacred precincts of the cemetery.

When the crowd was gone, Kanah the beadle systematically gathered up the remaining food and carried it into the house. He had already gathered up all the presents, all the gifts of cash; the latter he counted now and thrust the money into his pocket.

"Children!" he said, generously. "Tonight you may sleep in the beds. I shall sleep this time on the oven."

Zivyah flung herself, all dressed, on her bed. The day had exhausted her; she had eaten, gabbled, danced with the liveliest of the guests. At other times she might still have had strength left; in her present condition it had all been used up.

Yoshe did not move toward his bed. He stood erect near the door, listening to the double snoring, one a deep, choking bass, the other a thin snarling. He heard the rustling of the trees outside, and at intervals the shrilling of the grill behind the oven. A long time he stood motionless. Then, when the clock gathered up its works and sounded out many hours, he shuffled over into a corner, and began to fumble for his old clothes. In the dark he changed. He found his stick and his sack, and made certain that in the sack still lay his phylacteries and the stone to give the bottom of the sack weight. He went quietly to the door and slipped out.

In the morning, when Zivyah woke and saw the bed opposite her empty, she let out a wail which roused her father out of his sleep. Instinctively Zivyah felt that something dreadful had happened.

Kanah the beadle crawled down from the top of the oven, picked up his staff and his lantern—though it was already light outside—and went out hastily.

First he looked through the cemetery. From the cemetery he ran to the synagogue, and from the synagogue though all the streets which Yoshe covered when he called the Jews to prayer. There was no sign of Yoshe. Kanah ran to the house of Abish the butcher, and Abish woke all his fellow-butchers and sent them out at once on all the roads and lanes leading away from Bialogura.

They did not find Yoshe.

Kanah came home that evening with the knowledge that Yoshe would not return.

"There'll be no more Yoshe," he said to his daughter. "You are an *agunah*—an abandoned wife."

He made his daughter put a poor, gray shawl on the wig above her shaven head, and a broad apron on her stomach—like all married women. In the city they no longer called her by her father's name, but by her husband's.

"Zivyah, Yoshe the loon's Zivyah," was her name.

BOOK THREE

21

In nyesheve, in the big wooden synagogue which had been erected temporarily after the great fire, but which, after fifteen years, had not been replaced by a synagogue of stone, hundreds of out-of-town Chassidim were assembled.

It was the twelfth day of the month of Tamuz, the anniversary of the death of the most famous Rabbi of Nyesheve, the grandfather of the present incumbent, Reb Melech. On this day innumerable candles were lit round the grave of the saint, and Jews came from scores of towns and villages to place their prayer-notes in the tomb. Scribes sat at tables in the open, writing the notes rapidly and chaffering over the price. Suppliants paid according to their ability, or according to the obstinacy of the scribe. Women, their heads and half their faces covered with shawls, lingered in the rear of the crowd, afraid or ashamed to push themselves forward in the presence of so many men. They stood at a distance from the grave, like beggars at a wedding. On the outskirts of the crowd peddlers sold paper and ink, candles, cakes and even small bottles of whiskey. It was meritorious to take a drink and to wish Jews good luck here, on sacred soil.

Rabbi Melech himself came that day to visit the grave of his grandfather. He was a very old man now—somewhere in the eighties; his wrinkled skin was greenish with age; his beard and ear-locks were like thick white dust which gathers in neglected corners of a room. When he walked, two men supported him, one at each side, holding him under the armpits.

That day, as he came into the cemetery, Israel Avigdor preceded him, calling out continuously: "Jews! Order! Make a path! The Rabbi is coming!"

Israel Avigdor's beard was now more gray than red; but his body had lost none of its vigor. He took stronger and stronger snuff, which he soaked in whiskey and mixed with fine pepper. He drank great quantities of mead.

His devotion to Rabbi Melech had grown with the passing of the years. The Rabbi was a weak old man. Very often he failed to recognize his oldest Chassidim—even the richest and most important of them. His sons, elderly Jews, had waited long and impatiently for their day; and having waited too long, they now anticipated their rights. They were no longer afraid of their father. They held court openly, gave feasts, attracted followers of their own, dispensed blessings and distributed favors. They competed with one another and with their father for the great following of the Rabbinate of Nyesheve.

Israel Avigdor had watched all this with impotent rage and pain. He knew that a Rabbinic court was—he spat out piously when he made the base comparison—like a royal court. The power of the dynasty should always be concentrated in one man; a divided territory becomes the prey of outsiders. He also knew that he, Israel Avigdor, was hated by all the sons and daughters of Rabbi Melech; and he returned their hatred in full. They were also afraid of him; he knew too much. But the Rabbi was very old. And Israel Avigdor guarded him like the apple of his eye.

When the Rabbi returned that day to his apartment, the Chassidim remained assembled in the wooden synagogue. Newcomers joined them, and the place grew more crowded. There was a babble of voices; while some prayed, others talked business, and still others drank and wished themselves and one another and all the Jewish people good luck.

A strange figure was suddenly perceived at the door of the synagogue—a tall, lean Jew, with coal-black beard and ear-locks, and big, deep-set black eyes. His tattered clothes were covered with the dust of the road. Round his waist he wore, instead of a girdle, a piece of plain rope. The sack which was flung over his shoulders was as patched and as dusty as his clothes. His shoes gaped. He leaned with his right hand on a heavy, knobby staff, which was too high for him. At the door, with a hundred pairs of eyes on him, he paused, transferred his staff to his left hand, and with his right touched the *mezuzah* on the door post, then kissed his fingers. Slowly he let the sack slip to the floor, walked over to the barrel of water, turned the tap and washed his black hands.

A number of Jews approached him.

"*Sholom aleichem,*" they said.

"*Aleichem sholom,*" he answered.

"Where do you come from?"

"From the world."

The abrupt words and the low, decisive voice had something disturbing about them. They stared at him and put other questions, but the stranger turned from them without an answer. They watched him take out of his sack his prayer-shawl and phylacteries. They saw him slip the prayer-shawl over his head in a way of his own, and noticed with some awe that he had double phylacteries. The stranger stood alone near the door and prayed in silence.

When he had finished and had folded up the prayer-shawl and phylacteries, they approached him again and offered him a piece of cake and a glass of whiskey. He shook his head, saying nothing.

"You may take," they said. "Today is the anniversary of the great Rabbi's death, his memory be a blessing to us."

"I know," the stranger said.

He turned from them, lifted his sack, and took out several pieces of dried bread and some salt wrapped in a rag. These he put down on the bench, went over to the barrel and washed his hands again. Between washing and eating he repeated long prayers silently. Then he dipped the bread in the salt, and ate. He went again to the barrel and drank from the copper ladle. When he had finished the benediction after eating, he wrapped up his food again and turned to the nearest Jew.

"Is Israel Avigdor still *gabbai* here?" he asked.

"Certainly!" several voices answered.

"I wish to see him."

"He'll be here soon," they answered. "He is with the Rabbi now."

"Send someone for him," the stranger said, "and tell him to come at once. Tell him he has a visitor."

His quiet command overawed them. Without further question, two or three Jews left the synagogue and went across the yard. Meanwhile the stranger looked round, at every corner of the wooden building. Then he turned to the astonished Jews with a question.

"Was this built after the fire?"

Young boys, who did not remember the fire, smiled. Older Jews gave him the answer.

"Yes—after the fire, God save us!"

When Israel Avigdor came in, the stranger strode up to him and proffered his hand.

"*Sholom aleichem*, Israel Avigdor."

Israel Avigdor looked the tattered stranger up and down, and his face blazed with anger.

"Who are you?" he asked sharply, addressing the man in the contemptuous second person singular.

"A visitor," the stranger answered, as if unaware of the insult.

"What do you want?"

"I want to see the Rabbi."

The blood flowed from behind Israel Avigdor's ears into his face.

"What!" he snapped. "Nothing less than that? Is there anything else you would like? The Rabbi's waiting for you, of course!"

Israel Avigdor glared first at the stranger and then at the crowd of Jews standing in a circle. But not a single face showed any response to his angry irony.

"Israel Avigdor!" the stranger answered. "Go at once to the Rabbi and tell him I am waiting. I have come a long way."

The blood retreated from Israel Avigdor's face. He turned pale. The stranger's composure, his fantastic appearance and his fantastic words—"I have come a long way"—smote him suddenly.

Something like fear seized him. Israel Avigdor had been *gabbai* in Nyesheve a great many years. He was not easily imposed upon. But he had drunk with dozens of Chassidim that day, and it was the anniversary of the most illustrious and the saintliest of the Rabbis of Nyesheve.

Queer thoughts began to dance in his head under the steadfast look of the stranger, recollections of legends concerning the thirty-six hidden saints, who appear among men in all guises, of legends concerning Elijah the prophet himself, who took on unexpected forms and surprised Jews at the unlikeliest times and in the unlikeliest places. He thought even of the dead. . . . "*I have come a long way.*"

His anger was gone.

"Very good," he said. "What name shall I give the Rabbi? Who wishes to see him?" Israel Avigdor no longer used the contemptuous singular form.

"A Jew—a visitor."

He led the stranger respectfully across the yard into the anteroom before the Rabbi's apartment. Bewildered and frightened, he delivered the message in the stranger's own words.

"Tell the Rabbi I am waiting. I have come a long way."

The fear that was in Israel Avigdor's heart communicated itself to Rabbi Melech. He questioned the *gabbai* several times.

"A man in tatters?" he repeated. "With a sack on his shoulders? A visitor?"

"Yes, Rabbi."

"Well, let him in," the Rabbi answered at last. He put his heavy hat on, over his skull-cap. The day was hot, but he felt a sudden chill.

Israel Avigdor went out to the stranger.

"The Rabbi is ready for you." And as the stranger picked up his sack, Israel Avigdor added respectfully: "If you would like to leave your sack here, it will be perfectly safe."

"No," the stranger answered, and slinging the sack over his shoulder stepped past Israel Avigdor. The latter, utterly confounded, followed him slowly and closed the door.

When the stranger came into the Rabbi's room, he put down the sack and looked round; he looked first at the walls and at the bookcases; finally he looked at the Rabbi. The Rabbi's face was like the moss-covered bark of an old, old tree. His bushy eyebrows almost hid his eyes. The stranger stared at him closely, as if trying to remember something.

"*Sholom aleichem,*" the Rabbi said. "Come closer. My eyesight is not very good."

The stranger approached and touched the Rabbi's hand.

"Who are you?" the Rabbi asked.

"Nahum," the stranger answered.

"Who?" The Rabbi leaned forward, thrusting his ear forward with his hand.

"Nahum," the stranger repeated. "Your son-in-law."

Rabbi Melech fell back, shuddering, in his leather armchair. Israel Avigdor ran to him, but the Rabbi leaned forward again and addressed the stranger in a voice shaking with fear.

"I do not know you!" he said.

"I went away," the stranger said, "on the seventh day of the month of Adar, in the year *tov resh lamed aleph,* and it is today the twelfth day of the month of Tamuz, *tov resh mem vov*—fifteen years."

"Where have you been?" the Rabbi asked, dazed.

"In the world."

"Why did you run away?"

"It had to be."

"Why did you desert my daughter?"

"I had to do that."

The Rabbi felt chill again. "Israel Avigdor, give me my lined dressing-gown."

Israel Avigdor brought out the velvet, fleece-lined dressing-gown and helped the Rabbi change. The Rabbi rose slowly, and with much difficulty, from the depths of his chair. Leaning on Israel Avigdor, he approached the stranger and looked long at him from under his vast eyebrows.

"Have you come here to play the fool?" he asked, angrily.

"No. I have come to my wife, Serele."

"By what signs can you prove that you are Nahum?"

"Shortly before I went away—less than a twelve-month before —I studied, together with you, the book *R'ziel ha-Malach*. The eighteenth page was folded over. The mark may still be there."

"Israel Avigdor," the Rabbi said, trembling again, "get down the book *R'ziel ha-Malach*."

The Rabbi continued to examine the stranger from head to foot. He even put out his hands and felt him, as if he were a dead thing. Then, when Israel Avigdor brought the little volume, he opened it with shaking hands. He could scarcely separate the pages; but he found the eighteenth page—and it was folded over. The Rabbi clutched the book and reeled. Israel Avigdor steadied him and led him back to his armchair.

"Can you give other signs to my daughter?" the Rabbi asked. "Signs as between husband and wife?"

"Yes," the stranger said.

"Israel Avigdor," the Rabbi commanded, in a voice that had suddenly become firm. "Bring my daughter Serele here. But say nothing to her."

Serele came in, frightened, her hands crossed on her breast. She wore a gray shawl on her head. She was big and heavy. The stranger turned toward her as she came in, and stared at her steadfastly. She did not look back, but fixed her eyes on the floor.

"Serele," said the Rabbi. "Go closer to this man, and look at him well."

Serele approached the stranger and looked at him once.

"Do you know him?"

Serele started with fear, looked a second time at the tattered stranger and answered weakly: "No."

"And you, visitor," the Rabbi asked. "Do you recognize her?"

"Yes," the stranger answered in a low, firm voice. "It is Serele, my wife."

Serele uttered a faint scream. She looked round quickly for a chair, but before she could move toward it, she fell. Israel Avigdor was about to run to the door, to call the women, but the stranger stopped him and knelt down at Serele's side. She had not lost consciousness. The stranger commanded her to get up, and, taking her hand, helped her. The firm voice, the security and warmth of the man's hand, gave her new strength. The stranger led her to the chair and bade her sit down.

"Are you better?" he asked.

"Yes," she answered, in a whisper.

"Serele," the Rabbi said, "this stranger says that he is Nahum, your husband. Look at him again, closely, and say if you recognize him."

Serele stared up at the pale lean face, at the black beard, at the hard bony limbs which almost stuck out of the rags. She became agitated; she tried to speak and could not. Her face reddened slowly.

"I don't know," she gasped.

"It would be hard to know him," the Rabbi said. "When he left, he was young, without a beard; and now . . ."

"Yes," Serele muttered. "Fifteen years."

"Stranger," the Rabbi said. "What signs can you mention to my daughter, to prove that you are her husband?"

"I fasted for two days before I left."

"It's true!" Serele said, quickly.

"And on the day when I left, I would not eat even at night."

"It's true!"

The stranger turned to Serele and talked to her, with the familiar "thou."

"You thought I was sick, and you wanted to call the doctor."

"Yes. I asked you to go to bed . . ." but while she acknowledged this, she addressed the stranger in the distant and respectful plural.

"I would not have it," he answered. "I wanted to go on studying. So I went upstairs, to my room in the attic."

"And never returned—" she added.

The Rabbi rose again from his armchair. He approached Serele. "You remember all this?" he asked.

"Yes. I remember everything. I even remember what I cooked for supper—porridge and milk. It was the terrible day when poor Malkah, God rest her soul, was—was—"

She did not finish. The Rabbi nodded and muttered to himself. Serele took up the story.

"And I carried a glass of milk and a flat cake up to Nahum's room, because he hadn't eaten all day. But he wasn't there any more. There was only a book on the table."

"The Psalms," said the stranger.

"Yes, the Psalms," Serele repeated.

She thought sadly and went on: "I left the milk there. It was never touched."

"Serele!" the Rabbi commanded. "Look at the man again! You must not accept such a thing lightly. Look at him. Do you recognize him?"

Serele went closer to the stranger than she had done before. She stared steadfastly into his coal-black eyes. The roads he had traversed were written in his eyes; the dust of them was on his clothes.

"Yes," she said suddenly, in an access of faith. "Yes! I recognize him."

The Rabbi lifted his heavy eyebrows. "Serele! Perhaps you have other signs. Do not be ashamed. Signs on his body . . ."

Serele let her eyes drop. She was silent.

"My daughter," the Rabbi went on. "You are an *agunah*, a deserted wife. Speak!"

"Yes. He has a scar on his left side; he had an operation when he was a child." Then, after a difficult pause, she added: "He has two strawberry marks on his back, close to each other."

"Israel Avigdor," the Rabbi ordered. "Go with the stranger to the ritual bath, and examine him. Serele, you will wait here."

The stranger and Israel Avigdor left the room. Serele, waiting for their return, perceived the stranger's sack. She lifted it, examined it and felt, with eager fingers, its coarse, patched material. The examination changed into a slow, rhythmic fondling; she did not look at the sack any more; her eyes were filling with tears. The Rabbi uttered no sound.

In a few minutes Israel Avigdor burst into the room, the stranger following him.

"Rabbi! It is true. All the signs. I examined Reb Nahum thoroughly."

Israel Avigdor's face was radiant. The same radiance spread over Rabbi Melech's face. He rose again and said, loudly:

"*Mazel-tov!*"

Then, approaching his daughter, he said to her, quietly: "Remember—you must always be a pious, observant daughter of your people. I shall tell Israel Avigdor when the ritual bath must be heated."

Serele crimsoned. She could not lift her eyes from the floor. She heard her father saying something to Israel Avigdor about new clothes for the returned wanderer. She could have interrupted, to tell them that for fifteen years she had kept Nahum's clothes, had guarded them from the moths; and if they were too small now, they could be made over. But she could not bring herself to say anything. She could not even utter the two words which had haunted her all these years: "Nahum! Why?"

In a low voice she murmured to the dark man: "Perhaps you would like to eat something?"

For the first time, she addressed him with the familiar "thou."

22

THE NEWS THAT NAHUM, SON-IN-LAW OF THE RABBI OF NYESHEVE, had come home after his absence of fifteen years spread like wildfire through the Jewish towns and villages on both sides of the border. In thousands of Chassidic homes, followers of the Nyesheve dynasty, there was rejoicing and drinking and exchanges of congratulations.

That week-end the housewives of Nyesheve purchased the finest raisins and cinnamon to make Sabbath puddings, which they sent to Serele. Little boys and girls brought them, and said what they were taught to say: "Our love to your guest!" Serele gave the messengers almonds and nuts. So many rich puddings came in that she had to distribute them in the court, and the fat of the puddings ran down dozens of beards in the Nyesheve court that Sabbath.

Richer householders of Nyesheve sent her bottles of wine.

The Rabbi's sons and daughters, too, sent presents of food, wine in silver bottles and fruit in silver baskets. They congratulated Serele. But their hearts were not in their presents or their congratulations. They did not like this strange man who had returned to the Rabbinic court of Nyesheve.

He was secretive, silent, incomprehensible. He never spoke, either concerning his absence or the motives for his return; he said nothing about the places he had been to or the kind of life he had lived. When his relatives came to greet him, he merely returned the handshake and was silent. He had nothing to say even to Serele. Only once, to the Rabbi, had he offered this much:

"I had to do it."

The stern silence of the returned man spread around him an atmosphere of mystery and even of fear. Chassidim began to feel that this uncommunicativeness guarded more than ordinary experiences and memories; something of the other world and of its unutterable secrets clung to the new Nahum. And as he was chary of his words, so he was chary of his presence. He remained hidden. He did not join the congregation at prayer, and did not even attend the banquets of the Rabbi. It was told of him that he was, most of the time, locked in his old room in the attic, poring over books, or pacing to and fro. A few times he was seen, very early in the morning, slipping like a wraith across the yard to the ritual baths. And sometimes, it was said, he went walking in the fields and in the cemetery of Nyesheve. But he came and went without speaking to anyone; and his sudden, silent passages cast a fear on all who beheld him.

The Rabbi's sons, too, began to fear him.

The Rabbi was growing visibly older from day to day. From day to day his sight and hearing grew worse. And in the court of Nyesheve there was no peace or harmony among the successors to Rabbi Melech—nothing but intrigues, slanders and rapacity. They fought among themselves for their father's following; they lowered themselves in the eyes of the Chassidim. And now they began to be afraid that the strange, returned man would snatch away from them, at the last moment, their long-coveted prizes. The Chassidim would pass over to him in a mass and leave them with their little intrigues and ambitions.

Israel Avigdor threw all his energies into the new situation. For him it was a matter of life and death that the Rabbinic dynasty of Nyesheve should maintain its great following intact. He knew the Rabbi's sons well; the imposing heritage of generations, the court and following of Nyesheve were nothing to them. They would reduce it to fragments and scatter the fragments to the wind. But to Israel Avigdor the return of Nahum was providential. He did his best to heighten the effect which the behavior of Nahum was producing. Circulating among the Chassidim in the synagogue, and paying particular attention to the rich and influential, he would offer his snuff-box and point significantly in the direction of the attic, where the Rabbi's son-in-law was known to pass his days. In a low voice Israel Avigdor would say:

"I tell you, Jews, there's more in this than you think."

"True, Israel Avigdor," they answered; "it is not a simple matter."

The old Rabbi, too, was filled with awe and astonishment.

Even he had been able to elicit nothing from the returned man. He no longer had the old insistence and energy; speaking was a strain, and Nahum's silence was deadly and complete. The Rabbi told him how his father and mother, the Rabbi of Rachmanivke and his wife, had died grieving over the loss of their only son. And the stranger said: "I know"—and added not another word.

The Rabbi sent for Serele, and asked her:

"Does he behave like a husband toward you?"

"Sometimes."

"Does he speak with you?"

"No. He locks himself up with his books. I'm afraid to speak to him, and he never says anything to me."

The Rabbi had nothing more to ask.

"I tell you," he said to Israel Avigdor, "the man is not to be understood."

Israel Avigdor caught up that phrase and spread it far and wide

among the Chassidim. "He is not to be understood." A legend of
sanctity sprang up almost overnight around the returned man.

The women began to seek him first. To them he was a saint, a
wonder worker. They had almost given up seeking the intercession
of the old Rabbi. He had never been very patient with women, and
in his old age he had given up ministering to them. He had instructed Israel Avigdor never to admit a woman to his presence,
and not even to let the women gather on the threshold of his
house. Israel Avigdor tried to obey, but occasionally a desperate
woman would offer him a large bribe, and then Israel Avigdor
ignored the Rabbi's orders and admitted her. But the Rabbi had
nothing to say.

"I will not see you," he told the woman. "Go. I have no more
strength."

And if the woman was obstinate, and demanded to be heard,
Rabbi Melech would curse her and bid her seek out another Rabbi.

"Begone!" he growled. "Are there not enough Rabbis in the
world that you must pester me?"

The Rabbi's sons were glad to receive the women and take their
prayer-notes and their money; but soon after the stranger's return,
the women stopped coming to the Rabbi's sons, and began to seek
out Nahum. They stood under Serele's window, weeping for ad-
mission, stood there for hours, though no one replied, and begged
for the intercession of the holy man.

The fame of the new saint spread rapidly to other towns, and
Jews came long distances in the hope of catching a glimpse of the
son-in-law of Rabbi Melech. Scholars wanted to consult him;
young men who were thinking of abandoning their wives and children in order to give themselves up completely to sanctity wanted
his advice; adepts in the Kabbala suspected that here was an adept
greater than all others. But the returned man received no one and
spoke with no one. He remained locked in his room; and the
longer he held out, the more insistent grew the new following.

The Rabbi's sons were in despair. They knew that such things
had happened before. More than once in the history of Chassidism
the entire following of a great Rabbi had turned away from his
sons and heirs to go after a stranger, often not a member of the

Rabbinic court. Above all, this was likely to happen where a Rabbi had many sons, and, living too long, had become a commonplace to everyone. A Rabbi, they knew, should not show himself too often, should not cheapen himself. Their father had been seen too long; and they themselves had shown themselves too easily, too eagerly, too freely. To the world they were still "the Rabbi's children"; elderly men, with long beards, they were—and still "children." And in their despair they even united, made some sort of peace among themselves, in order to stand together against the stranger.

They did not know this man, nor did he ever give them an opportunity of finding out what he was like. He did not accept their invitations to their apartments. When they came to see him, he merely answered the greeting, then turned away and remained silent. But without knowing him they understood clearly that he had one purpose in mind: the usurpation of the Rabbinate of Nyesheve. Unlike themselves, he was not aiming for a part of it; he wanted it all, intact, leaving them, the true heirs, nothing at all. How else were they to understand his sudden return? How else could they interpret his careful and calculated seclusion, his strange and effective behavior?

Some of them tried to imitate the new man in their own way. They made themselves incomprehensible, let fall mysterious words, adopted extraordinary practices. No one was interested; no one spread the story. The Chassidim continued to flock to the returned man.

"I tell you," they said to one another, "he will even take over the Rabbinate during Father's lifetime. The Chassidim cling to him more closely from day to day. And no wonder. Father hardly ever receives anyone. . . ."

Above all, they were afraid of the approaching High Holidays, the Days of Awe, the New Year and the Day of Atonement. At that time of the year the hearts of men are opened and they are ready for signs and wonders and portents.

On the second and third days of the month of Elul several hundred young Jews arrived in Nyesheve in order to pass the penitential month in the presence of the Rabbi. And on the first day before the midnight prayers there arrived groups of Jewish scholars and men of substance. Shortly before the New Year, they began to pour in by the hundred. From Galician villages came Jews with *capotes* and ear-locks; from Vienna and Prague came German Jews in silk hats; from Hungary came heavy Jews who kissed the Rabbi's hand and studied Talmud in Hungarian. They came from Russian Poland too, Jews with little hats and big beards, Jews whom the Chassidim of Nyesheve considered no better than Lithuanians: skeptics, heretics, atheists even.

They came in hordes across the frontier, stealing across in the night, crawling through fields and woods, wading through streams, risking their lives, in order that they might pass the days of the New Year and of the Atonement in Nyesheve. Some of the richer Russian Jews came legitimately, with passports, and traveling second class. Never had so many Jews assembled in Nyesheve. And every Jew that came hoped to get a glimpse of the Rabbi's son-in-law—"the returned man."

But throughout the week of the midnight prayers, the stranger did not show himself. In the synagogue, Jews waited patiently, and so often as the door was opened, thousands of eyes were turned toward it.

"What is this? Does he even say the midnight prayers alone, without a congregation of ten?" They could not understand such a thing.

"*He* knows what he's doing," Israel Avigdor said, mysteriously.

On the eve of the New Year he appeared suddenly in the synagogue—lean, bony, black-bearded. He swept swiftly, almost unnoticed, through the throng, made his way into a corner and, keeping his face always to the east, presented only his back to the other worshipers. Throughout the services the eager Chassidim saw nothing more than the motionless, shiny satin of his shoulders. Not once did he sit down; he stood as if hewn out of stone. For the first time in many decades it was not the broad back of Rabbi Melech which was the center of attraction; the Rabbi's sons noticed it clearly; and in the midst of their pious responses, they wondered how far it would go.

When services were over, the returned man attempted to sweep again through the synagogue, as he had come in. But a solid wall of Chassidim—deeper by far than the one which temporarily detained the Rabbi himself—blocked his way. A hundred hands were stretched out toward the black figure, and a hundred voices said, in the immemorial formula:

"Thy name be written down for a good year."

He took a step forward, but the crowd did not yield. The Rabbi's sons, pale with envy and helplessness, felt that the decisive moment of their decline had come. They saw the faces of the Chassidim burn with devotion, awe and affection toward the returned stranger. It was his decisive apotheosis.

And then, in the midst of that enthusiasm and joy, a dreadful thing happened.

A voice, alien, raucous, out of all keeping with the spirit of the Holy Day, an angry and a vulgar voice, broke through the tumult of good wishes.

"Jews! God help me! What are you doing?"

For an instant the Chassidim thought that a man had been thrown down and was being trampled in the crowd—such incidents were quite common at Chassidic demonstrations. But the voice, instead of growing weaker, grew stronger, and it was not the voice of a man in physical pain.

"Jews! What are you doing? Desecration is being committed."

The mob of Chassidim turned. In the center of the synagogue stood a tall, emaciated Jew, with a vast gray beard and with a fiery red nose. His arms were raised to heaven, and he was shouting at the top of his voice.

"Reb Shachnah of Bialogura!"

They knew the man well in Nyesheve—knew him and hated him. He had been a frequent visitor of late; for with the death of Reb Meir'l he had made a bid for the Rabbinate of Bialogura, and followers of the Rabbi of Nyesheve in Bialogura had opposed him, because he was not of the sect of the Chassidim. Therefore he had come to Nyesheve to demand of Rabbi Melech that he order his followers not to oppose him. And Rabbi Melech had refused to see him—and Reb Shachnah had returned again and again, with his complaints and his insults and his demands for justice. He had even threatened to cite the Rabbi before a special Rabbinic court. And here he was now, with his arms raised to heaven, yelling in the synagogue on the eve of the New Year.

"Jews! Shame on you! Jews, I will not be silent! It is desecration!"

A number of Chassidim grabbed him, but he tore himself free, thrust his way furiously through the crowd and running up to the Rabbi's son-in-law, pointed a finger in his face and shouted:

"Yoshe! Yoshe the loon! Woe is me!"

For a moment there was the silence of paralysis. Then voices were heard:

"Take the man out! He has gone mad! Take him out! The man is an unbeliever, an enemy of ours!"

Hands were laid on him, but the old man showed amazing physical strength. He could not be moved. Still standing in front of the returned man he shouted, again and again:

"Jews! Know that you have been fooled, swindled! This man is not the Rabbi's son-in-law. He is Yoshe the loon of Bialogura, a sinner in Israel!"

Shuddering, some of the Chassidim covered their ears, not to listen to the blasphemy. Others shouted: "Bind him! Stop up his mouth!"

At this point the Rabbi's sons, who had lingered in the synagogue after their father had been conducted back to his apartment, intervened to save Reb Shachnah from violence. They made a ring round the threatened man, and the oldest of them shouted:

"Do not lay your hands on a Rabbi, a man of learning and piety. Let us hear what he has to say. This is the New Year!"

In an instant Reb Shachnah was on the pulpit, hammering for silence.

"Jews!" he cried, hoarsely. "Know that I am not mad, but in possession of all my senses. And I swear by the holiness of this day, and by the sanctity of the New Year, that the man whom you have greeted as the son-in-law of the Rabbi of Nyesheve is none other than Yoshe, called the loon, of Bialogura. He sinned, God save us! by committing adultery with the daughter of the beadle of the Great Synagogue, Reb Kanah. And because of this sin the community of Bialogura was visited by a pestilence. A Tribunal of Bialogura compelled him to marry the girl he had led into evil. And he left her, the night of the marriage, an *agunah*, an abandoned wife. Jews! I swear all this to you by the Holy Ark. And I will bring an entire city to bear witness to what I say."

As swiftly as he had ascended the pulpit, he now ran down, lifted both his fists in the face of the returned man and cried:

"Deny it! Deny that you are Yoshe the loon!"

The returned man did not utter a word. With eyes wide open, seeing nothing, he turned once in the direction of Reb Shachnah, and then away from him. Then swiftly, with long even strides, he left the synagogue, passing between the petrified onlookers.

The silence was broken by a hundred voices.

"Jews! To the Rabbi!"

The entire congregation streamed out of the synagogue toward Rabbi Melech's apartment.

23

THE CRY OF REB SHACHNAH OF BIALOGURA MADE THE RABBINIC court of Nyesheve tremble to its foundations.

When it reached the ears of Rabbi Melech, the old man rose to his feet as if he had been twenty years younger and, in a voice that had suddenly become powerful again, thundered curses against the accuser.

"Unbeliever and infidel!" he shouted. "Drive him from the court like a mad dog! Not a speck of dust shall fall upon the head of my Nahum!"

The lust of battle glared from his eyes. Israel Avigdor, astounded and delighted, ran from his presence to spread his fiery words among the Chassidim.

And now open rebellion broke out in the court of Nyesheve. The sons of the Rabbi met in conference. Every memory of ancient differences was obliterated. Without waiting for the festival days to end, they decided on their course of action. Every one of them contributed to a war chest, and out of the funds the greater part was turned over, as soon as the two days of the New Year were past, to Feibish Meir, the Jew whom they had chosen to take the first step for them.

"Feibish Meir! With this money we bid you go to Bialogura in the company of Reb Shachnah. In Bialogura you will see Reb Kanah and his daughter, and you will persuade them to come with you to Nyesheve. And if they will not be persuaded, you will lug them here, bound hand and foot. Do not dare to return without them!"

Feibish Meir had for years aspired to the post occupied by Israel Avigdor, but he knew that his only hope lay in a change of rulership. He hated Israel Avigdor for being what he himself wanted to be, the guardian of the gate, the chief intriguant, the principal bribe-taker in the court. The fury of all the hungry years filled him now with courage and hope. He undertook the commission eagerly. And the day after the festival he set out with Reb Shachnah of Bialogura.

Reb Shachnah was even more determined than Feibish Meir. "God help me," he kept repeating all the way to Bialogura, "if I have to turn beggar for it, and knock at doors, I'll stand by what I say. It's Yoshe the loon, none other. The world is not coming to an end."

When Reb Shachnah arrived early in the morning in Bialogura with his companion, he did not go home. The two men rushed at once to the Great Synagogue, where the men were assembled for first prayers. Without waiting, Reb Shachnah rushed up to the pulpit, smote it to obtain silence and cried out in a loud voice:

"Jews! A fire burns in the court of Nyesheve! Yoshe the loon is living with the Rabbi's daughter!"

The furious struggle which was to divide an entire people into two camps began there and then. For in Bialogura there were followers of the dynasty of Nyesheve and followers of the dynasty of Gorbitz—deadly enemies from of old. And that morning blows were exchanged in the Great Synagogue of Bialogura.

Kanah the beadle did not have to be persuaded, much less bound hand and foot. In his haste and eagerness he did not realize that a fund had been raised to bring him and his daughter to Nyesheve; he assumed he would have to pay his own way, and Feibish Meir did not have to rip open the little sack he had brought with him.

Reb Shachnah was more restless, more impatient, than anyone else. He forgot his Rabbinic aspirations. He forgot the intrigues against him. He would not speak about anything but the unspeakable evil that was being done in Nyesheve. He was returning with the others, leaving the city without a Rabbi. And when a deputation waited on him, protesting, saying that he was needed in case of ritualistic disputes, he answered:

"I say there is a law in this world which even Rabbis must observe. I say I will not let this pass. But I will go through the whole world and cry that in Nyesheve the Rabbi's daughter lives with a man who is the husband of another!"

The fury of Reb Shachnah was transmitted to others. Plain Jews closed their shops and prepared to accompany him. Followers of the Nyesheve dynasty were among the first; they knew that this was an outrageous plot against the good name and the glory of Nyesheve, hatched in the evil brain of an unbeliever, an enemy of Chassidim, whose private ambitions had been thwarted. They knew that Reb Shachnah would be driven in humiliation from Nyesheve a second time. Or he might be taken and whipped in public first. That would be a spectacle! Something to tell children and grandchildren! But with followers of the Nyesheve dynasty went followers of other Rabbis and dynasties—chiefly the followers of the Rabbi of Gorbitz. *They* expected something else; they expected the final humiliation and destruction of that hated center called Nyesheve.

Abish the butcher was among the first to enroll. He left his shop, his blocks, his cleavers and his customers. "Yoshe the loon?" he cried, continuously. "He's got too much sense, I tell you; that's what he's got."

On the very day of the Fast of Gedaliah the whole company left in wagons for the frontier. There had been no time to obtain frontier permits, much less regular passports. The travelers were to be smuggled across the border, and their guide was to be that same Reb Zanvil Moilecher who had turned the cemetery of Bialogura into a warehouse for contraband. Reb Zanvil had his arrangements with the commander of the frontier guard; a ruble a head for every passenger, a small barrel of Austrian cognac to distribute among the soldiers, and one extra silver ruble for the commandant—to get himself a girl with.

"No girl, no crossing," he explained to Zanvil. "Because with nothing to keep me busy I'm bound to hear you."

For several hours the entire company lay in a peasant barn, quarreling in whispers.

"Nyesheve donkeys!" said the faithful of Gorbitz.

"Gorbitz heathens!" retorted the faithful of Nyesheve. "Wait till we get to Nyesheve, you'll have the lesson of your lives."

Zanvil the smuggler swore and spat. "For the love of God, keep your mouths shut! Do you want all the country to hear you?"

Around midnight he led his company through the shallow river which divided the two countries at this point. The commander of the guard heard not a single splash. When the company emerged on the further bank, Zanvil said: "We're in Austria. Take off your boots and dry your feet."

But they paid no attention to him. In the distance they saw the glimmer of the oil lamp outside the tiny village station house, and they set out for it as if the train were waiting for them. All night long, in the station and on the train, they continued their quarrels.

From early morning almost until evening the visitors from Bialogura besieged the Rabbi's apartment, without being permitted to enter.

Israel Avigdor was on guard there, and he was in no hurry. "I can't let you in," he told them angrily. "Later. Perhaps tomorrow."

Israel Avigdor was ill at ease. Reb Shachnah was one man, easily dealt with. Here was half the city of Bialogura, and he was shaken. His uneasiness communicated itself at once to the Nyesheve faithful who had come from Bialogura. They did not like his uncertainty; they did not like the atmosphere in the courts; it was impregnated with gloom and mourning. And as their spirits fell, those of the faithful of Gorbitz rose correspondingly. They did not beleaguer the door as persistently as the others; in Nyesheve itself they found a few followers of Gorbitz, and among these they prepared an impromptu little banquet, an advance celebration of victory.

"To life!" they toasted. "God send us good news."

Kanah the beadle and his daughter sat all day near the well in the yard. Feibish Meir sent out dishes from the court kitchens, roast duck and breast of chicken; and from morning until late in the afternoon, the two of them sat eating, throwing crumbs to the fowl. Abish the butcher found his way, without invitation, into the kitchens themselves. There he was in his element; he showed the women new ways of scraping a calf's foot and of cleaning cows' livers. Within an hour he was part of the household.

Only Reb Shachnah was like a lost and restless spirit. He marched up and down the yard blowing his nose furiously, and shouting: "I tell you, the world is not coming to an end. There is a law for Rabbis too!"

Toward evening the Rabbi's sons took a hand in the matter. In a body they went to Israel Avigdor to remonstrate with him. They spoke haughtily, like men anticipating victory.

"Israel Avigdor! How dare you let worthy Jews wait a whole day under the open sky? Is this Nyesheve justice, or Nyesheve hospitality? Let them in! Do you think that this court is your plaything?"

Israel Avigdor looked through narrowed eyes at the "heirs." For an instant the blood crept out from behind his ears, and the yellowish hair on his hands seemed to bristle. He wanted to fling back that as long as the Rabbi lived—and that would be another hundred and twenty years, please God!—he, Israel Avigdor, was master of the door. But he did not utter the words. There was something new in the bearing of the Rabbi's sons! Yes, that wretch from Bialogura had started something which would not so easily be brought to an end. This was not the time for an open declaration of war. Israel Avigdor backed down and said apologetically:

"I am not the master here. I am merely obeying the wishes of the Rabbi."

A few minutes later he admitted them to the waiting room, and then led them, one by one, before Rabbi Melech.

Rabbi Melech was not alone. Three other Rabbis were with him, one from Nyesheve itself, two from neighboring towns, visitors for the High Holidays. The three Rabbis constituted a regular Tribunal. In a corner of the room, deeply absorbed in a book, and apparently indifferent to the storm, sat the returned man.

Rabbi Melech's face was dark with unsuppressed anger. There was life in it again, battle, the old imperiousness.

The first man to be led in by Israel Avigdor was Reb Shachnah. Rabbi Melech did not ask him to sit down. He glared at him for several moments, and suddenly burst out:

"I understand that you are the man who has suddenly appeared in our city and has stirred up trouble with the scandalous accusation that my son-in-law, Reb Nahum, who sits here in front of you, is not my son-in-law at all, but somebody or other by the name of Yoshe—called the loon—of the city of Bialogura. You stand now in the presence of a Tribunal of three Rabbis. Do you still dare to repeat here what you said in the synagogue on the eve of the New Year in the presence of thousands of Jews?"

"Yes!"

Rabbi Melech rose from his seat.

"You answer too off-handedly. Approach that man and look well at him, and repeat the same thing face to face with him."

Reb Shachnah strode up to the sitting man, looked into his face and said in the harsh voice he had used when he sat in his own Tribunal in Bialogura:

"I say, in all truthfulness, before the Tribunal of three Rabbis, that this is Yoshe, of Bialogura, whom they call the loon, the assistant beadle of the Great Synagogue, the man whom the community of Bialogura married to the daughter of Kanah the beadle, and who fled the night of the marriage and left her an abandoned wife."

The firmness of his tone sent a shudder of fear through the three Rabbis. But the returned man, at whom the accusing finger was still pointed in petrified rage after the accuser had ceased speaking, seemed unaffected. He did not lift his head; he did not move a limb.

After Reb Shachnah, other Jews of Bialogura were admitted, one by one. Israel Avigdor gave first place to the Chassidim of Gorbitz; his own partisans he kept to the end. And one by one the Jews of Bialogura stepped up to the returned man, looked him straight in the face, and exclaimed:

"Yoshe the loon!"

The Rabbis of the Tribunal were pale.

After the Chassidic followers of Gorbitz, the other Chassidim of Bialogura, followers of Nyesheve, were admitted. Nothing remained now of their courage and high spirits; they were as pale as the Rabbis on the bench. They could not even speak. Only their terror spoke for them. Some even tried to cover their eyes, in order not to be compelled to bear witness; but it was too late. Others, looking at the returned man, only exclaimed: "God help us!" and turned away.

The last to be admitted were Kanah the beadle and his daughter. Kanah tried to edge his way in together with the girl, but Israel Avigdor compelled him to wait until she had been cross-examined. When Zivyah came in, Rabbi Melech rose again, to get a better view of the strange, half-witted woman. Never had he looked at any human being with such contempt and hatred as at the fleshy, grinning, stupid face before him now.

"You!" he thundered. "You are in the presence of three Rabbis. Be careful of what you say. If you do not speak the truth, they will tear the flesh off you with red-hot whips in the next world. Take a look at that man, and say who he is."

Zivyah approached the sitting man and began to neigh with delight.

"Yoshe!" she exclaimed, amid her giggling. "Yoshe the loon, you—Yoshe—"

The Rabbi stepped up to the babbling woman.

"What signs can you give that this man is your husband?"

She did not answer him. She kept looking at the returned man and giggling hoarsely: "You—Yoshe—husband—Bialogura—" She went closer to him and snatched his hand. There was a mortal stillness in the room. The only one who was unaffected was the returned man. Israel Avigdor thrust Zivyah away, shouting:

"How dare you touch his hand? Have you no respect? Fool!"

Rabbi Melech went back to his seat. His anger seemed to have given way to scorn. He paid no attention even to Kanah the beadle, when the latter added his testimony to that of the other witnesses; but when he was finished, he turned once more to the fiery Reb Shachnah, and, without addressing him by name, asked sharply:

"Was your Yoshe the loon, of Bialogura, a man of learning or an ignorant man?"

"He was a man who could only chant Psalms."

The Rabbi almost laughed aloud. "And I assert before this Tribunal that my son-in-law, Reb Nahum, is a learned man and an adept in Kabbala!"

The three Rabbis stared.

"Israel Avigdor," the Rabbi called. "Tell the Tribunal what you yourself saw and heard when Reb Nahum returned to Nyesheve."

Israel Avigdor planted himself before the three Rabbis and said loudly: "In these dread days of penitence, between the New Year and the Day of Atonement, in the presence of three Rabbis and of my own Rabbi, I will report what I heard and saw, and I will neither add anything nor leave anything out, nor say anything which is only my opinion."

In a clear, almost jubilant voice, he recounted in detail the events of the first interview between the returned man and Rabbi Melech; he mentioned the folded page in the book, the testimony of Serele, the examination of the returned man's body. He forgot nothing. And as the recital continued, the face of Rabbi Melech became more and more joyous, while on the faces of the three Rabbis terror and astonishment struggled for mastery. Only the returned man sat unmoved.

When Israel Avigdor had finished speaking, the Rabbi sent for his daughter.

"Israel Avigdor," he said, "bring in the wife of Reb Nahum."

He did not utter his daughter's name; he called her by the title of her husband, to heighten the effect. Israel Avigdor opened the door, and Serele, pale but firm, stepped in amid such a silence that the rustle of clothes was heard when heads were turned in her direction.

In her bearing was visible the determination of a woman prepared to battle against a whole world. With certain steps she approached the Tribunal and remained standing at a respectful distance from the bench. The Rabbi bade her come closer.

"My daughter!" he said in a gentle, loving voice which she had never heard from him before. "The woman standing over there, the daughter of a beadle and gravedigger in Bialogura, in Russian Poland, states that Reb Nahum, your husband, is not Nahum, but that he is one Yoshe the loon, who married her in the cemetery of Bialogura in the time of a pestilence, and then abandoned her. Speak out before the Tribunal and say what you know concerning your husband Reb Nahum. Speak, and hide nothing."

Before answering, Serele turned and looked steadily at the woman in the corner, the woman who was at the center of this unspeakable conspiracy to rob her of her husband. She pushed back on her forehead the silk kerchief which she had put on the day of her husband's return, as the sign of her restored status. Her lips were contorted for a moment in an expression of fierce contempt. Then remembering her own shame—that she, the daughter of the great Rabbi, should have to fight for her husband with this creature—she turned again toward the Tribunal. But before she had uttered a single word, there was a patter of feet, and Zivyah charged down upon her, snarling like a wild animal whose cubs have been threatened. There was no time to head her off. A cry of horror went up as the unclean finger nails of the enraged woman plowed into Serele's face.

"No!" Zivyah screamed. "My Yoshe, my loon!"

Israel Avigdor was, in spite of his years, the first to intervene. He leaped across the room like a boy, and with a trick which had remained with him from the distant time when he used to help his father, the inn-keeper, throw out drunken, brawling peasants, he seized Zivyah with one hand by the throat, while with the other he pinched her flesh so that she let out a squeal of pain and almost fainted.

"Bitch!" he roared, and swung her away from Serele toward the door. Someone opened the door for him and he pitched her out, so that she fell face forward.

Rabbi Melech had risen to his feet, and his face blazed.

"Out of this house! Every one of you! My curse, and God's curse, upon the man or woman who dares to say evil against my son-in-law Reb Nahum. Begone!"

Terrified and bewildered, the audience rose and streamed from the room. Outside, near the door, lay Zivyah, baying like a lost dog, heedless to the comforting words of her father.

24

Reb shachnah of bialogura, together with his protégés and witnesses, left Nyesheve within a few hours after he had been ejected from Rabbi Melech's room. But Reb Shachnah did not return home; from that day on he was dedicated to a single, consuming purpose—a holy war against the Rabbinic dynasty of Nyesheve.

He went from town to town, from synagogue to synagogue, from Rabbi to Rabbi, and there was one cry on his lips:

"Jews! A fire is burning in Nyesheve!"

He forgot his home, his ambitions and his private grudges. His wife wrote to him frantically, begging him to take pity on her and return; his congregation pleaded with him; he had become such an important man that the opposition to him could easily be defeated; the Rabbinate of Bialogura was his now for the asking. They complained that the ship was without a rudder, the flock without a shepherd, the city without a light. Reb Shachnah had one answer:

"Though I have to turn beggar, and go from door to door, I shall make justice prevail. The daughter of the Rabbi of Nyesheve lives in sin with the husband of an abandoned wife. I say that the world is not coming to an end."

He prepared a petition at the end of a long sheet of paper. In tiny script which bristled like himself he wrote out his accusation; he filled it with learned quotations of famous cases, with opinions of illustrious Rabbis, with sayings from the Talmud and the Sages; and he closed it with a demand that the Rabbinate of Nyesheve root out the evil from its midst. He took a roll of linen and gummed his petition to it, to make it durable; and wherever he went he gathered signatures of Rabbis, scholars and influential Jews, who called upon the Rabbi of Nyesheve and his daughter Serele to submit to trial before a great Tribunal of the learned.

Burning with the zeal of a prophet, he suffered the fate of one. Followers of the dynasty of Nyesheve persecuted him. In the synagogues they threw books at his head; in the street they threw stones. They reported him to the police as a disturber of the peace. His wife refused to send him his old overcoat, and he went about in his satin *capote* shivering with cold. He had no linen and no money. Dirty, haggard and hungry, he begged his way from town to town, slept on earthen floors, wheedled rides from impatient wagoners, or, failing that, followed the long roads on foot. Single-handed he waged his war against the mighty dynasty of Nyesheve. He traversed Jewry like a firebrand, leaving behind him a trail of smoke, unrest and dissention.

He did not travel alone. Just as he had abandoned his Rabbinate in Bialogura, so Kanah had abandoned his synagogue and cemetery, so that, together with his daughter, he might accompany the avenger. But Kanah did not travel like Reb Shachnah. Kanah was much more practical. He carried, sewn into his undervest, a sum of money, part of his takings as beadle, thefts from charity boxes, bribes given him by smugglers. He spent his coins reluctantly, but neither he nor his daughter would put up with the hardships which Reb Shachnah suffered. Kanah and his daughter were heavily clad. They were much more ingenious than Reb Shachnah in taking advantage of housewives, innkeepers and servants. Kanah, moreover, could bluster his way, in every town, into the company of beadles and grave-diggers; he knew their language and their ways. So that, traveling with Reb Shachnah, he maintained an economy of his own for himself and his daughter. But he was always on hand to be introduced by Reb Shachnah, and he had his little speech, the speech of a plain and simple man:

"Rabbi! I am Kanah the beadle of Bialogura; and this is my daughter Zivyah, the wife of Yoshe the loon, who today lives in the Rabbinic court of Nyesheve as the husband of the Rabbi's daughter."

There were times, however, when Reb Shachnah and Reb Kanah and his daughter fared exceedingly well.

Many Jewish householders who were counted among the Chassidic followers of this or that Rabbi, and who attended Rabbinic courts regularly, nourished a secret hatred of the rich and snobbish religious hierarchy. Having neither the initiative nor the courage to rebel, they were glad of this warfare against one of the most powerful of the Chassidic courts, and their dissembled contempt and resentment were transformed into an indignant demand for justice. In homes like these Reb Kanah and his daughter were treated royally. In exchange for their story—which Kanah repeated a hundred times with the same manly simplicity and vigor —they were given the best rooms; and on the Sabbath a feast was prepared for them. Relatives and friends were invited, to hear at first hand the recital of wrongs; and between questions and answers, Kanah stuffed himself methodically with rich food, and encouraged his daughter to do likewise.

In such homes, Reb Shachnah hardly tasted anything. He was a man possessed with an idea. When the golden Sabbath bread was placed in front of him, he would dip the same piece ten times in the salt before he remembered to carry it to his mouth. He took the parsley off the soup, intending to throw it away because he hated the taste of it; but instead of throwing it away he put it into his mouth and chewed it. Eating had become a burden to him, a digression and a waste of time. He could not even bear the traditional singing with which it was customary to follow the Sabbath meal. He wanted to talk only of one thing, Yoshe the loon and the sinful court of Nyesheve. And he wanted no one to ever think of anything else.

His fury was inexhaustible. He returned again and again to the charge, quoting a host of authorities, cajoling, threatening and denouncing. His eyes seemed to shoot out sparks.

Sometimes his hosts pleaded with him.

"Reb Shachnah, leave it alone until the evening. You know it is forbidden to a good Jew to torment himself on the Sabbath. Reb Shachnah, take a piece of fish."

Reb Shachnah did not hear them.

"I say the world is not coming to an end. There is such a thing as the Holy Law."

Some even dared to poke fun at him.

"Reb Shachnah, the fiery river Sambattyon itself rests on the Sabbath. Will you not?"

Reb Shachnah was not offended, chiefly because he was not listening. He never listened when the subject was not Yoshe the loon.

He became leaner from week to week. His eyes sank deeper into their sockets, his beard became grayer and stiffer, his hands bonier. His voice became hoarse. But he felt nothing and saw nothing. The vision was with him always, the sin of Nyesheve which he, Reb Shachnah of Bialogura, had been called upon to root out.

Hell fire, pestilence and destruction were on his lips. There would be no peace and no blessing in Israel until the evil had been removed.

"Jews! A fire burns in Nyesheve! Jews, the Holy Law is the same for all men, for the cobbler and the Rabbi. A fire burns in Nyesheve and the flames of it will consume—God forbid!—all Israel. Jews, be warned in time, and save yourselves!"

The rage of Reb Shachnah of Bialogura kindled a storm in the Jewish community on both sides of the Austro-Russian frontier.

It began among the non-Chassidic Rabbis, the scholars and intellectual leaders of orthodoxy.

From of old there had been enmity between the regularly ordained and learned Rabbis—those who were fitted by long training to conduct communal affairs—and the wonder-working Rabbis of the Chassidim. Of late the wonder-working Rabbis had,

however, been overstepping the boundary. Instead of confining
themselves to their own field of religious enthusiasms and thauma-
turgy, they had actually begun to compete with the regular and
traditional Rabbinate in such serious matters as the interpretation
of the Law. Rarely was a Chassidic Rabbi capable of speaking
intelligibly on that difficult subject; but this did not prevent most
of these Rabbis from settling disputes and issuing decisions.
Often, like Rabbi Melech himself, they kept a learned and quali-
fied assistant for the purpose, in order that Jews might have less
and less recourse to the regular Rabbinate. The assistant was
paid a miserable wage, and the fee was added to the revenues of
the Chassidic Rabbi.

Nyesheve had been a great offender. Reb Melech had steadily
encroached on the prerogative and privileges of countless regular
Rabbis. Moreover, he had, by intrigue and bribery, pushed relatives of his own into vacancies created by death. And as soon as it
became evident that this incident of Yoshe was not a momentary
disturbance, but had the capacity of developing into a major public affair, the Rabbis were the first to take a hand in it.

Letters began to pass across the Austro-Russian frontier; they
contained long, involved questions; they inquired concerning
precedents and regulations. These letters, from one scholar to another, always started out with tremendous flourishes, titular cour-
tesies which took up ten lines of tiny script and ended with a
similar extravagance of modesty in the signature of the writer.

The Gaon or Genius of Przemysl, he who was known, from the
title of his most famous book, as "The Growling Bear," was the
first to write. And he addressed himself in a learned epistle to
the Gaon of Lublin, the author of "The Pleasant Baruch."

"Great Light," wrote "The Growling Bear" to "The Pleasant
Baruch": "Mighty Hammer, you who pick up millstones and rub
them into sand, Mount Sinai, Only One of our generation:
Happy are we that such beauty lives in our time! Greatest of the
Great, Shelf laden with books, Rabbi of all children who are in
exile, Tearer-up of Mountains of Crags, let your Light shine forever, Rabbi of the City of Lublin, Holy Congregation which is a
mother in Israel, let Zion be rebuilt, Amen . . ."

After several more lines of adulation the writer launched into his subject, which was approached in the same style. The letter was crammed with quotations, hints, technical abbreviations—the kind of letter which only a learned anti-Chassidic Rabbi could write or read—and it wound up with several lines of violent self-deprecation:

"From me, the groveling worm, the less than human, the ignorant in the Law, the lowest of the low, the little and young one, the smoky candle, which is extinguished by the light of your torch, the author of 'The Growling Bear,' Rabbi of the Holy Congregation in Przemysl."

In a letter which was even more learned, which began with even more extravagant praise and finished with even more violent self-deprecation, "The Pleasant Baruch" answered, indicating his profound and agitated interest in the matter.

When it was known that the mighty had begun to exchange letters on the subject of the extraordinary case of Nyesheve, the smaller fry followed suit. From Mohilev on the Dnieper to Cracow on the Vistula, from Lemberg to Dinaburg, from Pressburg to Brisk in Lithuania, there was a mighty outpouring of correspondence and compliments. Tiny and obscure Rabbis of hamlets exalted each other to unbelievable heights, and flagellated themselves with superfluous derogation. There was a perceptible increase in postal business between Lithuania and Poland, between Galicia and Russia; Czechoslovakia and Jerusalem also felt the effects. The fever of interest spread even to remote places like London, Prague and St. Petersburg; foreign scholars in outlandish cities had something to say. Salonika was mightily interested, and Turkish Rabbis in Constantinople, who called themselves not Rabbi but *Haham*, wrote in their own curious style of Hebrew to investigate and to comment.

From the Rabbis the storm spread to unofficial scholars, to ordinary householders and even to simple workers. The interest grew from week to week and month to month. Jews neglected their business, their studies and even their prayers. Chassidic followers of Nyesheve and Chassidic followers of Gorbitz were at one another's throats, and scandalous scenes took place. Business rivalries were exasperated into frantic hatreds by the injection of the new issue. Communities and groups excommunicated one another in solemn style. Matches were broken; parents recalled their married sons and daughters, and compelled them to divorce their partners. Nyesheve enthusiasts would not buy meat slaughtered by an enemy of Nyesheve, and vice versa. Such meat, each side argued, was undoubtedly unclean. They would not purchase wine from each other for benediction. And they would not be buried next to each other in the cemeteries.

From the men the storm spread to the women.

Here was something to talk about, to embroider, to exercise the imagination on! In the market-place and in the women's gallery of the synagogue, in the kitchen and bedroom, at mending clothes or stuffing cushions, they talked Nyesheve, Nyesheve, Nyesheve! Their eyes blazed, foam gathered at the corners of their mouths, hatred woke in their hearts. The mysterious name of Yoshe the loon was everywhere. Wives who had been abandoned by their husbands ten and twenty years, women who had not only given up hope, but had even forgotten that they had ever had husbands, pricked up their ears. It might be—such things had happened!—it might be none other than their own man. . . .

There were women who sold their last possessions to buy themselves a railroad ticket to Nyesheve; and for weeks they hung about the yard of the Nyesheve court in order to get a glimpse of the returned man—the man who hid himself from the world behind seven bolts, but of whom the world continued to speak day and night. Israel Avigdor drove the women from the yard, and becoming tired of it, hired a burly peasant to keep them out. Some of the women left Nyesheve in despair, without a glimpse of the Rabbi's son-in-law; but others refused to leave. They continued to haunt the precincts and to wail for a glimpse of the stranger.

Women who had their husbands at home were seized with doubt and fear. Young husbands out on a business journey were afraid to come home an hour late, lest they should find their wives in hysterics. The face of a new man in any town or village set the women by the ears. Was he another of those who had abandoned their wives? The man might have the most plausible story. He might be a merchant traveling with samples, a salesman for sewing-

machine factories, an accredited insurance agent—he became at
once the center of a conspiracy. Several such men were actually
claimed by excited women who had forgotten what their errant
husbands looked like; they were dragged before the Rabbi; they
were stripped for identification.

Skeptics and infidels, Jews notorious for their lack of piety and
faith, village atheists and minor rebels, were happy to find new
ammunition against the godly. Talmud students wrote sarcastic
letters to Hebrew newspapers, and signed themselves with lofty
names from the Bible. The modernized intellectuals wrote to the
Yiddish papers, employing a mock-heroic near-German and inter-
spersing their contributions with quotations from Schiller and
Lessing. A well-known apostate in a small town—a lawyer by pro-
fession—wrote up the whole story in an anti-Semitic German
paper, and a schoolmaster in Brody wrote a long ballad which he
set to a popular melody and printed on broad sheets which sold
by the thousand. Servant girls, wagoners and seamstresses sang the
new ballad in homes, on the roads and in the workshops.

The followers of the Gorbitz dynasty were not the only ones
within the camp of the Chassidim to take up the battle against
Nyesheve. Other courts had long envied the power and influence
and income of Rabbi Melech. But he himself was not the real
object of their envy and hostility. Rabbi Melech was an old man;
he could not last more than a few years. It was his empire which
they wanted to destroy, in order that they might appropriate its
fragments. They wanted to cover the name of Nyesheve with ridicule and ignominy, so that Chassidic Jews would be ashamed to
be associated with it. They wanted the court of Nyesheve to become desolate, so that the stream of its followers might be di-
verted in their own direction.

And therefore the correspondence of the regular Rabbis was
paralleled by a similar correspondence, but on a lower level of
learning, between the Chassidic Rabbis and wonder workers. Here
the Hebrew was far from faultless, and the calligraphy clumsy.
But what they lacked in learning they made up in titular grandilo-
quence. They called each other Angel, Man of God, Pillar of Fire
and Flame, Lightning, Voice of Thunder, Divine Light.

Finally the government itself was dragged into the whirlwind.

Jews wrote indictments of each other to officials—little Jews to little officials, big Jews to big officials. The complaint was that in the Rabbinic court of Nyesheve lived a bigamist; the counter-complaint was that the public peace was being disturbed. The little officials declining to interfere, the original complaint traveled through rising circles of the hierarchy until a solemn petition was sent to the Royal and Imperial *Stadthalter* in Lemberg. And when the Royal and Imperial *Stadthalter* declined to send a commission to Nyesheve, money was collected to send a delegation to the *Kultus* Minister in the Imperial City of Vienna. A statement was prepared, and several important Rabbis, learned in the German language, traveled to Vienna to present it at a personal interview. They came to demand that the Imperial Minister defend the honor of the Jewish religion against the insult which had been placed upon it by the Rabbi of Nyesheve.

The red-headed Assistant-Secretary for Jewish affairs, the apostate Hofrat Pesheles, tried to intercept the delegation and to spare the Imperial Minister the painful interview. But the learned Rabbis, after listening politely to the long list of State problems which was absorbing the Minister, insisted humbly that none but the Minister himself could do them justice.

In their new silk *capotes*, made specially for this journey, with new satin skull-caps on their close-cropped heads, and with ear-locks hanging down, they resembled tall black bottles with tiny handles. Obsequious but immovable, they made the apostate Pesheles arrange an interview with the Minister.

Count Kerwitch Navratni, the *Kultus* Minister, was an elderly, Teutonized Czecho-Hungarian. He was a tall, pallid man, and his stupidity and aristocracy—the combination by virtue of which he had been made *Kultus* Minister—were written large on his face. He swore in a mixture of German, Hungarian and Czech when Pesheles reported to him that the Jews would not budge without a personal interview; he swore at the Jews specifically, all the way back to Abraham's father, Terah; but he could not refuse to receive a delegation of religious leaders. His Royal, Imperial and Apostolic Majesty might hear of it and be angry. His Majesty treated all religious leaders with great respect. Besides, the *Kultus* Minister's work consisted of nothing but the reception of delegations. Therefore Count Navratni put on a pious face and bade his assistant introduce the reverend gentlemen.

When they entered the ministerial cabinet the Rabbis, highly flustered, bowed with more enthusiasm than grace, and loudly repeated the benediction which praises God for having conferred so much glory on a man of flesh and blood. In their nervousness they forgot that this benediction is uttered only in the presence of Royalty. The Minister, not understanding a syllable of the Hebrew benediction, blushed faintly and said:

"Gentlemen, I am deeply touched."

In a strange language which was a mixture of Galician Yiddish and High German, and in a voice which slipped unconsciously into the traditional chant of Talmudic studies, the chairman of the delegation recited the story of Yoshe the loon and the Rabbi's daughter. The Jews, the faithful and obedient subjects of his Imperial Majesty, were deeply concerned by the flouting of the law. They begged for the intervention of the Government.

The Count listened to the long recital, understanding less than half of it. He did not quite know what the Jews wanted of him. He felt sleepy.

Before leaving, the chairman handed the Count a huge document, and the delegation lifted its hands and conferred a blessing upon him.

"For your grace in receiving us, we will ever pray for the welfare of his Royal and Imperial Majesty, and for the welfare of your Excellency, the great and noble Premier. . . ."

"I am not the Premier," said the Count with a light sigh.

"Your Excellency will be," said the chairman, quickly. "Whoever deals justly and kindly with the Jews is exalted to the right hand of the King—so say our holy and learned Talmudists."

Shortly after the visit of the Rabbis to the *Kultus* Minister in Vienna a serious riot, attended by bloodshed, broke out among the partisans and enemies of Nyesheve. It happened in the following manner:

From one of the large Hebrew schools in Lemberg a group of ushers had been expelled for indecent relations with a cleaning-woman. Having nothing better to do, the group decided to turn to the theater. One of them had written a comedy entitled "The Saint of Nyesheve, or, Yoshe the Loon and His Two Wives," and the unemployed ushers tried it out in a low tavern frequented by servant girls, wagoners, shoemakers, bakers' assistants and the like. The play, in which the Rabbi of Nyesheve, Yoshe the loon, Serele the Rabbi's daughter, and other leading figures were represented in the flesh, was a great success, and the ushers decided to tour the provinces.

They went from village to village, appearing everywhere in the cheapest and most disreputable taverns before the dregs of the population, and wherever they went the songs and lines created a furore. One scene in particular, where Zivyah went down on her knees before the proud Rabbi's daughter, and wept for justice, took the country by storm. Encouraged, the actors had the temerity to include a woman in their troupe, to take the part of the wronged woman.

Wherever the play came, the town or village was in a turmoil. Followers of Nyesheve tried to have the performance stopped. The young people, especially of the kind which frequented these taverns, raged against this interference. And riots took place.

In the town of Sandz, a Hebrew teacher declared a war to the death against the troupers.

A performance having been announced in the casino of the town, the Hebrew teacher flew through the streets rousing pious Jews, housewives and youngsters to action. Armed with broomsticks, shovels, rolling pins and other impromptu weapons, the mob streamed toward the casino, and found it guarded by a cordon of workingmen, determined that the performance should take place.

"Jews!" the teacher yelled, "we shall fight for our sanctity like the heroes of old! We shall die for our faith! We shall let no one insult our saint!"

His followers, less devoted than he, and alarmed by the grim aspect of the guard about the casino—brawny, heavy-limbed wagoners and bakers—pleaded with him to turn back. But the teacher would not listen. He rushed to the attack.

He was flung back with such violence that he flew through the air and landed, head first, on an ugly heap of stones. He did not get up. His frightened followers came close, saw the blood streaming from a fatal wound, covered him and sent for the police.

A cry of alarm went up from the Jewish communities of Austrian Galicia. Jewish blood had been shed in the Nyesheve fight, and who knew if this was not merely a beginning.

Repercussions of the Sandz riot spread to the non-Jewish world. In the Viennese newspapers there were lively articles about the furious civil war among the "Ear-lock Jews," the fanatics of Galicia. Special correspondents were sent down to Nyesheve and other centers of Chassidism. In the Parliament in Vienna one Deputy, a priest, interpellated the Government.

"Does the Minister of the Interior," he asked, "know of the intestine warfare among the Chosen People in Galicia because of a case of bigamy in one of the Rabbinic courts? And if the Minister knows, what steps does he intend to take?"

That same day the telegraph wires between Vienna and Lemberg carried a demand for an investigation from the Minister of the Interior to the Royal and Imperial *Stadthalter* Count Kutchebitski.

The walls of the stronghold of Nyesheve were beginning to crack.

25

REB SHACHNAH OF BIALOGURA TRIUMPHED.

Shortly before Passover the walls of the Jewish streets in the towns of Galicia and Russian Poland were plastered over with a great proclamation signed by seventy Rabbis and scholars—the number which made up the Sanhedrin of old—calling upon Rabbi

Melech of Nyesheve to submit the case of his son-in-law to trial before a Tribunal of Holy Law.

From houses and synagogues, from slaughter-houses and ritual baths, the proclamation stared down upon the Jews. Jammed in among all sorts of notices about Sabbath candles, *kosher* utensils, hot-water day at the ritual baths, lost and found articles, among advertisements of book dealers and scribes who offered to inspect *mezuzos* and phylacteries, of healers who cured the most various diseases without medicine or operations, but solely with a special kind of belt, among warnings by bakers that after a certain hour on Friday afternoon they would accept no more dishes to be kept warm over the Sabbath, and announcements by peddlers that they had brought to town a new stock of cheap story-books, skull-caps and girdles, among all sorts of appeals, protests and declarations, public and semi-public, religious, commercial and moral, the proclamation, in Hebrew and Yiddish, dominated the scene, and, from morning to evening, held its own circle of readers.

"With the help of the Supreme, praised be His Blessed Name, we, the undersigned, call upon all our brethren throughout the world to listen to our words, which are as the words of Heaven, our sages have said. Likewise we say unto our brethren that a convened Tribunal is like unto the Almighty Himself, for our Holy writings say that when our mother Rebecca went to Shem and Eber she went to the Almighty.

"It is not in a spirit of dissension, or of hatred against any person, that we issue this call, for we know that dissension is like idol worship, God protect us from both. Nay, we have made this proclamation only because our eyes are no longer able to look upon that which they have seen, and our ears no longer able to listen to that which they have heard. For a great desecration, God help us, has appeared in the tents of Jacob, and in its train has brought warfare and denunciation. In the Houses of Prayer there is no more studying, but only quarreling, particularly at the moment when the Holy Law itself is being read forth; and for such things, the Zohar says, God turns away from His people. Likewise it has come to our ears—woe is us!—that we have fallen so low that one Jew denounces another unto the Gentiles. Likewise we know that certain Jews have written books filled with mockery and impiety, and have caused the mass of our people, the vulgar ones, to sin; for the servants and the servant girls and the women of the people read these books, and sing insulting and low songs about our God-fearing saints who are our cedar trees. Woe is us, for we have become a mockery among the Gentile peoples! For they read in their public prints about our shame, and of things among Jews the like of which have not been known before. And how shall we be able to lift our heads among the princes and mighty ones in whose shadow we live? For, say our holy sages, we should pray for those who govern us, inasmuch as without them men would swallow each other alive; and particularly should we pray for the welfare of our Sovereign, the King and Emperor, may his might and glory increase. For they will ask: If a fire rages among the fir trees, what shall be said of the moss which is on the walls? If the Saints can do such things, what shall be expected of the vulgar people? A trembling is in our bodies and a weakness in our hands, for innocent blood has been shed in our midst, God have mercy on us!

"With broken hearts and with weeping voices we call upon his high honor the Rabbi of Nyesheve that he bethink himself and appear before the Tribunal, for he is called thereto by seventy Rabbis, which is like unto a Sanhedrin.

"God forbid that we should, beforehand, say anything or pronounce sentence. But an evil report has come to our ears that a certain man, who has been recognized by a great number of decent and God-fearing Jews as one Yoshe (the loon), the assistant beadle of the Great Synagogue of Bialogura, and who was married to the daughter of the beadle of that synagogue, Reb Kanah, and who abandoned his wife, that this same man has given himself out as the son-in-law of the Rabbi of Nyesheve, and now lives in that city with the Rabbi's daughter, a married woman. We do not, God forbid, say that this report is true before the matter has been made clear by a Tribunal. But we demand that his high honor the Rabbi of Nyesheve shall not rely upon his own opinion, and shall not harden his mind. For if only one man were to call him before a Tribunal he would be bound to appear; how much the more, then, when he is called by seventy Rabbis and scholars? Let not thy mouth smile with scorn, nor thy lips utter mockery, even though thou art in the right. In the eyes of the Holy Law the great man is not more than the mean man. And even King David (his virtue plead for us in Heaven, Amen!) when a blot fell upon him—and the Sages have said that he who accuses King David of having sinned is in grievous error—the prophet came to him and punished him, and the child died.

"With the power of the Holy Law and with the sanction of Rabbis and mighty scholars, we call upon his high honor that he submit himself to a Tribunal of Seventy Rabbis, not later than the beginning of the month of Iyar. For the honor of the great Rabbi of Nyesheve, and because of his age—God spare him—and also because the complainant must come to the defendant, the Tribunal will come, with the help of God, to Nyesheve, though the trouble and the expense will both be heavy. But until the time when the Tribunal shall render decision, the strange man shall not, God forbid, be permitted to live even one moment with the daughter of the Rabbi, in that there is suspicion of shameful sin. They shall be separated and shall not even be permitted to dwell under one roof. These are the words of those who speak with broken hearts and humbled spirit. And those that will heed these words shall be blessed."

Seventy Rabbis signed this proclamation, each one with the name of himself and his father and his congregation. Rabbi Melech could not withstand this mass protest, the less so as the Royal and Imperial *Stadthalter* had informed the Jews that unless they settled the matter through their own courts, he would be compelled to interfere in person. Rabbi Melech agreed to appear before the Tribunal on the first day of the month of Iyar, and he designated a number of his own Rabbis, followers of Nyesheve, to sit in the Tribunal of Seventy.

Soon after Passover the streams of Jews from both sides of the frontier set in toward Nyesheve.

There came big-city Rabbis of Galicia and Russian Poland, imposing figures in their wide satin mantles; they were accompanied by beadles and assistants, and their baggage consisted of magnificent leather cases; there came likewise—independently of the trial itself—swarms of lean and obscure little clericals who had grievances of their own, and saw here an opportunity to enlist the sympathies of the mighty. There came Jews of influence and wealth, public figures and leaders of communities, in silk hats and furs, who had to be part of every activity. High-class beggars, fathers gathering dowries for their daughters, authors in search of spiritual and financial support, came likewise. A few signatures from among the famous who would be in Nyesheve could be the life-long support of a needy scholar. There were also fathers of daughters whose reputations had been blown upon, seeking vindication; and desperate husbands of impossible wives wanted the signature of a hundred scholars declaring that their partners were insane, and the marriage could be declared invalid. Young men studying for the Rabbinate came in the hope of wheedling ordainment out of a prominent Rabbi. Precocious geniuses were brought, to achieve fame with an exhibition, and scholars-at-large came in the hope of winning praise and perhaps a bride with a decent dowry. There came marriage brokers, eager to take advantage of the concourse of representatives of mighty families, and widows of Rabbis, who wanted their congregations to give the vacant post to a young man who would take one of their daughters. Book dealers came, with rare and precious volumes, printers looking for customers among authors, and a swarm of ordinary peddlers, hat-makers, tailors, caterers. Young German businessmen, in frockcoats, and carrying canes, sought Rabbinic permits for their wines, sardines, oils, cakes. There came even a Gentile chemist who had a depilatory which made unnecessary the use of the forbidden razor. And over and above all these there came the hordes of the believing, village Jews and Jewesses, dark, oppressed, weary creatures with diseases and difficulties of all kinds, seeking in the concourse of Rabbis and saints the salvation they could find nowhere else.

The last to arrive were the most illustrious of the regular Rabbis.

"The Lion's Head" of Dinaburg came. He was a thick, stumpy little man who looked and dressed like a small-town shopkeeper;

but he had enormous, restless eyes which reminded one of the eyes of a caged lion. "The Genius of Lublin" came, an old man whose snow-white beard, descending to his waist, made the beholders think of pictures of Father Abraham by Gentile painters. "The Saint of Lizhane" came, famous more for his piety than his scholarship; in the little books which he wrote in great numbers, he was always forbidding and enjoining. His reputation was very great; Jews wanted to turn him into a wonder-working Rabbi; they wanted to visit him after the Chassidic fashion, but he would not have it. But the greatest among all the Rabbis, as well as the oldest, was the Rav of Cracow; he was so old that no one really knew his age; he was a tiny, withered figure, and he could not walk unless one man on each side supported him under the armpits; and whether he walked or sat, his head trembled above his skinny throat, so that he seemed forever to be saying: "No, no! It is forbidden."

Half the city of Bialogura came with Kanah and his daughter. The last two looked exceedingly well-fed and contented with themselves. And Reb Shachnah strode about in the streets of Nyesheve, his nose redder than ever, his gaunt features expressing the bitter happiness of his triumph.

When he arrived in the city, he was not at all sure that the Rabbinic demand for the separation of Yoshe and the Rabbi's daughter had been met. He therefore made close inquiries, eavesdropped in the court and did not rest until he discovered that the man and the woman had been separated, and that they did not even live under one roof. Satisfied, he turned himself into a reception committee, met every one of the incoming Rabbis, greeted them heartily and expressed his gratitude.

"*Sholom aleichem*, Rabbi. God be thanked that the matter has been brought thus far. Yes, the world is not coming to an end."

Three days the Tribunal of Seventy, like a Sanhedrin, sat in the synagogue of Nyesheve; and during these three days the scales of the balance swung up and down opposite each other, lifting and lowering each of the contending parties in turn.

The President of the Tribunal was the Rabbi of Cracow, oldest and most learned in that assembly. He sat at the head, in a huge armchair, on top of several cushions, so that he might be able to reach the table. The constant trembling of his head disturbed the assembly with its suggestion of negation. With withered hands he thrust his old ears forward, to catch what was being said.

Nine and sixty Rabbis sat at the two long tables which ran parallel to each other at right angles to the head table. They sat in order of precedence, the greatest next to the President, the least important, furthest away. At another table sat Rabbi Melech. They tried at first to put him side by side with the President, but he would not sit in the midst of these enemies of the Chassidim.

"I'll sit with my son-in-law Nahum," he said.

He said this aloud, as if to indicate his defiance of the Tribunal, and a murmur went up from the assembly. All eyes were fixed then on the figure of the stranger, who looked at no one, but read constantly in the little book which he held open. Next to Rabbi Melech, erect and alert like a soldier on guard, stood Israel Avigdor.

Opposite them, on a bench, sat Kanah the beadle and Reb Shachnah. The latter could hardly be said to have sat. During the three days of the trial he was mostly on his feet, gesticulating even when not talking, blowing his nose, glaring at the assembly and the judges. Kanah the beadle was self-possessed; he had not the slightest doubt as to the outcome of the affair.

On several long benches sat witnesses for the prosecution and the defense. The women witnesses were put into a corner, and a curtain separated them from the view of the assembly. The remainder of the synagogue was jammed with visitors. The doors and windows were crowded with forms and faces.

Great candles, black and white, stood on the pulpit. On the pulpit table lay a ram's horn, likewise a prayer-shawl and a white robe to be donned by anyone taking the oath. In one corner of the synagogue stood the board for the washing of the dead. The assembly kept their eyes averted from that corner.

The first witnesses to be called were the Jews of Bialogura, among them Abish the butcher.

"Jews," the President of the Tribunal said, "you know that in our Law no oath is administered to a witness. But you know, too, that to speak before a Tribunal is equivalent to having taken an oath on the Holy Scrolls. You are in the presence of a Tribunal of Seventy, which is as if you stood in the presence of the Great Sanhedrin itself. Think well before you speak. For wide is the gate which opens into Gehenna, and narrow the door which opens outward therefrom. Life and death are in the power of the Word. Have you all understood me?"

"Yes, Rabbi," the witnesses murmured, awestruck.

"Approach, then, the man under judgment," the President said to each witness in turn, "and say who he is."

"Yoshe the loon, of Bialogura."

"How do you know that he is that man?"

"By his looks."

"Do you not know that two men may resemble each other very closely?"

"Yes, Rabbi."

"Perhaps you are deceived?"

"No, Rabbi."

"Are you quite certain?"

"Yes, Rabbi."

"If there is the slightest doubt in your mind, do not be ashamed to confess it."

"No, Rabbi. Not the slightest doubt."

So they went, one after the other, and as testimony was added to testimony, the scale of Bialogura sank deeper and deeper with the weight of it.

"Reb Shachnah," the President called, "you are a Rabbi, and therefore you know without my telling you what it means to testify before a Tribunal of Seventy."

"I know," Reb Shachnah answered. And blowing his nose fiercely, as if in special salutation to the august assembly, Reb Shachnah lifted up his hoarse voice.

"I testify before this Tribunal of saints and scholars, that the man under judgment is the assistant beadle of the Great Synagogue of Bialogura, Yoshe the loon. I testify that in Bialogura a Tribunal sentenced him to marry Zivyah, the daughter of Kanah the beadle of the same synagogue, for she bore witness before the Tribunal of Bialogura that she was pregnant by Yoshe. The marriage took place in the cemetery of Bialogura, and in the presence of the whole city Yoshe took Zivyah to be his wife. On the night of the wedding he fled, and left Zivyah an abandoned wife. I testify before this Tribunal that this is the same Yoshe."

The scale of Bialogura, full weight and overweight, could sink no further. In the synagogue rose a loud murmur.

"Silence!" the President called.

"Silence!" all the other Rabbis cried after him.

After Reb Shachnah came Israel Avigdor of Nyesheve, and his testimony sent the Bialogura scale up into the air again.

Israel Avigdor uttered his testimony with great pomp. Before speaking a word he washed his hands, as if he were preparing to pray. He straightened out his skull-cap and his hat, flattened his girdle, and approached the President's table as if he were advancing toward the pulpit to read the Law. Then, closing his eyes, he spoke slowly, clearly:

"Before this Tribunal, before my Rabbi and before this congregation of Jews, I, Israel Avigdor, son of Feige Leah, testify that the man under judgment is Nahum, the son-in-law of my Rabbi. He took exile upon himself, and on his return he gave signs by which he was recognized. I myself examined his body and verified those signs which he gave to Serele, the daughter of the Rabbi. And with the permission of the High Tribunal, I shall repeat all the signs."

"Speak," said the President.

Then Israel Avigdor repeated, without faltering once, all that he had witnessed on the return of the stranger; he told of the volumes of *R'ziel ha-Malach*, of the glass of milk, of the marks on the body. He left out nothing. Then, when he had ended, he gave the scale of Nyesheve a final, downward thrust with his peroration.

"Gentlemen! I am no longer a young man. Before long I shall stand before that Greatest Tribunal of all. And by this gray beard of mine I say that this testimony is as true in every word as the Holy Word of God!"

Questioned in every detail by the Tribunal, Israel Avigdor stood firm. No, he could not be mistaken! The scale of Bialogura swung so high in the air that Reb Shachnah trembled from head to foot.

Zivyah, the daughter of Kanah, was the next to be led before the Tribunal.

Her old acquaintances of Bialogura were astounded by her appearance not less than by her manner. Her travels had shaken some of the animal stupidity out of her; contacts with new faces and new people had awakened in her whatever intelligence had lain dormant under the contempt and indifference of her home surroundings. She seemed to understand every word that was spoken to her; she replied almost without stammering, and she hardly ever giggled or whinnied.

"Woman!" said the President. "You stand in the presence of Rabbis. Do you know what that means? You must tell nothing but the truth, or else you will burn in hell-fire. Do you know that?"

"Yes."

"Approach that Jew sitting at the table, and say who he is."

"Yoshe the loon."

"Who is he?"

"My husband."

"Have you any signs by which you can declare him your husband?"

"I know Yoshe," she said, simply.

"Could you swear that with your hand upon the Holy Scrolls?"

"I swear."

After Zivyah came Serele, the daughter of the Rabbi. Israel Avigdor conducted her to the table respectfully as if she had been the Rabbi himself.

Pale, red-eyed with much weeping, she looked first at the table where her father sat with the husband from whom she had been separated by the order of the Rabbis. Her father returned her look, but not her husband. He did not lift his eyes from the book. She swayed slightly, and Israel Avigdor brought forward a chair.

"Daughter of the Rabbi of Nyesheve," said the President. "Do you know what a Tribunal of Seventy is?"

"I know. It is like a Sanhedrin of old."

"True," said the President. "You know the Five Books of Moses, do you not, even if only in Yiddish?"

"Yes."

"You know, therefore, what shall be done to a woman who lives with the husband of another?"

"She shall be stoned to death."

"True. You know also that since our Temple was destroyed, the Sanhedrin no longer has the power to stone a sinner. But you know too that the punishment of Heaven remains, even on this earth."

"I know," said Serele. "It punishes with early death."

"True. And now approach the man under judgment and say who he is."

"My husband, Reb Nahum," said Serele, firmly.

"How can you be certain it is your husband? Your husband was absent from you fifteen years. How did you know it was he?"

"He gave me signs."

"What signs?"

Serele lowered her head.

"Do not be ashamed. You are in the presence of a Tribunal. Were they signs between husband and wife?"

"Yes."

"Was it not possible that another knew of these signs? Have you at no time told any of your close friends?"

"No."

"Perhaps your husband told these signs to some man, and that man made use of the knowledge."

"There were signs on his body," said Serele, in a low voice, the blood mounting to her face. "My father the Rabbi had them examined."

A murmur spread through the synagogue.

"Silence!" the President cried.

"Silence!" the Rabbis cried after him.

Serele was led back behind the curtain, and her place was taken by Kanah the beadle.

"Reb Kanah," said the President, "you are a party to this case, in that you are the father of the Bialogura *agunah* who claims that the man sitting here is her husband. According to our Law, a party to a case must take the oath; but inasmuch as our Law does not permit a woman to take the oath, you, her father, will take it for her. Can you, under oath, maintain that this man is the husband of your daughter?"

"Yes, Rabbi," Kanah said vigorously.

The head of the Rabbi of Cracow trembled more than ever.

"An oath is an awful thing," he said, solemnly. "For a false statement under oath, and even for an error under oath, Gehenna itself is not punishment enough. If there is any shadow of doubt in your mind, declare it."

"I will take the oath," Reb Kanah asserted. "I am not afraid, since I speak the truth."

"Beadle!" said the President, addressing himself to the official of Nyesheve. "Put out the white candles and light the black ones."

The beadle obeyed.

"Bring the purification board to the pulpit."

The assembled Jews became pale. Kanah the beadle did not even look around. He was not impressed by a board for washing dead bodies.

"Reb Kanah! Go wash your hands, then mount the pulpit and put on the white robe and the praying-shawl."

Kanah the beadle obeyed imperturbably.

Supported by two other Rabbis, the President approached the pulpit and struck the table with his hand.

"The whole world shook," he said, "when from the height of Sinai the Almighty said: Thou shalt not bear false witness against thy neighbor. All sins that mortals commit can be forgiven, but not the one of bearing false witness. For other sins, the sinner himself suffers, but for the sin of bearing false witness, his children and his children's children shall also be punished. Nor does Heaven wait for the final Tribunal, but metes out punishment at once."

The President lifted his eyes to the assembly; a host of dumb, frightened faces stared back at him.

"Sound the *Shofar!*" he cried.

A Jew, wrapped in praying-shawl, blew the ram's horn.

"Repeat every word after me, Kanah, son of Henye Peshe!"

The beadle of Bialogura repeated word for word:

"I, Kanah, son of Henye Peshe . . ."

But he got no further. At that instant Rabbi Melech, who had been sitting all the time in his praying-shawl and phylacteries, sprang to his feet and uttered a fierce shout.

"Stop!"

There was deadly silence in the synagogue, and even the President could not utter a word. Massive and terrible, the Rabbi of Nyesheve faced the assembly.

"I will not permit the bearing of false witness under oath in my city!" he cried.

The silence broke for an instant. Men turned to one another, amazed, bewildered. Rabbi Melech lifted his hands, and silence was restored.

"I, Melech, the son of martyrs, bear witness in my prayer-shawl and phylacteries, that the man under judgment seated here is my son-in-law Reb Nahum. When he returned after fifteen years, I did not recognize him. He went away, young and beardless. He returned a full-grown man, with beard and ear-locks. But he gave me signs in which there could be no error. He reminded me of the book we had last studied together, and said that the eighteenth page of the book *R'ziel ha-Malach* was folded over. I looked and it was so. He gave me other signs, ordinary things which had to do with the food which was prepared for him the day he left. . . ."

Reb Melech snatched down the phylactery from his head, and clutching it frantically to his bosom, cried:

"I swear it! I swear it by the head-phylactery!"

In the silence which followed, the President made a sign to Kanah the beadle to step down from the pulpit. Completely bewildered, Kanah took off the white mantle and the prayer-shawl and walked back to his seat.

It seemed now that the scale of Nyesheve had triumphed; nothing could disturb the effect of that appeal. But when the Tribunal, restored to order, called up the man under judgment, the balance was again destroyed, and before long the scales were dancing up and down so swiftly that none of the judges could follow their motion.

"You who are under judgment," the President called him, not knowing what name to use. "Who are you?"

"I do not know."

"You do not know?" the President repeated, astounded. "If you do not know who you are, who shall know?"

"No man knows who he is," the stranger answered.

"This is impossible," the Rabbis murmured. "I do not understand."

"But I understand," said the Rabbi of Nyesheve, rising. "Reb Nahum," he addressed the stranger. "I understand you well. But here, in the presence, you must speak simply and clearly, and say whether you are Reb Nahum."

"I am Nahum," the other answered.

"When was it that you married my daughter?" the Rabbi asked.

"On the Festival of the Thirty-third Day in the year *tov resh chav tes*." The voice of the stranger was like a remote echo.

Rabbi Melech rolled his eyes around the assembly.

"Who was present at the wedding of my daughter to my son-in-law Reb Nahum?"

Dozens of voices answered: "I was!"

The Rabbi looked back at the stranger.

"My son-in-law, do you remember the sermon which you preached at your own wedding?"

"Yes."

"Repeat it now in the presence of the Tribunal."

In his far-off voice, which did not seem to issue from a living body, the stranger repeated the sermon from beginning to end.

Voices cried out: "Yes! It is true! I remember!"

Rabbi Melech looked with contempt at the hosts of Bialogura witnesses.

"Reb Shachnah of Bialogura," he cried, "was your Yoshe of Bialogura a learned man or an ignoramus?"

"He recited nothing but Psalms," Reb Shachnah answered.

"Jews," cried Rabbi Melech, "my son-in-law is a learned man and an adept in Kabbala!"

"This is beyond human understanding," the President was heard to mutter.

"Beyond understanding," the other Rabbis echoed.

Rabbi Melech sank back into his chair, his eyes gleaming with triumph. At the same instant Reb Shachnah sprang to the front and addressed himself to the man under judgment.

"Yoshe!" he cried. "Declare before the Tribunal that you are not Yoshe the loon of Bialogura."

The stranger was silent.

"You do not answer," Reb Shachnah shouted. "You do not deny. And that means that you admit it."

Reb Shachnah turned to the Tribunal.

"Gentlemen! He is silent now! He was just as silent when he was brought before the Tribunal in Bialogura. In that city a terrible pestilence—God guard us!—had broken out. The daughter of Reb Kanah the beadle testified that he, Yoshe the loon, had sinned with her. And he was silent, did not confess, did not deny! And they compelled him to marry her in the cemetery, and he fled that night. Let him deny it!"

A shudder went through the synagogue.

"You who are under judgment!" the President addressed him. "Have you heard what Reb Shachnah of Bialogura has declared before the Tribunal?"

"Yes."

"What have you to say?"

Silence.

Reb Shachnah danced with rage and impatience.

"Deny it!" he screamed. "I declare that you are not Nahum, but Yoshe, Yoshe the loon. Deny it!"

The stranger did not even look at the screaming accuser.

The head of the Rabbi of Cracow, the President, trembled as if it were about to tumble off his shoulders.

"You who are under judgment," he asked, "who are you?"

"I do not know."

The President was aghast.

"You have said that you are Nahum, the son-in-law of the Rabbi of Nyesheve. Why did you abandon your wife?"

"I had to do that."

"Where were you?"

"Out in the world."

"Name the cities which you visited."

"They cannot be enumerated."

"Do you know of a city called Bialogura?"

"Yes."

"Were you there?"

"I was everywhere."

"What were you doing in your wanderings?"

"I do not know."

The President sat down, almost fainting. He could not go on.

"Gentlemen," he said to the Rabbis around him, "you carry on."

The first to follow the President was "The Lion's Head" of Dinaburg. But he could wring nothing from the man under judgment. Hasty, impatient, tricky, leaping at conclusions, he only brought confusion into the court.

"You who are under judgment!" he said, furiously, while he rubbed his forehead. "One of the two parties here is lying! That is clear. For if you are Nahum, you cannot be Yoshe, and if you are Yoshe, you cannot be Nahum. Reuben cannot be Simon, and Simon cannot be Reuben. You will admit that, will you not?"

He looked wildly at the stranger, as if he had clinched the matter. But not waiting for an answer he began to cite cases and quotations. But the stranger did not even look at him.

But, as the Tribunal was growing restless, the Saint of Lizhane, he whom the Jews wished to exalt into a wonder-working Rabbi, and who had refused to let them do it, rose and interrupted "The Lion's Head."

"Reb Samson Raphael," he begged. "Be good enough!"

Something in his voice caught the attention of the assembly. "The Lion's Head" could not be silenced at once. He went on for a few minutes, carried by his own momentum, until he realized that all eyes were turned upon the Saint.

The manner, as well as the name, of the Saint of Lizhane, struck awe into the assembly. He had closed his eyes, and a mystic expression was on his face. His voice was low and pregnant with unutterable secrets. Something new was about to happen; a dread revelation was about to be made through the lips of this strange and unfathomable intimate of heaven.

The Saint of Lizhane began to recall the witnesses, but the questions which he put to them baffled and startled the assembly.

He called back first Serele, the wife of Nahum.

"Daughter of the Rabbi of Nyesheve," he asked, "when your husband returned to you, did he prove himself a man like all other men, or not?"

Serele did not answer.

"Does he ever speak to you?"

"No," she said, mournfully.

"What does he do?" the Saint of Lizhane asked. "What are his habits?"

"He stays locked in his own room."

"What else?"

"Often, in the night, he goes into the fields, and stays away many hours."

"In the field many hours?" the Saint repeated softly, his voice growing more tense. "Where else does he go?"

"To the cemetery."

"To the cemetery." The Saint looked closely at Serele, and asked suddenly: "Does he ever live with you as a man should live with his wife?"

Serele looked at the floor.

"Answer," the Saint insisted. "The Tribunal must know."

"Sometimes," she answered, in a whisper.

The Saint spoke more slowly now, and his low, clear words carried to every corner of the synagogue.

"Have you ever seen him undress?"

"No."

"Does he conceal himself from you?"

"I do not know."

"Have you ever seen his feet?"

"No."

"You may go," the Saint said.

He called next for Zivyah the daughter of Kanah the beadle.

"Woman," he said, "was Yoshe in the house of your father in Bialogura a long time?"

"A long time," said Zivyah.

"Did you ever see him in the night?"

"Yes."

"What was he doing?"

"He was crying."

"Crying," the Saint repeated. "Did he ever go out nights into the cemetery?"

"Yes."

"Did he ever speak to you?"

"No."

"Did he ever laugh? Was he ever happy?"

"No."

"Did you ever see him undress?"

Zivyah began to giggle.

"Woman!" the Saint cried. "Do not dare to laugh. Have you ever seen his feet?"

"No."

"Did he conceal himself from you?"

Zivyah did not understand, and the Saint did not insist. He released her, and called upon the Jews of Bialogura one by one.

"Whence did this Yoshe of Bialogura come?"

"I do not know."

"Did he behave like a normal man, or was he an idiot?"

"He was a simpleton, and therefore we called him Yoshe the loon."

"Did he ever trouble anyone?"

"No, never. Even when they used to hit him, he remained silent."

"Did he ever speak with anyone?"

"No. He was silent, and always kept himself apart."

At the next question the Saint of Lizhane looked intently at the witnesses.

"Did you ever see him undress?"

"No."

"Have you ever seen his feet?"

"No."

When the last witness had been released, the Saint of Lizhane thrust his hat back upon his head, and closed his eyes again. When he opened them again and spoke, his voice trembled.

"Gentlemen! It is as clear as day that neither side in this case has borne false witness before this Tribunal. The Rabbi of Nyesheve, in prayer-shawl and phylacteries, had sworn that the man under judgment is his son-in-law. Who will dare to doubt the word of the Rabbi?"

"True!" the assembly whispered.

The Saint of Lizhane was shaking from head to foot.

"You who are under judgment!" he cried. "Who are you? Answer!"

"I do not know."

"But I do know!" the Saint of Lizhane cried. "You are a reincarnation, the wandering soul of a dead man!"

A shudder of horror passed through the assembly.

"Yes, yes," the Saint of Lizhane continued, and he fixed his eyes piercingly on the stranger. "A dead soul! You wander from place to place, to mock the living, and you yourself do not know what you do."

The assembly was paralyzed with fright.

"You are Nahum and you are Yoshe; you are a scholar and you are an ignoramus; you appear suddenly in cities and you disappear suddenly from them; you wander in the cemeteries in search of your own kind; and you steal through the fields at night; and wherever you come you bring with you disaster, terror, pestilence; you unite yourself with women; you flee from them and you return. You know not what you do; there is no taste in your life or in your deeds, because you are nothing yourself, because—hear me!—you are a dead wanderer in the chaos of the world!"

Like blind men who feel suddenly that they are about to see, and who are terrified by the prospect of the light, the Jews in the synagogue stared in front of them. A choked sigh passed through the assembly.

"Deny it!" the Saint of Lizhane cried.

The stranger was silent. Calmly and coldly he looked back at the Saint, out of eyes that saw nothing.

The assembly was silent with him, but it was a silence pregnant

with storm. Suddenly Rabbi Melech stood up in his place and
turned toward the stranger. The eyes of Rabbi Melech were glazed
over; his mouth was open, black like a gaping grave. He took a
step forward.

"Nahum!" he croaked.

In that instant he reeled and fell with all his bulk upon the
wooden floor. A hundred hoarse voices cried out: "Rabbi!"

Before anyone else could reach the fallen figure, Israel Avigdor
was at its side. With more than human strength he lifted the
body of his Rabbi and placed it in the chair. But the moment he
removed his hands, the body fell forward, rigid and horrible. Amid
the silence of the assembly two men lifted Rabbi Melech and
carried him to the pulpit. They laid him down slowly and tenderly,
as a great Scroll of the Law is laid down, and they covered him
with a praying-shawl. Then Israel Avigdor rose and said, in a
steady voice:

"Blessed be the True Judge!"

One single voice, a man's voice that sounded like a child's, a
voice filled with despair, rose in the synagogue, in terrifying
lament.

26

THE NEXT MORNING THE ROADS LEADING TO NYESHEVE WERE BLACK
with Jews. They came on foot and in wagons—individuals,
groups, families, clans, men and women and children—to be
present at the funeral of Rabbi Melech.

All day long the rain-drenched telegraph posts in Galician fields
and villages hummed with the messages passing through the wires
overhead, and shepherds gathered round the posts to wonder what

cataclysm had wakened the sleeping sentinels. All day long the news was passed from point to point: the Rabbi of Nyesheve was dead.

Five sons stood that day round the Rabbi's grave and said the first *Kaddish* for him, and five lapels were ripped in sign of mourning. Then, round each of the sons, a group of the faithful gathered, and voices were raised:

"Long life to you, Rabbi of Nyesheve!"

But the largest group, with Israel Avigdor at its head, looked in vain for the man whom they considered the rightful heir of the Rabbinic court. They called: "Reb Nahum! Where is Reb Nahum, the rightful Rabbi of Nyesheve?"

They did not find him.

For the man they sought was already far from Nyesheve. In rags, with a patched canvas sack on his shoulder, with a stone inside the sack to hold down the prayer-shawl and phylacteries, with a staff in his right hand, he was striding swiftly along the road, his back to Nyesheve. Village dogs ran after him, and shepherd boys threw stones at him, and shouted: "Hey! Sheeny!" He did not seem to be aware of them. He strode on past fields and meadows, past lakes and windmills.

In the evening he came to a Jewish village and made his way toward the synagogue.

In the twilight, on the village street, they recognized him and fled from him. They slammed the doors of the houses. When he came to the synagogue, it was locked and barred in his face, and voices shouted at him from the interior:

"Demon! Dead man's soul! Begone!"

He passed out of the village to the cemetery, the Eternal House. There he placed his folded sack on a stone, and lay down and slept.

The moon shone on his face and kept watch over him.

SCHOCKEN CLASSICS

THE TRIAL

by Franz Kafka, translated from the German by Willa and Edwin Muir

The terrifying story of Joseph K., his arrest and trial, is one of the great novels of the twentieth century.

"Here we are taken to the limits of human thought. Indeed everything in this work is, in the true sense, essential. It states the problem of the absurd in its entirety."

—Albert Camus

0-8052-0848-8 paper, $6.95

THE METAMORPHOSIS, THE PENAL COLONY, AND OTHER STORIES

by Franz Kafka, translated from the German by Willa and Edwin Muir

This powerful collection brings together all the stories Franz Kafka published during his lifetime, including "The Judgment," "The Metamorphosis," "In the Penal Colony," "A Country Doctor," and "A Hunger Artist."

0-8052-0849-6 paper, $7.95

LETTERS TO FELICE

by Franz Kafka, edited by Erich Heller and Jürgen Born, translated by James Stern and Elizabeth Duckworth

Kafka's correspondence with Felice Bauer, to whom he was twice engaged, reveals the writer's complexities as a lover and as a friend.

"The letters are indispensable for anyone seeking a more intimate knowledge of Kafka and his fragmented world."

—*Library Journal*

0-8052-0851-8 paper, $13.95

THE FAMILY CARNOVSKY

by I. J. Singer, translated from the Yiddish by Joseph Singer

This family saga traces the lives of three generations of German Jews, up to the Nazis' rise to power.

"A titanic, overwhelming novel . . . filled with life, with people of every conceivable type, with suffering, and yet with an unbreakable optimism." —Joyce Carol Oates

0-8052-0859-3 paper, $11.95